another piece of my heart

ALSO BY JANE GREEN

Straight Talking

Mr. Maybe

Jemima J

Bookends

Babyville

To Have and To Hold

The Other Woman

Swapping Lives

Second Chance

The Beach House

Dune Road

Promises to Keep

another piece of my heart

JANE GREEN

St. Martin's Press
New York

ANOTHER PIECE OF MY HEART. © 2012 by Jane Green Warburg. All rights reserved. Printed in the United States of America. For information, address St. Martin's Press, 175 Fifth Avenue, New York, N.Y. 10010.

www.stmartins.com

Library of Congress Cataloging-in-Publication Data

Green, Jane, 1968–
   Another piece of my heart / Jane Green.—1st ed.
        p. cm.
    ISBN 978-0-312-59182-3 (hardcover)
    ISBN 978-1-4299-6273-5 (e-book)
   1. Stepmothers—Fiction.   2. Stepdaughters—Fiction.   3. Fathers and daughters—
Fiction.   4. Jealousy—Fiction.   5. Childlessness—Fiction.   6. Marital conflict—Fiction.
   7. San Francisco (Calif.)—Fiction.   8. Domestic fiction.   I. Title.
   PR6057.R3443A56 2012
   823'.914—dc22

                                                                                    2011041347

First Edition: March 2012

10 9 8 7 6 5 4 3 2 1

Acknowledgments

For their support, encouragement, kindness, or simply because they helped me on the journey this past year:

Jennifer Rudolph Walsh, Anthony Goff, Louise Moore, Clare Parkinson, Katya Shipster, Matthew Shear, Jen Enderlin, and the new, shiny team at St. Martin's Press, for whom I am endlessly grateful. Marie Coolman, Elizabeth Dyssegaard, Tish Field, Josephine and Len Finnochio, Robin Kall, Ranjeev Khush, Victoria Love, Cathy McKenna, Julia Obst, Celia Offir, Sue Redston, Robin Roberts, Jill Schwartzman, Lorilee Strate, Ken Sunshine, and Keleigh Thomas.

To the many women who so generously shared their stories; to the forums where I learned so much about women I don't know, dealing with the challenges of stepparenting; and to Wednesday Martin, whose book, *Stepmonster*, proved an invaluable resource.

And finally, for my Beloved, Ian Warburg, for everything he is. Thank you.

Happiness is not having what you want,
but wanting what you have.

—ANONYMOUS

another piece of my heart

Part One

. . . .

ANDI

One

. . . .

The sheets are drenched. Again. Andi takes a long time to wake up, drifting in and out, aware she is hot, then freezing, then finally, when she moves into a state of consciousness, wet.

Opening an eye, she looks at the clock—4:02 A.M. It's always four in the morning, these nights when she awakes, when she cannot get back to sleep. She turns her head to see Ethan, his back to her, his body rising and falling in deep sleep.

Lucky.

In the bathroom, she pulls the wet T-shirt off, slides the PJ bottoms down, and pads naked into the closet, pulling a dry T-shirt and boxer shorts off the shelf. But that leaves the sheets. Warm and wet.

The linen closet is in the hall, at the other end of the corridor, where the girls' bedrooms are. Andi knows she shouldn't open their door, shouldn't check up, but she is being a mother, she tells herself. This is what mothers do. A stepmother may not have the same rights, but she is trying, has tried so hard to turn this into a proper family, and that includes treating the girls as if they were her own.

How she wishes she had children of her own. Still. Even though she is in her early forties, on a good day she could surely pass for thirty-six.

Every month, she keeps her fingers crossed that this might be the month, this might be the month a miracle happens. Every month, she swallows her disappointment and hopes for the next time.

She pushes Sophia's door open gently to see her, fast asleep, the bald teddy bear that she cannot sleep without, now lying on its side, on the floor next to her bed, Sophia's hand curled out toward it, as if she is waiting for the bear to jump back in. Andi stands in the doorway and smiles, feeling a wave of love for her stepdaughter. Her daughter. And Sophia *is* her daughter.

She was eight when Andi and Ethan met, and instantly fell in love with Andi. Sophia now tells people she has two mothers, no differentiation in her head between Andi and her real mother.

That first family date, they had gone into the city, dim sum in Chinatown, then walked down to the ferry and taken it out to see the sea lions around the bay. Sophia had grabbed Andi's hand, skipped alongside her, and when they sat down for ice cream, she climbed on Andi's lap and leaned into her, like a much younger child, as Andi stroked her hair, thrilled.

Emily, on the other hand, at twelve, had sulked the entire day. She had squinted evil eyes at Andi, and when Andi had attempted to engage her, asking her questions about school, attempting to share some of her own stories about going to school in New York, Emily had just grunted.

"What is she?" she had sneered at her father, at one point, with a savage gesture toward Andi. "Your *girlfriend?*"

"She's my friend," Ethan had said. "That's all." Which wasn't true. They had, by that time, been sleeping together for seven weeks.

On their first date, Ethan talked about his children nonstop, which was, as far as Andi was concerned, an unexpected bonus.

They met through Match.com, a continual embarrassment to Andi. But where else did anyone go to meet people? she wondered.

She had done a series of evening classes with what she thought was a masculine bent—Fundamentals of Investing, Estate Planning 101, and Beginner's Best Barbecue. (Which was a dud. What red-blooded American man, she realized, as she sat in an empty classroom, would admit to not being able to barbecue?)

None produced so much as a date. There were, admittedly, random times she would meet men, or be flirted with in a coffee shop, but they never led to anything permanent.

At thirty-seven she realized, with a shock, she had to be proactive. Sitting back and assuming, as she always had, that she would be married with a large group of smiling kids wasn't the natural order of her life, and unless she took the bull by the horns, she was possibly going to find herself single, frighteningly, for the rest of her life.

It wasn't as if her life wasn't full. Her twenties were spent working in interior design, for a small store in Fairfield, Connecticut, where she had grown up. As she approached thirty, her mother suggested she get a real-estate license, and although Andi enjoyed selling houses, it was what she had to suggest to the homeowners they *do,* in order to sell their houses, that was her true passion.

Andi loved design. She saw how the addition of new rugs and curtain panels, and moving furniture could transform a home. She started offering her services as a "home-stager"—someone who would come in and beautify the interiors, for minimum cost, in order to sell. Soon she had a warehouse filled with furniture she would rent out to her clients, and reams of fabrics from which she could have curtains, or pillows, or bedspreads quickly made.

It wasn't long before it was her primary business.

Her mother got sick after that. Breast cancer. She fought hard, and won a reprieve, for a while. She assured Andi that moving to California

with Brent, the man Andi thought she would marry, was absolutely the right thing to do.

Even when the cancer returned, spreading to her bones, then finally to her liver and lungs, she insisted that Andi stay in California. She knew that Andi had found a peace on the West Coast she had never found at home.

It was true that one week after landing in San Francisco, despite having spent her entire life on the East Coast, Andi knew that at heart she had always been a West Coast girl, through and through.

The sunshine! The warmth! How laid-back everyone was! San Francisco! The Pacific Coast Highway! The redwood forests! The wine country!

The list was endless.

Brent married someone else: in fact, the woman he had started sleeping with almost as soon as he began his new job in San Francisco, and Andi stayed, staging homes all over the East Bay.

Match.com was fun for a while, then disheartening. She always prepared for a date, terrified he wouldn't like her, that somehow, although she was blond, and green-eyed, and girl-next-doorish, they would be disappointed.

All of them wanted to see her again, but she rarely wanted to see them. Until Ethan. He seduced her with his open face, his wide smile, his easy charm. They had met for drinks, which had become dinner, and when he left to go to the bathroom, Andi had watched him walk through the restaurant with a smile on her face. *He has a great butt,* she found herself thinking, with shock.

He had been divorced three years. His little one, Sophia, was great, he said, but Emily was harder. His eyes had welled up as he talked about Emily—how much he loved his firstborn, how difficult this had been for her, and how he would do anything, *anything,* to bring her some happiness.

I will help you, Andi had thought, her heart spilling over for this

sensitive, kind, loving man. One date led to two, led to them sleeping together, led to Andi realizing, very quickly, that for the first time in years, she could see herself spending the rest of her life with a man. With this man.

She could see herself building a life with him, having children with him. He was clever, and creative, and hardworking.

Ethan was supposed to have been a banker, he told her soon after they met. Or have run a large corporation. He was supposed to have done something that would make his parents proud, not to have started a landscaping business in school—merely to pay off his loan—a business that became so successful, so quickly, he had decided to devote himself to growing it once he had left school.

He'd started mowing lawns himself, paying a cheap hourly rate to Carlos and Jorge, who had recently made the arduous trek from Mexico.

"I was a clean-cut college kid with good ideas." He dismissed Andi when she said how talented he must have been. "And I was willing to work hard. That was all. I'd show up with some men to mow a lawn and start chatting with the homeowner, asking the wives if they'd ever thought of planting a lavender bed next to the path, or the husbands if they'd ever considered a built-in barbecue, or fire pit."

"I bet they always said yes." Andi's eyes sparkled in amusement.

Ethan just grinned.

He took on a mason, and by the time he had graduated from Berkeley, he had four full-time crews working for him.

When he met Andi, he had six. Now he has ten, plus a thriving landscape-design business.

Andi couldn't have imagined a more perfect man for her had she tried.

He cooked her dinner at his house in Mill Valley; during the appetizers she silently redesigned the whole place. She would

remove the 1950s windows and replace them with French doors spilling out to a gravel terrace with olive trees and lavender.

The kitchen wall would come down, opening up into one great big kitchen/family room, a place where kids would be happy, a giant island with a host of kids lined up on stools, tucking into pancakes she would be happily flipping as the children laughed.

They would be, she thought, a great combination of the two of them. Would three children be too much to ask for? Five in total? She shuddered at the thought and reduced it to two. A boy and a girl. The boy dark, like Ethan, and the girl a towhead, much as she had been.

She tuned out Ethan for a while, so caught up in the fantasy, so convinced this would be her future, she couldn't think of anything other than how to create the house she had always wanted for the family she would now have.

Coming back to earth, she noticed there were photographs all over the house. Ethan and his girls, all of them laughing. Gorgeous girls, dark-haired, dark-eyed, who clearly adored their father. Andi had picked up one of the photos, Emily hanging around her father's neck with a huge grin, at around seven or eight years old.

Difficult? she thought, looking into the laughing eyes of the girl in the picture. No. She just needs love. She needs the security of a loving family, of brothers and sisters, of a stepmother who will love her.

Ethan didn't talk much about his ex-wife, which Andi liked, not being the sort of woman who needed to know everything. He had said that his ex was damaged, and cold. That he realized he couldn't carry on without affection, with the constant negative sniping, that he felt he might die if he stayed.

"How about the girls?" Andi had asked. "How is she with them?"

Ethan's eyes clouded over with sadness. "Distant," he had said. "And disinterested, although she would never admit it. She prides herself on not having a babysitter, on being there for her kids, but when she's not at work she's out with her drinking buddies."

"She drinks?"

Ethan had nodded.

"You didn't go for sole custody?"

"I wanted to," he said. "I tried. But she cleaned up her act for a while, and I agreed to joint. The girls want to be with me all the time, but she won't let them. She'll scream at them and guilt them into staying, even if she's going out."

"You can't do anything?" Andi was horrified.

He shrugged. "I'm doing the best I can. I'm trying to provide a loving, stable home for them, and they know they are welcome here all the time. They're both reaching ages where Brooke won't be able to control them, and if they want to stay here, she won't be able to stop them."

They need love, Andi had thought. Love, and care, and a happy family. And I will make them happy. I will create the home they have always wanted. I will create the perfect family.

Even when Emily had been rude, and difficult, and squinty-eyed that first meeting, Andi had known she could get through to her.

Children loved Andi. It helped that she looked vaguely like a fairy-tale princess, or at least, had the correct hair and eye color. She was fun, and bubbly, and cool, and kids had always gravitated toward her.

But Andi loved children more. As a little girl, she couldn't wait to be a mother. Couldn't wait to have a family of her own, wanted to fill the house with children. Ethan's already having two children of his own was a bonus, and when he said, initially, he would have more children, better still.

On their next family date, Ethan had made the mistake of quietly taking Andi's hand as they walked side by side, the girls walking in front of them, Emily scuffing the pavement as she walked, hunched over to hide the changes puberty was bringing her.

Emily had turned around briefly, and had seen them holding hands. Ethan dropped Andi's hand like a hot stone, but Emily came whirling back and literally, physically, shoved Andi aside and grabbed her father's hand.

Andi, shocked, waited for Ethan to say something, but he merely looked adoringly at his daughter and gave a resigned smile to Andi.

Other times there were tantrums. Many of them. Emily would explode in anger, with a rage that left Andi shaking in fear and bewilderment.

"I hate her," she would hear Emily scream. "She's ruined our life. Why? Why, Daddy? Why, Daddy? Why, Daddy? Whhhhhhhhyyyyyy?" Her voice would become a plaintive moan, rising to shrieks and wails. "If she stays, I'm going," she would shout.

Ethan, bewildered and guilty at his child's pain, would sit and talk her through as Andi sat alone in bed, quaking, wondering why no one stood up to this child, no one stated that this behavior was unacceptable. And then she understood.

Ethan was as scared of the screaming as she was.

Emily had all the power.

And yet . . . and yet. Amidst the tantrums, the screaming, the slamming doors, and those first, tumultuous years, were moments of glory. Moments when Emily would come and sit next to Andi on the sofa and lean her head on Andi's shoulder, when Andi would feel herself overcome with love to the point of crying.

Moments when Emily knocked gently on the door of their bedroom and asked to snuggle. Ethan would be in the shower, and she and Andi would watch funny animal videos on YouTube, and giggle together, tucked up in bed.

Andi would take the girls shopping, and buy them anything they wanted, within reason. She spoiled them: American Girl dolls for

Sophia, and cool teenage clothes for Emily. All Andi wanted was for them to be happy.

And to have children of her own.

They married two years ago and stopped using protection on their wedding night. Ironically, that was the first night Andi woke up drenched.

Her next period hadn't arrived, and she had never been late. Andi had run out to the pharmacy and come back with a pregnancy test, knowing the pink lines would indicate pregnancy. She peed on the stick with a huge smile on her face, staring at the stick in disbelief when it came back negative.

Twenty-four sticks later, all negative, her period came. She had looked at the blood and burst into tears, at a client's house, in the small half bathroom to one side of the mudroom. She hadn't wanted to come out, and the client had eventually knocked on the door and asked if everything was okay.

It wasn't.

They kept trying. Several months later, Andi, who hated going to the doctor unless she thought she was truly dying, went to the doctor. The night sweats, she had decided, after spending an afternoon on the Internet on various medical websites, were cancer.

She wasn't sure which kind, but she was sure it was cancer. Ever since her mother's diagnosis, every ailment, every mole, every headache was something more.

It was the fear that always hung over Andi. A headache was never just a headache, it was a brain tumor. A stomachache was pancreatic cancer, and so on. Except Andi never actually went to a doctor about it, instead using the Internet as her unofficial diagnostician. She would convince herself she had something terrible but would not go and see a doctor, and after a few days, she would have forgotten about it entirely.

But these night sweats were bad. Usually whatever symptom it was she was worried about would go away, but this was happening more and more often.

"Will you just go to the doctor?" Ethan had finally said. "If nothing else, it will just put your mind at ease."

And so she had.

Dr. Kurrish had peered over her glasses at Andi and asked a series of questions. Had her periods changed? Yes, Andi had admitted. They either came every two weeks, or sometimes not for six, and when they did, they were shockingly heavy.

How were her moods? Dr. Kurrish had asked. Terrible, Andi had said, but that was largely due to a stepdaughter who hated her most of the time, who had started coming back drunk at fifteen (although she didn't actually tell the doctor that part), and to a husband who refused to do anything other than tell his daughter he understood her pain.

Any unusual changes in hair? Her hair had become thinner, she said and, with embarrassment, admitted she had taken to plucking out a few stray whiskers on her chin.

"I think," Dr. Kurrish had said, "you are going through perimenopause."

"Menopause!" Andi had exclaimed, louder than she intended. "But I'm only forty-one. I'm trying to have children. How am I going through menopause?"

"Not menopause." Dr. Kurrish smiled. "Perimenopause, the period leading up to menopause, and it can happen to women even in their thirties. It doesn't mean you *can't* get pregnant," she said gently, although the expression on her face told a different story, "but it's unlikely. Your ovulation is much more erratic, and it becomes harder . . ."

She stopped at that point, as Andi started to sob.

. . .

She and Ethan talked about IVF, but the chances of its being successful, given her age and the added bonus of the perimenopause,
were slim, and not worth the vast expense.

They talked adoption, although vaguely. Ethan wasn't a fan, and
eventually he pointed out that they already had two children, that although Emily was difficult at times, Sophia loved and adored Andi,
and perhaps . . . wouldn't it be better . . . might she find a way to be
happy with the family she had rather than the one she didn't?

She agreed to try to reconcile herself, still hoping that she would
be one of the lucky ones, that despite the advancing menopause, it
would still happen, but the hope was fading. She would wake up in
the middle of the night, particularly those nights when she woke up
cold and wet, feeling an empty hole in her heart.

They hadn't used protection ever, and still, every month brought
disappointment. There were times she cried; couldn't stop herself
gazing longingly at the young mothers in town, with newborn babies
cradled in slings around their necks. She felt a physical pang of loss.

She loves the girls, Sophia particularly, but the longing for a child
hasn't gone, and these nights, as she moves quietly around the house,
looking in on the girls, she feels it more strongly than ever.

Andi moves quietly from Sophia's room, stands for a while outside Emily's. Emily is seventeen now. She drives. The tantrums have
lessened, but there have been other problems.

Last month she lost her car for a week, for coming home drunk.
She wasn't driving, was a passenger that night, but still, there had to
be a consequence.

"I hate you!" she'd screamed, this time at her father. "You can't tell
me what to do! I'm almost eighteen! I'm an adult, not a fucking child!"

"Don't swear at me," Ethan said, sounding calm, although the
muscle in his left cheek was twitching, always a giveaway. "And I am

your father. While you are living in this house, you will follow the house rules."

"Fuck you!" she shouted, throwing the car keys at her father, who ducked, so they hit the door frame, leaving a small chip and a grey mark. Emily stormed out while Ethan just sank down on the sofa, looking dazed.

"You can't let her speak to you like that," hissed Andi, standing at the bottom of the stairs with her arms crossed. "It's disgusting. I've never heard of a child speaking to a parent like that."

"What am I supposed to do?" His voice rose in anger. "You're always telling me how to deal with my child, but you have no idea what it's like."

There was an icy silence.

"What's that supposed to mean?" Andi asked slowly. Her voice was cold.

"Nothing." He shook his head, burying his face in his hands. "I didn't mean anything. I just mean I don't know what else to do."

"You did the right thing," Andi said eventually, breathing through her anger, for she knew what he meant: she wasn't a mother. She couldn't understand. "You took the car away for a week. Now you have to stick to it."

Ethan nodded. "I know."

"Really," Andi warned. "When she comes to you tomorrow, crying and saying how sorry she is and she'll never do it again, you can't do what you did last time, you can't give her the car back."

Ethan looks up at her sharply. "Last time? I've never done this before."

"No, but last time she was drunk you told her she couldn't go to Michaela's party, and when she apologized, you said she could."

Ethan sighed. "I'm trying," he said eventually. "I'm just doing the best I can."

The latest transgression resulted in a curfew being imposed. Midnight. This is for two weeks. Starting three days ago.

S ome of the time, when Andi wakes up drenched, she changes and goes straight back to sleep. Tonight is not one of those nights. Back in bed she tosses and turns before sighing deeply and reaching over to click on the bedside light.

Next to her, Ethan moans slightly and rolls over to face away from the light, but he doesn't wake up. Damn. Her book is downstairs.

Reluctantly—sleep is no longer an option, and what else will she do—she climbs out of bed again, padding out of the bedroom to go downstairs.

The woven wool carpet is warm and comfortable, and she braces herself for the cool wood floors of the hallway, making yet another mental note to buy some slippers.

At the far end of the hallway, Andi notices a light coming from Emily's bedroom. Strange. Surely she should have been asleep by now. Perhaps she has fallen asleep with the light on. Andi moves down the hallway and gently pushes open the door, shaking her head in dismay as she surveys the chaos.

Crumpled clothes are strewn all over the floor. A pyramid of makeup, with a fine dusting of face powder covering the carpet, lies by the mirror. The comforter on the bed is scrunched up, and it is hard to tell whether there is anyone in it until Andi, gingerly stepping over odd shoes, bowls half-filled with days-old encrusted food, draws closer.

The bed is empty. Emily is nowhere to be seen.

Two

. . . .

As if on cue, downstairs, the sliding door to the yard creaks open, and there are slow, uneven footsteps. Emily. Home. Andi freezes. With her own children, she knows she would go straight down and confront, but this is not her own child, and she isn't sure that, at four thirty in the morning, she is ready to take on the tantrum that will undoubtedly ensue.

If she does go down, Emily will beg her not to tell her father, but how can Andi not tell him? He has to know. This is not okay, and she cannot withhold it from him, not least because she is worried for Emily, terrified that her life is spinning out of control, and the only person who may be able to stop it is her father.

Through the balusters, Andi sees Emily weave through the hallway, a smile on her face. Andi tiptoes back to her bedroom, pulling the door until there is just a crack, and watches as Emily trips up the stairs, recognizing the smell as soon as Emily drifts past the door.

This time, she is stoned.

Again.

. . .

This isn't within Andi's frame of reference. She wasn't a kid who
did such things. Perhaps if she had been, she wouldn't be so discombobulated by Emily's increasing preference for alcohol, or drugs,
when she goes out. The only kids Andi knew in high school who
were potheads dropped out, then went on to . . . nothing.

Other than Gary Marks, who became an Internet bazillionaire.

But Emily is still a child. She is seventeen, young for her grade,
and has decided not to go to college this year, but to take a year off
instead, a year in which to mature.

Thus far, she hasn't applied anywhere; the more time that passes,
the more Andi realizes that Emily's throwing her life away is a very
clear, and terrifying, possibility, increasingly becoming a probability.

Emily is clever. And funny. She is the sort of girl whom everyone
thought would always be at the head of the class, but the teenage
years derailed her, and the rebellions seem to be more than the classic
teenage kind.

The friends Emily had when Andi first met them have long since
disappeared. Samantha, and Becky, and Charlotte are still the golden
popular girls, the girls Emily once whispered with and went to dance
class with. The same girls Emily now hates.

Emily's crowd is now what Andi would call *goth*, but what she
thinks might today be called *emo*. They dye their hair jet-black, and
have piercings. Emily came home with a pierced nose last month. It
could have been worse, Andi thought. It could have been a pierced eyebrow, or lip, or, like so many of Emily's male friends, giant holes in
their earlobes that they stretch every few weeks by inserting bigger
discs in their ears.

She tried to ask them about it. Just last week, Andi came home
to find Emily in the kitchen making scrambled eggs for two boys,

sitting at the kitchen counter. They looked like twins, in their grey drainpipe jeans, raggedy sleeves hanging over their fingers, their hair, the requisite blue-black, covering their eyelinered eyes almost down to their pierced and sulky mouths.

"Hi!" Andi said brightly, putting the grocery bag on the counter. "I'm Andi. Emily's stepmom."

"My father's wife," Emily muttered, belligerently, from the stove. Andi didn't respond, putting her hand out to shake hands with the boys.

The first looked down at the hand as if he'd never seen one before, then warily took it and sort of held it limply before dropping it quickly. "Hey," he said.

"Hi," said the other. "I'm G-man."

There was something familiar about him. "G-man?" Andi peered at him.

"Yeah," he grunted, looking down.

"George!" she exclaimed suddenly. "George Mitchell?"

He shrugged.

"Oh, my goodness! You've . . . changed. I haven't seen you for years. How are your parents?"

"Dunno." He shrugged again as a hot red blush filled his cheeks. *Oh, God,* she thought, wondering if Beth Mitchell was going through the same hell as she was, wondering what had happened to her sweet, clean-cut son. She hadn't seen Beth in at least a year, not since she had run into her at a Bikram Yoga workshop (which Andi hadn't been able to complete, thanks to almost passing out from the heat halfway through).

"Is your mom still teaching at Red Dragon?"

George grunted something that sounded like a yes.

"Well, tell her I said hi," Andi said, peering at the black bone hoops in his ears, which had stretched the original piercing hole to half an inch, half an inch through which Andi could clearly see the French

doors at the other end of the room. "So Geor . . . G-man." She frowned, unable to tear her gaze away. "Can I ask you a question? What is it about the holes in the ears? I know I'm old, but I just don't get it."

All three teenagers looked at one another in horror as George shrugged, and mumbled in embarrassment, "It's just what everyone does."

And what will you do when you are my age? Andi thought. *What will you do about the inch-wide holes in your ears? What do you think your children will think, and how in the hell do you correct it? Can a plastic surgeon sew your ear back together?*

A vision appeared, of thousands of middle-aged people, all walking around with giant holes in their ears, giant earlobes dangling, swinging as they walked, getting caught on things and ripping.

"Do you, like, need anything in here?" Emily turned to her in exasperation. "Because we were having a private conversation."

The urge to laugh was suppressed. *A conversation? These kids can barely talk.*

"You want to put my groceries away?" Andi kept her voice light.

Emily paused, then: "Okay."

"Great. Thanks. I'll get out of your way. Don't forget to wash the dishes when you're done." She quickly walked out before Emily could say something else, but Emily called out just as Andi reached the hall.

"Hey, Andi?"

Andi turned, rare for Emily even to call her by name, and watched Emily leave the boys in the kitchen and come out to the hallway by herself, her hand extended.

"Do you know what this is?" Emily dropped her voice as she pointed out a rash on her fingers.

Andi peered closely. "I think it's just from dry skin," she said, "or maybe an allergy. Do you want some cortisone cream?"

Emily nodded. "You're sure I don't need a doctor?"

"I'm pretty sure, sweetie. Let's try the cream and, if it's not better tomorrow, we'll go to the dermatologist. How's that?"

Emily smiled, and her face lit up. "Thanks, Andi," she said, disappearing back into the kitchen, leaving Andi stilled by her sweetness, her turning to Andi as a mother, wishing she could hold on to these moments rather than have this constant pendulum, hate to love, to hate again.

At times like this, Andi feels a surge of all-consuming love for Emily, but more often it is a surge of dislike. Andi refuses to use the word "hate," at least out loud. But when Emily is screaming, and Ethan is paralyzed with fear, and Andi is railed against over and over, with no one standing up for her, this is what she thinks.

I hate you. I hate you. I hate you.

And during those times, when Ethan refuses to get involved, when he sits on the bed, looking miserable, looking from one woman in his life to the other, one of who is screaming, the other who is trying to get a word in but can't because she is constantly shouted down, this is what she thinks:

I hate you, too.

She doesn't. Of course she doesn't. But just as Emily blames her father for choosing Andi over her, it is hard, sometimes, when Andi is tired, and drained, and despairing at having to deal with the constant drama, for her not to feel that Ethan, in disappearing for hours to try to heal Emily's pain, has also abandoned her.

And when Andi is hurt, or abandoned, her natural inclination is, has always been, to run away; to make the hurt disappear by disappearing herself.

Emily is all she and Ethan ever fight about. All they have *ever* fought about. And five years on, in her deepest, darkest moments, Andi wonders for how much longer she can do this.

Whether it is worth it.

. . .

Emily weaves down the hall as Andi watches from behind the safety of the bedroom door; then Emily walks into Sophia's room. *Oh, God. Please don't wake her up.*

Andi hears Sophia's voice, sleep-filled, as the light is switched on, and now Andi has to intervene. She has no choice.

She walks firmly down the hallway, her heart already pounding with anxiety, and walks in to find Sophia sitting up groggily in bed, with Emily sitting on top of her.

"What the hell are you doing?" Andi says, her voice loud with anger. "Sophia was fast asleep. Get into your own room."

"Oh, chill," Emily says. "I just wanted to give my baby sister a kiss good night."

"Leave her alone. She was fast asleep," Andi says. "And wait until your father hears about you breaking curfew again."

Emily gets up and pushes past Andi in the doorway, pausing to lean her face in close to Andi's.

"Big fucking deal when my father finds out. What's he going to do? Take my car away again, then give it back when I cry? I don't care. The only thing he can do to hurt me is stay with you. Bitch." And she walks into her bedroom, slamming the door and leaving Andi shaking in the corridor.

Are you okay?" Sophia, still fuzzy with sleep, appears next to Andi. She nestles in close, leaning her head on Andi's shoulder and taking her hand.

Andi closes her eyes for a few seconds. She is the adult. She is the one in charge. She is the one who should be looking after the children. Instead, a thirteen-year-old is comforting *her*. This is not the way

it should be, and she has to pull herself together, if nothing else than for Sophia's sake.

"I'm fine." Andi smiles down at Sophia. "Don't worry so much. And get back to bed, young lady. You need your sleep."

"You know she doesn't mean it." Sophia frowns. "She means it at the time, but . . . not really. It's like a habit."

"Bed!" Andi points to the bed. Her world is topsy-turvy. A thirteen-year-old is asking her if she is okay. It should be the other way around.

"Okay, okay. Are you going to bed now, too?"

"Sophia"—Andi waits for Sophia to climb into bed, then pulls the covers up and tucks her in, Sophia scooching over to the side so Andi can sit down—"I will probably go back to bed, or I may read for a bit because I am not sleepy." She smiles down at Sophia as she smooths the hair back off her forehead, continuing to stroke her hair as Sophia opens her mouth in a huge yawn.

"Want me to stay with you for a bit?" Andi asks as Sophia nods with a sleepy smile.

Within minutes, Sophia gives the nod: Andi can go; she is almost asleep.

Oh, if only Emily were as easy as this.

What's going on?" Ethan is standing in their bedroom doorway as Andi pulls Sophia's door closed and walks down the hallway toward him, his hair tousled with sleep. "What's all the noise?"

"Emily just got in." Andi tries to keep her voice down, not wanting Sophia to be further disturbed. She gestures to Ethan to keep it down, then walks into the bedroom before continuing.

"Emily's either drunk or stoned, and she just woke Sophia up. I told her to go to her room, and she called me a bitch."

Their bedroom door is suddenly flung open. "That's because you

are a bitch!" Emily is there, in their room, glaring daggers at Andi, who feels nothing other than exhaustion.

"Yes, I know," Andi says wearily. "I've ruined your life, your life is hell, you hate me. Yeah, yeah, yeah. I've heard it all before." She turns to go into the bathroom, knowing the usual litany is coming, too tired to deal with it.

"I wish you'd die," Emily screams. "I wish you'd get hit by a car and die."

"Emily!" Ethan interjects. Finally. "Enough! You don't mean that."

"I do!" She now bursts into hysterical tears, which is usually enough to get her way. "I do. You don't love me anymore. Ever since she came on the scene, you stopped loving me. You don't care about me, and you're a terrible father now. I wish you'd all die." The sobbing increases as Ethan lays a hand on her arm.

"I do love you," he starts, his voice gentle as Andi watches in disbelief. Ethan looks up at her, and Andi shakes her head in dismay, turning to leave, knowing that she won't be seeing Ethan for the next hour while he calms his daughter down, putting his arms around her to rock her to safety as she sits on the bed.

It doesn't matter that Emily broke curfew and might be drunk and stoned. It doesn't matter that Emily just screamed terrible things. What matters is that Emily is upset, and Ethan, in these moments, exists only to comfort Emily.

Sure enough, just before she reaches the stairs, Andi turns to see, through the doorway of their room, Ethan, his back to Andi, holding a sobbing Emily, her head on his shoulder. Emily, in a creepily prescient moment, raises her head just then and locks eyes with Andi.

She gives her a small, triumphant smile.

D o you not see what this is?" Andi laments later to Ethan, who is tentatively sinking down on their bed, having finally calmed

Emily down by walking her to her own room and lying next to her on the bed, stroking her hair until she fell asleep.

Emily is asleep. Ethan is exhausted. There is no way in hell Andi can go to sleep now. She is as wound up as a spring, and any attempt to read now would be futile: she cannot focus on anything other than her fury.

"She has you wrapped around her finger," Andi insists. "What she said tonight was appalling. That she wishes I were dead? And you didn't say anything. As soon as you said 'enough,' she turned on the tears because she knows you feel so damned guilty that all she has to do is cry, and you'll sit there and give her all the attention she wants."

"I did say something. I talked to her about it," Ethan says weakly.

"Oh, for God's sake." Andi's exasperation is clear. "You talked to her about it? She comes in at four in the morning, stoned, when her curfew is midnight, wakes her younger sister up, tells me she wishes I were dead, and all you can do is *talk* to her about it?"

"What do you want me to do?" Ethan's voice suddenly rises in anger. "I'm fed up with this. With all of this. I'm trying to be the best father I can be and trying to be a good husband, and I'm constantly being put in the middle of the two of you. Why can't you just work out this problem between you? Why can't you just find a way to get along?"

"You think this is a problem between *us*? Everything I do is to try and make Emily happy. I buy her things, I take her out, I try to talk to her. I spend half my life thinking of what I can do that will make Emily's life nicer. Not Sophia. I barely think about Sophia because so much of my damned energy goes into Emily. And then I am repaid with her screaming that she wishes I were dead? And you think this is a problem between *us*? Are you kidding me?" Andi's voice is a scratched, loud whisper.

"Look at you." Ethan gives her a withering look. "You're react-

ing in exactly the same way as her. If you were calm and loving with her, she wouldn't be like this. She needs an adult in her life, not another teenager."

"For your information, I am calm and loving 99 percent of the time. I only lose it when I see how manipulative she is with you. When I walked away, and she was 'sobbing,' she smiled an evil smile at me. She knows she won tonight."

"Oh, don't be so stupid." Ethan looks at Andi in amazement. "*Evil smile?* What are you? Ten?"

"Okay. *Triumphant.* It was a triumphant smile. She knew she'd won because she got you to herself, which is all she wants."

"Oh, for Christ's sake." Ethan shakes his head. "Now you're the one being childish."

"Do you realize that she only ever throws these tantrums when you're here?" Andi continues. "When she's on her own with me, most of the time she's fine. Some of the time, she's even delightful. But as soon as you're here, she has to turn me into the evil stepmother again, and she starts acting up to get your attention. She'll do anything to make sure you choose her."

There is a long silence as Ethan looks at his hands.

"I can't deal with this tonight," he says. "I'm going out."

"Don't walk away," Andi says. "We need to talk this through."

"I'm done with talking." Ethan stands up, his voice weary as he pulls on some shorts and slides his feet into flip-flops. "I'm going for a walk," he announces, and Andi listens disbelievingly as the front door closes.

They have fought before. Many times. But this is the first time Ethan has ever left the house afterward.

Three
· · · · · · · · · ·

H ey, Andi!" Her neighbor Drew looks up from where he is replacing the cilantro that had bolted in the herb garden. "Where are you off to?"

Andi, about to go for a hike in Madrone Canyon, changes course and walks across the front lawn, stepping over the low rosemary hedge, into Drew's garden, and bends down to plant a kiss on his cheek.

"Hello, love." He stands up slowly, hands on his back. "God, I hate getting old," he groans, stretching. "I've been meaning to ask you, have you spoken to your friend Isabel?"

"Don't you mean, *your* friend Isabel?" Andi grins. Isabel is a childhood friend who landed in San Francisco a year or so before Andi. They bumped into each other one night in a restaurant, and despite not having seen each other for years, are now firm friends.

They don't see each other as often as either would like but have enough of a shared history for that not to matter. Months can go by, and when they do get together, it is just as easy and comfortable as if they had seen each other yesterday.

When Isabel excitedly announced she was marrying her long-term boyfriend, Greg, she asked Andi whether she knew of any great venues. Andi didn't, but she knew a man who would.

Drew not only found Isabel the perfect spot to get married, he has also ended up organizing the entire event, and, as a result, is now best friends with Isabel.

"*Our* friend," Drew says. "How's that? Is she happy? Does she like what I've picked for the lanterns?"

"Like? She *loves*! If it makes you feel better, she cannot stop talking about how beautiful everything is and how incredible you are!"

"It makes me feel better," he says, suddenly peering more closely at Andi. "You look like you had a rough night. Is everything okay?" Andi shrugs, is about to say everything's fine, but her expression gives it away.

"Come inside, love. Let's have a coffee. Or vodka perhaps? You look like you need it."

"You have no idea," Andi says, gratefully following him inside.

When Andi first moved into Ethan's house, next door there was a crotchety old couple who wasn't the slightest bit interested in being friends with Andi or Ethan and seemed to hate all children, particularly ones whose screaming could be heard across the neighborhood.

Andi still feels guilty at being relieved when they died. Mr. Whitehall died a few months after they moved in, shortly followed by Mrs. Whitehall, and the house was put up for sale.

No one wanted the 1930s cottage, which was unsurprising given that it was like a miniversion of Grey Gardens, but without the cats. Litter was piled up everywhere, it was filthy, and broken. Everyone who came in was horrified.

The Realtors tried to persuade the Whitehall children that they

would need to put a little money in to sell it, but the children were as unpleasant as the parents and too busy fighting over probate to want to contribute a penny, even to do the bare minimum to help facilitate a sale.

The house sat for months, and this was when the market was high. Everything else was selling, but no one could see past the years of neglect, until Drew. He arrived first, a former art director for a huge ad agency and now househusband with a spectacularly good eye, and saw, immediately, what it could be.

His long-term partner, Topher, came that evening, and despite his horror trusted Drew. On the plus side it was well below their top limit. It would mean they wouldn't be house-poor, they could buy the house, do it up, and still be able to head to Bacara for their regular rest and relaxation.

Andi brought them chocolate-chip cookies when they moved in, dying with curiosity about who had bought the house.

She caught a glimpse of Drew one afternoon—his six-foot-two frame and handsome, Spanish features hard to miss—and felt they might be friends. When they opened the door—Drew first, an expectant but warm smile on his face, with Topher, a cool blond prepster in khakis, a Ralph Lauren cashmere sweater wrapped around his shoulders, behind him, she knew she was right.

The long renovation had been more expensive and more time-consuming than either of them had realized, they told her, within five minutes of meeting her, but it was all worth it. Would she like to see? Would she, by any chance, be interested in a tour?

Walls had come down, windows put in, the space had been opened up. They walked from room to room, these two, tall, handsome men leading the way, brimming with excitement at their new home as Andi fell in love.

It helped that they had done exactly what Andi would have done herself, only with a more masculine design, and were working on

plans for a beautiful garden—gardening, Drew confessed, was his true passion.

Several hours later, Andi hadn't left. She found herself sitting at their kitchen counter downing peach mojitos and laughing more than she had in years. When Ethan texted her to find out where she was, she told him to come next door, and a firm friendship was formed.

Even Emily liked them, which was something of a first. When they did the garden, they put a hot tub in the corner, with grey wooden sun loungers on a gravel terrace, under the shade of a large eucalyptus.

They told the girls to use it whenever they wanted, and the girls took them at their word. Andi was terrified they would overstay their welcome, or that *the boys,* as they had come to be known, would regret their kind invitation; but they truly loved having the girls there, to the point where Drew removed one of the fence panels in the backyard, and put in a wooden gate so the girls could just go straight there.

The boys were a huge port in the storm that was Emily. They loved her, and seemed to understand her, and she was sweet with them, and chatty, and revealed things, in a way she never would with Andi, choosing instead to shut down when Andi was around.

"It's almost like a veil that comes down over her face," Topher once said. "I totally get what it's like because I've seen it."

"Can't you talk to her about it?" Andi pleaded.

"I just do it subtly. Talk about how much we love you, what a wonderful person you are. The couple of times I asked, she just goes into a bit of a diatribe, and we can't seem to get through."

"Oh, God," Andi had groaned. "I don't want to know."

"You really don't," Topher said. "Not because it's bad, but because it's just classic teenage hating the parents stuff. It's meaningless. And it will pass."

. . .

Topher is a recovering alcoholic. He will happily mix the mojitos but won't drink them. He has been sober for nine years, and his life, he says, has never been better.

Andi knows his routine. Three meetings a week, Tuesday mornings, Thursday nights, and Sunday mornings, seven A.M. If he misses a meeting, which he tries not to do, he will go to one the next day. Nothing is more important than his sobriety, he says.

Drew, as his partner, goes to Al-Anon. He doesn't commit to it quite as seriously as Topher does to AA, but certainly in the early days, when Topher was getting sober, Al-Anon was his support system, teaching him how to live with someone using drugs or alcohol, teaching him how to get on with his life instead of becoming enmeshed in Topher's.

In much the same way Andi's life is becoming enmeshed with Emily's. For when Emily is sweet, Andi is sweet. When Emily is angry, Andi is angry.

It is the very definition of codependency, as Drew gently pointed out, after months of listening to Andi talk.

They couldn't get involved when it came to Emily's accepting Andi as her stepmother, but they could get involved when it came to drugs and alcohol. That is something they both knew about, and with Ethan refusing to take it seriously, refusing to do anything about Emily's drinking and, Andi suspects, drugs, the boys are the ones she turns to.

Maybe the boys can tell her what to do.

Four
· · · · · · · · · ·

T his is not good," Drew says sternly, handing Andi another
cappuccino from the giant Gaggia sitting on the counter.

"Which bit?" Andi pauses from her reenactment of the
scenes from last night's drama to take a tentative sip, com-
plimenting Drew. "Delicious."

"None of it, but I really don't like that you and Ethan haven't spoken since then."

"I know." Andi stares down into her cup, then back up at Drew,
fear flashing for a moment in her eyes. "It's the first time he's walked
out."

"But he came back, right?"

"He had to shower and stuff, so we saw him, but it was just cold
and awful."

Drew shakes his head. "It's not insurmountable," he says finally.
"But you have to communicate. If you leave these things, they build
into bigger resentments, until the resentment is so big there's no way
to get beyond it. You cannot let this relationship get to that point.
You have to talk about this."

"Resentment." The word emerges from Andi's lips in a long, low whistle. "That's how I feel. All the time. Resentful. I resent that he doesn't stand up for me. I resent that he allows his daughter to treat me like shit. I resent that he thinks I am somehow culpable in this, that I have a part."

"Maybe you do."

"Drew!" She looks up at him sharply. "You know how I am with Emily. I don't deserve any of this."

"I didn't say you deserve it. I said that maybe you have a part. Not even consciously, but from her point of view, she had her daddy all to herself. She was his leading lady until you came along. Her real mother might not be interested in her, but she's still going to feel an intense loyalty to her, and how disloyal would it be if she loved you? How would that make her mother feel?"

"I do get it." Andi sighs. "I know all of that, but Drew, I couldn't be any nicer, I couldn't do more for this kid, and I'm at my wits' end. I don't know what else to do."

"You could try setting boundaries," he says.

"How?" Andi's voice rises. "Ethan can't set a boundary to save his life. He'll set a curfew, then not enforce it. Take away her car and give it back when she says sorry and turns on the tears."

"Honey? This isn't about Ethan's setting boundaries, this is about you. You can't change him," Drew muses, "it's true. But you can set boundaries of your own."

"I try," she says, "but . . ." and she trails off.

"What?"

"I'm as scared of her damned screaming as Ethan is. He'll do anything to keep the peace, give in to anything to keep her happy, and I just want to . . ."

"What?" he says gently.

Andi looks up at him with tears in her eyes. "Leave."

. . .

Oh God. She said it. She can't believe she actually said it out loud. Until this moment she wasn't even aware she had actively thought about it, but now that it's out there, hovering in the shocked silence, she knows it's true.

But it's not *always* true. That pendulum swinging from love to hate, the pendulum driven toward hate by resentment and fear, can come just as swiftly back to love, back to safety and security.

The nights Emily and Sophia are with their mother, supposedly one night a week and every other weekend, are the nights Andi looks forward to the most, the nights she doesn't have to worry about being held hostage by a teenage terrorist, doesn't feel the weight of dread sinking upon her as they pull in the driveway, not knowing whether they will find good Emily or bad Emily.

The weekends when they go hiking, or poke around the farmer's market in the CVS parking lot, or run down to Sausalito for sushi and a game of pool at Smitty's. Then they are just another couple strolling around the bay, looking at the boats, hand in hand, Ethan pulling her in for regular kisses.

"Do you know how happy I am?" he says, smiling down into her eyes.

"Do you know how happy *I* am?" She'll reach up and kiss him. And in that moment, it is true. In that moment, those moments, Andi knows they will be together forever. She didn't marry until her late thirties, and when she did, she married because she found a partner. Unlike so many other women she knows, she wasn't driven by fear: not having children; being left alone. She married because she found a man she loves, a man who makes her happy.

The qualities she loves about him are the same qualities she resents in his relationship with Emily. His kindness, generosity, calmness.

His selflessness, thoughtfulness, willingness to talk about any problems until they are resolved. When he is kind and generous with Andi, helping her sort out life's problems, she is grateful, but when he does the same for Emily after one of Emily's screaming tantrums, Andi feels exasperated that Emily has deliberately acted out knowing it will give her Ethan's attention.

But why can't he be more firm when it comes to his children? Why can't he learn to say no? Andi may not have children of her own, but she is a child, a beloved only child of parents who doted on her but still had rules, and who were strict, and firm.

Why can't he be more like her father?

D rew is first to break the silence. "You don't mean that," he says finally.

"You're right," she says. "I don't. But . . . sometimes I do. Sometimes I do just want to . . . leave. I'm tired, Drew. I'm tired of the drama, the screaming. I didn't sign up for this. I waited thirty-seven years to find the right guy, and he is. There's no doubt in my mind that he is the right guy, but the stepkid situation is just . . . too much. I can't deal with it." Tears fill her eyes as she sits. "I just don't know for how much longer I can do this."

Drew reaches out and puts a hand on hers, squeezing it. "Take a breath," he says, "and know that this will pass."

"I know," she says. "Until the next time. And the next. And the next."

"Andi, breathe!" he commands sternly, and this time she does. Closing her eyes, and with him, inhaling deeply, then exhaling as he counts.

After a minute, she opens her eyes and looks at him. "Thank you," she whispers.

"I need to say three things to you," he says. "The first is that you

need help. Not just you and Ethan, but the whole family system. You need to be seeing a therapist."

"I know, but Ethan doesn't want to."

"If the thought of leaving is even occurring to you, you're at a crisis point, and he may not have a choice."

Andi nods.

"The second thing is that we are not talking about a young child here. Emily is almost eighteen. I know she's taking this gap year to travel, but after that, she's going to college, right? And then she's gone. She's a grown-up. It's not like you have all these years ahead of you with her being at home. She's almost gone." He shakes her hand, smiling. "You still need help, but she's almost gone."

"I know. I know." Andi smiles. "You're right. I needed to hear that. I need to be reminded of it. When I'm in it, it's just so all-consuming, I can't think of anything else, I can't see a way out."

"I know, but it always passes, and you can always, always come and talk to me. Or Topher. We love you, and we love your family."

"So what's the third thing?"

"I'm having lunch with Pete, my trainer, and he's totally cute and flirty, and straight. I think you need some fun, so I'm sending you home to get some makeup, then you are putting your game face on and coming with me, and no, I won't take no for an answer."

Five

. . . .

Kids on stunt bikes are gathered around a bench, showing off tricks to one another making their bikes hop and skip as Andi and Drew weave out of the way, crossing over to the Depot Bookstore for lunch.

Andi smiles an okay as the kid shouts an apology over, then she pulls on Drew's sleeve to bring him to a stop.

"Explain to me again why you're having lunch with your trainer? And why I'm accompanying you, narrowly avoiding being run over by a BMX bike?"

"Because he's cute?"

"Yes. Other than that."

"Because he's been working me out for a year, and we've become friends. I think I may be his gay best friend. He wants to charm me into finding him some new clients, and I thought you might be interested."

"So that's your ulterior motive." Andi grins. "You think I'm getting a flabby ass."

"No, I think your ass is peachily perfect. But nobody's ass is stay-

ing peachily perfect after forty-two without a bit of help. Anyway, it's good for you. I know you totally hate exercise, but he'll work you out on the weights, and he'll go running with you, and I swear, you'll love it. He's fun. There he is!" Drew calls out to a man standing at the end of the counter, examining the homemade delicacies.

He is not very tall, and not what could be described as classically handsome, but there is something immediately compelling about him. When he turns to them and looks at Andi, she finds herself standing stock-still, startled.

He has amused, clear blue eyes, but it isn't that. Nor is it the strong but broken nose. It isn't his chin, with a scar running down the left side, or his short, dark hair, with just enough gel to brush it back over his head. It looks spiky but soft. Andi instantly wants to reach out a hand and touch it.

God he's handsome, she thinks. Then blinks. He isn't, she realizes, but there is something about him that is mesmerizing. She finds herself suddenly self-conscious, on the verge of blushing, when he reaches out to shake Drew's hand.

"So this is why you brought me here," he says, shaking Drew's hand, then engaging in the claspy man-hug thing that Andi has noticed everyone doing these days. "To torture me with all the refined sugar and white flour."

"We have organic, vegan, gluten-free cookies," the girl behind the counter pipes up. "If you're interested."

"I think chili's more my thing," Pete says. "But thanks. Hey"—he turns, finally, to Andi, who, willing herself to act normal, is stunned at the reaction she appears to be having to this man—"I'm Pete."

"Andi." She is shocked at the warmth of his smile, a warmth that travels up her arm, along with a slight warning bell that makes her shake her head ever so slightly, as if to dislodge the nugget of disquiet that has, without invitation, entered her being.

"Nice invite." Pete gives Drew an approving smile as Andi blushes.

"She's married." Drew shoots Pete a withering look. "To the greatest guy ever. And she's happy. But you're allowed to flirt because I know you're completely incorrigible, but don't get any ideas, okay."

"Either of you," he whispers to Andi as they follow Pete to a table on the terrace outside.

Later, when they've finished lunch, and are basking in the warmth, lingering over herbal teas, Pete says to Andi, "You look like you're in great shape," clearly lying.

"Great way to get new clients," Andi teases. "Tell them they're in great shape and don't need your services. For the record? I'm in terrible shape."

"I didn't say you didn't need my services." Pete reaches over and takes hold of her arm. "You're what, a size six?"

Andi, who ranges anywhere from a ten, to a more usual eight, to a very, very occasional six, and only ever for brief periods in her life, nods.

"You look awesome. You don't need to lose weight, but you could tone. See here?" he gently holds out the pudgy skin on Andi's arms as she cringes. "That would be gone in just a few sessions."

"Any other flaws?" Andi tries to hide her embarrassment. "Can you get rid of cellulite?"

"You don't have cellulite." Pete shoots a look down to her crossed legs, her shorts having ridden up when she sat down, then grins. "Trust me. I already looked. And no. This isn't about pointing out your flaws. It's just about toning up. You'll feel so much better."

"Well, thanks. I can see why you're good, but I don't have the time."

Drew frowns at her.

"What?" she looks at him. "Drew! I have a business to run, I'm a

wife, a mother, I can't fit the gym in on top of the other stuff I already do."

"I don't know you," Pete interjects kindly, "but I know you have time. We all have time to do the things we want to do, and if we don't, we make it. You only run out of time for the things you don't want to do."

"He's right," Drew says. "Look at you! You've wasted a whole morning and now a lunchtime with me, when you could have spent an hour of that in the gym."

"Okay, okay," she grumbles. "But now I'm feeling guilty at not doing any work today. I have to go." She stands up and gives Drew a hug, extending a hand to Pete.

"I'll take the hug, thanks," he says, and she awkwardly steps in, patting him on the back and wanting to leave as quickly as possible.

I'm married, not dead, she says to herself later, all the way home. *I'm married, not dead.*

"It's fine to be attracted to other people," she has heard herself saying to friends who have confessed to feelings they shouldn't be feeling for men who are not their husbands. "It's just not okay to do anything about it."

She hasn't found anyone even remotely attractive since meeting Ethan. She hasn't felt the thrill of attraction for anyone other than her husband for five years. She doesn't want to feel anything for anyone other than her husband, isn't looking to feel anything, isn't the slightest bit interested in other men.

I am being stupid, she tells herself; *I am reacting to the fact that a man, single, straight, and cute, paid attention to me, flirted with me ever so slightly.*

I am married, she repeats, over and over. *I am married to a wonderful man and, who knows, maybe one day soon I will find myself pregnant.*

And think what a beautiful child we would have together, a celebration of our love.

Please, God, she silently prays, *please let me be pregnant, please let me fall in love with my husband again, please, please, let life be good.*

It is good, she tells herself, forcing herself to focus on Ethan. *Soon,* soon, *Emily will be out of the house, and we will have the relationship I know we can have. He is a good man, I will not find better. He and I are meant to be.*

With great and grave effort, she manages to push Pete out of her head, but it is only when she gets home and finds Ethan clearing out the garage that Pete leaves her head completely.

W hat are you doing?" Fear courses through Andi's body as she approaches the driveway. It looks as if he is packing. It looks as if he is leaving. *She* might have thought about leaving, might have thought that she hadn't signed up for this, but she didn't expect, never expected, Ethan to pack up and leave.

"Organizing the garage." Ethan looks up. "Why? Did you think I was leaving?"

Andi feels a wave of shame and stupidity. "No."

"You did?" Ethan stands then, closing the box. "You really did? Because of last night?"

"I just got scared," Andi admits.

"Oh, love." Ethan walks over to her, extending his arms, and Andi gratefully sinks in.

"I love you. I hate these fights, these moments that happen when we disconnect from each other so completely, but that isn't what de-fines our relationship." He steps back to take her shoulders and look her in the eye.

"What defines our relationship is trust. And love. And communi-cation. I hated this morning. I hated that we didn't resolve it. I know

we need to talk it through, which is why I came home early, but I would never leave you, Andi. I love you."

"I'm sorry," Andi says. "I'm sorry I thought that, and I'm sorry for what happened. I just felt so resentful. It seemed like such a manipulation."

Ethan hangs his head. "I'm not saying Emily can't be manipulative. And she was wrong. And she said terrible things to you. I've spoken to her mother, and she's taking the girls this weekend."

"Really?" Andi feels a weight lift. "But it's our weekend to have them, and we have Isabel's wedding."

"I know. I already texted Isabel to say the kids wouldn't be coming. I told Emily I didn't want her around until she can conduct herself better. I told her it's fine to feel the way she feels, but it isn't fine to express it in the way she does. Not to mention the consequence of her breaking curfew. That's why she's going, very much against her will, to be at her mother's this weekend."

"How did she take it?"

His eyes flicker away. "You don't want to know."

"But you didn't cave?"

"I'm not as weak as you think I am."

"Thank you," Andi says, reaching up on tiptoes as she snakes her arms around his neck. "I love you so much."

Ethan gives her a half smile. "Does that mean I can tempt you upstairs for a spot of afternoon delight?"

Andi checks her watch. "We've got twenty-five minutes until Sophia gets back from camp. Think you can delight me enough in twenty-five minutes?"

A throaty laugh emerges as Ethan hauls her over his shoulder and runs upstairs, throwing her on the bed as her laughs turn quickly to slow, satisfied sighs.

Six
· · · · · · · · · ·

When Sophia comes home from tennis camp, Andi avoids Emily by putting Sophia in the car and taking her to the showroom. Sophia has a natural eye for design and loves nothing more than putting together sample boards in Andi's office.

Technically, Andi still calls herself a home-stager although most of the clients who go on to sell their homes thanks to Andi's staging then ask her to help them decorate their new houses.

The business has grown to the point where she now has a large warehouse—four times the size of the one she had when she ran her business on the East Coast—filled with furniture and accessories and furnishings that are rented out to turn houses into homes, with one corner devoted to bolts of fabrics and books of wallpaper for the interior decorating clients.

Andi answers e-mails, returns calls, and rings her suppliers while Sophia curls up on the sofa and leafs through old interior design magazines, tearing out pictures of rooms she loves, gravitating, naturally, toward children's bedrooms.

"I love this!" Sophia will gasp, holding something out for Andi to look at. When Andi goes over to the marble counter on which stands a kettle and a glass apothecary jar filled with tea bags, to make some tea, Sophia comes to stand next to her, wrapping an arm around Andi's waist.

"Promise me you'll let me work with you when I'm old enough," she says, leaning her head on Andi's arm.

"I promise. I already told you next summer, when you're fourteen you can work as my assistant." Andi smiles down at her and kisses the top of her head.

"I just love it here." Sophia sighs happily. "I'm so lucky I know what I want to do when I'm older."

"Interior decorator?"

"Mmm-hmmm."

"How about Emily?" Andi ventures, for the only way they know anything about Emily these days is by subtly asking Sophia. "What do you think she wants to do?"

Sophia shrugs. "All she's interested in these days is her boyfriend."

Andi is surprised. "She has a boyfriend?"

"Mmm-hmmm. Although I don't, like, know who it is today."

"There's no 'like' in that sentence. Who was it yesterday?"

"No! It's like, last . . ."

"No 'like' in that sentence."

"Sorry. Last week it was G-man, but this week it's li . . . sorry, it's someone else. She changes all the time."

"She does? She really has a lot of boyfriends?"

"Yeah." And Sophia turns away. Bored now.

We are so unaware, Andi thinks. *We think of them as children, long after they are children.* On some level, of course, they know that Emily must be sexually active, but is she really? Who with? Where?

It's not as if Emily makes any effort to be attractive to boys. Her raven black hair is stringy and greasy, her nail polish chipped, her clothes loose and voluminous to hide her ever-growing figure.

"Puppy fat," Ethan once said.

"At seventeen?" Andi countered.

"It'll go," he said, unconcerned.

Emily has a lot of boyfriends, Sophia said.

Who are they? And what, Andi wonders, do they see in Emily. Every day she has to hold back a nugget of judgment. Put your hair back, she thinks. Remove the eyeliner that has smudged into deep dark shadows underneath your eyes. Wash your hair. Stand up straight. Smile. You're so pretty when you smile, do you have to look so damned miserable all the time?

But she doesn't say it. Any of it. She holds her tongue and looks away.

Seven

. . . .

G od, I love it out here." Andi puts down the printout of the driving directions to look out the window as they drive past the sunlit open fields of Sonoma County: miles and miles of vineyards; rows of grapevines snaking dramatically up hillsides, disappearing over the crest. Itinerant workers, wide straw hats shielding them from the glare of the midday sun, hold baskets, carefully picking the grapes as they move slowly down the rows.

The valley gives way to the mountains. The roads become narrower, and darker, gnarled manzanitas and huge eucalyptus trees lining each side. Ethan slows to navigate the hairpin bends, each turn causing Andi to gasp in delight as she glimpses panoramic vistas through the trees, the sparkle of water in the far, far distance.

"This is amazing!" Andi turns to Ethan in delight, all drama and discord of the past few days forgotten. There is nothing like the sheer beauty of this state to lift her spirits. Whether it's the graceful curve of the Golden Gate Bridge, the smell of Stinson Beach, or the power of the skyscraping redwood forests, all of it brings Andi a feeling of deep peace.

Ethan grins. "I wish I could appreciate the views. I'm terrified of these damned turns!"

"Liar. You're fine," she teases.

"You're right. I love it out here. I always wanted to buy someplace in the country."

"I know. I used to think Mill Valley was the country."

"Yeah, right." Ethan shoots her a look, and they both laugh.

"So what would you have bought? A vineyard or a farm?"

"Farm, probably. With maybe a small vineyard, just enough to make wine for family and friends. I prefer it up here, though. Or Cazadero. Rustic and beautiful, not too precious."

"Could we have miniature sheep?" Andi muses. "I love those. And donkeys. And maybe a horse."

"A horse? You ride?"

"Oh, my God." Andi starts to laugh. "How is it we've been together five years, married for two, and you don't know I ride?"

"I guess you didn't tell me. What kind of riding? Western?"

"You are such a California boy!" She laughs. "I grew up in Connecticut, remember? I took riding lessons for years. I was obsessed with horses. The only fantasies I ever had at thirteen were of having my own pony."

Ethan shoots her a look. "Are you suggesting Sophia is having fantasies about something else? Because I'm a little freaked out right now."

Andi laughs. "No. She's got a couple of years to go. I'm just saying. I always wanted a horse. Look!" She points out a building, a private home turned into a winery, Mediterranean style, yellow plaster with a red tile roof, ivy tumbling down every wall. "Isn't that beautiful?"

"Beautiful. I bet it's only worth eight million."

"Really?" She turns to him aghast. "But we're in the middle of nowhere."

"It's still Sonoma County, which is pure wine country. Maybe where we're going is more affordable, but this whole area is so beautiful."

"Could we afford it? Even the cheaper areas?"

"No." Ethan laughs. "But it's fun to fantasize, and even more fun to look."

"Maybe I'll get a huge commission this year to do the interior design of a giant hotel, and they'll pay me a fortune, and they'll bring you in to do the landscaping, and we'll suddenly have a few million dollars spare. Whaddya think?"

"I hope the money gods are listening." Ethan shakes his head as he turns onto an old, narrow dirt road, slowing to avoid the potholes and peering out the window. "Where the hell are we?"

Andi looks down. "This is right. Just keep going for four miles, then it's on the right."

A split-rail fence appears, marking a driveway, at the end of which are several people milling about. As Ethan pulls in, they turn and wave.

"Oh look! There's Greg!" Andi presses the window down. "Hello, groom!" she calls, as Greg comes to the car. "How are you feeling?"

"Great." He smiles. "Excited. Drew and Topher aren't with you?"

"No." Ethan leans over to explain. "Drew hadn't finished making the wedding cake so he was in a panic. He said he'd be here by three."

"That's good," Greg says, spying dishes on the backseat. "What did Isabel have you guys make?"

"Greek chicken kebabs and tzatziki dip. I have *slaved*!" she jokes. "Honestly, do you know how many hours it takes to skewer chicken? I am now an expert chicken-skewerer. I'm thinking of starting a new business."

"I'm happy we could help." Greg laughs. "Seriously? You're amazing. Thank you. It's so mind-blowing how all our friends are

helping us with this wedding. It makes it real, you know? Intimate and warm, and wonderful. Thank you. We're parking in a field over there." He gestures to a bumpy field in the distance. "Can I help you bring the food over?"

"Absolutely not," Andi says. "You go and concentrate on your wedding. Don't worry about us."

In the field adjacent to the parking area are huge metal sculptures that spin lazily in the sun, changing as the light hits different parts. Guests are wandering through, standing beneath giant sculptures, fantastical half-man, half-beast goliaths, gazing in awe.

"This is *awesome*," Ethan murmurs, looking around him in wonderment. "What is this place?"

"See that barn?" Andi points out a large barn in the distance, with old broken-down tractors outside, piles of scrap metal, large aluminum bins. "Isabel says there's an artist who leases the barn, and this is his work. He makes stuff for Burning Man."

"Cool." Ethan whistles. "It's beautiful. I thought you didn't even know what Burning Man was." He is teasing, reminding her of when she first moved here and had never heard of the biggest arts festival on the West Coast. "Want to go sometime?"

Andi gives him a hard look. "Do you *know* me? I love you, mister, but a camper I am not."

"What about if we rented a luxury RV? Then you'd be comfortable. It's amazing."

"If you'd asked me twenty years ago I might have jumped at the chance," Andi says. "But I'm just too damned old."

"Bullshit. It's all ageing baby boomers and Generation X-ers like us."

"Speak for yourself, my love."

"I know, I know. You can take the girl out of New York, but you can't take New York out of the girl."

"Now you're learning!" she says, patting him on the butt. "Let's go and put the food down."

They find Isabel helping to string lanterns from the branches of a huge old apple tree, under the leaves of which she and Greg will be getting married.

Other friends are stringing Japanese paper lanterns from tall posts in the field—lanterns Drew found for next to nothing in Chinatown—zigzagging over long trestle tables, benches on either side, with simple burlap runners down the middle, jelly jars of cottage flowers, zinnias, and stock, and phlox and lavender, dotted down the center.

It is a hive of activity, friends and family members coming over to say hello, all helping with the cooking, the decorating, the music. Kids run through the busy adults, weaving in and out between their legs, two teenage girls on babysitting duty, trying to herd the kids down by the creek, where large flat stones let the water rest, forming a natural swimming hole.

There are a series of buildings, barns, outbuildings, one of which contains a basic kitchen. An old commercial stove, and a barbecue made from oil drums cut in half, on which marinaded chicken drumsticks are spitting. Dusty strings of colored fairy lights are strung between old Victorian gaslights, wrapped around beams, looped around vintage cowboy posters.

Someone is pouring homemade lemonade into a giant glass dispenser, another is pounding mint with a pestle in a large mortar, adding sugar for the mojitos that will be poured into jelly jars and handed around to the guests.

"This is amazing!" Ethan turns to Isabel in amazement. "How did you find this place?"

"How do you think?" She grins.

"Drew?" Ethan ventures.

"Of course." Isabel shrugs.

"He is amazing!" Ethan shakes his head with a laugh as Andi gives him an I-told-you-so look. "Is there anything he doesn't know?"

"Lots. But when it comes to hospitality and cooking, and especially finding the perfect spot for your wife's oldest friend to get married, he's the best," Isabel says.

"He wouldn't tell me anything," Andi says. "I've been trying to get details for weeks. What are you wearing?"

Isabel leans in. "Want to come and see?"

"Am I allowed?" Andi can't hide her surprise.

"No, but I love my dress so much, I can't stand it. I have to show my favorite girlfriends. Come." And, grabbing Andi by the hand, she pulls her toward one of the outbuildings. "Sorry, Ethan!" she yells over her shoulder. "I'll only steal her for a little while."

Oh, Isabel." Andi gently runs the ivory chiffon through her fingers. "It's beautiful."

"I know!" Isabel says. "I know it's a bit much, and I never thought I wanted a proper wedding dress, but I saw this and just completely fell in love. I can't wait for Greg to see it. I know he thinks I'm wearing some hippie dress, which I was planning to, of course. He'll be amazed."

"You're going to be so gorgeous." Andi reaches over and tucks one of the curls back behind Isabel's ear. "What are you doing with your hair?"

"Totally messy, but up. Loose curls." She gathers her hair up with her hands. "Basically, just this, held with a big clip. But," she says shyly, "I have fresh flowers I want to wind in. I was going to ask a couple of friends to do it for me. Would you be one of them?"

"Help you get ready for your wedding?" Andi feels a lump in her throat as Isabel nods. "Are you kidding? It would be an honor!" And Isabel throws her arms around her as the two women envelop each other in a tight embrace.

. . .

I t is so different from Andi's wedding, and hers was so different from
the weddings she attended back in New York back in her twenties
and early thirties.

Andi didn't want what so many of her friends had had, the perfect
fairytale wedding, the opportunity to be princess for a day. They
took over the Maidstone Arms in East Hampton for beach weddings,
the New York Botanical Garden or the Knickerbocker Club in New
York for formal, elegant affairs.

Two hundred guests were always invited; three hundred; four.
The wedding was organized by their mothers, with Vera Wang dresses,
and catering by Abigail Kirsch. It was never about the couple, Andi
thought, even then, but about presenting an image to the world, an
image of who they were going to be, this new couple, forging a new
and fabulous life together.

It is one of the blessings of not getting married until she was almost forty, she thinks. She didn't need the big dress, or the hundreds
of attendees, or the day that was all about her. Ethan had done that
the first time around, and Andi didn't want that kind of wedding.
Their ceremony was small and intimate, about them, and their family, and, of course, everyone walked on eggshells around delicate
Emily.

Andi had taken Emily shopping to buy whatever dress she liked.
She hoped Emily would choose something lovely, but didn't try
to dissuade her when Emily chose a floor-length stretchy black
jersey dress that was less *The Wedding Party* and more *The Addams
Family*.

She had asked Emily to be her maid of honor, had bought her and
Sophia each a delicate pearl necklace, with a tiny pearl-and-diamond
pendant. They were expensive, and beautiful, and when Emily "lost"
hers before the wedding, Andi didn't say anything.

Emily cried throughout the ceremony, sobbing throughout the vows, hiccuping loudly throughout the "I do's."

She had run out, loudly and dramatically, crashing through the doors, immediately after Ethan put the ring on Andi's finger, and Andi had grabbed on to Ethan's hand to stop him from running after her, flashing him a warning look with big eyes. To his credit, he had stayed, but he kept looking toward the door. Physically, he was in the room next to her; but emotionally, he was outside, with his arms wrapped around his daughter.

Andi's mother was still alive then, fighting her way through chemotherapy, her magnificent hair now gone, a chic bobbed wig in its place.

"My love," she had said to Andi when they were milling around, the immediate family and their four closest friends. "You have your work cut out for you."

"Oh, Mom." Andi turned to her, scared. "Is it going to be okay?"

"Yes, my darling," she said. "He is a wonderful man, and that is what is important. Emily is a teenager, so these years, these difficult years are nearly done. I'm sure things will change once you settle down into your new life. It's one thing to create drama before you are married. *That* I understand—she is trying to prevent it from happening—but once you are married, then what? Then she'll have to accept it. It will all be fine, you'll see." But her eyes were filled with doubt.

Andi shakes the memories of her own wedding out of her head. It wasn't a day of happiness and joy, as she had hoped, but of tension and upset. She had been glad when it was over, when Ethan's parents had taken the girls to drop them off at their mother's, when they were finally on a plane headed to Zihuatanejo.

Had it been a premonition, she sometimes wondered, in her darkest hours. But no, she refuses to believe it. A car honks a short burst, disturbing her thoughts, and she looks up to see Topher's car kicking up a cloud of dust as he pulls into the driveway.

"Cake, anyone?" he hollers out the window and, with a large smile, she goes over to see what he has pulled off. He's giving her strange looks as she approaches, but she has no idea what they mean.

"Look who I found!" Topher's voice sounds suspiciously—almost deliberately—cheerful, Andi realizes, slowing as she reaches the car.

Peering through the window, trying to decipher Topher's tone, Andi sees Drew in the passenger seat and, slumped in the rear seat, her mouth in a sulky frown, Emily.

mily?" Andi says with a sinking heart, trying desperately to sound bright and cheerful. "Aren't you supposed to be at your mom's this weekend?"

Emily shrugs. "I was bored so I came back to Dad's."

"And we found her there all by herself, so we threw her in the car and brought her with us." Drew steps out the car and walks around to the trunk to get the cake. "Kids were starting to come over, and we were worried."

"What do you mean, *kids?*"

"Just . . . cars pulling up. We sent everyone away and locked up the house. Don't worry, but Emily refused to go back to her mom's, and we thought this was the best thing."

"It was. Thank you," Andi says, squeezing his hand. "I just . . ."

"What?"

"I just needed one weekend to ourselves." She turns her head and drops her voice to a whisper, ensuring Emily doesn't hear. Tears fill her eyes as she shoots a look at the black-haired figure frowning in the backseat. "I needed a weekend without the filthy

looks and the sarcastic comments and the rudeness. I just needed a break."

"We're here with you," Drew says quietly. "We'll look after you. Topher already told her she has to behave."

"He did?"

"You know my husband. He's pretty damn tough when he needs to be."

"She didn't throw a fit?"

"No. I think the kid is desperate for some boundaries."

"Tell that to her father," Andi says.

B oundaries." That loaded word is bandied about by people who think they know everything about parenting. It is the word that Andi uses more than any other when she and Ethan are talking, or *arguing* about what is wrong with Emily.

As a child, Andi was never aware of the word "boundary." It wasn't talked about; her parents did not sit with other parents and discuss how every child needed to know where the limits were in order to feel safe. Andi did not plead and whine and beg for something she wanted, long after her parents had said no, in the knowledge that if she created enough of a scene, in all likelihood she would get what she wanted.

She was the only child of older parents who had given up on the desire to have children. At forty-four, entirely unexpectedly, Judith and Oliver Fieldstone found themselves pregnant.

Andi was adored and revered from the beginning, but she knew her place. Her parents had her eat dinner with them every night, with a beautifully set table in the dining room, joining in the adult conversation. They talked about their days, and about museums they had gone to, books they had read, plays they had seen.

When they had finished eating, Andi would clear the table and dry

the dishes her mother washed. If she misbehaved, or got "fresh," a stern look would usually be all it took for remorse to flood her small body as she apologized.

"No" meant no. If ever Andi didn't listen, her mother would start counting, the threat of "three" being so terrible, Andi always did whatever she was supposed to have been doing by "two."

The boundaries were invisible, never talked about, but were absolutely there: lines she would never dare cross, too frightened of the consequences.

Despite this, Andi knew she was loved. At night, before bed, she would sit in her mother's lap, their fingers intertwined as her mother read her a story. When Andi would look up and catch her mother gazing at her, there was infinite adoration in her eyes.

The family home, with all its invisible boundaries, was her mother's haven, a place filled with quiet and calm. Andi knew she was loved, and in turn loved her parents, but she wished—oh how she wished— they were younger, like all the other parents.

She wanted them to be young, and hip, to be interested in pop music and parties, not opera and the ballet. She wanted brothers and sisters. She wanted her parents to be invited to the neighborhood barbecues that seemed to be a constant occurrence during the summer—a roving party at someone else's house every night of the weekend.

She wanted to eat dinner at a stool at the counter, at five o'clock. She wanted PB & J for dinner, and macaroni and cheese, and green bean casserole made with Campbell's Mushroom Soup, not the fresh, grilled steaks and salad, the Sôles Veroniques the coq au vins that they sat down to on a regular basis.

Andi wanted friends to come over and tear through the house as their mothers sat with her mother at the kitchen table, drinking coffee and smoking, and barely raising an eyebrow at the children.

Her parents were only in their forties when they had Andi, but back

then, that made them ancient, at least one generation older than the other parents.

And when the parents of her class friends got together for impromptu barbecues and drinks, Andi's parents were never included. When Andi's friends came over, her parents didn't gossip at the kitchen table over coffee but attempted to engage her friends in discussions about what books they loved, or what plays they had seen.

Andi was mortified. Why couldn't her mother be like all the other moms? When Andi had a sleepover, her mother had packed them a midnight feast, but instead of dime-store candy and chocolate like all the other kids, she had made sandwiches, and given them apples. One time there was cottage cheese. Andi wanted to die.

When she grew up, she determined at a very young age, she was going to have a huge family. Tons of kids, and all their friends. She was going to have a freezer filled with pizza, and a pantry filled with Campbell's Mushroom Soup and Lipton's Onion Soup Dip. She was going to fill her house with people, and she would let her kids have the basement all to themselves, and once they were down there, she was never going to disturb them.

And she would never, *ever*, ask them their opinions on books or current affairs.

As an adult, Andi adored her parents. She used to tease them that she grew into them, but in part that was true. They were educated, sophisticated and, as she discovered when she was older, tremendous amounts of fun. None of which were qualities she was able to see, or appreciate, as a child.

When she was small, Andi decided she was going to have the life she couldn't have when young. Even though she didn't meet Ethan until her late thirties, even though he already had two daughters, even though one of the daughters hated her, and she is going through perimenopause, which means her moods are horrific, and she probably

won't ever have children, she still thinks there is some hope for them to be the happy family she has always wanted.

If Ethan would only set some boundaries. If Emily would only learn to accept her and be happy. If . . . if . . . if. There has to be a way. Andi is almost, *almost* sure of it.

Emily, honey?" Andi, determining to make an effort, leans into the car. "Want to come with me and see Isabel's dress? It's so beautiful. She said she—"

"Where's Dad?" Emily interrupts, sharply.

"I think he's helping set up the bar," Andi says as Emily climbs out, deliberately pushes past her, and walks off.

"See?" She turns to Drew. "See? I try my damnedest to be nice all the time, and she's just a total bitch." She inhales sharply. She may think the word, but she doesn't ever say it out loud.

"She is," Drew says, as Topher walks around the car. "I agree. You were being lovely, and she was awful."

"Maybe that's part of the problem," Topher says slowly.

"What do you mean?"

"You try too hard. Emily knows she's got you wrapped around her finger. She knows she has all the power because you give it to her."

Andi shakes her head. "How? How do I give her the power?"

"*Emily, honey?*" Topher does a surprisingly good imitation of Andi, and Andi instantly hears the fearful, pleading tone in his voice.

"Oh, God," she says. "Did I sound like that? I was just trying to be loving."

"I heard fear, which means so did Emily, and that empowers her."

"So what do I do? Ignore her?"

Topher shrugs. "That's a good start, I'd say."

"But . . . I was kidding. I can't just ignore my stepdaughter."

"Yes, you can. Right now, you're giving her total control of your mood. Try detaching from her. She is who she is, which is nothing to do with you. You didn't cause her mood, you can't control it, and you certainly can't cure it."

"But I always think if I'm supernice she'll love me."

"I know," Topher says kindly. "That's the root of all codependency. You think it's something to do with you, but it really isn't. Detach with love. Let her do whatever she's going to do and try not to focus on her. You're here for Isabel and Greg, and you're here to have a good time."

"But look." Andi gestures over to the far side of the field, where she can see Ethan talking to someone. Hanging off him, her arms around his neck, pulling him down, is Emily. "How can I ignore that? Now she's going to spend all evening dragging him away from me. Not to mention the inappropriateness of a seventeen-year-old hanging off her father like he's her lover."

"It is a bit weird," Drew interjects.

"No it's not," Topher says. "I mean, in our world it is, but Ethan feels constantly guilty about who Emily is, that the divorce might have caused this, and so he doesn't say no. He doesn't know whether this is appropriate or not, he just knows that this is what Emily does, and if he pushes her away, she's going to think he doesn't love her."

"Can't you say something to him?" Andi says.

"No." Topher laughs. "I can't triangulate. You could say something. Or . . . you could just let it go."

Hi, baby!" Ethan turns with delight as Andi walks over, Emily's having wandered over to the fence to see the horses in the field. "What's the matter?"

"I just . . . I need to wrap my head around Emily being here."

"I get it," he says. "But I'm so glad she's here rather than at home.

I just texted her mom. Brooke didn't even know she wasn't in the house. I worry about Sophia. I don't know." He shakes his head. "It makes me want to go back and change the custody agreement."

"Sophia would tell us if things got bad," Andi says. "Listen, I know we've talked about this before, but there were a couple of raised eyebrows about the way Emily was draping herself all over you just now."

Ethan looks aghast. "*What?* From who? It's my *daughter.*"

"Ethan, she was practically climbing on top of you."

There is a silence during which a cloud passes over Ethan's face. "Don't start this again now," he warns, his voice low and steady. "Just leave it alone."

"Leave what alone?" Andi's voice climbs. "Do you have any idea how inappropriate it is? She isn't being your daughter when she hangs off your neck and nuzzles against you. She's being your lover."

"Oh, stop," Ethan barks suddenly. "I'm fed up with hearing this. Frankly, I'm pretty disgusted that you would even think such a thing. She's a kid. My kid. She's just showing me affection."

"Oh, for God's sake," Andi snorts. "You have no idea how inappropriate her behavior is. When you sit down and she curls up on your lap, nuzzling your neck . . . you think that's cute, but it's not cute, it's inappropriate because she's trying to replace *me.*" Andi stops, shocked at the whine in her voice, and turns away as Emily appears, standing squeezed up against Ethan and taking his hand.

"Daddy," she sings in a little-girl voice. "Will you come and see the ponies with me?" She rests her head on his shoulder as she glares at Andi.

"In a minute," he says, removing his hand and stepping aside as Emily's eyes brim with hurt. "Andi and I are just finishing a discussion."

Emily stands there, waiting.

"Emily, we need a moment."

"Why? There's nothing you can't say in front of me."

"Yes there is," he says. "Please. Just give us a moment."

"It's always her," Emily sneers. "You always choose her. *Andi* needs a moment, *Andi* needs me, *Andi* wants me to do something with her. You've become a terrible father. I used to love you, I used to be proud to call you my dad, but now it's clear you hate me and Sophia, and you know what? We hate you, too." Emily turns on her heel and storms off.

Ethan looks at Andi, his lips pressed together in a thin line, shaking his head.

"Thanks," he says. "Really. Thanks a lot." And he turns to go after Emily.

"No." Andi grabs his arm. "Okay, I'm sorry. I didn't mean that, but Ethan, please don't go after her. Just leave her. This tantrum is for you, and if you go to her now, the evening is ruined."

"I can't just leave her," he says.

"Why not? What's the worst that can happen? She gets depressed and bored and comes back?"

Ethan shakes his head, torn. "I . . . I don't know."

Topher suddenly walks up, a cold beer in each hand, one of which he hands to Ethan.

"Hey, buddy," he says. "What's up?"

Ethan shrugs. "Not much."

"Emily's in a bad mood, and Ethan was just about to go after her," Andi blurts out. "I was telling him to leave her."

"Teenagers." Topher rolls his eyes. "I'd leave her to it. She'll get over it."

Ethan hesitates as his shoulders sink in defeat. "Okay," he says finally. "Cheers." And he takes a long, cool sip, unable to look Andi in the eye.

One of Greg's friends plays the guitar, and the air is suddenly filled with beautiful music, indicating that the guests should gather around the tree.

Another friend stands up and sings a Carole King song, then Isabel appears, gliding gracefully out of the barn, her chiffon dress gathered in one hand to keep it from draping on the floor, a huge smile on her face as she looks from one guest to another, her gaze ending on Greg, who is already wiping a tear from his eye.

They stand together, holding hands as Drew, who qualified as a minister in order to marry them, offers his words on marriage, commitment, and love. He quotes Kahlil Gibran, then speaks from his heart, offers lessons he has learned, talks about why the love between Isabel and Greg is so special.

Andi and Ethan, furious at each other, stand side by side with acres between them, but as Drew speaks, they both find themselves softening, remembering why they married, why they love each other. When Isabel starts to softly say her vow, Andi slips her hand into Ethan's.

"I'm sorry." She reaches up and whispers into his ear.

"That's okay," he whispers back. "I'm sorry, too," and he gives her a sad but loving smile.

"I do love you, you know," she says, squeezing his hand.

"I love you, too." He squeezes back.

The music strikes up again after the wedding, and Andi leaves Ethan talking to friends as she wanders around the property. She is concerned about Emily, as much as she doesn't want to admit it, and wants to, if not talk to her, at least see that she's okay.

She crosses over the fields to the one with the sculptures in it and stands for a long time, mesmerized by the sun slowly setting behind the trees, lighting up the majestic creations.

There are voices coming from the barn. Laughter, which sounds like it might be Emily's. Andi carefully picks her way around the objects that are scattered around the barn—found metal, oil drums,

bicycles, old farm equipment—and stops at a crack in the shiplap sides, through which she sees the source of the laughter.

There are two boys, one standing, one sitting. The standing one has a buzz cut, the seated one a long, dark ponytail, a beard, and piercing blue eyes. Even from a distance, Andi recognizes the sexual energy emanating from him.

He is in jeans and boots, an oversized shirt, leather bracelets on his wrist. She wouldn't have expected him to be Emily's type, but Emily cannot take her eyes off him. She is Emily at her best, smiling, laughing, teasing.

God, she is so beautiful when she smiles, when her face lights up, Andi thinks.

"You should really come," the bearded guy is saying as he reaches for his beer. "It's totally awesome. Just filled with beautiful art and beautiful people."

"You're such a hippie," the boy with the buzz cut says. "I've gotta carry on with that welding. I promised Ken I'd finish it today."

"I think it's so cool you're artists' assistants," Emily says. "But when are you actually going to be artists?"

"Oh, man." The bearded guy laughs, shaking his head. "We already are. I have a ton of stuff I work on at home, but working with Ken is the most unbelievable experience. That's what I meant about Burning Man. I'd never get to meet the people I did, or have the experience I had if I weren't there as Ken's assistant. It doesn't mean I'm not already an artist, though. If you have a creative soul"—he touches his heart with a nod and a serious expression—"it doesn't matter what you do, that will always come out."

Emily nods sagely. "Yeah. I get that," she says. "I'm supposed to be going to college in a year, but I don't know. I'm thinking I might learn more at the University of Life." She laughs.

"Oh, yeah, baby." Bearded Guy laughs. "I hear you. So what are you doing this year?"

Emily shrugs. "I'm supposed to be traveling and working, but I haven't really done much about it."

"You should come hang with us," Bearded Guy says. "Starting with Burning Man."

"You're really trying to convince me to come?" Emily says, her doubtfulness giving away her youth.

"Well, yeah. You're cool. It would be fun to have you."

"Cool?" Emily gives him a long, slow look. "I thought I was hot . . ."

Andi, watching from outside, catches her breath. This is an Emily she hasn't seen before, an Emily who is fully cognizant of her sexuality, who knows exactly how to use it.

"Well, that goes without saying," the bearded guy says slowly, and as Andi watches, he leans forward and kisses Emily.

Andi jumps back as if burnt, hesitates for a moment, then walks quickly back to the party.

W here've you been?" Ethan says, extending an arm to draw her close.

"I went for a walk. I found Emily."

His face grows serious. "How is she?"

"She's . . ." No, she won't tell him. "She's great. She's found some people her own age, and she seems to be having fun."

"Really?" Ethan's face lights up. "Where is she? I'll go check in on her."

"No. Don't. She didn't see me. She's doing her thing, and she's fine. Let's just enjoy the party."

Ethan nods. "Sounds like a plan."

Nine

. . . .

A ndi puts down her book and listens hard. Next to her, Ethan is sound asleep, his breath escaping in a stream of air with an occasional snore.

They didn't get home from the wedding until almost one in the morning, but Andi can't sleep without reading at least a few pages. Ethan has always been asleep within seconds of his head touching the pillow, but without a book to quiet her mind and still her racing thoughts, Andi would be awake for hours.

She picks up the book again, then hears noise. Slipping out of bed, she pads quietly to the door, opening it to hear the unmistakable sounds of retching.

Emily.

They had not seen Emily all evening, and when she had finally appeared, after Andi had called her name in the general vicinity of the barn, she had been disheveled and, Andi was certain, drunk.

"You okay?" Ethan had asked, concerned, after Emily had lain down on the backseat of the car.

"Just really tired," she mumbled, closing her eyes.

"She's drunk," Andi mouthed to Ethan, who gave her a look of disdain.

"Do you always have to be so negative?" he mouthed.

Andi just shrugged and spent the entire car ride home looking out the window. She imagines that Ethan must have roused Emily and gotten her to bed, while Andi walked straight into the house and upstairs, shutting the bathroom door to brush her teeth and get ready for bed. Alone.

Now, though, Emily is sick. Andi walks down the hallway, sniffing the faintest smell of pot, growing stronger as she approaches Emily's room. The bathroom door is open, and Emily is squatting, with her arms draped around the toilet seat, retching into the bowl.

"Are you okay?" A wave of sympathy sweeps over Andi as Emily turns around and looks at her, shaking her head, her face a pale shade of grey, her eyes red-rimmed. Andi rubs her back and, with her other hand, gathers Emily's hair out of her face, holding it out of the way.

"What happened, sweetie?" Andi says, reaching over for some tissues to wipe Emily's mouth.

Emily finishes and collapses next to the toilet, closing her eyes. "I feel sick," she moans.

"I know, baby," Andi says, getting up and wetting a washcloth, pressing the compress on Emily's forehead. "How's that? Is that better?"

Emily nods.

"Oh, Em. I think you're sick because you mixed alcohol and drugs. Your body's rejecting it."

"Didn't," Emily mumbles.

"I can smell the pot," Andi says, not unkindly.

"Gonna be sick again." Emily reaches blindly for the pot and retches again, leaning her head on the seat in between. Andi rewets the washcloth, and holds it on the back of Emily's neck until she's done.

"Do you want to try and get to bed?" Andi asks gently, helping

Emily up. "I'll get you a bowl to keep by the bed. Here, let me help." And, with an arm around Emily's waist to steady her weaving, she walks her back into her bedroom.

Emily sinks into bed, and looks up at Andi, the color slowly returning to her face.

"Can you not tell Dad?" she manages to get out. "Please?"

"I won't tell him." Andi doesn't know why she agrees, but Ethan doesn't need to know. She sits down on the bed, next to Emily, and strokes the hair out of her eyes, holding the compress down before standing up to get a bowl.

"Where are you going?" Emily's eyes flash open in a panic.

"I'm just going to get a bowl," Andi says. "I'll be right back."

As Andi places the bowl next to the bed, Emily looks as if she might have fallen asleep, and Andi quietly turns to leave when a small voice says, "Don't go."

Andi turns around and goes back to the bed.

"Can you stay with me? I'm scared."

"Oh, Em." Andi's heart bursts open. "Of course." And when Andi sits down, Emily slips a clammy hand into Andi's and turns her head, closing her eyes.

"I'm sorry," she whispers.

"It's okay," Andi says. "These things happen."

"No, I mean I'm sorry for being so mean to you."

Andi wants to say something. Is trying to say something. But the lump in her throat is so big, it won't let any words emerge, and she silently strokes Emily's forehead, the dislike, irritation, and yes, sometimes hate she so often feels for her stepdaughter having disappeared like a puff of smoke.

Andi knows that when the girls are at their mother's house, they are lucky if there is any cereal in the pantry for breakfast.

Sophia tells Andi how she gets herself up, dresses, packs her backpack, and makes her own snack. If there's food at home for breakfast,
they help themselves, and if, as so often happens, Brooke has not
managed the grocery shopping, Sophia counts off the hours until
snack time, whereupon her teacher will dispense crackers for the kids
who forgot a snack.

Sophia has even confessed to sometimes "borrowing" food from
her father's, hiding it in her bedroom at her mother's, doling out
crackers, or cookies, for both of them to take to school, or munch
on when Brooke is too drunk to think about dinner, and there isn't
any food in the house anyway.

It breaks Andi's heart. Often, Andi will drop a snack off at school
on the days the girls are with their mom. She knows that Brooke sleeps
late, usually hungover, rousing herself occasionally to plant a hazy
good-bye kiss on Sophia.

She just doesn't know quite how bad it is.

When the girls are with their dad, Andi makes sure she is up, well
before Sophia, and has breakfast all ready. Waffles, pancakes, bacon,
strawberries, French toast. She makes different breakfasts every day,
always something hot. Sometimes oatmeal, fruit salad, scrambled
eggs, with orange juice and a beautifully set table.

Sophia loves it. Emily usually sleeps through it, although in her
junior year she always grabbed something when she thought Andi
wasn't looking, stuffing it into her bag for later.

Children need a good breakfast. Andi's mother's words echo in her
head as she cracks the eggs in the bowl, pausing to pour herself some
fresh coffee, checking to see she still has fifteen minutes to herself
before she wakes Emily.

These children, in particular, need a good breakfast. Children
who are so neglected when they are at their mother's, who, if they're
lucky, manage to get enough money to go down to the deli and get
their own dinner.

And look at how appreciative Sophia is! See how she comments on the delicious smells as she walks into the room, look how her eyes light up when Andi places French toast and bacon in front of her.

If their own mother won't do it for them, Andi will. And she will do it better than anyone else.

Andi and Brooke do not have a relationship. She has heard the entire story from Ethan, and lately, from Sophia, who would never directly criticize her mother; but Andi can hear Sophia on the phone, hears the sharp barbs Brooke constantly shoots at her daughters, and the upset in Sophia's voice.

On some level, the girls know that their mother is an alcoholic. A couple of years ago, when they were having friends for dinner, Sophia, who had been about to turn eleven, had wandered into the kitchen just in time to hear Ethan ask one of their friends what they would like to drink.

"She'll have wine." Sophia had grinned. "All grown-ups drink wine all the time!" Her voice was a singsong of innocence. "It's like"— she paused, thinking—"it's like the grown-up version of juice!" She was delighted with her explanation and didn't see the look that passed between Andi and Ethan.

"No," Ethan quickly said. "That's not quite true."

"It is!" Sophia had giggled. "Mommy drinks wine *all* the time!"

Later that night, Andi left their guests to go and tuck Sophia in. "Not all grown-ups drink wine all the time," she said. "I know sometimes it seems like that, and some grown-ups drink more than others, but many don't drink at all. Look at me. I hardly drink wine at all. It gives me headaches."

Sophia thought for a while. "So what do you drink?"

"My favorite is cranberry juice and seltzer," she said, thinking vodka martinis were probably not what was called for here.

"I love those!" Sophia said. "And ginger ale and cranberry juice!"

"Yum! You have to understand that all grown-ups are different, and some drink wine, but many don't."

Andi didn't know how else to explain to Sophia, sweet innocent Sophia, that there is another path; not all adults are like her mother; not all adults drink wine like water, and please God let Sophia choose the other fork.

Andi has met Brooke less than a handful of times, and then, mostly, by mistake.

Long before they met, she read the e-mails Brooke would send, accusing Ethan of being a terrible father, blaming him for her financial woes, telling him she would take him back to court to get full custody.

Or Brooke would phone the house, leaving slurred, drunken messages on their voice mail, telling the girls they had to do something, reminding them to hand in some homework,

It felt, always, as if she was staking her claim. She refused to accept Andi as an equal: *she* was the mother of the girls, and she wasn't about to let Andi forget it.

"Tell your father's wife," Brooke would say disdainfully to the girls, never referring to Andi as their stepmother.

The first time they met was in Whole Foods. They were on their way back from a hike, and ran in, dividing and conquering as soon as they got through the doors—Andi to the fresh produce, and Ethan to the dairy section.

Arms full of vegetables, she came across Ethan, talking to a woman whose face was hidden by a mop of thick, curly blond hair.

"Hey." Andi walked over. "I wondered where you'd gotten to."

Ethan looked stunned.

"Oh, I . . ."

"Hi." Andi put him out of her misery, extending a hand to the woman, smiling and realizing, as she looked into her eyes, exactly who she was, for she looked like Sophia. Only sexy. And older, of course. "I'm Andi," she said more tentatively.

"I'm Brooke," Brooke said, with a pained smile that did not reach her eyes.

"I figured." Andi forced a smile. "You look exactly like Sophia."

"So they tell me," Brooke said. "I was just talking to Ethan about the schedule."

"Okay," Andi said, standing there, waiting for them to finish. Brooke just looked at her.

Oh, no way, Andi thought, realizing that Brooke was waiting for her to disappear. *No way am I going to make myself invisible. I am his wife now, and stepmother to your daughters, and you will not dismiss me like this.*

She shifted weight onto her other foot to get more comfortable, and with a smile on her face, merely nodded and looked pleasantly at Brooke.

"So is there more?" Ethan said eventually, unable to deal with the discomfort of the extended silence.

"Yes. I guess I can phone you later," Brooke said.

"Oh, please, feel free to finish your conversation," Andi said.

"No, forget it," Brooke said. "I have things to do. Nice to meet you," she tossed over her shoulder, not looking at Andi as she turned her cart and disappeared around the corner.

"Wow." Andi stood still, stunned. "Was I just . . . dismissed? Was that really as horribly uncomfortable as it felt?" She turned to Ethan, shaking her head in disbelief. "Did that really happen?"

"That was awkward," Ethan murmured, running his fingers through his hair.

"Awkward?" Andi said. "Could she have been any ruder?"

"Well, yeah. She could have been a hell of a lot ruder. At least she was sober."

. . .

S he isn't what I expected," Andi mused on the way home.
      Ethan shrugged.

"She's so different to me. Sexy." She frowns. "When you said she
was Waspy, I thought she'd be stiff, not earthy and wild. But . . . wow!
She was so rude. I'm shaking."

Ethan, wisely, chose not to say anything, just squeezing her hand
from time to time as he let her vent most of the way home.

"I'm having such a hard time picturing you and Brooke married.
Married!" Andi swivels in the passenger seat to look at him. "Seriously. I just cannot imagine the two of you together in a million years.
She seems so weird. I never expected her to be . . . that. Although I
guess, listening to those messages she leaves, I shouldn't be surprised."

"I know." Ethan sighed finally. "That's Brooke. She's bitter, and a
pain in the ass, but you know what? She's also the mother of my children, and I need to just get along with her for the children's sake."

"You're right. I'm sorry. I just feel horrible for the girls, and I
never expected her to be so rude when she met me. I'm the stepmother to her daughters. I know she may hate that, but at least pretend
to get along, for the sake of the children if nothing else. Would you
maybe say something to her?"

"Right," said Ethan. "Because that'll be well received. Look, I
agree the two of you don't have to be friends, but it's easier if you just
accept that her behavior has nothing to do with you. Isn't that what
Topher always says to you? She is who she is, and you need to move
on. She drives me nuts, as you well know, but I've learned to always
stay calm. I yes her to death, then do whatever I want to do."

"Urgh. Do I have to?" Andi said grudgingly.

"I know," Ethan said wearily. "But it works, okay? You were

pretty amazing with her today, by the way. You were gracious and friendly. That's why I love you, because you were able to rise above it."

"Is that the only reason you love me?"

"No." He shoots her a sly, sideways look. "I love you for your body as well."

"I was gracious, wasn't I?" Andi says gleefully. "I was channeling Jackie O. But honestly, I was stunned at how different she was to my mental picture." And she didn't mention another word until she suddenly remembered she had to borrow a stick of butter from Drew, and spent a good hour sitting at Drew's kitchen counter regaling him with the whole story.

Subsequent meetings have been better, in terms of Brooke's behavior. There is a hint of a smile behind her tortoiseshell glasses, a pretense at politeness, but Andi can't forgive her being drunk in front of her children.

"It's just such a shame," she says to Ethan on a regular basis. "They get no attention, no love, no care when they're there. She's just drunk and angry. No wonder Emily's drinking. What other model does she have?"

"She has me," Ethan points out. "And you. Thank God. I need you to stop focusing on the negative. Think of all the good."

"I know, I know," Andi murmurs.

Most of the time, she manages fine. Most of the time Brooke has very little to do with their lives. But there are times when she phones drunk and Andi refuses to pick up. One night, Ethan turned the ringer off, too tired to deal with Brooke, and in the morning they scrolled back through caller ID to see how many times she'd called.

Thirty-seven times.

Between eight P.M. and half past midnight.

"What for?" Andi was bemused.

"Yes." Ethan shrugged. "That's why we turn off the ringer. Also," and he grinned, a naughty, five-year-old's grin, "nothing infuriates her more than not getting hold of me exactly when she wants to."

Now, when Andi is listening to her messages on the home voice mail, hearing Brooke's angry, slurring voice, she presses erase without even listening. The messages are always for Ethan, or the girls, and she figures nothing is that important.

Yet Brooke is the mother of her stepdaughters. While Andi is not friends with her, is mystified and upset at her behavior, she would never, never, let the girls know.

However conflicted they may be, however much Brooke also drives them crazy, particularly during these teenage years, she is still their mother, and they love and hate her in equal measure.

Sophia is only just starting to see her mother in a negative light. At thirteen, her hormones are changing; she is beginning to realize that her mother is not like all the other mothers. It used to be that when her mother would phone to criticize, or accuse, or berate, when her mother would point the finger of blame, it always bypassed Sophia and landed firmly on Emily.

Now, though, Sophia is finding she is more frequently in the line of fire, for no other reason than she is the one who is there.

Unlike Emily, she doesn't fight back. She doesn't scream, and shout, and slam doors. She tries to make it better. She offers to make her mother tea, or do the shopping, or urges her mother to sit down and let Sophia take over.

Which only serves to infuriate Brooke further.

I am okay, Sophia tries to tell herself. *This has nothing to do with me.* Except she worries that it has everything to do with her. That if she becomes the perfect daughter, if she does everything Emily can't,

if she is better, and sweeter, and more helpful, then her mother might start loving her again.

Her mother might get well.

"I want Mommy to get better," Sophia will say to Ethan when they are by themselves.

"I hate Mom," Emily will say to Ethan when they are by themselves.

Whatever they are saying, and whoever is saying it, Andi is careful never to say anything negative, or critical, or judgmental about Brooke. Not in front of the girls.

She has seen this happen. Remembers a mother in Sophia's class, divorced and struggling as a single mother with three children, talking about her child's distress that morning after he returned from his father and stepmother's house.

The stepmother had spent the morning asking the child why the mother was so cheap, why she never contributed anything, telling the child the mother had lied about money to get more in the divorce settlement.

And the child, sweet-natured Katie, naturally, was devastated, spending the entire day at school in tears.

Andi may disapprove of Brooke's drinking, but she would never even drop a hint that she felt that way. She tries not to talk about Brooke at all, and if she does, it is never negative, and never charged with emotion.

She saves those conversations for when she and Ethan are alone.

And the children. These poor, damaged children. Andi puts the bread in the toaster oven and slides the door closed, thinking about Emily last night, sleeping with her hand still in Andi's, wondering if Emily has a hope in hell. What would it take for Emily to be happy? To feel safe, and secure, and loved?

The Emily she glimpsed through a crack in the barn siding was

the Emily they all want her to be, all the time. Not angry, and sulky, and unhappy, but charming, and fun, and clever.

It still remains a miracle to Andi that Emily is not flunking her way through school. Her senior year was spent partying mercilessly, and it is only thanks to Emily's excellent memory that she actually managed to scrape through.

And scrape through she did, with SATs that were so bad, they have put off college for a year, during which time she will be traveling briefly, working, studying, and retaking the test to enable her to go to a decent college, to please, God, *please, please,* God, get a shot at having a decent start in life.

Already, though, Emily has done nothing about getting a job. She hasn't figured out travel plans, hasn't thought through the year, despite Ethan's sitting down with her and attempting to go through ideas with her.

"She has to do it herself," Andi says, watching Ethan try desperately to engage a bored Emily. "If she wants to screw it up, it's her life, you have to let her."

"She's my child," he says. "And right now she needs some help to get her on the right path. She needs our help and support. Both of us." He gave Andi a hard look.

P lease let the Emily she saw last night be the start of a new path. Please let that glimpse of a lovely Emily be the Emily she decides to be.

Ten

. . . .

'll get her up," Ethan closes the fridge door wearily, checking his watch and sighing. "Emily has to be on time for this and we're already leaving it later than I'd like."

"Want me to make eggs?"

"Sure," Ethan says, making his way out the room to rouse his sleeping daughter.

When younger, Emily had always expressed an interest in writing, and Ethan, scrabbling wildly to try and find something that would engage his daughter, has set up an interview with a small publisher who is looking for an intern.

Ethan knows nothing about publishing, but the last time they flew East to visit Grandpa O, he flew home earlier, alone, and found himself sitting next to a woman he is hoping may change his life.

Or at least, Emily's.

Robin Kall turned and introduced herself as soon as they sat down, and although Ethan wasn't in the mood to make small talk with a

stranger on a plane, her smile was so genuine, her warmth so enveloping, he found himself quickly enthralled.

She was passionate about books, with a radio show and a Huffington Post column he had read. She made him laugh with stories of the authors she interviewed on Reading with Robin, then moved him to tears when she talked about her mother's death from breast cancer, and the money she and her sisters, Laura and Jennifer, had raised as a result.

Her enthusiasm for everything in her life was infectious, and when Ethan mentioned that one of his daughters, Emily, had always loved reading, Robin instantly offered to introduce him to people to help her find a job.

She had a publisher friend in San Francisco, and although it had been some time, they had finally coordinated schedules to set up an interview for Emily.

The plan had been to collect Emily from her mother's this morning, but having Emily show up yesterday was something of a hidden blessing, for it is unlikely that Emily would have even been awake, let alone up and ready to go, had she stayed at Brooke's house.

At least this way, Ethan has more control.

"Morning."

Emily shuffles into the kitchen as Andi greets her tentatively, still glowing from last night's sweetness, from Emily's apology, her hand-holding, her vulnerability in showing Andi that she needed her, and more than that, she *wanted* her. Andi remains hopeful that last night marked a turning point in their relationship.

Emily doesn't respond, merely scrapes a chair back with a scowl as Andi, with sinking heart, slides a plate of scrambled eggs in front of her.

And Emily gags.

Pushing her chair back quickly, she runs from the room. Andi hears her retching in the powder room, and when she returns, she is grey.

"Just tea?" Emily nods, self-conscious suddenly, as Andi removes the plate. "Try some dry toast, sweetie," Andi says gently. "My mother always said it was the best cure for sickness. Black tea, dry toast, and lots of water to flush your system out. Can I make some toast for you?"

"Cool, thanks." Emily nods, not meeting Andi's eye.

Half an hour later, Emily is feeling a little better, both mentally and physically.

Ethan has run out to pick up Sophia from her mother's, since Sophia has softball early that morning, and Brooke can't be relied upon to get her there. When he walks back in he plants a kiss on Andi's shoulder as she puts the plates in the dishwasher before planting a kiss on the top of Emily's head.

"How's my girl today?" he says. "You were tired last night!"

Emily and Andi exchange a small smile. "I was," she says. "But I'm good now."

"Great. Ready to meet Bob Foster? He'd definitely be open to using you as an intern, he said. He wants to find out what you're reading and who you like. Did you prepare?"

"Kinda," Emily says.

"So tell me. Practice now."

"No, Dad! I'm not a child. I'll be fine, I don't need to practice with you."

"Okay." He acquiesces. "So did you have fun last night? We didn't see you all evening!" His voice has taken on a false cheerfulness that

he so often adopts when talking to Emily, as if by sounding happy and upbeat all the time, he will somehow make her happy and upbeat.

"It was awesome." She surprises them with her effusiveness. "Those sculptures were incredible, totally inspiring."

"Wow!" Ethan laughs. "You sound like you were really moved."

"I was. I thought it was mind-blowing. I met the artist and his assistants, and they were telling me all about Burning Man."

Ethan starts to laugh. "God. Burning Man. Those were the days."

"You've been?" Emily and Sophia say it in unison, both shocked.

"Of course! You don't get to grow up in California and *not* go to Burning Man. I went a couple of years, with a group of guys from school. It was a blast. It's an incredible place."

"Now I feel stupid," Andi says. "I know I've lived here for years, and I'm always hearing people talk about Burning Man, but I still don't completely understand what it is. I always think of its being like Woodstock, is that right?"

"Kind of." Ethan nods. "If Woodstock had been about art rather than music, and if it had been held in temperatures of well over a hundred degrees in the Nevada desert."

Andi shivers. "Sounds horrific," then corrects herself as she catches a familiar withering look from Emily. "I mean, it sounds hot."

"It is, but it's cool, forgive the pun. It's like landing on another planet. It's all about community, and self-reliance, and this incredible art, installations that are constantly moving and changing, everywhere you look."

Emily's eyes are wide. "The guys last night said it was the largest outdoor art gallery in the world. Forty thousand people. And they have villages, and streets."

Ethan nods. "I remember that. It's amazing that this huge town is erected in the desert, from nothing, for one week." He shakes his head, eyes misted over with the memory of years gone by. "I had a blast at Burning Man."

"So." Emily is wriggling with excitement. "Can I go?"

"What?" Ethan's reverie is interrupted. "When?"

"Next week. It's next week. They invited me to join them. Oh, Dad, it sounds life-changing, I really, really badly want to go."

"Who are these people?" Ethan asks.

"Dad"—Emily looks at him—"I'm not a child anymore. I'm almost eighteen. Soon I won't even have to ask you."

"You will if you expect me to pay for it," snorts Ethan.

"True, but you had an incredible time, right? How old were you?"

"Older than you. Nineteen? Twenty?"

"So only just older than me. And I bet there were tons of younger people there. I just . . . I feel in my bones there's something about Burning Man that's going to change me. I know we're going to see your client about publishing, but maybe art is my calling. Maybe I should be thinking about art school? You know how creative I've always been and how I love photography. I get it from you, right?"

Flattery will get you everywhere, thinks Andi, noting the discomfort on Ethan's face. *He wants to say no but with no good reason.*

"I think she should go," Andi says simply, seeing Emily's eyes widen with delight. Ethan looks at her.

"It sounds like it *could* be life-changing," continues Andi, "and what's the downside? It's one week, right? Next week?"

Emily gulps and nods, looking to her father.

"If I were to say yes, and I haven't said yes," Ethan warns, "but if I were to, there would have to be some rules."

"Of course, that's fine. I totally understand."

"I would have to meet the people you are going with, and I have to approve of them."

"No way, Dad. I get that you have to meet them, but you can't base this decision on liking them or not. That's not fair."

Ethan looks at Andi, who shrugs. "I kind of agree with her."

"But I have to meet them. And I have to have contact numbers and addresses for all of them."

"Does that mean yes? Does that mean I can go?" Emily is almost squealing as Ethan draws out the pause before finally exhaling with a long sigh.

"Yes."

"I love you, Dad!" She flings her arms around him and squeezes him hard as he laughs, then turns to Andi and, bubbling with uncontained excitement, throws her arms around Andi and squeezes her, too. Sophia shakes her head, smiling, and buries herself in her book.

"Oh, God." Emily runs out of the room, thumping up the stairs. "What am I going to pack?"

"Pack later," Ethan shouts up after her. "We have to leave here in ten minutes."

That was a nice thing you did," Andi says as Ethan gets his coat. "I know you didn't want to say yes, but it was good. It shows her you trust her."

"I know," he says. "And I have to admit, it feels amazing to see her so happy. I just hope she can be trusted. I hope she can't get into too much trouble. I hope she makes responsible choices." He stops and looks at Andi with panic suddenly in his eyes. "Oh, God. What the hell was I thinking?"

"It'll be okay," Andi says. "It may be life-changing after all. You'd better go."

"I'll see you later." He leans in for a quick kiss. "You're out tonight, right?"

"Yup." Andi does a quick roll of her hips. "Salsa dancing with the girls."

"You sure you don't want me to come and embarrass you?"

"Very sure, thank you. Girls' night out means no men allowed. I'm sorry, did I say no men? I mean no husbands allowed."

"Just you behave yourself," Ethan says.

"As if I would do anything else." And she gives him a wave as he goes to the foot of the stairs to shout for Emily to hurry up or they're going to be late.

S ophia?" Andi calls up the stairs. "Are you ready?"
    "Coming!" Sophia's voice floats down, and seconds later there she is, jacket on, backpack packed, book clutched tightly in hand.

"How did you manage to be so grown-up and responsible?" Andi shakes her head with a laugh. "Seriously? I have never come across two girls as different as you and your sister. How did it happen?"

"Seriously?" Sophia says.

"Seriously."

"Seriously, I think I'm a changeling."

"What?"

"You know. A fairy child who was swapped with a human baby. Somewhere out there, the real Sophia is being brought up by fairies, and I bet she doesn't have an evil older sister who tries to make her life a misery."

Andi barks with laughter. "I bet she doesn't, but your explanation suddenly makes perfect sense. I always knew you were an angel, and now I know why." She puts an arm around Sophia and plants a smacking kiss on her cheek as Sophia, giggling, pulls away and runs to the door.

A ndi initially thought that being first the father's girlfriend, then the stepmother, would put her in an awkward position at school. The mothers of Sophia's classmates had already had years of an established relationship with Brooke. Andi presumed Brooke would have

bad-mouthed her to the extent that no one would be interested in befriending her.

As a consequence, in the beginning, Andi tried not to get involved in Sophia's school life, stepping in only when she was sure there would not be a conflict with Brooke, or when Brooke was definitely not going to be turning up at a school event.

But as regular playdates were set up, and Andi got to know the mothers, she realized that Brooke wasn't true friends with any of them. She was far too self-involved and damaged, and the few that had reached out had ultimately found that a friendship was too difficult—Brooke would always end up blaming them for some small grievance, and she quickly developed a reputation.

It seems she had moved through the class, forming instant best friendships, only to have them inevitably explode a few weeks later.

Andi, on the other hand, is easy to get along with, and although it took time, slowly, slowly, some of those mothers had become her friends.

It is often like the schoolyard, she thinks, when she is in school. Brooke's role, Andi has come to realize, is as victim, and the women who did surround her, in a bid to help her, play into that. *Good luck to them,* Andi thinks, looking at the woman who is, apparently, Brooke's latest greatest. *Thank God for the friends I have found,* she thinks. *The friends who have provided a constant light in the tempest that comes in the form of Emily.*

Good luck to them, and thank you, Lord, for the friends that I have had the grace and good fortune to find.

Tess is Australian. She writes children's books, has a mouth like a trucker, although she claims to be training herself out of it, and is married to a bazillionaire, not that anyone would know it to look at her. She rarely wears makeup, lives in Patagonia and Reef flip-flops,

and has a mouth that looks as if she is always on the verge of laughter, which she often is.

She and her husband, Steve, a dot-com entrepeneur, live in a small glass house on Roscoe, with incredible views over the bay. They cycle everywhere, and when forced to drive, show up in a Prius, or Jeep.

Travel is their indulgence. They fly by private jet to their home in Aspen, or their villa in Mexico. They don't have a sitter for their two children, Griffin and Sydney, who is one of Sophia's best friends, but they have a cook and a cleaner who come every day.

Andi had no idea how much money they had until they invited her and Ethan skiing. That they were traveling for free on Steve's jet was jaw-dropping, then to see Tess and Steve's wooden house, tucked into the mountain, walls of glass with spectacular views, was awe-inspiring.

"They must be worth fortunes!" Andi whispered to Ethan that night as they showered in Tess's marble bathroom, laying their clothes on her freshly laundered Pratesi sheets.

"They are." Ethan laughed. "You didn't know? Steve is one of the biggest names in the dot-com field. Even I know who he is, and I'm just a landscaper."

"Wow. I just didn't expect . . . I don't know. She seems so normal. They're so . . . unpretentious. I always think people with vast amounts of money must be dripping with diamonds and driving Maseratis."

"That's because you're a New Yorker." Ethan smiled. "Out here in California, you can never tell. That's the beauty of living here. That's why I'll never leave."

Deanna is a yoga teacher and, of late, Andi's closest friend, the one to whom she turns if ever she needs to talk. Tall and willowy, she has curly blond hair that is always haphazardly shoved up on the top of her head with a large spider clip.

Ten years ago, Deanna became a Buddhist, and has always been

the calm one of the group, the girl who listens instead of shouting everyone else down in their exuberance and excitement, the one who thoughtfully and calmly imparts words of wisdom.

She has one child, Francesca, whom Sophia was superfriendly with in fourth grade, before they went their separate ways. Deanna and Andi have been trying to get the girls together ever since, but neither of them shows much of an interest in the other, and their mothers have accepted that if it is meant to be, it will be, and that it need not have an impact on the independent friendship they have forged.

Sophia turned to Andi just the other day and suggested having Deanna and Francesca over for tea.

"I thought you weren't friendly with Francesca anymore," Andi said as Sophia shrugged.

"I'm not really, but I think we should try because our moms are so friendly."

Andi had started, in shock. "Your mom's friendly with Deanna?"

"No!" Sophia laughed. "I mean you!" A warm glow filled Andi's heart as she put her arms around Sophia and gave her a hug. *If only this beautiful child were enough,* she thought. If only she could be happy with having these children, but the beauty of Sophia only makes her want a child of her own even more.

When her period is due, she is stressed and nervous, praying that it won't come, praying for the blue line. Deanna was the one who gently suggested Andi would benefit from yoga. Although Andi does, from time to time, attend classes, she doesn't really get it. Andi lives on nervous energy: constantly moving; constantly doing. When she exercises, she likes to feel it, and with everything going on in her life, she doesn't have the time for exercise.

Or perhaps she just can't be bothered.

Either way, yoga has always seemed too damn slow. She finds herself pushing up in downward dog and fighting the irritation. *Bored now.* She wants to move.

. . .

The first time Andi went to an event at the school, a school play, she stood in the reception area, sick with nerves, not knowing any of the other parents and aware of the looks she was getting, aware that she was, as the new girlfriend, an intruder. A few yards away, she caught the eye of a wiry blond woman who flashed a huge smile at her and beckoned her over.

I love her, she thought instantly, drawn by the twinkle in her eye. *I have no idea who this woman is, but I want to be friends with her.*

Tess's warmth enveloped Andi like a comforting blanket; they quickly became inseparable. Tess brought her new clients and had Andi decorate her den so she could show her off to others and bring in new business.

They went together to Deanna's yoga class after Deanna posted flyers around the school, and stood chatting with her for almost an hour after the class, decided then and there they would all have to get together.

Five years later, these women, together with Isabel and Drew and Topher next door, are Andi's family, although Tess has removed her children from the public school and sent them to Greenwood, so they see her less and less. Andi misses her, but Deanna has stepped in to fill the void, and Andi thinks of her as the sister she never had.

These women, together with Ethan, were the ones who surrounded her and eased her pain when her mother died. Andi thought she was prepared, had accepted that this time her mother couldn't win the fight. She flew to Connecticut to say her good-byes, holding her mother and whispering words of love, hoping that, despite the coma, her mother might be able to hear, hoping everyone was ready.

But how can you ever prepare for the loss of your mother?

Andi flew back home after three weeks, and found herself sinking into a deep well of grief. Those women, and Deanna in particular,

brought her trays of lasagna and chicken Marbella, drove the girls to their classes, sat and drank wine with her as she cried what felt like a never-ending river of tears.

Who is left, after all? No brothers and sisters, no grandparents, just her father, still in Connecticut, in the house that held all the memories of years gone by.

He is Grandpa O now, to everyone who knows him. The stern but loving father of her youth has been replaced with a little old man who is soft and smiley, whose eyes crinkle when he catches sight of the girls, particularly Sophia. He might be in his late eighties, but he is sprightly and spry, still managing to visit "his beloved girls" twice a year.

Andi had never thought about how not having her own children might have impacted her parents, until seeing them with her stepchildren. They were so loving, so warm, so entirely accepting, it filled her with a fresh sense of longing.

"I'm Grandpa O," her father introduced himself, not thinking for a moment that he should be anything other than a grandpa, nor treated by them as anything other than a biological grandparent.

"And I'm Granny J," her mother had said. There had never been any question of their being anything else. To Andi's amazement, they had morphed from the formal, reserved, rather awkward parents of her own childhood, to wonderful, warm, natural grandparents who showered the girls with love.

And the things Andi found so different as a child—the way they always treated her like a grown-up; the questions with which they bombarded her; the expectations they had of her being able to discuss grown-up affairs—the girls loved.

Especially Emily.

Granny J recognized the difficulties with Emily, saw how much Emily struggled with accepting Andi, yet she never treated Emily with anything other than love. Emily, in turn, adored her.

On the day she returned to California, after her mother's death, Andi curled up in bed, in the fetal position, and cried. She heard the bedroom door open, felt Ethan sit on the bed, stroking her back, for a long, long time. Eventually, when her sobs abated to lurching hiccups, then finally calm, Andi turned to thank Ethan, who hadn't stopped stroking her back the entire time.

But it wasn't Ethan. It was Emily, with tears streaming down her face. Andi had taken her in her arms, and this time it was Andi's turn to comfort Emily.

Her mother's death left a hole Andi hadn't anticipated. During the illness, she thought she was prepared for the end. Andi had lived on another coast for years, was used to not having her parents be part of her daily life. She would speak to them on the phone a couple of times a week, but days would go by when she didn't give them a second thought.

Nothing could have prepared her for those final days. For the tragedy and shock of seeing her mother after weeks of radiation, shrunk to nothing, a weak and whispery shadow of herself.

Nothing prepared her for the grief that took hold, the tears that came so unexpectedly when she was caught up in the mundanities of life, the sobs that wracked her body while she stood in the checkout line at Safeway.

Ethan was gentle and caring. Even Emily gave her a reprieve, after an outburst in which she accused Andi of not being the only one to suffer.

Andi turned to Ethan with tears, to her friends for laughter, for a reminder that life still needed to be lived.

Tess didn't stand on the doorstep with sympathetic eyes, asking plaintively, "How *are* you?" She pushed her way in and filled the fridge with food her cook had made for them, a huge box of See's chocolates, and turned to Andi, stating firmly she needed a drink, before pulling a bottle of tequila and a margarita mix out of her bag.

"I know it's sugary shit," she said, pouring margaritas for all of them. "But sometimes in life, you just need some sugary shit."

Deanna, who ate no sugar, refined flour, or meat, wordlessly stood up from her position on the kitchen stool, pulled open the fridge door, and pulled out the box of chocolates.

She ripped off the cellophane cover, threw the white corrugated paper resting on top of the chocolates on the floor, and grabbed, at random, three chocolates, before stuffing them in her mouth.

"She's right," she mumbled, her mouth full. "Sometimes you just need some sugary shit." And the three of them had sat there and laughed before, much to Ethan's horror, polishing off the entire box.

Eleven

. . . .

ndi opens the door, twirling with delight as Drew puts a hand to his chest.

"Wow!" He grins in approval as she grabs a purse and heads to his car. "You really look gorgeous. You should dress up more often."

They are going to a new salsa club in San Francisco. As a non-drinker, Drew is the designated driver, picking up Tess and Deanna en route. For their salsa lessons in Mill Valley, Andi wears black leggings and sloppy T-shirts, but for a club, she has gone whole hog.

A cherry red wrap dress, with Capezio T-bar shoes. Her hair in a chignon, possible only because she added a fake ponytail from CVS to her own short, sparse ponytail, twisting the thick bunch up and pinning it into a meaty bun. She considered adding a red fabric flower but decided it was too much.

But she couldn't resist the slick of glossy red lipstick, a color she would never normally wear.

"You know what you need?" Drew says as he opens the car door for her. "A red flower in your hair."

Commanding him to wait, Andi runs back inside, up to the bathroom, and grabs the flower, pushing it into the bun. Passing Ethan in the kitchen, she gives him a quick kiss as he tells her to have fun, then runs back into the car.

"Perfection." Drew claps his hands in delight as she turns her head before pulling out of the driveway.

Clubs are not the chosen destination of any of these women, not anymore, and Andi is grateful that growing older means you no longer have to pretend to have the desire, or the energy to go.

But salsa is different. When Deanna persuaded Andi to try out a new class a few months ago, Andi intended to go only once to keep Deanna happy. She never intended to catch the bug, but she felt the magic in that very first class and, toward the end, when she finally got the movements, felt it take hold, the music became a sensual throb that moved through her body and transported her to another place.

In the salsa class, she loved watching herself in the mirror in the studio, the way all of them moved their hips as they rolled from front to back, emulating José in his tight black pants as he encouraged them to be sexy and gorgeous.

"Feeeeel the beat," he said in his seductive Spanish accent. "Feeeeeeel it in your entire body. Move those hips, think of your looooover . . ." The first time he said this, Andi immediately pictured Ethan, in his cargo shorts and Reef flip-flops, a faded baseball cap on his head, and almost started laughing.

She caught Tess's eye, then Deanna's, and they all burst out laughing, all thinking of their unsexy husbands.

"Okaaaaaay." José had grinned. "Do not theeenk of your lover. Theeeenk of your dream lover. Theeeeeenk of Javier Bardem," the name sounding exotic and sensual, spoken in his native accent. "Theeeenk of him taking you by the hip, looking deep into your eyes, and spinning you around."

The women had stopped smiling and started thinking, all of them breathing a sigh of contentment as the music washed through them, and they started to realize what it was all about.

Now proficient, able to be led by a partner, they do occasional trips to salsa clubs—dark, and sweaty, and filled with swarthy good-looking men eyeing the women up and down. They realized quickly that what was missing from these clubs was a threat. The men weren't eyeing the women seductively, but rather to see who was a good dancer, whom they would choose next, not as a lover, but merely a partner in the sensual beat.

Deanna was the best. She rarely got a chance to leave the dance floor. When one song ended, another suitor would be waiting, smiling and nodding politely as the previous dance partner melted into the background. Deanna had a natural rhythm, and a flexibility that allowed these men to fling her around. She whipped her head back and forth and gazed into their eyes in an act of seduction that was truly an act, ending when the music stopped.

Occasionally, she had met prospective boyfriends at salsa clubs, had gone on dates, but never a relationship. She didn't mind. One of the things Andi appreciated most about Deanna was how she loved and accepted her life.

Deanna didn't think it would be better if she were married, or spend her time winking endlessly at people on Match.com. She didn't ask girlfriends to set her up, then sit over coffee relaying every detail about the night.

When she had dates, she was quiet about them. Tess and Andi had to drag information out of her, teasing her mercilessly about her reticence.

She was friends with her ex-husband, friends even with his long-term girlfriend. The only time she seemed to truly let her hair down, have fun, stun those around her with her sensuality and passion, was dancing salsa.

Tess, on the other hand, was dreadful. She had no rhythm but loved it anyway. She was only ever asked to dance by men who had just entered the club, who hadn't had a chance to watch her on the floor, and, of course, by Drew, who was brought into the salsa club for precisely that reason.

Andi does not have the confidence of Deanna, but she has the rhythm. She dances in a quieter way, loving the freedom salsa affords her.

She has been dancing with a tall man who does not speak English. Protocol requires they introduce themselves, but the music is too loud; she doesn't hear his name. The music fades, and they step apart, smile at each other as Andi feels a tap on her shoulder.

Turning, she finds herself face-to-face with Pete. The trainer. Drew's friend. He holds his hand out to lead her to the center of the floor, and she is grateful for the dark lighting so that he doesn't see her flush.

"At least I don't have to ask your name." He leans in close to her ear so she can hear him as the music starts, their bodies moving in unison.

"What are you doing here?" she says as he spins her away, then pulls her sharply back in.

"Same as you, no?" He laughs. "I'm here with friends. I just saw Drew. But I've been watching you. You're really good."

"Thanks. You're not so bad yourself."

"I bet you say that to all the boys." He grins. Andi looks away. *Focus on the music,* she tells herself. *Focus on the dancing. This is just a dance partner. Ignore the tingle of electricity I'm sure I feel.*

I'm married, not dead, she thinks. Again. *I'm married, not dead.*

"Your husband's a very trusting man," Pete says, pulling her in again, putting his lips so close to her ear they brush it ever so slightly. She shivers.

"He has good reason to be." She regrets that it comes out sounding like a schoolmarm, both prim and prissy.

"I'm not sure I would be so trusting if you were my wife," Pete says.

"This is just your schtick." Andi gathers her composure and leans in to say it close to his ear. "Flirting for new clients. Does it work?"

"No," he says firmly, spinning them both around. "I don't flirt for new clients. Ever. I only flirt with gorgeous women."

They dance, Andi struggling for a comeback, unable to think of anything to say.

"You do know I'm married, right?" she says eventually.

"I do. And I think you look unhappy. Relax. We're just having fun." And with a small smile, he pulls her close, then pushes her away.

The music stops, and Pete bows his thanks, disappearing without giving Andi a chance to explain herself, to ask what he meant, to put the record straight.

I am not unhappy, she wants to say. *I love my husband. My husband loves me. Why do I look unhappy? What is it that makes you say that?* But Pete quickly chooses someone else with whom to dance, and Andi heads over to the bar, where Tess is watching her with amusement.

"Jesus H. Christ!" Tess leans over and shouts in her ear. "I could smell the sexual chemistry from here. What the hell was that all about?"

"What do you mean?" Andi looks away, looks for a distraction, tries not to meet her eyes.

"You know what I mean. There was heat coming off the two of you. Who is he?"

"He's a friend of Drew's." Andi attempts nonchalance. "Some trainer, I think."

"If I didn't know better . . ." Tess teases.

"I'm married, not dead." Andi goes for lightheartedness, but it comes out in a bark.

"Jeez. Excuse me. You like him."

"Well, he's cute, right?" Andi finally concedes.

"Is he ever. Just don't do anything I wouldn't do . . ." Tess winks, unaware that Andi is feeling unsettled. Excited. As if she is on a precipice, deciding whether or not to jump.

Twelve
. . . .

Andi cannot settle. She dances with other men, drinks her drinks, laughs with her friends, and all the time her eyes are roving, looking to see where Pete is, what he is doing, whether he is still there.

She is hyperaware, her senses heightened, conscious of where he is at any given moment, as if there were an invisible thread connecting them. She watches him say good-bye to Drew and feels a sharp pang of disappointment in her stomach.

"I'm in the gym all week," he says into her ear as he leaves. "Come see me." And brushing his lips against her ear, causing a shiver that reaches down to her toes, he steps back, looks at her, a question in his eyes instead of a smile, and leaves.

He wants me as a client, she tells herself, over and over, seeing the club suddenly as a dark and somewhat seedy place, now that the unexpected light has left.

Stop imagining this is something more, she tells herself, over

and over, as she goes to the bathroom to take a break from the noise.

God! she berates herself in the bathroom mirror. Could you be any more *predictable*? You're a middle-aged married woman who's completely discombobulated because a thirtysomething cute man seems to be flirting with you.

Andi stares at herself in the mirror, astonished at how different she looks tonight. It is rare for Andi to examine herself, and when she does, she might describe herself as looking cute. Or neat. Or attractive.

Who is this gorgeous, sexy creature staring back at her with a spark in her eye? Andi feels, suddenly, sexy in a way she hasn't in years. *Alive.* And it shows. She loves Ethan, but the toll of marriage, of raising children, the stress of dealing with Emily, the stress of accepting that she cannot have a child, all have led to her putting her sexuality to bed.

They still have sex, of course, but it is hardly the wild, passionate lovemaking that was the signature of their early time together. It is quick, and . . . pleasant. It fuels their intimacy but could never be described as sexy.

It happens in bed, with Ethan pulling her nightgown up. Or occasionally in the bathroom, as she drops her flesh-colored underwear in the laundry basket before getting into bed, Ethan will walk in and grin. At times she will be thrilled—when she is ovulating, when this presents another possibility for her child. Other times her heart will sink as she eyes her warm, cozy nightgown, but when he moves behind her and wraps his arms around her, leaning down to kiss her neck, she will acquiesce. And it will be quick, and . . . pleasant.

When did I stop feeling sexy? Andi wonders, unable to tear her eyes away from this new, improved Andi staring back at her in the mirror. When did sex with my husband become so dull?

Perimenopause, Dr. Kurrish had explained, could lead to a loss

of sexual desire. *Could,* Andi remembers thinking. It won't happen to *me.*

Her libido, however, had different ideas. In the beginning, when they were first married, she was still attached to the possibility of getting pregnant, still excited by the prospect of creating a new life, still delighting in the prospect of being a wife, having a husband, sharing the intimacy of making love.

There are no babies now. Nor will there be. Andi walks on eggshells in her own house, a house in which chaos and drama reign. The nights when Emily throws tantrums, when Ethan spends hours trying to calm her down, leave Andi empty and cold.

And Dr. Kurrish was right. "Sexual desire"? She can barely remember what those words mean. She no longer thinks of herself as sexual, or desirable.

Until now.

This man is so different from her world. He makes her feel like she did before all of this, before drama and chaos, and the gradual acceptance of her infertility made her feel middle-aged and sad. He made her sexy, and that brings with it possibility.

Does it mean anything that this thirtysomething man is making her feel like this? Is this something more than recreational flirting? If it is merely recreational flirting, why is it making her feel so damn special?

Stop! She turns away, guilty. *It's who he is. It's what he does. It isn't about you. He's no more interested in you than he is in Drew: a potential client, and this, clearly, is what he does.* He knows how to get the bored housewives interested by flirting, by looking deep in their eyes, by promising them an excitement their husbands aren't giving them.

But Ethan . . . Ethan. Ethan is everything she had never dared hope or dream she'd find. Her relationship with Ethan is the kind of relationship she thought existed only in the movies, in books. It was

always loving, warm, companionable, and since their wedding, had settled into something peaceful, comfortable, easy.

She is content, she realizes. She has found contentment. Has loved saying good-bye to the excitement, the drama, the constant ups and downs of the dating world. So why, so suddenly, when she is so happy, is she beset by this craving for excitement that had appeared in the form of a young, flirtatious trainer?

There are those who say that in order for someone to stray, in order for an affair to take place, there has to be something wrong in the marriage.

But isn't there something wrong in everyone's marriage? They may be happy, in love, settled, but isn't there always the slightest of fissures through which a view of the road not taken can be glimpsed?

I am not the sort of person who would have an affair, Andi tells herself, sipping from an ice-cold margarita and trying to focus her attention on Deanna, who is telling them a story as they sit around a low round table in a corner of the club.

Is *anyone* the sort of person who would have an affair? Who likes to think of themselves as the sort of person who would commit adultery? Who likes to think of themselves as the sort of person who could, *would* betray and lie, smash their wedding vows into meaningless pieces?

What if I could be happier with Pe— someone like Pete? Andi drifts off, imagining a life without Emily, a life with no drama, a life in which she and Pete, or someone much like him, hung out, saw friends, threw parties, made love.

She shivers at how cold she is being, brings her thoughts back to Ethan. *I love him,* she thinks, picturing his sweet smile, his strong, capable hands that can fix anything in the house, that have redesigned the garden, that have brought her hours and hours of pleasure.

But is love enough, she wonders, lost in thought as she stares at Deanna, pretending to listen, smiling and shaking her head in all the right places, copying the others. Is love enough to save us? Will we ever be rid of the chaos of Emily?

It is a constant roller coaster. When Emily is lovely, as she can be, Andi tumbles head over heels in love with her. After their trip to Santa Rosa for the wedding, Emily was so *sweet*. She *apologized*—something she has never done before, asking Andi to stay, to look after her. Andi felt, still feels, in those moments, a surge of blinding love for this child, of what might be, of how things still could all work out.

Those moments are fewer than they were. Andi came into this relationship with such high hopes. All Emily needed, she thought, was love and attention. If Andi loved her enough, gave her enough kindnesses, did enough for her, Emily would come around; Emily would love her; all would be well.

Her phone buzzes in her purse. She feels it only because her foot is touching her purse at the time and, leaning down, she pulls it out to find a text from Ethan.

CALL ME NOW.
NEED TO GO TO POLICE STATION. NOW.
SOPHIA ASLEEP.
COME HOME. CALL FIRST.

"What's going on?"

"Where have you been? I've been calling you for hours." Ethan is furious, his voice a loud attack when Andi gets through.

Andi's heart jumps. "What is it? What's the matter?"

"Jesus, Andi. You'd think you might have checked the phone."

"I'm sorry, okay? I didn't think to check the phone. It's loud inside. What is it? What's going on? Tell me!" Her voice rises with an edge of panic.

Ethan's voice is shaky when he next speaks. "Emily's been arrested. She was with other kids. I'm not clear on who was driving, but they were all drunk. I just hope to God Emily was not the driver. Jesus. DUI. Underage. Alcohol in the car. It's not good."

"Oh, Christ." Andi whistles. "That's . . . terrible. That affects college, jobs, every . . ."

"I know! Okay?" Ethan blurts in anger. "I need to get down to the police station, and I can't leave Sophia. Topher's out, so you need to come home."

Andi takes a deep breath. "Why don't you let Emily spend the night? It's the obvious natural consequence. She needs to know she's in deep trouble . . ."

"Oh, for Christ's sake!" Ethan explodes down the phone. "She already knows she's in deep trouble. She's seventeen years old and she's just fucked up big-time. She's terrified. She's been sobbing on the phone, and she needs someone there. Now is not the time for consequences, okay? We'll deal with that later."

Andi recoils at his anger but takes a deep breath, doesn't react. "I'll go," she says.

"What?"

"You stay with Sophia. I'll leave now, and I'll go straight to the police station. I'll go with Drew."

There is a long pause. "I think I should go," Ethan says.

"No. Let me. She's been very sweet with me recently. I think she may want me there as another woman, a mother figure."

Ethan does not want to agree, but an opportunity for Emily and Andi to bond, even under these terrible circumstances, is not to be missed.

Andi is not offering because she is intent on cementing their newfound bond, although granted, that would be a welcome side benefit. She is offering because the histrionics that will ensue when Ethan walks into the police station do not bear thinking about.

Ethan has already said, again, that Emily is a child, she is already upset, she does not need to be upset further. Ethan is probably already thinking about how he can get her off, what explanation they can come up with that can make it all okay for Emily.

Andi is thinking about the consequences, what could be done to show her how grave this is, although zero tolerance will probably take care of that.

Worst-case scenario? If in fact she was the driver, surely that she will be charged with an underage DUI, and perhaps a regular one. Her license is likely to be suspended for a year. She will attend compulsory safety and alcohol-abuse classes. She will have to list it on all college applications and all job applications.

Andi knows she shouldn't wish this on Emily, shouldn't wish this on anyone, but isn't this what she needs? Couldn't circumstances as grave as this finally shock Emily into giving up the alcohol and the drugs? Force her to grow up, to follow a different path than her mother?

She thinks of today's young stars, the celebrities who surround themselves with lawyers able to reduce the severity of any consequences, able to ensure that they will continue their lives, screwing up over and over, because nobody ever holds them accountable.

Doesn't Emily need someone to say, "No! Enough! We're watching?" Doesn't she need an intervention before it's too late?

Thirteen

· · · · · · · · · ·

W e've been pouring coffee and water down her," the
officer says, shaking her head. "She should have
sobered up by now."

Andi follows her mutely, noting that the place is
enough to sober anyone up. She has been into the police station from
time to time, but not back to the cells. This is where the criminals are
kept, Andi thinks, reminding herself she is in Mill Valley, where the
greatest crimes tend to be, indeed, DUIs.

The officer gestures to the end of a corridor and draws out a key.
"Sorry about this. We only put her in here because she wanted to
sleep," she apologizes. "And she was getting hysterical."

"It's fine," Andi reassures her. "Don't worry." But she suppresses a
gasp at how serious this now feels, Emily behind bars.

"Your mom's here," the officer says. Emily, asleep on the bench,
groans slightly before opening her eyes, but Andi, staring at Emily's
sleeping form, finds herself frozen in shock.

· · ·

Emily, in all her goth glory, wears black flowing clothes, the looser the better. In recent months, she has put on weight, wrapping cardigans around her thickening girth, buying skirts with elasticized waists.

Andi does not say anything. Emily is not her daughter, it is not her place to say anything, and even if Emily were her daughter, she would not want to give her a complex about weight, would not dare say anything to Emily other than that she looks lovely, or her makeup is great, or she likes some new outfit.

Emily only criticizes, herself and others. "I'm so fat," she'll mutter. "I'm so ugly." "I hate my thighs."

Andi corrects her, telling her she's womanly and pretty, but Emily just rolls her eyes and walks out.

But here, tonight on a bench at the back of a cell in the Mill Valley police station, Emily lies on her back, her body no longer hidden by swathes and drapes of clothing, her stomach sticking out proudly, Emily still half-asleep, unaware that Andi is transfixed by her stomach, her swollen breasts.

She's not fat, Andi realizes, with mounting horror. She's pregnant.

Where's Dad?" Emily wakes up and coldly stares through Andi. "He's at home with Sophia. I was already out, so I came to get you."

"Great," Emily mutters witheringly, shaking her head. "Just what I need."

"Would you rather stay the night here?" Andi is in shock, and suddenly, instead of feeling frightened of Emily, as she so often does, she is angry. "Because I can leave. That's fine." And she turns to go.

"No." Emily mutters. "I'll come."

"How about a thank-you?" Andi says as they walk down the corridor.

"Thank you," Emily parrots, adding, almost under her breath, "It's all about you."

Andi stops. "Excuse me?"

"Nothing." Emily carries on walking.

"Do you have any idea how much trouble you're in?"

"Yes," Emily says, dripping with sarcasm. "Thanks for the support."

"You don't get it, do you," Andi says, unable to hold the frustration in any longer. "You have no idea how this is going to affect the rest of your life. College applications, jobs. If you are charged, this is going to be a problem forever."

"I know!" Emily explodes. "I fucking know, okay, but I wasn't driving. Get off my fucking back, all right? Jesus. I can't believe my bitch of a stepmother comes down to get me when all I wanted was my dad. He couldn't even do that for me. I get the one person in the world I fucking hate. Great."

Andi feels anger rising as she looks at Emily's sullen face. *Don't do it*, she tells herself, but this anger, this raw rage isn't something that can be contained. Andi does everything with Emily in mind, thinking constantly of what she can do to make Emily happy, and instead of a thank-you, instead of gratitude, she gets insults and criticism. All the time.

Andi has had enough.

"How dare you!" Andi finally, *finally* explodes. "How dare you always be so rude, so surly, so damned *horrible*. Your father does everything for you, and now, heaven forbid, he is staying with your younger sister, who doesn't deserve the shit you put her through, the shit you put us all through all of the time. I have never in my life come across a girl as ungrateful and unpleasant as you. You're a spoiled, entitled little brat, and don't think I don't know that you have your parents wrapped around your finger. Your mother's too drunk to give a shit, and your father's so terrified of upsetting you, of your throw-

ing one of your tantrums, he'll do whatever you want. But not any longer, young lady. Do you get it? Your father's had enough. This has pushed him over the edge."

"How dare you say anything about my mother," Emily screams. "You're not worth the ground she walks on. She's an amazing, sweet person, and how dare you say she's drunk. You're the bitch, you've been a bitch since you walked in and stole my father. All you care about is him. You pretend to love Sophia, but I know you don't. You're the most selfish person I've ever met. We were all happy before you came into our lives, and I hate you more than I've hated anyone. You're just this big fake. *Oh, Emily, your hair looks so pretty,*" she mimics. "*That's a cute skirt, is it new?* You think I don't know how fake you are, that you only say those things in front of my dad so he thinks you're nice to me? You have ruined all of our lives."

There is a long silence as they look at each other, and, as quickly as it appeared, Andi's rage goes. The fight goes out of her as she stares at Emily, seeing her as a terrified little girl.

"No, Emily," she says quietly, looking pointedly at Emily's stomach. "You're the one who has ruined her life. What are you? Three months pregnant? Four?" She looks back up to see a flicker of fear in Emily's eyes.

"What are you talking about?" she says disdainfully, but there is fear in her voice.

"When was the last time you had a period, Emily?"

Emily's eyes look upward for a second, and Andi suddenly realizes that Emily doesn't know, is thinking about when her last period actually was. Perhaps, on some level, she suspected, but she doesn't *know*, is thinking perhaps that if she buries her head in the sand deep enough and long enough, it will all go away.

The color drains from Emily's face. "I'm not pregnant," she says.

"Wishing it were so doesn't make it so." Andi sighs. "So when was your last period?"

"I'm not fucking pregnant, okay?" Emily yells, and runs out of the room, slamming the door.

They drive home in silence, Emily hunched up in the passenger seat, her sweater tightly drawn around her, arms crossed to hide her stomach.

Andi silently berates herself all the way home. How could she not have seen? How did she not realize? She thought it was puppy fat, teenage weight, the freshman fifteen a little earlier than planned. And the throwing up. Now it makes sense. Those times she thought she heard Emily throwing up, putting it down to drugs, or alcohol, she now realizes were due to morning sickness.

And the drugs! The alcohol! What about fetal alcohol syndrome? Andi thinks of the way Emily has abused her body these last few months, the way Andi suspects she has abused her body, and shivers with horror.

There is termination, she tells herself, mentally calculating in her head. What choice does she have, a seventeen-year-old who has been drinking and doing God knows what drugs during a pregnancy. She will have to terminate.

And then, *What if I am wrong?* What if I have jumped to terrible conclusions? *Please, God,* she prays silently, glancing at Emily out of the corner of her eye. *Please, God, for Emily's sake, for all of our sakes, let me be wrong.*

Fourteen

. . . .

"What the hell's going on?" Ethan looks first at Emily, then at Andi, seeing an expression in her eyes he has never seen before.

"Are you going to tell him?" Andi's voice is calm and quiet. She looks at Emily as Emily howls and smashes her hand into the wall.

"Shut up!" she screams. "Shut up! Shut up! Shut up! I hate you."

Ethan's eyes widen in shock. He expected a tearful, contrite Emily, not this bundle of rage, and this insane accusation.

"Emily, stop." He tries to grab her arm, but she tears away from him and starts pulling her own hair, shrieking all the while, "Shut up! I hate you! I hate you!"

"Emily?" Ethan's pain is obvious, seeing his daughter in a place he can't reach, and he turns to Andi with fury in his eyes.

"What the hell have you done? What has happened to my daughter? I knew I shouldn't have let you go."

Andi is too tired to take umbrage. She's too tired to be offended. She's had enough.

"Ethan," she says quietly. "Look at her. Look at her stomach."

Emily turns to the wall, screaming, "No!" so he can't see.

"What? What are you saying?" He is stricken as he pulls Emily around to face him, his eyes dropping. "Oh, sweet Jesus. Emily? You're pregnant?"

"Leave me alone." Emily tears herself away, spitting like a trapped cat. "Shut up!" Emily continues screaming. "I hate you! I hate you!"

"Emily!" Ethan roars. "Stop! *Are you pregnant?*"

Emily, with a howl of pain, runs up the stairs, into the bathroom, and slams the door, locking it firmly, where she continues to scream and bang her head against the tiles.

Andi stands, shaking, the shock threatening tears for her, a gulf as wide as Mexico now between her and Ethan.

"Do you have a pregnancy test?" he says finally. Quietly.

Andi nods, and wordlessly she goes up to her bathroom, each step feeling as if she is treading on cotton candy, her whole body woolly and trembling from the force of Emily's rage and fear.

Ethan is waiting outside the bedroom when she comes out and hands it to him silently. She hears him go down the corridor. More screaming, more sobbing, and finally, a brief lull of silence before the wailing starts again.

An hour goes by. Two. Suddenly, Andi hears footsteps down the hall, and Ethan appears, exhaustion pulling him down, making him seem ten years older than he is.

"Is . . . ?" She looks at him expectantly.

Ethan sits down on the bed, looks at her, nods.

Then he bursts into tears.

Fifteen

. . . .

than's body heaves, the only sound being occasional gasps
of air as Andi sits wearily beside him, laying a hand on his
back, rubbing in small, gentle circles, finding her own eyes
filling with tears that spill down her cheeks.

She has never seen him cry before, had not expected to cry herself,
but she is crying for different reasons.

Andi sits, silent. Terrified that if she opens her mouth to speak, it
will open the floodgates for her to sob next to him, and if she starts,
she is not sure she can stop. She wants to put her arms around him,
pull him in close, comfort him, but . . . but . . . she cannot do more
than this right now, rubbing her hand on his back as the sadness pulls
her deep, deep down.

She is not done. Not yet. But close. This is too much for her: the
drama, the screaming, the hatred and rage that fly around this house,
that fill her with dread each time she comes home.

She doesn't want to think about how she will leave, when she will
leave, but listening to Ethan cry, Andi is overcome with exhaustion

and numbness. She wants to sleep. Forever. She wants to be in a small, cozy bed, in a quiet apartment, with a cat.

She wants a life that is peaceful. Happy. Simple.

There were such high expectations with Ethan, expectations that haven't been fulfilled; some of that is okay. She is trying to deal with the fact that they cannot have children of their own, trying to deal with not being a mother herself, but she cannot deal with the daily fact of being hated; cannot deal with the fear that descends upon her every time she pulls into her own driveway—what will Emily's mood be today, what is waiting for her on the other side of the front door.

Ethan, so accustomed to Emily's tantrums, cannot understand how they *undo* Andi, who cannot do this for very much longer. That is the only thing of which she is certain, the thing that is now weighing her down on the bed, forcing her eyes closed with sadness and grief.

She isn't leaving tonight. Nor tomorrow. She needs to figure it out in daylight, when the night terrors aren't overwhelming, when everything seems more manageable. It is weeks, she thinks, not months. A few weeks.

If she can last that long.

Finally, she leans her head on Ethan's shoulder, closes her eyes, and allows the tears to fall.

The next morning, Andi manages to avoid almost everyone. Ethan kisses her good-bye, early, as she wonders if he feels the same emptiness. There is a gulf of sadness between them. She assumes he must have a sense of what she is feeling, but they don't speak other than to make arrangements for Emily.

She and Emily will meet him at her OB/GYN later today. She has not yet made an appointment but, given the circumstances, they will get in.

Ethan calls to Sophia, asking her where she wants to go for break-
fast, and Andi hears Sophia's light footsteps approaching their bedroom.
Father and daughter stand in the hallway just outside the bedroom as
Andi puts down her makeup brush to listen.

"What's the matter with everyone?" whispers Sophia.

"What do you mean?" Ethan is trying to make his voice as normal
as possible. It doesn't sound normal. It sounds strained and false.

"There's a very weird atmosphere in the house. It feels like something has changed."

"Nothing has changed." Ethan forces a laugh, but Andi knows he
feels it, too. She hears Ethan usher Sophia downstairs, then, from down
the hall, Sophia saying, "Wait! I'll be just a minute."

Her footsteps run back to the bedroom and into the bathroom,
where she flings her arms around Andi.

"I love you!" she whispers into her ear, clasping her tight.

"I know, sweetie." Andi blinks back the sudden tears, wondering
why Sophia is choosing to say it now. She used to say it to Andi all the
time, but since becoming a teenager, while still surprisingly affectionate, she no longer says the words themselves.

"I just wanted you to hear." Sophia looks her in the eye, then picks
up her backpack again and runs down the stairs to her father, waiting
in the car, leaving Andi in the house, saddened that Sophia must
sense that something is wrong. Why else would she offer those words
now?

It will be hours before Emily wakes up. She sleeps until lunchtime
every day, leaving Andi to enjoy the peace, the only time Andi
feels relaxed in her house. She showers, dresses, grabs an apple and
a Clif Bar from the pantry, then heads out to her studio, making calls
in the car, shouting into the Bluetooth speakerphone that muffles
everyone and has never worked properly.

Her phone buzzes as she steps out the car. A text. Deanna.

"How's Emily? Are YOU okay?"

Andi pauses. Normally she would text back, but today she needs a friend. Today she needs Deanna. She dials and then holds the phone to her ear.

"Want to come to the studio for coffee?"

Deanna glides in, swathed in layers of jersey, two cups of something hot in her hand, one of which she places on the table in front of Andi, leaning down to kiss her cheek.

"Soy chai latte," she explains. "It's what I drink when I need comforting."

"Tha—" Andi starts, then bursts into tears.

Deanna doesn't say anything. She leads Andi to the sofa, sits her down, hands her a tissue, then sits next to her, sipping her tea quietly and waiting, one hand resting on top of Andi's, her thumb gently stroking Andi's fingers until Andi's sobs reduce to breathy hiccups, slowing down, finally, to sadness.

"I can't do it," Andi says eventually, quietly, with tears still brimming. "I can't do this." She takes a deep breath before turning to Deanna. "I've had enough."

"What happened last night?"

"It isn't even what happened last night. It's everything. It's this girl poisoning everything she touches. I hate her, Deanna." Her voice fills with passion. "I hate her. I hate her for destroying us."

There is a silence as Deanna considers. Finally, gently, she says, "Have you thought that she is just being who she is? That as hateful as her behavior may be, and I'm not saying it's anything other than that, but that you are the only one who can give her the power to destroy you."

"Drew and Topher say the same thing, but I don't know how to

detach. She fills the air with her poison, and one drama after another."
Andi's shoulders slump. "The latest drama? She's pregnant."

"She's . . . what?" Deanna is shocked.

"I know. Seventeen, drinking and doing God knows what kind of drugs, and pregnant."

"Oh, Lord. Poor child."

"She's not a child," Andi snaps. "She's a spoiled, entitled, ungrateful little bitch."

"This will pass," Deanna says. "You've had dramas before and come out of it."

Andi shakes her head. "This time it's different. Every time we have one of these things, every time she screams at me how much she hates me, every time her father defends her and lets her scream those terrible things, I shut down a little more. Everyone has their limit, and I think I may have"—she gulps—"reached mine. I didn't expect to feel this. I don't *want* to feel this, but I can't deal with it anymore. I can't live like this, with this constant fear. I'm frightened to be in my own house when she's around. Do you have any idea what this is like for me?"

Deanna shakes her head.

"I love Ethan." The tears spill over again. "He's the best man I've ever met, but it's not enough. It's just not enough, and it's not enough to sacrifice myself. I'm a good person, Deanna. I spend all my time thinking of what I can do to make Emily happy. All I wanted was a family, and kids, and I was so convinced that I could make this work, that we would all live happily ever after." She snorts derisively at her own naïveté. "Having Emily is like this poison that seeps into everything, and I kept thinking that she would grow up, move out, go away, and we'd be fine, but it's not going to happen."

"What do you mean it's not going to happen?"

"I mean people like Emily don't grow up. They don't stop having dramas. There's always going to be something. And I'm realizing I

could be happier, I *would* be happier, on my own. I just made a huge mistake, marrying someone with kids. I can't have kids of my own, and now I know, if I'm with anyone at all, I need to be with someone who doesn't have kids."

"She will grow up," Deanna says calmly, trying to calm Andi down, for Andi seems now to be bordering on hysteria, her words tumbling out as fast as light, her energy edgy and nervous. "Emily won't be in your lives forever and, as you said, Ethan is the best man you've ever met. He's wonderful. You won't find better."

There is a silence as Andi thinks. "You're right," she says after a while. "I won't find better. But I will find different."

Deanna cocks her head. "Different like that friend of Drew's you were dancing with last night? The one who was flirting with you?"

Andi looks away quickly. That was exactly what she had been thinking. That she would indeed be far happier with someone like Pete. No kids. No ex-wives leaving ranting drunken messages on the answer machine at home. No husband who has to leave in the middle of the night to collect the kids, or drop everything at a moment's notice because their mother hasn't shown up. Again.

A man like Pete, who has no baggage. Oh sure, he might have some—who doesn't?—but not the kind of baggage that is cluttering their lives on a daily basis; not the kind of baggage that brings drama, and turmoil, and poison into their home, into their lives.

"Maybe a man like him. Not him"—Andi feigns nonchalance—"but yes. I wouldn't be with someone with children again. Not after this. I want someone who has no ties."

"No one has nothing. Not at this age," Deanna says. "That guy? Pete? That guy may look like the answer to your problems, but I promise you, he isn't. You may be lying in bed thinking about Pete, or . . . a man like Pete . . . and when you are going through a painful time, another man can be a great distraction, but I promise you, it is not a reason to end a marriage."

"I *know*!" Andi says. "This isn't about him. This is about the family dynamic. It's about Emily."

"But thinking about another man saves you from problem-solving," Deanna insists gently, knowing she is right. "It removes you from your life, and places you squarely in fantasyland. If you end this because you think another man, Pete or someone else, is the answer to your prayers, you're very much mistaken."

Andi says nothing. There is nothing to say because Deanna is right. She is choosing to shift her focus from what is wrong in her marriage to a fantasy of what it could be like with Pete.

"I once knew someone," Deanna says quietly, "who had a wonderful husband, and a small baby. She and her husband were childhood sweethearts. They met at camp when they were teens, and had always known they were going to get married and be together forever. They had a great relationship, until the baby came along. He didn't know how to adjust to fatherhood, so he threw himself into work, and was hardly ever home. She was left on her own with this screaming, colicky baby, in a new town where they'd recently moved for his work, and she started to hate him." Andi sits forward, rapt.

"She would lie in bed at night and dream about divorce, wonder whether she could make it as a single mom. Because she'd just moved to town, she didn't have close girlfriends, she didn't know whether other women were going through the same thing. She just thought she was the loneliest girl in the world, and nothing was as lonely as loneliness in a marriage. Eventually, she found a student who would come in every day and babysit for a couple of hours, giving her some time to herself. At first, she didn't know what to do. She'd go to the grocery store, and walk around town, window-shopping, not remembering what she used to do with her time in the days before she became a mother. She started going to the library. There was a sofa by a big picture window, with a great view. She started reading again, something she hadn't been able to do since the baby was born, and every

day she'd curl up for a couple of hours and lose herself in a great book." Andi watches as Deanna's eyes mist, thinking back to a long-ago time, knowing she is finally hearing the story that Deanna, fiercely private, had only ever hinted at before.

"There were tables in the room, and a few people sitting around working. She started to get to know them. They'd nod at one another, then smile, and after a while they'd find themselves sitting near each other in the café close by, and they'd start a conversation.

"One of them was a writer. He was published, and even though she didn't recognize him, she knew his name, and she was drawn to his quiet intelligence. They started meeting at the café by chance, and he asked her questions. He made her feel . . . special. At a time when she felt like a harassed mother who had lost all sense of self, he made her feel beautiful."

Andi wants to reach over and tell her she is beautiful, that how could she ever think anything else, but she stays silent. Listening.

"She started to look for him. On the days he wasn't at the library, or the café, she felt a wave of disappointment, which she tried to bury in the pages of the book, but it was hard. She'd find herself thinking about him at home. She'd be making dinner for her husband, who would always get home later than planned, and she'd think of something the writer had said earlier that day, and she'd find herself smiling. Soon, they were e-mailing each other. At first short, pithy e-mails, but they quickly became long and involved. She found herself revealing herself to him in a way she had never done with anyone else, the privacy of the computer screen creating a sense of intimacy that she had never found anywhere else."

Andi nods. She knows the power of e-mail.

"She started to think of him as her best friend, refusing to admit she couldn't stop thinking about him, that he had become the focus of her every waking thought. It carried on like that for months. She

would never have had an affair with him; she'd never been unfaithful in her life. It just felt so good to have someone who could see into her soul; it felt so good to feel . . . complete. They were walking in the park one day, and he turned to her and told her he thought she was his soul mate. It threw her completely. She was furious with him for saying the words, and she stormed off and spent the rest of the day in tears. She tried not to see him, which she managed for about a week. A week in which she was plunged back into the loneliness again, a week she spent trying to hide the tears in front of her child. They met after a week, and vowed not to let it change. Said that a mutual attraction didn't mean they would *do* anything about it. He was separated, but he didn't want to ruin her marriage. They made a pact that they would never have an affair. A month later, they slept together for the first time. It was wonderful, and terrible. She became the woman who climbed out of her lover's bed and into her husband's. She felt sick with the betrayal."

Andi lays a hand on her arm to interrupt her. "How were things with her husband?"

"The same. Ships that pass in the night. The only way he knew how to deal with the shock of fatherhood, the change in their relationship, was to throw himself into work and distance himself further and further. He didn't notice that she wasn't present in their relationship anymore. I think mostly he was grateful that she seemed to be happy again. She started to think that she had made a terrible mistake with her husband. He had been her childhood sweetheart, but he had grown into someone she didn't recognize, and it was clear to her that neither of them could make the other happy. She didn't know how to leave him, though. Even though the writer wanted to build a life with her, and even though she wanted to build a life with him, she was terrified of actually telling him, of changing her life so dramatically, of causing so much upset."

Andi is now so wrapped up in the story, she can feel Deanna's

pain as if it were her own, and her voice comes out in a whisper: "Her husband found out?"

"Of course. He knew about her friendship with the writer, and started to suspect, eventually going through her e-mails. She thought she had hidden them well enough, but he found them. All the pent-up passion and longing was in their e-mails. He read them all. She came home from being with the writer and found her husband sitting at the kitchen table with a pile of e-mails printed out, and tears running down his cheeks."

There is a long silence. This time, Andi is the one to reach over and squeeze Deanna's hand.

"She left him?"

Deanna shakes her head. "No. As soon as she saw her husband, she knew it was a terrible mistake. She knew she didn't want the writer. Maybe she had never wanted the writer; she just wanted to be . . . seen? Acknowledged?" Deanna shrugs. "She wanted to stop being so lonely, and it seemed that he was the perfect man to do that. She'd removed herself from the marriage by fantasizing about the writer, about all that their life would be, how perfect it would be, how happy she would be if she were with the writer instead of her husband. She was so lost in the fantasy, she never gave reality a chance."

"What happened?"

"Her husband left. He cried all night, and in the morning he packed his things and walked out. She felt sick, and scared, and all of a sudden, the comfort the writer was willing to provide didn't seem so comforting. They tried to continue their relationship for a while, but once her husband had gone, she didn't want the writer anymore. She wanted her husband, who was also"—Deanna gives Andi a pointed look—"the best man in the world. She threw it all away for a fantasy." Deanna blinks, and looks Andi straight in the eye.

"He never gave you another chance?" Andi had heard rumors that

Deanna had once had an affair with a famous author, but she had never offered her story, and Andi had never asked. Until now.

Deanna shakes her head. "He said he could never trust me again."

"You regret it. Clearly."

"Oh Andi. It was the biggest single fuck-up of my life. I miss my husband to this day. He's married now, to Theresa, as you know, and she's great. She's amazing to my kid, they're blissfully happy, but you know what? It should have been me. And every time I pick up my kid, every time I pull into their driveway, I know that she is living my life, and the only person I have to blame for it is me. Andi, my sweet?" Deanna's tone is urgent, intense. "I love you. I care about you. And I believe that Ethan is one of the greats. If you were married to someone else, I might have different advice, but Emily will not be at home forever, and don't, please don't, make the mistake of thinking your happiness lies elsewhere, or with someone else. Don't make the same mistake as me."

Andi holds Deanna's gaze, then sinks her head in her hands. "Oh, God," she says with a groan. "It's just all so damned hard."

"I know." Deanna gives a wry smile. "It is all so damned hard."

Sixteen

. . . .

mily sits at the other end of the row of seats in the waiting room, her arms crossed protectively over her chest, staring at the ground, refusing to acknowledge Andi and Ethan.

Ethan shoots Emily worried glances every few seconds, pretending to watch CNN on the TV screen high up in the corner, from time to time making attempts at humor, looking at Emily to try to include her, draw her out of her funk, but she will not look up, will not meet his eyes.

Andi pretends to watch the television screen, jittery with anxiety. They are here to discuss what to do, and although nobody has uttered the word "abortion," it is the unspoken cloud that is hovering above all their heads. Andi's thoughts keep coming back to it, no matter how hard she tells herself they are here only to explore the options, and she is so upset, she cannot look at Emily.

She cannot believe she is here, cannot believe that the possibility of a baby is right here, at their fingertips, and instead they might be going to destroy a life.

What would I do? she thinks. *What would I do if I were seventeen and*

pregnant. Would I have an abortion? Could I? She doesn't know. She only knows that now, as a woman in her forties, desperate for a child of her own, the thought of abortion makes her feel ill.

Now, as a woman in her forties, she would do anything, *anything*, to have a child. They talked, early on, when they first learned pregnancy was no longer a probability, about adoption. Ethan determined it wouldn't be the right thing for them to do. To this day, she knows that Ethan didn't want to adopt not because he didn't want more children but because it would have upset Emily.

Emily had made it quite clear, from the beginning, how disgusted she would be, how she would leave home and never speak to him again if he dared to have another child.

Ethan had laughed her down, but behind the forced laughter, his fear was palpable. Andi knew that he regarded her loss of fertility as a hidden blessing, a welcome relief. When she brought up adoption, which she did regularly in those early days, he changed the subject, or just said he wasn't ready, that they should just enjoy being together for a while.

When Andi pushed, he said they already had two children, that they were lucky they were healthy and happy (although Emily had never exactly been happy), and that he was done.

He didn't want to be a father to a baby in his late forties, he said. He didn't want to be in his sixties with a child graduating from high school. He was tired, and there were enough moving parts without having to add another to the mix. He loved Andi, and he knew it was hard, and it would be one thing if she somehow, miraculously, became pregnant and they then had to deal with it, but another thing entirely to adopt. It wasn't something he could do.

He was sorry, and he loved Andi, but no. Adoption wasn't an option.

She still harbored a hope that a miracle would happen, and she would indeed somehow, miraculously, become pregnant, but short of

that, she had grudgingly, sometimes resentfully, come to accept that she wouldn't have a baby, a child of her own.

Until now.

She was driving through town when the thought came to her. What if . . . what if Emily had the baby. What if Emily gave the baby to them, if she and Ethan adopted the baby, raised it as their own.

The fantasy grew, Andi's heart filling with anticipatory joy, until she remembered that the mother would be Emily. Emily would never let that happen, would never give Andi the one thing she really wants. It isn't even worth thinking about.

Here they are, in the waiting room, with Emily hating everyone and everything, wishing she were anywhere but here, Ethan feeling like his life is spinning out of control with no idea how to get it back, and Andi seeing her last chance at happiness being snatched away from her.

Three people sitting feet apart, separated by a mile of hurt.

Doctor Kurrish is kind, and gentle. She does not ask specifics of the situation, but instead does blood work before taking Emily to a room down the corridor for an ultrasound. Alone.

"You can go in in a minute," she tells Ethan and Andi, who sit outside, staring mindlessly at CNN without hearing anything, looking up expectantly every time someone enters the room.

Finally, their doctor appears, leading them to her office, gesturing for them to sit and gently closing the door, turning to them with sympathy in her eyes.

"She's very scared," she says. "And I can't get much out of her. I don't know when she last menstruated or when she last had relations. She keeps saying she doesn't know, and she's having an emotional moment in the other room. You can go in to her, but first I want you to

know that I think she's far more advanced than she thinks she is. My guess would be she's around six, maybe seven months pregnant, but we'll be able to get a more precise answer when we do measurements during the ultrasound."

Ethan and Andi both gasp, Andi reaching over for Ethan's hand to steady herself.

"I'm sorry. This is a shock, I know. You thought it was much earlier?" They nod. "I know Emily expressed a desire for termination, but that isn't going to be a possibility. She is going to have this baby."

"Oh, God," Ethan groans. "Oh, God."

"I'm sorry," the doctor says. "But Emily is not the first young girl I've seen in this position, and she definitely won't be the last. My suggestion to you is to start looking into adoption. There are so many families who are unable to have children, who would give this child a loving and wonderful home. You would rest assured that this baby is going to be loved, and Emily can go back to being a teenager, can get on with the rest of her life.

"We have leaflets on adoption I can give you today," she says. "And a counselor on hand who can talk to you and Emily about it, answer any questions you may have." The doctor lays a hand on Ethan's, who is now as white as a sheet.

"This is not the end of the world," she says, "although I know it feels like it right now. There are women out there who are longing to be mothers, who would give anything to be in the position Emily is in right now."

I know! thinks Andi. *I'm one of them!*

And she bursts into huge, heaving sobs.

There is nothing to say on the way home. Emily sits in the back, sniffing and gulping, clutching the prenatal vitamins she has been sent home with.

Emily had refused to look at the scan. The sonographer had conducted the scan in silence, clicking the measurements as Emily kept her face turned to the wall, eyes closed, tears streaming down her cheeks.

The doctor had set aside the kindness to talk to Emily about drinking.

Fetal alcohol syndrome is a huge concern for the doctor: what Emily has put her body through these past few months. Andi thinks about the drinking, the pot smoking, the God knows what else, and shudders.

"Fetal alcohol syndrome can be caused by one drink, or many. Sometimes we don't see it at all even when we expect to. It is entirely unpredictable," the doctor warned.

"What about drinking up to now?" Andi asked reluctantly.

"Let's not worry about that. No more drinking. The markers look good. There are several indicators of FAS, which are not showing. You have to remember"—the doctor sighed—"it is mostly alcoholics who have babies with FAS. Moderate drinking can be okay. Emily sounds like she has done some binge drinking, but it's not regular, is that right?"

"Right," Andi says.

"I think, I hope, it will be fine, but she cannot have any more alcohol."

"She won't listen to me," Ethan said finally. "We've tried. Will you tell her?"

"Oh, don't worry." The doctor nodded. "I'll put the fear of God into her." And she did, hence Emily's refusal to speak all the way home. She slouched down in the backseat, sinking her chin into her chest, her mouth set in a determined line as she squinted out the window, refusing to talk, refusing to look at them.

When they pull up in the driveway, Emily is first out of the car.

She runs into the house, slamming the door behind her. From the driveway, they hear the door to her room slam, then silence.

What are they supposed to do now?

I can't believe this," Ethan whispers, the color still not having returned to his face. He looks down at his hands, splaying his fingers and staring in amazement as they tremble. "I'm a mess," he says, looking at Andi, both of them still sitting in the car, unwilling to go inside.

"I know." She dabs away her own tears and takes a deep breath. There is something she has been thinking about all the way home, the same thought that came to her driving through town. She has been only half concentrating on Emily, the thought growing until it has taken up all the space in her head.

It is the obvious solution. So simple, she realizes, it is practically genius, and Ethan, she is certain, will agree. Her dismay and disappointment at Emily's pregnancy, has morphed, during the car ride home, into excitement and joy.

"I have an idea."

Ethan just looks at her.

"I know this might sound crazy, and I know you probably won't say yes right away, but . . . I've been thinking . . . this is your flesh and blood, your *grandchild*, and I don't know if I could forgive myself if we gave a member of our family away. . . ." Her words come out in a rush. She pauses, aware of her heart pounding, hoping she is saying the right thing, the words that will make Ethan say yes.

"I was thinking that maybe the best solution for everyone would be if . . . you and I . . . raised this baby." She looks at Ethan for a reaction, but there is none. He stares at her, in silence. "Emily would still be around, but this baby becomes *ours*. This is the baby we always

wanted. And we can do this!" Her words start to flow as she gains confidence.

"I know you never wanted to adopt, and I understand, I really do, all the things you used to say about not wanting to have a baby in your forties, and not wanting to be putting a child through school in your sixties, but neither of us ever anticipated *this*. I have accepted that you and I aren't going to have a child together. I know you have never understood this . . . craving I have, this *need* to have a child, and even though it has never gone away, I've learned to accept it, and I've learned to live with it, and it's okay. It wasn't what I wanted, but it was okay. But this? This is a gift from God. This is our baby, Ethan. This is the baby we are *supposed* to keep. We need to do this. This is the right thing to do."

The more Andi speaks, the calmer she grows. Hearing her thoughts out loud, they make even more sense. She is astonished at how practical she sounds, how obvious this solution.

Who would even think of doing anything else? She settles back and watches him expectantly, her head already filled with visions of a bundled blanket of love in her arms.

Seventeen

. . . .

Andi can't have heard correctly. Her lips are already poised in a half smile, ready to throw her arms around Ethan and weep tears of joy, for hasn't this been the one thing she has always wanted? Isn't this their destiny?

"No," he says again. "I know how much you wanted, *want*, a child, but this isn't the right thing to do. It isn't the right thing for Emily, and it definitely isn't the right thing for us."

Andi stares at him, bewildered. "How can you say that? It is the right thing for us, and Emily doesn't care. This is the one thing I wanted. The only thing I ever asked for . . ."

"Andi, I can't go over this again. You know how I feel about adoption and at this stage in my life, in *our* life, I don't want to be starting again with a baby. I just don't. I haven't got the energy, and we're just starting to get our own lives back. I don't want the responsibility. I'm sorry. I know how much you want this, but I also know that you had accepted it."

"I haven't accepted it," Andi bursts out. "I still cross my fingers every month, praying that this might be the month when a miracle occurs and I actually find myself pregnant. I don't have any idea

these days when my next period is going to be coming, and each time it doesn't come on time, I pray it's not the goddamn perimenopause, and I'm pregnant, and if I was, we *would* have a baby. You wouldn't have a choice. You wouldn't be able to just give it away because it wasn't the right time for you, and you didn't feel like raising a baby. What about me, Ethan? It's not just about you. *What about me?*" She is on the brink of tears, desperate to change his mind, to make him see sense.

"This isn't about me," he says eventually. "And it's not about you. This is about what is best for both of us, and this isn't it. I'm not going to change my mind. Adopting Emily's baby is madness, and it's not going to happen. I am not going to turn all our lives any more upside down than they are already. Jesus, Andi. Enough. Please. Another two months, and this will all be over and we can just carry on with our lives as normal."

"I don't want to carry on with our lives as normal!" Andi is now sobbing. "I want this baby!"

Ethan stares sadly at her, with a small shake of his head, reaching out to comfort her, wincing as she recoils from his outstretched hand, twisting her head, her whole body, away from him.

"I have to tell Brooke," he says quietly. "Please come in. Please don't do this, Andi. I love you. Please."

Andi looks away from him, not moving until he has closed the car door and disappeared into the house.

Her tears fall hard and fast as over and over again the same words come to her:

How am I going to forgive him? How am I ever going to get over this?

An hour later, Andi is still in the car. Numb. She cannot think anymore, can't move. All she can do is sit, staring into nothingness, feeling nothing, until a sharp rap on the glass makes her jump.

Drew peers in through the window, concern on his face. "Andi? What's going on?"

It jerks her out of her reverie, and she opens the door, looking up at Drew with puffy, red-stained eyes.

"Oh, sweetie." He crouches down next to the car and takes her hand. "What happened?"

Andi wants to tell Drew what is going on. She tries to tell him. She forms the words in her mind, thinks about opening her mouth and letting them come out, but nothing comes. She can't speak. She can't do anything other than sit in the passenger seat, one hand on the handle of the now-open door, and stare straight ahead.

"Can I get in?" Drew asks gently. Andi manages a slight nod.

Drew closes Andi's door, walks around the car, climbs into the driver's seat.

"Shall I drive us somewhere?" he asks after a while.

Andi manages to nod again.

Drew drives through town, and out through the suburbs. Past familiar buildings, and streets, and on until the Pacific Coast Highway. The buildings disappear, leaving only the winding coastal road, the rough scrub of trees leading down to the choppy waves. It is the landscape that lifts Andi's spirits, the smells of sea, salt, and pine, the huge expanse of space always calming her down.

Not today.

Drew takes the winding road smoothly, changing the radio station to an easy listening one filled with hits from the seventies. He sings along to Carly Simon and Neil Young, and eventually, as they drive, Andi sings along, too.

They do not talk until they get off the highway high on a cliff above the ocean. Drew parks the car on the top of a cliff with an incredible view. Miles and miles of open land, hills, and valleys fading into a silvery grey in the distance. The wind is up as they wordlessly climb out the

car and sit, side by side, on a large rock at the side of the road, staring out into the distance.

"Emily's pregnant," Andi says after a very long silence, which is entirely comfortable. "Seven months. I have to begin meeting prospective couples who will adopt this baby."

"Oh, love." Drew's face creases in sympathy. "I'm sorry."

"This baby, who is Ethan's grandchild, is going to be given away to a couple who are desperate for a baby but who can't have one. I want to raise this child. This is our baby. This is supposed to be mine, but Ethan says no. He won't do it. He doesn't want a baby."

Drew reaches over and holds her hand as the tears come out.

"I can't stand it," she moans. "I don't know how we look after her and lead her through this pregnancy knowing we are giving this baby away. I don't know how to be that selfless, and I don't know if I can do it." She trails into silence.

"How is Emily?"

"How do you think she is? Miserable."

"So what else is new?" Drew says, and Andi, who would normally smile, shrugs. "Have you spoken to *her* about keeping the baby?"

"No. Ethan won't even consider it. All he can think about is himself. That's *he's* happy with his life the way it is, that *he* doesn't want to raise another child, that *he* thinks it's too much of a disruption. He doesn't give a damn about me or what I want. He won't keep this baby because he's protecting Emily. God forbid anything should upset Emily, even though this could be the solution, this could be a win-win for everyone. If we raised this baby, Emily could go to college, could finally leave, and we would have a baby."

"Don't you think Ethan will come around?"

Andi shakes her head bitterly. "No. I don't. Emily wants to brush this under the carpet and forget about it, and that's why he won't consider keeping this child." She turns to Drew, fire in her eyes.

"I never thought I'd say this, but right now? I hate him!" She spits the words.

"No you don't," Drew says gently.

"I do! I know you think it's impossible, but I swear on my life, cross my heart and hope to fucking die, right now, I hate him, and I don't even know how I'm going to walk back in that house and be in the same room as him."

"It will pass," Drew says. "I believe you feel that now, but this is Ethan, your husband. You love him. You know his blind spot is Emily, it always has been, and you've always accepted that. This is a terrible situation for all of you. I can't even begin to imagine how it feels, but Andi, this baby isn't supposed to be yours. If it was, it would be. If you were supposed to keep this baby, you would. We always talk about how everything happens for a reason, and you have to accept that everything in God's world is exactly where it is supposed to be. I know it's painful. Oh, love, I know this is the worst thing that's ever happened to you, but you will get through it."

"But I don't want to get through it anymore," Andi bursts out, feeling as if she is becoming completely unhinged, but no longer caring. "I'm *done!*" she cries. "I'm *done!* I don't want to get through it, to walk on eggshells until the next damned drama. I'm already so angry I don't know how I'm even going to look at Ethan again. I don't want to be around him. I'm tired of being hurt. I'm just done."

Drew looks at her mutely. He doesn't know what else to say.

FAMILY

· · · · · · · · · · · · · · · · ·

Part Two

Eighteen

. . . .

often wish I could turn the clock back. Sometimes, when I'm lying in bed at night, I think back to the last time I was happy, and I play those memories in my head, constantly rewinding, like watching a favorite old movie.

The memories are so sparse. I seem to have only a handful from when I was a small child. Sometimes I wonder if things were so bad that somehow I blocked them out, but the things I remember are good; I just wish there were more of them.

I remember Mom waking up and actually being fun! Her crazy mop of hair would be sticking up everywhere, and she'd pretend to be blind without her glasses, feeling our faces and making us giggle like mad. Even Dad.

I remember cuddles, and love, and both of them taking turns to come up and kiss me good night, my dad always telling me not to let the bedbugs bite before tucking the comforter tightly around me.

My childhood should have been happy, at least until I realized my mom wasn't like all the other moms, that the other moms didn't slur their words once the sun went down, that their moms didn't explode

with rage at the tiniest thing, or lurch toward us with raised arm, ready to slap, before tripping over the coffee table.

When we were small, from the outside, our family looked happy, but even then, I never was. I never felt like I belonged; I was awkward in my body, uncomfortable in my skin. I was on the outside looking in, wanting to be one of the gang, wanting to be the same as all the others, but I never was. I never am.

Still.

I am not . . . enough.

I was always aware that I was different. Not different *better*, and I'm not sure I ever thought it was different worse, not consciously, but I have never felt like the others.

When the girls chose who to play with at recess, I was never picked unless it was a last resort. I remember wanting to be petite, and little, and pretty, like all the other girls, but I was always taller, chubbier. Even today, although I think I can look really good with a ton of makeup, I'm the first to admit I look pretty damn rough first thing in the morning.

I like my eyes. And I like my teeth, although I hated wearing the braces that led to them looking like this. They used to call me Buckeye, before the braces, and I was so excited to finally get braces, thinking it would make me cool, but it just gave me sores in my mouth; I couldn't wait to get them removed.

My mouth is okay. I wish my lips were bigger. Since I became more goth, I started using black lipstick, and I like that I can change the shape of my lips with black eyeliner. I have a picture I found of an old singer called Siouxsie Sioux that I keep in my drawer because her look is awesome, and I try to copy it although I won't cut my hair.

I love my hair, especially now that it's raven black. It's soft, and silky, and falls down my back. Michael Flanagan always loved my hair, said it was the softest thing he'd ever felt, even though it was just regular dull old mouse brown at the time.

When we'd lie on the pillows, head to head, in the tree house, he'd play with my hair between his fingers and draw strands of it under his nose, brushing it over his lips, a million times. It was weird. But cute.

Michael Flanagan.

I've seen him only occasionally this summer. He's been working at Woody's, and Sophia is totally addicted to the cable car chocolate frozen yogurt, so we go there quite a lot. I try to stay in the car, because I don't know what to say to him anymore. Andi's all, *Hey Michael! How's the job? Emily's in the car, I'll tell her you said hi!* Which drives me nuts. I'm in the car because I don't want to see him, and he doesn't say hi. Not anymore. He ignores me.

The thing is, I befriended Michael way before he was *Mike.* I went out of my way to get to know him because both of us were the class outcasts, and I figured we might as well be outcasts together.

I took pity on him. He used to sit at his desk and pick his nose when he thought no one was looking, but of course everyone knew. He was skinny, and little, and he smelled kind of sour although that didn't bother me. And he was adopted, so the other kids would say that even his own mother didn't want him. I felt so bad for him.

So one day I went up to him during recess and offered to split a Twix with him. We weren't supposed to bring chocolate in, healthy snacks only, but I had it, and his face lit up. I told him there and then: You have to stop picking your nose because it's gross. He was embarrassed, but he stopped.

I hadn't ever had a best friend before, and I loved having one. I know we were an odd couple—I was twice his size, but he made me laugh so much. Sometimes the two of us would get the giggles so badly, my cheeks would hurt, and he'd clutch his stomach, moaning.

He had this tree house that his dad had made when he was small. You had to climb a ladder to get up there, and he had pillows and blankets for sleepovers. We'd take a ton of food up and just lie on

the pillows and talk for hours. I told him everything. He was the best listener.

When my parents divorced, he was the one who totally got me through. He knew what pain was like because of being adopted. I know some kids are totally fine with it, and he always said that he loved his mom and dad, that he was really lucky and they were amazing, but he always had this nagging fear that his real mom, his *birth mother,* gave him up because he wasn't good enough.

We were more alike than you might have thought.

If I wasn't at his house, which I was almost all the time, we'd sit on the phone. He'd walk over and meet me every morning, so we'd get the bus together, and we'd do homework together every day after school. If it hadn't been for Michael, I don't even know if I would have got through it.

But then in eighth grade things changed. He went off to camp that summer, and I wrote to him every day—long, funny letters filled with silly stuff I'd seen, or done, things I thought would make him laugh.

I think I maybe got three letters from him all summer, and even calling them letters is a push. They were notes, totally impersonal.

Hey Em!

Having a great time! I learned to sail, and I'm playing football— can you believe it! You would totally hate it here ☺ *See you when I'm back. Later, Mike.*

I should have known. *Later?* What the hell was *that?* What happened to *Love?* And when did he become Mike? Of course, the minute he got back I saw that he'd become Mike at roughly the same time he grew a foot, his hair was bleached blond from the sun, and he suddenly seemed . . . built.

He didn't look like weird, skinny, smelly, adopted Michael Flanagan anymore. He looked like Mike, a jock. He looked, in short, like one of the popular kids.

Maybe it's as simple as that. I'd never stopped to think about it, but maybe it is as *lookist* as that: if you look like one of them, you *are* one of them. All I know is that I spent the summer before eighth grade missing my best friend desperately and writing to him every day, and we started eighth grade, and I lost my best friend.

I still don't get it. How do you go from one day being virtually inseparable and telling each other everything, even those embarrassing awful stories that you would never tell anyone else, to being virtual strangers?

I'd pass him in the hall, surrounded by the pretty, popular blond girls. He'd look up and catch my eye, and I'd pause, expecting him to break away, to come and talk to me, but he'd just look away, as if he was embarrassed to know me.

I started hanging out with the emo/goth crowd, and the more involved I became with them, the more distant I felt from Michael.

For a while we'd pass each other in the hallway and if neither of us were with anyone else, we'd do that *"Hi, what's up"* thing, then, after a time, we'd just smile, then we'd nod, and suddenly we stopped even acknowledging each other. If I saw him at the end of the corridor, I'd change direction. If I absolutely had to pass him, I'd suddenly remember something I had to get out of my bag, so I'd be busy getting something, or texting someone . . . something, *anything* that meant I didn't have to meet his eye.

By the way, he was doing the same thing. I saw him change direction many times. He didn't get busy with his bag, but he got his phone out or pretended to be on it. I only know he pretended because there was this one day when he thought I hadn't seen him. He put his phone to his ear and started having this fake conversation.

As he passed me, saying, "Yeah, it was a totally cool night," his phone started to ring. I swear. His damned phone started to ring. He looked embarrassed, rightly, and I just gave him this withering look.

"God you're lame," I said. I know I shouldn't have done it, but I had to. It was just so pathetic. I will say for a second he looked like the Michael of old. He looked sorry, and sad, and I just wanted to be back in the tree house, laughing.

He looked at me for a long time, then he said, "Em, I don't even know who you are anymore."

"Me?" I gasped. "Me? You're the one who became this big freaky popular jock."

"And you became this weird, miserable goth." He stared at me then while I felt the knife turn in my heart. "And your hair. Your beautiful hair."

"What? What about my hair?" I snapped.

"Why did you dye it?" He reached out and touched, actually touched my hair with such incredible gentleness, and I knew I was about to cry. I could feel the lump in my throat, and I turned so he wouldn't see, and the tears started running down my cheeks, and he didn't see.

"Fuck you," I threw over my shoulder as I walked off. When I got to the edge of the quad, I turned around. He was still standing there, looking at me. But not close enough to see the tears.

I guess that's when it all started to go a bit wrong for me. I started drinking in ninth grade. We'd steal liquor from our parents' cabinets and go up to the canyon and get wasted; we started smoking weed, too.

I loved how both took me out of myself, numbed me to the point that I didn't care about my parents, didn't care that my mom was totally disinterested, and usually drunk herself. I didn't care that my dad hasn't wanted to have anything to do with me since Andi came on the scene.

I didn't care that I had lost my best friend, and that there was no-body in the world who knew me anymore, and nobody in the world who loved me. There were times when life was so painful that I al-most couldn't get out of bed. I would want to hide under the covers forever, and just . . . disappear.

But my friends were doing the same stuff as I was.

Andi knew more than Dad. She's always watching me. For the record, Sophia's always watching me, too; but it's different. I know she loves me, and I know she doesn't judge me. Sure, she hates me some of the time, like I hate her some of the time, but at the end of the day, we're sisters.

Put it like this. She might drive me nuts by being oh-so-mature and Miss Goody Two-shoes, but let me tell you, if anyone was ever mean about her, or did something to her, I would kill them. Seriously.

That's why the watching doesn't bother me, and anyway, it's not just me. Sophia watches everyone and everything. She's the one who usually warns me about Mom when she's about to throw a shit fit. I have no idea how Sophia knows it's coming, but she always does, and she'll text me and tell me to stay out of the way.

Sophia knows more about my life than anyone else in my family, but I don't tell her everything. I know she doesn't judge me, but there's no way I would tell her about sex, for example. Or who I've had sex with. No way.

The judging thing is a big problem with Andi. Huge. I can get away with almost anything with my dad—he's always willing to see the good, to believe the good—but Andi's ready to jump on the worst, always sees the bad in every situation. At least when it comes to me.

I feel like she's always judging me, and I'm always disappointing her. But then . . . there are other times she can be so nice, it confuses me. When I'm sick, or really depressed, or . . . today. I was so scared today, I am so scared by this whole pregnancy thing, and Andi is be-ing amazing.

Every time I look in my dad's eyes, I see this massive disappointment, but Andi doesn't seem to be judging me, and when I was in there getting a scan, and they were rubbing the gel on my stomach, I was embarrassed and ashamed, and I really, really wanted Andi in there with me.

I kept my eyes closed the whole time because I wanted to pretend I was somewhere else. Anywhere else. Going through anything else. I wanted to pretend I was back in third grade, or fifth, Michael and I in the tree house, or going out to Stinson Beach for the day, shrieking with laughter as we jumped the waves.

I thought about that day Michael reached out and touched my hair, and how I was left with this tremendous loss, and I squeezed my eyes shut in that doctor's office and didn't move, not even to wipe away the tears that were streaming down my cheeks.

The thing is, it isn't going to be okay. My whole life my parents have told me things were going to be okay, and they always have been. Even the divorce, which was awful, ended up being . . . okay. Dad meeting Andi was pretty fucking awful, and my life isn't exactly great, but I deal with it.

Andi is a total bitch, but she can sometimes be nice. When she and my dad first got together, she used to do a ton of things with me. I hated that he had a girlfriend, but I liked what she did with me, and all the stuff she bought me. All I'd have to do was pause in a store and pick something up, say how much I loved it, and she'd buy it for me as a surprise.

Things haven't changed that much, except she can't buy me anymore. She never could, but for a while she seemed to think it was possible, so I let her.

I know Andi's not a bad person, I just think she's pretty fake most of the time. She pretends to like me, pretends to be interested, but I know she'd be much happier if I just disappeared. She loves Sophia,

not me. She loves Sophia because she's well behaved, and pretty, and slim. She looks a lot like Andi, in fact—like the daughter Andi always says she wanted. She looks like what she is: one of the popular girls.

But the real issue I have is that Andi makes everything about herself. Even this pregnancy. I bet she's thinking that she and my dad could keep this baby. I can see a look in her eye every time we talk about adoption, and I know she's thinking about it all the time, but she wouldn't dare say it.

She'd better not say it because there's no way in hell that would ever happen.

And that's why I can't stand her: from the moment she walked into our lives, everything had to revolve around Andi.

If Andi says jump, my dad asks how high. Sophia will do anything she asks. I'm the only one who refuses, who sees what's really going on. Except . . . except those times, like today, when she was caring, and it felt real, and genuine. Those are the times when I think I could almost . . . almost love her.

When she was stroking my arm and put an arm around me afterward as we were walking out the clinic, and pulled me in tight, kissing the side of my head, I wanted to let her enfold me in her arms.

I wanted to believe her when she said it was all going to be okay.

But this isn't something that's going to be okay. It never was. Dad kept asking me how I didn't know, but how are you supposed to know if you've never been pregnant?

Also, I had periods pretty much throughout. They were much lighter than normal, but there was still blood, and I had wicked PMS, but I seem to have that all the time anyway.

How was I supposed to know?

Maybe it crossed my mind, but not seriously. It was only hooking up. It wasn't supposed to lead to . . . Oh, God. A baby. Yeah, yeah, I know how biology works, but my group and I just hook up for fun, and because we're bored. It's just . . . what everyone does. And the guys always pull out before . . . well. They say that makes it safe, but obviously *that's* not true.

I didn't even think about it as *sex*. It's not like I particularly enjoy it that much. It's just something we do. The guys seem to get far more out of it than the girls although Justine says she comes. I don't know. I don't think I ever have. I have no idea what it feels like, but I'm pretty sure I'd know if I'd feel something other than wondering when it will be over.

And that's the other thing. My dad keeps asking me who the father is, but I don't know. We've all had sex with everyone in our group, and sometimes other people. There are a couple of guys who are older who hang out with us, and I've done it with them. So has Justine.

I just can't believe I'm about to have a baby. It doesn't feel real. Andi's downstairs now, on the phone to adoption agencies. I looked at the leaflets the doctor gave me but didn't read them properly.

My dad and Andi are talking about adoption as if it's decided. They have decided I'm not going to keep this baby, we're going to find some nice couple who will take this baby and raise it and give it a life filled with love.

But here's the thing. This is *my* baby. It's growing inside of me, it's part of me, and no one else has the right to tell me what to do with my baby.

I may be seventeen now, but I'll be eighteen by the time the baby comes, and I know I can love this baby. I know that I have so much love to give. All the love that's pent up that I've never been able to let out? The love I used to have for my father before he betrayed me by marrying Andi? I could give it to this baby.

And she would love me back. I already know it's a girl, and she

would love me with all her heart. All children need is for someone to love them and listen to them, and I would do that. I would love her more than anyone else in the world.

I want to keep her.

I'm going to keep my child.

Nineteen

· · · · · · · · · ·

There is nothing in the world Brooke hates more than hearing the words *We need to talk*. They inevitably sound ominous, inevitably remind her of her father calling her in, reprimanding her for something she's done of which she was entirely unaware. It doesn't matter if they're from a lover, a teacher, or her ex-husband. They always fill her with fear.

She knows this is something to do with her daughter. This is *always* something to do with Emily. Up until a few weeks ago, she would have reached for the vodka, drunk herself into oblivion, fed up with the constant crises and dramas that her daughter brings, removing herself from it all, drinking and sleeping the pain away.

But today—for today—she is celebrating sobriety. Forty-three days today. She hadn't planned on getting sober, had always thought A.A. and rehab was for losers, and anyway, she wasn't a drunk. She just liked a drink. That didn't make her an alcoholic—there was a huge difference.

That was before the night she fell.

Forty-four days ago.

At two o'clock one morning Anne, Brooke's next-door neighbor, heard water running, followed by a loud thump. Unbelievable that Anne was even up, but she was coming back from a fiftieth birthday party that had gone on far later than anyone had planned, was letting herself into her house when she heard the thump coming from the house next door.

Anne had paused; something had told her to check. The lights were on in Brooke's house, so Anne had rung the bell, and when there was no answer, she had reached behind the heavy iron pot on the doorstep, pulled out the key that was hidden there, and let herself in.

Upstairs, she found the bathwater overflowing, Brooke on the floor, lying unconscious in a pool of her own vomit, with blood gushing from her forehead. She must have fallen while running the bath and cut herself. Whether unconscious from drink, the cut, or both, thank God Anne was there.

Brooke woke up in the hospital with sixteen stitches in her head. She had no recollection of anything, knowing only that this time, she needed help. If that party hadn't gone on late, if Anne hadn't happened to be in the driveway, hadn't happened to hear Brooke fall . . .

The doctors told her how lucky she was. Had she not been found, she might have died. She needed to get help. And fast. They sent an addiction counselor into her hospital room; by the time she left, she had signed up for the A.A. program at the hospital. Her first meeting was that afternoon.

"Ninety in ninety," they said. Ninety meetings in ninety days. She got a sponsor—a woman named Maureen who had fifteen years of sobriety: serenity and wisdom poured from her every pore. Brooke's own newfound sobriety was shaky, but steady.

She still wasn't sure she wanted to be sober, but she looked around the meetings at all the people who were sober, envied them their lives. She envied them their calm, their wisdom, their positive outlook on life.

When they spoke of where they had come from, the blame, the resentment, the anger, the self-pity, she related. It was where she had been living for years, and it was that, more than anything else, that kept her coming back. She didn't want to live in a haze of anger and blame anymore. She wanted to see the glass as they seemed to: half-full.

She speaks to Maureen once a day, has been told to call Maureen at any time. Day or night. Whenever she feels alcohol calling, or . . . for anything at all. Any problems, anytime she doesn't know what to do.

Right now would be the perfect time to call Maureen. Her ex-husband is coming over because they "need to talk." Dread has settled around her shoulders like a hair blanket, itchy and uncomfortable, too heavy for her to move.

She looks at the phone but can't pick up to call Maureen, as much as part of her wants to. Brooke has always felt isolated. She describes herself as a hermit although it wasn't always like this. When she was young she remembers being sociable and social, remembers loving meeting people, loving building a life.

It was once she was married she started to lose herself, trying to be someone she thought she was supposed to be. She had the not-fitting-in gene, the never-feeling-good-enough trait, the same one she sees in Emily; she sees so much of herself in Emily, it almost breaks her heart.

Ethan was supposed to rescue Brooke, to be her knight in shining armor, but once she was married, the inadequacies, ones she had been able to hide for a while, kicked in full force.

She would stand in the hallways outside Emily's preschool classroom with a fake smile stuck to her face, neediness emanating from every pore, wanting so badly to join in the conversations about gym programs, or babysitters, or kids' clothes outlets.

She was barely in her twenties at the time, so much younger than the other mothers, all of who seemed to be in their thirties. But she wanted to be one of them, she wanted them to accept her.

Sometimes she would try to join in, feeling awkward and wrong. She remembers hearing about a playgroup that had started with a selection of other mothers, hearing them plan whose house to meet at next, then talking about a mom's night out they had held.

Nobody thought to invite her. Even when she was standing there, a polite smile fixed on her face, nobody seemed to notice her. It was around that time she found a glass of wine during "the witching hour" made her feel a whole hell of a lot better.

Everybody had a glass of wine during the witching hour. Didn't they? She heard the other mothers laugh about it. Brooke had never been a big drinker so tended to drink the wine quickly, more like water than wine. She refilled. A glass and a half.

The glass and a half became two. For a long time she had two glasses every night. But two crept up to three, crept up to four, and more. Every night.

Everyone did it, she told herself, as she grew adept at hiding the empty bottles of wine, stashing them in the garage under the empty crates, taking them to the recycle bins at the grocery store the next morning.

Ethan would sit and watch her, disapproval etched on his face, but she wasn't hurting anyone. If anything, she was better when she was a bit . . . tipsy. More confident, more fun. Looser.

After a while, she stopped being more confident, more fun. She started being angrier, critical, negative. She would look at Emily, so like her when she was young, and feel fury.

"Get it together, Emily!" she'd shriek. "Lose weight, for Christ's sake! Look at you! Who'd want to date you?" She wouldn't realize she was holding her stunned daughter by the shoulders, shaking her.

Resentment set in. Why should she help them with their homework? Jesus, she was a mother, not a teacher. It was the school's job to ensure that her children knew what they were doing, not hers.

Why did she have to make dinner every damned night? She wasn't a

cook. She had other things to do, Goddamnit. No, I didn't make dinner tonight, you can damn well make something yourself.

Ethan stepped in to fill the void. He'd come home from work to greet the kids off the school bus, trying to contain his mounting sadness that Brooke was already well on her way to being incapacitated.

He'd stop at the market on the way home, buy prepared food, knowing full well there'd be nothing in the fridge, and late at night they would have fights. Ethan would say he would leave if she didn't stop drinking; she would tell him to leave, knowing that he wouldn't, until, eventually, he did.

She stopped drinking then. For three weeks. She needed to prove to Ethan, and to herself, that she could. That was her test, for surely an alcoholic—that was what he called her—couldn't stop drinking for three weeks. An alcoholic couldn't stop drinking for two days. How could she possibly be an alcoholic?

They went back and forth for a while, until Ethan left. Permanently. Whatever love and affection was left had trickled out by the time he walked out for the last time.

Brooke continues to blame him, to blame everyone else. She is still negative, and critical, and judgmental. Everything to do with Emily is Ethan's fault, as Brooke is, in her own mind, an exemplary mother. She goes to *most* events at school, doesn't she? She shows up, mixes and mingles with the other mothers. Surely that's enough?

When Brooke's life isn't good, it is Ethan's fault. Emily being . . . *Emily,* is Ethan's fault. Brooke's being a single mother who is struggling to get by, despite the generous alimony and child support she gets, is Ethan's fault.

Her inability to work, because how on earth could she possibly get a job when the whole world is against her, is Ethan's fault. Her subsequent inability to fly to Boston for her high school reunion and dreamed-of old boyfriend reunion is, naturally, Ethan's fault.

And with such a terrible husband, and such high-maintenance god-damned needy children, is it any wonder she has a drink or two at night, just to ease her nerves?

I t is a familiar feeling, Ethan's heart jumping into his mouth as he stands on the doorstep waiting for Brooke to come to the door. Emily is in the car, refusing to get out, and there is not much he can do about it.

He just lost it in the driveway, roaring at Emily to get out of the damned car. She shook her head and sank farther down into her seat. Short of lifting her up, which he doubts he could even manage, there is nothing else he can do.

He notices that Brooke's house looks more kempt than usual. The planters on either side of the front door have been planted with chrysanthemums to welcome the fall. For years they have been filled with overgrowing weeds, which Ethan, on his rare visits, cannot resist plucking out, but now they are properly planted. He is surprised.

The door opens, Brooke looks at him, leaning to one side to look past him to the car.

"I thought you were bringing Emily. Is she coming in?"

"No. She's here, but she refuses to get out of the car."

Brooke frowns. "Do you want me to talk to her?"

Ethan shakes his head. "I think she needs to be left on her own for a little while." He highly doubts this, but Andi's words echo through his head: that Emily creates these dramas for attention from her parents, that she doesn't do it if her parents are not around, and right now he is too tired, too fearful of Brooke's impending rage, to focus on indulging Emily's tantrum.

Brooke seems different. He looks at her closely. Her eyes are clear and shining; she is neat and tidy. Usually, her hair is a mess of dry, tangled knots; unwashed, a mess. If she is wearing makeup, it is sloppy

and wrong—a red lipstick that never seems to stay within the lines of her lips, clothes that neither flatter nor fit her.

Today she looks . . . lovely, like a completely different person. Her hair healthy and clean, clipped back in soft waves. She is not wearing makeup, her skin is clear.

Simple cargo pants and sneakers, and a clean white T-shirt. That's it! She looks clean, and Brooke never looks clean. She even—he leans forward, taking a subtle sniff—yes! She even smells clean, which is something he hasn't smelled for years.

It is Ethan's turn to frown. Everything is different today, and it unsettles him. Andi has become the source of his stress, whereas Brooke is feeling like a refuge. This is upside down, the reverse of his usual life. It throws him off the speech he has prepared in his head, a speech designed to keep her calm, to redirect her inevitable rage.

"Come into the kitchen." Brooke leads the way down the hall. Ethan stares at the house in amazement as he walks through. Usually it is filled with stuff. Brooke is disorganized, messy, a hoarder. There are always piles of magazines, of books, of clothes. Coats are flung down, never to be hung up. Bills disappear in piles on the kitchen counter. Dust collects on the surfaces of tables covered with tiny china animals that Brooke cannot bear to throw away.

She was never particularly domestic, but it became so much worse after they split up. One of the reasons he tries to avoid entering her house is because it upsets him so much: to think this is how his daughters are forced to live when they are not with him.

Sophia assures him her own bedroom is lovely, and he believes her. Not because of anything Brooke will have had to do with it but because Sophia is naturally neat and tidy. Her mother's house might be in squalor, but she will ensure her bedroom is not.

That his children have to live in a filthy house, that they have to deal with a drunk mother, has been one of the biggest upsets of his

life. At times he has thought of going back to court, fighting for sole custody, but he doesn't want any further damage done to his daughters, and in truth they are with him far more than they are with their mother.

He looks around him. Today, everything is different. There are still piles, too much stuff in the house, but it feels clean. The house has been vacuumed, and dusted. There are no piles of filthy plates in the kitchen sink, encrusted food on the granite counter. Today, it is gleaming, with a jar of drying hydrangeas in the middle of the kitchen table.

"Can I get you some coffee?" Brooke asks nervously, gesturing to where a fresh pot of coffee is brewing.

"Sure," Ethan says, looking around for her omnipresent glass of wine, but she pours herself a coffee instead, then joins him, sitting opposite him at the kitchen table.

"You look like you're wondering what's going on." She attempts a smile.

"I guess I am. It looks great in here. Clean and fresh."

"I'm sober, Ethan," she says quietly.

"Great," he says cautiously. "Good for you." He doesn't get too excited. He remembers when they first split up, how she would stop drinking for a week or two, announce she was sober, and as soon as he came back, he would find bottles hidden in the trash.

"I know. You've heard me say it before. But I'm forty-three days sober. In A.A. I have a sponsor and everything."

Ethan looks at her closely, for suddenly he sees the difference. She is not announcing this with drama or flourish, but quietly and bashfully. And the evidence is all around them.

"That's really great," he says, and this time he means it.

Brooke gives a nervous giggle. "I feel great. Scared, but clear, for the first time in years. It's really different this time. I am an alcoholic, and I'm taking it a day at a time."

Ethan nods silently, looking up to find Brooke gazing at him intently.

"I'm really sorry," she bursts out suddenly. "I'm so, so sorry."

"What for?" He is shocked, hadn't prepared in the least for this.

"For messing everything up. For everything I put you and the girls through. I know, I know, you've totally moved on, and you probably don't even want to hear this, but I never meant to hurt all of you so much."

"It's fine," Ethan says awkwardly. "We're fine."

"Things are good with . . . Andi?" Usually Brooke calls her "your wife," with more than a hint of disdain.

"Great," Ethan lies. Even before today, before their conversation about keeping the baby—a conversation he now suspects, with dread, will have consequences—Andi has been drifting away from him, and he doesn't know how to bring her back. He is terrified he is losing her, for it feels as if that is exactly what is happening, but every time he broaches the subject or tries to talk to her, she says she is "fine," in her curt, dismissive way, and he cannot get through to her.

Nor have they made love in a while. He reaches over only to have her sigh with the inevitable shake of the head, telling him she is tired, or not in the mood.

She is never in the mood these days, it seems.

She no longer reaches out in spontaneous displays of affection, wrapping her arms around him and kissing his neck, burying her nose in his shoulder because she "just loves the smell" of him.

When he reaches out, she recoils. He has now retreated, hurt and wounded. He doesn't want to go through another divorce. He doesn't want to lose Andi. He just doesn't know how to make it all right.

"Emily's being better with her?" Brooke asks, bringing him back from his reverie.

"She's . . . Emily. Sometimes great, sometimes not."

There is a silence, which Brooke eventually breaks:

"You said there is something you wanted to talk to me about. I presume it's Emily?"

Ethan nods, a wave of nausea suddenly washing over him. God, how he is dreading this conversation.

"I don't quite know how to tell you this," he says, his prepared speech having long been forgotten. "We found out this week that Emily is . . . pregnant." He can't look Brooke in the eye until he realizes there is no shrieking, or screaming, and he raises his eyes to see what is going on.

Brooke's eyes have welled up with tears, one of them trickling slowly down her cheek.

He waits for her to say something, and when nothing comes, he continues.

"We were hoping it was early enough for her to have an abortion, not let it ruin her life, but we took her to the OB/GYN yesterday, and she is seven months."

Brooke gasps.

Forty-three days ago, she *would* have started screaming. Forty-three days ago she would have shrieked how dare they take her to the OB/GYN without telling Brooke, how dare they not tell her immediately; but newly sober, calm, able to react to things peacefully, Brooke feels only a huge wave of sadness.

"We have started looking at adoption agencies, which seems to be the only course of action open to us, but . . ." He sighs deeply. "Emily wants to keep this baby. She won't listen to us. We don't know what to do. I think she has no idea what being a mother entails, and having a baby now, at her age, will ruin her life forever."

Brooke is now openly weeping as Ethan trails off. He would never have dreamed of this reaction, has no idea what it means or how to react to it.

He waits as she weeps, blindly grabbing a tissue from a box on the hutch behind the table, blowing her nose as the tears continue to fall.

"I can't do this . . ." she sobs after a while. "I just . . . can't."

"You can't what?" Ethan has no idea what she means.

"I can't take care of Emily and take care of myself. I just can't."

"What are you saying?" Ethan is horrified. "I don't understand."

"Ethan." The expression on her face is the most pained he has ever seen. "I love Emily, but my sobriety is too precious for me to let anything derail it, and especially Emily. I am devastated, but I can't be there for her. Not now. I'm sorry." She sobs. "I'm sorry."

"You're . . . disowning her?"

"No! I just need some space. I can't live my life wrapped up in whatever Emily's latest drama happens to be. Even hearing it makes me want to reach for a bottle of wine. I can't do it right now, Ethan. I want to, but I'm frightened of what will happen."

"So . . . she's not . . . you don't want her sleeping here on her usual nights? You want the girls to live with me?"

Brooke nods. "You can't understand. I know it seems like I'm being a terrible mother, but for now you and . . . Andi need to look after them. Please."

"Okay." Ethan stands up abruptly, pushing back his chair. Jesus. This was the very last thing he expected, and the one thing he has wanted for years. To have his girls to himself, but the victory feels hollow, and he doesn't know what to do. "What do I tell them?"

"Tell them I love them. Tell them I've been sick, and I'm getting better. It's not forever. It's just . . . for now. I'll be in touch."

Ethan leaves Brooke sitting at the kitchen table, still sobbing. As soon as he closes the door, Brooke reaches for the phone and calls her sponsor as Ethan walks numbly over to the car, wondering how in the hell to explain to his daughters that their mother doesn't want them anymore.

Twenty

· · · · · · · · · ·

Today, my dad started talking about condoms in the car, which completely freaked me out. It's a bit late for that, right? I mean, I know I kind of wondered if I was pregnant, but I kept thinking it would be okay. I kept thinking that I would wake up, and I wouldn't be, and if I refused to accept it, which I do, then it would all be fine.

I still can't believe it's not. I can't believe I'm going to have a baby. Andi's downstairs now, on the phone to adoption agencies. I stood at the top of the stairs a while back to listen to her. No one can believe I didn't know, but they're not in my shoes. How can they possibly know what it's like?

The thing is, I know I have to give this baby up for adoption. Of course I do. I don't know who the father is and, as my dad keeps telling me, I have my whole life ahead of me.

But it doesn't feel like I have my whole life ahead of me. It feels like my life is pretty much over. I've got these stupid classes I have to take because of the underage drinking, and it's a major pain, and

the only thing that ever gives me hope, that makes me feel life is going to get better, is the thought of having a baby.

I try not to think about how I got here because it just freaks me out and makes me so mad I can hardly stand it, but my life was not supposed to be like this. If my parents hadn't got divorced, and my mom wasn't a nutcase alcoholic, and my dad hadn't fallen in love at an age when he should have been more interested in raising his daughters, none of this would have happened.

I wouldn't want to numb the pain of just being me by drinking and taking drugs and having sex with people I barely even know. Who knows, I might even be a normal, happy, well-adjusted teenager getting ready to go to college.

I screwed up my college applications this year, which is why I'm taking a year off although I'm a year ahead anyway, so this just evens things out. The thing is, I don't even know that I want to go to college. Of course, that's what every middle-class girl is supposed to do. How could I possibly think of doing anything else? But I just don't see myself going to a college.

I like writing, sure, but the thought of being a literature major fills me with horror. What I really like is photography. I haven't done it that much recently, and although art school is definitely more interesting to me, I don't know if I'm any good at it, not really. I used to think I was, I used to think I had a real talent, when my mom gave me her old Nikon, and I'd take tons of pictures on proper film.

I'd use Sophia as my model. Sometimes I'd take pictures of her back with her clothes just kind of draped, because it looked more artsy, like something you might see in black and white, framed and hanging on the wall of a cool modern house.

I never totally understood the whole aperture and shutter-speed thing, but I experimented and ended up taking some amazing shots at the beach. Manzanita branches twisting on the sand, cool shells, that kind of thing.

Andi got them blown up and framed as a surprise. I walked into the house one day after school and four of these shots I took were hanging in the hallway. They looked totally professional, and I felt so proud. Everyone who came over commented on them, but now they're not special anymore; they're just part of the furniture.

Sometimes I take photos of my friends, and I mess around with Photoshop, making the picture look so much better than it actually does. My friends say I'm really talented, but I don't know. It's just something I like doing.

There's this photographer, Nan Goldin, who took these amazing photographs of her friends in, I think, the seventies or eighties, in New York. I found one of her books at the library one day, and I couldn't tear myself away.

They're explicit, and raw, and beautiful. It's sex, and drugs, and rock and roll, and if ever I thought I stood a chance at being a proper photographer, those are the kinds of photographs I'd take.

My friends are all heavily into drugs now, and I have these great shots of them, but it's not as seedy as Nan Goldin's pictures. Popping OxyContin and Vicodin, and their parents' Ambien that they've stolen from the medicine cabinet, plus occasionally snorting the odd line of coke isn't quite as dramatic as someone's tying a tourniquet on their arm and shooting up some smack.

I kind of keep hoping that someone will do something a bit harder, so I can capture it on film, but even I recognize that's a bit sick. I just like hanging around and shooting what's going on, and I know that if someone chooses to do something stronger, I'll probably be there to capture it.

At least, that was before the Bean came along. I call her the Bean, even though it's not a bean, it's a baby. My dad and Andi said not to find out the sex because they still think I'm going to give this baby up for adoption and they don't want me to get too attached, and even though they didn't tell me, I know it's a girl.

And I'm already thinking about the kinds of photographs I could take of her. Like Sally Mann, but maybe not as provocative. Or Tierney Gearon. Photographers who captures these moments in their children's lives, all the sweetness and sadness that comes with childhood.

I won't do those dressing-your-baby-up-like-a-pea-in-a-pod kind of shots, though. They're just weird. But how awesome would it be to be able to capture your child's life with these beautiful images from the moment of birth onward. Obviously, though, I wouldn't be able to capture the moment of birth, but maybe just after.

Birth.

Ergh.

I have to say, that bit totally freaks me out. First of all, it means they're going to be looking at my, well, you know . . . That bit is just *beyond* gross. I think I might just die of embarrassment on the table.

I YouTubed videos of people giving birth, and it's not pretty. Plus, if some male doctor tries to stick his hand up there, I think I might slap him.

And the pain freaks me out. I've already said sign me up for every drug available. I'm not one of those martyrs who plans on natural childbirth and breathing. Christ, no. Stick that needle in my spine and fill me up with that epidural, baby. I don't want to feel a thing.

But here's the thing: it will all be worth it because right now, inside my body, is another life, and she's all mine, the one person in the world who's going to love me unconditionally, and the one person I'm going to love unconditionally. I'm never going to leave her, or do anything to hurt her. I'm going to make sure she feels safe and loved her entire life.

You think I don't know how to do it? You think that my mother was so crap I couldn't possibly be a good mother myself? Huh. The reason I *do* know how to do it is because of my mother. It's exactly because she never did it, because I see the disappointment in her eyes every time she looks at me that I know how to do it differently.

My mom is the most amazing mom in the world. When she's nice. Or sober. Or in a good mood. She's also the biggest bitch in the world when she's drunk, which is a lot of the time. She can look at me with love and say something really sweet, then, I swear, an hour later she'll come pounding up the stairs and crash into my bedroom and start screaming at me.

It comes from nowhere, with no warning, and when it comes, it's vicious.

"Look at you!" she screamed, right before I graduated. "You're a goddamned freak with that hair and makeup. And the size of you! Jesus, Emily. You're enormous. Who the hell is going to even look at you, looking like that."

When I was younger, and she used to start in on me like that, I'd just curl up in a ball and squeeze my eyes shut, pretending to be somewhere else. Anywhere else. But now I just scream back. Fucking bitch.

And then, the next day, she apologizes, and I can see she feels horrible about it when she's sober, and it isn't fake, it's for real. She puts her arms around me and croons to me as she rocks me back and forth, holding me tight, telling me I'm beautiful.

She didn't mean any of the stuff she said, and it was nothing to do with me, she says. And she is so sorry, and I mustn't listen to her when that stuff comes out of her mouth.

She says she has no idea why she's so moody, and I want to point out that three bottles of wine, or a pint of vodka may have something to do with it, but I don't. I allow myself to be a little girl, safe in her mommy's arms, and in those moments I know, I really do, that the woman spewing that hateful shit the night before is not my mom.

But now—get this—she's apparently been sick and can't see anyone while she's getting better. Not even her daughters! I'm worried, and I'm scared, and I can't believe that at this time in my life, my own mother has abandoned me.

And the thing is, I know it's not true. For the past few weeks my mom's been amazing. She said she wasn't drinking, but usually when she says stuff like that she's already reached the point of slurring, but this time I believed her. So how come she's suddenly sick? If I ever got sick, no matter what it was, even cancer, or anything, my Bean is going to be right there by my side, and I'm going to continue loving her, no matter how ill or tired, or drunk I am.

But I'm not going to drink anymore once Bean is born. I'm not drinking now. Bean and I are going to be this incredible team. I'm not going to even think about dressing her in anything pink. She's going to be the coolest kid. I might even give her a Mohawk when she's a toddler. She's going to wear black leggings and cute little black hoodies. I even found a website that sells these baby shoes that look like biker boots, and she is so totally going to wear those all the time, and we are going to do everything together. She's not going to be one of these kids that stops my life, she's going to be part of my life, she'll learn to hang out and sleep even if there's loud music.

I'm a little scared about the drinking I've done. I know the doctor said it was probably going to be fine, but I'm scared that I might have done something to hurt her, and I would never do anything to hurt her. It's not like I even *want* to drink anymore. I want to look after myself. I want to look after Bean.

Andi's been making me these protein smoothies, and big salads, and all this food that's supposed to be good for the baby's brain, and it feels like I'm being looked after.

In a weird way, Andi's being more of a mother to me right now than my mother ever was. I still want to hate her, and at times I get pissed at her because she's being so nice, which makes me resent my own mom, and that's not fair, but . . . it's nice. I wouldn't ever spontaneously kiss her—*God no!*—like I do my dad, or tell her I love her or anything, but she sometimes puts her arms around me if I'm sitting down, and puts a kiss on the top of my head, and I kind of like it.

It makes me feel safe.

I don't think things with her and my dad are great, though. For years they've been all sickly sweet together, and suddenly there seems to be tension between them. This should make me happy. I've been trying to get rid of her for years, but right now, especially with my mom abandoning me, I need Andi. I don't want them to split up until the Bean is born.

And you know what? I don't feel as angry at her. I hated her so much for stealing my dad, for ruining what was a perfect arrangement. I didn't want the divorce, but my dad was amazing afterward, he was with me and Sophia all the time; but then, once he met Andi, he wasn't, and I just wanted her to be gone.

But my mom isn't around, and I need someone who understands, and Andi's the closest thing I've got.

G-man comes over this afternoon. I hear him downstairs, hear Andi chatting to him, and then she comes up and knocks on my door.

I've been making playlists on iTunes for Bean, and I've found these collections with Tom Waits, Lisa Loeb, and Sarah McLachlan, playing music for kids. It's not the stuff I listen to, but it's better than that Disney crap. When Sophia was young, she used to love the Wiggles. Seriously. She was obsessed.

Mom and Dad used to sing the fruit salad song all the time, and even then I thought it was pretty awful. Bean isn't going to be that kind of kid. I'm going to raise her to appreciate good music.

"Emily? G-man's downstairs. Do you want to come down?" Andi waits outside my closed bedroom door.

I take the earbuds out and think about it. I haven't seen anyone for days, and with all this talk of adoption, I couldn't face anyone. I didn't want any of my friends to know I was pregnant, although honestly, if

I thought I was just getting fat, I bet they thought the same thing. I mean, no one would know the difference, right?

But now, I'm going to keep Bean, so it shouldn't matter if people know. I haven't told my dad yet. I know he's going to freak out. It's going to be the usual shit about ruining my life, and I have no idea what having a baby involves, blah blah blah.

The thing is, yesterday I spent the afternoon in the library, and I read a ton of books about what to expect, then what it's like the first year of your baby's life. I took a notebook and made notes, and it was kind of funny. I felt like I was studying for a test, and probably studying harder than I've studied for anything in ages. I was really into it.

But I do know what to expect, and my dad will get over it. He has to. He has no choice.

So when Andi hovers in the doorway I nod, pull my oversized sweater around myself, and head downstairs to see G-man.

W anna go out?" he says.
"Sure."

"Where are you going?" Andi's back downstairs, pretending to be busy chopping vegetables, but she's worried about what I'm going to do. I can tell. I look at G-man, and he shrugs.

"Town?" I say, and he looks at me quizzically. We don't usually hang out in town because there's not much to do there, or at least, not the kind of stuff we like to do. But I'm really determined not to drink, even though I know that bulge in G-man's jacket is a hip flask filled with whatever he's managed to steal from his parents' liquor cabinet, and I'm really determined not to smoke weed, even though I know on the other side of his jacket his pockets are probably holding two superthin joints of superstrong skunk, but in town I won't be tempted.

He shrugs eventually, and we leave the house, and I feel Andi's eyes follow me until we turn the corner.

Even then, I feel like she's still watching.

So where you been?" G-man says, shuffling beside me with his hands in his pockets and his head down.

"Kind of busy."

"Yeah? With what?"

And so here it is. Decision time. Do I tell him or not. If adoption is an option, I wouldn't tell him. I wouldn't tell anyone. I know that if I tell G-man, the word is out. No one I know can be trusted to keep a secret. The only person I ever knew who could keep a secret is Michael Flanagan.

He knows everything about me, and even now, when we don't speak, and we cross streets to avoid each other, I trust that he won't tell anyone anything. Just as I would never breathe a word about him.

And suddenly, as freaky as this sounds, I don't want to tell G-man. I don't want anyone in my so-called crowd of friends to know because it feels like this is a special secret between Bean and me, and the only person I want to tell, the only person I can trust, is Michael.

"Just hanging out," I tell G-man, suddenly wanting to get away from him, to get back home. "I can't stay long. I have a ton of stuff to do."

G-man shrugs. "Hey, you should have been with us on Tuesday. Man, we drove out to this farm in Sebastopol, and got so totally wasted. We built a fire, and Rockit brought his guitar. It was awesome."

"Great," I say, but my heart isn't in it, and I just want to leave.

An hour later, I get rid of G-man. It isn't hard. Everyone texts us while we're hanging out in town, and they're all going to Suki's

house because her parents are away, and I just tell him I'm too busy, and I promised Andi I'd get home to do stuff for her.

Instead, I go straight to Woody's, but they say Mike isn't working until that evening, and so I walk over to his house. There isn't anyone home there, either, and by the time I get there, I start to think I'm totally nuts and have no idea what I'm doing there.

I go into the backyard, and the tree house is still there, exactly the same, and it makes me literally cry with longing. Before I know it, I'm climbing the ladder up to the tree house.

I lie on my back, looking out the window at the canopy of trees rustling slightly as they brush the tree house, and it looks and smells the same. The pillows are still the same faded green and orange pillows that his mom gave us years ago, and there are still the broken rattan baskets we used to keep our stuff in. I take off a lid and—OH MY GOD—there are pictures of Michael and me, grinning and sticking our tongues out and stuff, pictures we used to take on the computer and print out.

We were so young! And look at me! I look so happy. That's when I start to cry, when I realize I haven't been happy for years and years; probably not since the last time I was up in this tree house, and that's when I hear voices down below.

I freeze. It's Michael, and one of the bitchy beautiful girls, Jenna, and they're walking over to the tree house, and I hear him say: "You have to see this. My dad made it for me when I was five," and I think I'm going to throw up.

Twenty-one
. . . .

Ethan pounds down Hillside at the end of his daily loop, his T-shirt drenched, but he's calm now, filled with purpose. It is the kind of day he used to love, the kind of day that makes him happy to be alive.

He slows down as he comes into town, pauses at a bench, and bends, clutching his knees, slowing down his breathing before standing up and stretching.

Usually he takes nothing with him on his runs, except perhaps an iPod strapped to his arm, but today he has a small fanny pack with money; today he has a plan.

Andi was fast asleep this morning when he left. Usually, she wakes up while he is in the bathroom; he emerges to find her sitting up in bed, checking her e-mail and looking at *The Huffington Post*.

But these past few days she has been . . . if not actually sleeping, then feigning sleep. Her breathing is too slow to be asleep, the most common mistake people make when they are faking, but she keeps her eyes closed, and when he leans down to kiss her good-bye, she mumbles something inaudible before rolling over away from him.

Even though he knows she is awake, he doesn't know what to do
other than leave, quietly pulling the bedroom door closed behind
him.

When he gets back from his run, she is usually making breakfast for
Sophia downstairs, busy packing snacks and lunch for camp, helping
her pack her bag, or chatting with her about what it will be like being in
seventh grade.

Ethan tries to join in, but Andi can barely look at him, only talks
to him if she has to. He knows she is still furious with him, and feels
helpless in the face of her hurt. He has tried to apologize but isn't
changing his mind, knows that nothing would make him willing to
raise this child.

Time will heal her wound. It has to. When the baby is born, when
a suitable family is found, she will forgive him. She will understand.

If only the chasm between them weren't growing larger by the
day.

He remembers this feeling once before. Years ago. At school,
when he fell in love with Tricia. They dated for two years, and he
thought he was going to spend the rest of his life with her.

They were together all the time her junior year, but toward the beginning of their senior year, something changed. At first, he thought he
was imagining it. She didn't pick up the phone, or she said she was going out with girlfriends when she had not been on a girls' night out for
years.

She came in late, and became suddenly critical of him. He worked
too hard on the landscaping business, he didn't have enough time for
her, he was too serious. Nothing he did seemed to be right.

When she said she needed space, he trusted she needed space. She
said she was going through some emotional stuff, and she just needed
space to figure out where she was; it had nothing to do with him, and,
no, he shouldn't worry at all.

He agreed, reluctantly, to a month off. She moved out and into a

friend's apartment, and stopped taking his calls entirely. A week after she moved out, he was dragged out by friends to try to drown his sorrows at the local bar.

He walked in and saw Tricia immediately. Nestled in a corner booth with a guy he vaguely knew—one of the basketball players. She was giggling, with her head on his shoulder. They shared an intimacy and a comfort that led to Ethan's knowing, instinctively, this had been going on for a while; this was the reason for her needing space.

She must have felt him staring. She looked up, and the smile on her face was instantly replaced with shock. Guilt. Remorse. She stood up and tried to push her way through the crowd to . . . what? Explain? He didn't want explanations. He was gone. To another bar, to get blind drunk. To figure out what had gone wrong.

To this day, he doesn't know what it was. He'd spent months thinking about what he could have done differently, how he could have saved their relationship, but he never figured it out. One day they were fine, the next it was as if she turned the switch to "off."

She was gone; there probably wasn't anything he could have done about it.

What terrifies him today, despite the fact he is no longer a naïve kid, despite the fact that he has been married, divorced, remarried, has two beautiful children, is that the way Andi is treating him, the sense of distance he now feels, is exactly what happened all those years ago.

It is as if that switch has been flicked again.

This time he is damned if he is going to let it go without a fight. Yes, things have been difficult. Of course, Emily has thrown drama after drama at them, and he has always been in the impossible situation of being in the middle, trying to keep his wife and his daughter happy when they both seem to hate each other, each wanting him to *choose her.*

But Emily was almost a grown-up; these terrible teens were al-most over. My God—was this really as naïve as it now felt—he *pre-sumed* that he and Andi would spend the rest of their lives together.

After the drinking and the drama that colored his first marriage to Brooke, Andi was his port in a storm. It wasn't the intense, passionate falling in love he'd had with Tricia all those years ago. If anything, it was slow and steady. He liked being around Andi. He liked who he became when she was there and the way she seemed to take every-thing in stride.

He loved how she was with Sophia, and how measured she was with Emily, even when Emily was behaving horribly. Occasionally, Andi would snap; complain to him—Emily was the only thing they had ever seriously fought about—but to Emily she was always calm. Emily would scream things at Andi, and she never took the bait. She just calmly said she wasn't going to be talked to that way, and she was sorry Emily felt that, and she would go out until Ethan managed to calm Emily down.

And things seemed to be so much better between the two of them. It seemed like, since finding out she was pregnant, Emily was turning to Andi more than to him. It was what he had always wanted: all his girls to get on.

Before Andi came into their lives, Ethan had always been the care-taker. He had looked after Tricia, then Brooke, then his daughters. Whenever anyone had a problem, Ethan was the one who stepped in to mediate and sort it out. It had never occurred to him that in a part-nership you take care of each other; it had never occurred to him that someone should look after him.

These past five years, Andi has looked after him. She doesn't stare at him disdainfully when other women talk of expensive vacations and ask him witheringly when he is going to make some proper money.

She doesn't pick up his hand when they are out, having dinner with friends, and drunkenly point out his less-than-clean fingernails, shuddering with mock horror and suggesting he might want to take a

longer shower next time, as their friends sit, frozen with mortification and horror.

She doesn't belittle and criticize, slurring that he shouldn't be so sensitive, and she is just joking, despite the anger and resentment in her voice.

Andi loves him. She believes him to be handsome, and clever, and brilliant, and in believing that, has changed the way he sees himself. She doesn't want him to make more money, or be more successful; she doesn't expect him to compete with some of the wealthier men in town.

Andi is happy with him exactly as he is. They talk about every-thing, have the same sense of humor, and are both of the opinion that the key to a successful marriage is not taking each other for granted. At this they have . . . *had* . . . been successful.

She cooks for him, for the girls, every night. Delicious meals that she presents with love. Sophia's favorite is her lasagna, his, her porcini-encrusted steaks. Emily professes to hate everything she cooks, but they all know she secretly loves Andi's Italian meatballs.

Andi has created something none of them had ever had before: a family. She has created a beautiful home, and warmth, and good food, and stability.

But it is more than that for Ethan. She *is* home. And losing her, losing everything, is something he cannot let happen.

When they first met, when they first became lovers, on weekends when they had no children to look after, he would go for a run and return with fresh croissants and cappuccino for her, fresh strawberries from the market.

The cappuccino would be lukewarm by the time they finished making love, but they would lie in bed, limbs intertwined, crumbs everywhere as they ate breakfast.

They haven't done that in years.

Life, children, domesticity have gotten in the way. This morning, as he completes his morning Mill Valley run, he is planning on bringing

her breakfast in bed. A small thing, but it will surely remind her of the past, of how good they are together when they do not let the turmoil of their life and their children intervene.

E than?"

Ethan turns from the counter, the croissants in hand, to see Drew waiting at the end of the line in the café.

"Hey!" They give each other a brief hug as Drew grins.

"So we live next door to each other, but I don't see you for weeks, and the only time I run into you is here? That's insane. You're working too hard."

Ethan is about to laugh, but he pauses. It's true. He has been working hard. He has taken on more clients than he ever thought he would, and the tensions at home have been overwhelming to the point where it is easier to be outside of the home, away from Emily and Andi and the discord that exists between them.

Perhaps that is part of the reason why things are bad with Andi. He needs to spend more time at home, he suddenly thinks. He needs to be present more.

"You're right," he says to Drew. "I have been working too hard. How are you guys? We should have dinner. The four of us haven't gotten together for ages."

"Why don't you and Andi come tomorrow night? I just got some organic short ribs, and I was going to braise them. Join us! Casual."

"Casual? Right!" Ethan snorts with laughter as Drew shrugs helplessly. Drew and Topher's idea of casual is anything but. When they entertain casually, it means Drew has dotted the house with beautifully arranged vases of green-and-white parrot tulips, armfuls of stock and nicotiana, creamy white roses.

Their house will be lit by candlelight, scented candles on every

surface, crystal dishes filled with nuts spiced by Drew, glistening in the light.

They will have a signature drink: whiskey sours, Manhattans, or dirty martinis, all the accoutrements for the drinks, including olives, and ice, and cocktail shakers assembled on a large, round, silver tray they will place on the antique marble-topped table in the living room.

Hours will have been spent on the perfect playlist: Ella and Count Basie, with some Buble and Mraz thrown in, drifting soulfully from the unobtrusive speakers behind the sofa.

Drew will have spent hours on the menu. He will serve thin slices of toasted baguette rubbed with garlic and topped with a teaspoon of whipped ricotta, a sliver of prosciutto, a drizzle of balsamic vinegar and fig jam.

There may be homemade cheese straws, made with the finest Dufour's puff pastry, and the best Parmigiano-Reggiano money can buy. They will be brought into the living room hot from the oven, where the delicate twists will be devoured in minutes.

They may sit with drinks and hors d'oeuvres for an hour, sometimes more. When they are ready, they will move to the dining table, covered with a crisp white tablecloth, small pots of lavender running down the center, ceramic lotus flowers holding fat white votive candles.

They will start with a beautiful salad: perhaps caramelized pecans, pears, blue cheese, beautifully arranged on simple white plates, all the better to show off the food. Drew will serve an artisanal bread perhaps, one he made that morning, with a delicate soup.

They may have short ribs as an entrée, but they will be balanced precariously on a round of creamed potatoes, surrounded with a drizzle of brussel-sprout purée, topped with a crescent of horseradish cream.

Their guests—and it may be just Andi and Ethan, or, as so often happens with Drew and Topher, there will be last-minute additions:

artists, and musicians, and finance guys, and cooks, and dot-com billionaires, and creative directors—their guests will take a bite and swoon with dreamy pleasure, and all will tell Drew that he is the next Martha Stewart, bemoaning the fact that someone doesn't give him his own TV show.

C asual?" Ethan laughs. "You and Topher don't do casual."
      "Usually we don't. But . . ." Drew lowers his voice and his face turns serious. "I know things are tough right now. I thought it might be nice just for the four of us to get together, quietly, sitting around the kitchen table."

Ethan feels an unexpected lump in his throat. How much does Drew know? He swallows hard and nods.

"How's Emily doing?" Drew quietly lays a hand on Ethan's arm.

Ethan doesn't trust himself to speak. Instead, he just nods and shrugs, as if to say, you know, it is . . . how it is.

"And how are *you* doing?" Drew then asks gently, and the lump is back, and Ethan cannot say anything, and if they were not in a public place, he might very well burst into tears. As it is, he stands, struggling, until Drew leads him outside without saying a word, then stands next to him, one hand on his arm, while Ethan struggles to compose himself.

"I'm sorry," Ethan says after a while, when the threat of tears has passed.

"Don't be. Sometimes it helps to let it out."

Let it out? Could Ethan let it out? he wonders. What would he say? That his life, which has felt so settled for the past five years, now feels as if it is about to turn upside down, and he feels utterly powerless; that he doesn't know what to do about it? That he wakes up most mornings so scared it is all he can do not to throw up?

"It's . . . rough," he says finally, assuming correctly that Andi

will have confided in Drew, that he will know most of what is going on.

"It must be," Drew says, for which Ethan is grateful. He is glad he didn't say "I know," because he couldn't know. No one could know unless he had been through it himself.

"I'm terrified," he says. "For Emily, and for what this means, and . . . for us. I feel like this is going to change everything. I'm not ready for this."

Drew nods.

"And Andi seems . . . so far away. I can't reach her." He gestures down to the bag he is holding. "I know it's stupid, but I'm bringing her breakfast in bed. I thought it might remind her of how things used to be."

"I think that's a great idea."

Ethan shrugs. "It's small, but . . . anything that will remind her seems like it must be a good thing. I just feel my life slipping away from me, and I don't know how to get it back."

"Can I give you a ride home?" Drew says as Ethan nods, and they start walking toward the car.

"It's a frightening time. But Emily's seven months, right?" Ethan nods as Drew speaks. "I know Andi thinks she's found a couple to adopt the baby, and Emily will get back on her feet. I think Andi's just struggling with everything. It will pass. When the baby has gone, things will get back to normal."

"You think so?"

"I think so," Drew says.

Except he really isn't sure at all.

By the time Ethan walks through his front door, he is feeling somewhat better. He has accepted the dinner invitation—Drew and Topher have always had an extraordinary amount of common

sense, particularly Topher, to whom he has turned on numerous occasions when he has been pushed to the edge of sanity by Brooke—and Drew has filled him with hope that this is all temporary, that this will pass.

Standing in the hall, he realizes he has created a romantic fantasy of what will happen when he walks in. Andi will still be asleep, or in bed, at least, and her eyes will fill with the soft warmth of forgiveness when he walks in with breakfast on a tray and a rose plucked from Drew's rosebush in a tiny vase.

She will tear up as she tells him she has thought about it for days and has realized he is right; will reach up, placing a hand behind his neck to pull him down for a kiss. They may or may not make love—Emily is in the house but likely asleep for many hours—but they will, at least, cuddle. They will talk softly, and smile, and hold each other.

They will reassure each other that the worst has passed, that whatever comes their way, they are strong enough to weather it together. And then, he supposes, they will live happily ever after.

Ethan organizes the tray, nervous suddenly, which feels ridiculous. This isn't a date he is trying to impress; it is his wife, for God's sake, and yet he is almost trembling, as if she were a stranger. Is this how far they have drifted? He shakes his head as if to dislodge the thought.

Upstairs, the bed is empty. He pauses, listening, but there seems to be no noise in the bathroom. He places the tray on the bed and walks over to open the bathroom door.

Andi is dabbing on lip balm, fully dressed, a scarf and light jacket to protect from the sudden chill in the late-summer air.

"You're . . . going out?"

"Client meeting," she says, not looking at him. "I'm late. Sorry. She wants to put her house on the market in two weeks and, apparently, it's a disaster. She wants to move all her stuff out and have me stage

the whole thing. In two weeks! Can you believe it?" She pauses. "Did you need me?"

"No," he lies. "I thought maybe we could have breakfast together . . ."

"Not today," she says, and her words feel hollow as she brushes past him in the doorway, not stopping to brush her lips quickly against his as she always, *always* does.

Did.

"I'll see you later, okay?"

"We're going to Drew and Topher's for dinner tomorrow night," he says. "Casual. I said yes, hope that's okay."

"Fine," she calls from the hallway. "Bye." And the front door slams.

"I love you, too," he whispers, standing alone in the master bedroom as he listens to the car engine revving up and his wife pulling out of the drive.

Pulling ever farther away from him.

Twenty-two

· · · · · · · · · ·

This is what a wild animal must feel like. Trapped. I'm stuck in the tree house, and Michael and Jenna are getting closer, and there is nowhere to run, and nowhere to hide, and I already know what's going to happen.

He's going to look at me in shock, and she's going to be right behind him, and she's probably going to give me that disdainful, dismissive look they give all the girls who pass them in the cafeteria who aren't in their clique; then she's going to text everyone she knows and say they found me, the freak, hiding in Michael's tree house.

It shouldn't matter. I steel myself, thinking, *It doesn't matter.* School is done. Everyone's going off their separate ways, most to college far away from here. I'm probably going away myself, with Bean.

I missed Burning Man—Bean took care of that—but she and I could still go someplace else. Seattle maybe. Or Austin. Somewhere far away from the bitchy girls at school, from the people who instinctively knew what I thought was my secret: I wasn't good enough.

So I prepare myself, hearing the steps on the ladder, the giggling from Jenna, and I realize she is flirting, and they may or may not be

hooking up, but she is totally into him, and he tells her to wait until he is up because the ladder might even have rotted, it's been so many years since he was up here, and I am tucked into a corner of the tree house, or as tucked as my ever-growing bulk can be, and my eyes are wide with fear, even as I try to talk myself into its not mattering.

It matters.

Michael is pushing open the doorway, but he's looking back, encouraging Jenna, then he turns and sees me, and this time it is his eyes that grow wide. With shock.

He stares at me, then turns again; this time his voice quieter.

"Wait!" he commands Jenna. "Go back down."

"What?" she says, her voice still giggly. "I want to see."

"No. It's . . . there's something up here."

I shake my head ever so slightly. *Don't tell her,* I plead silently. Don't tell her it's me. Please God, I'll do anything, I'll never touch a drop of alcohol or smoke again, just don't tell her I'm here.

"What!" The ladder is quiet; she has stopped climbing. "What do you mean? Like a dead animal or something?"

"Yes." She has inspired him. "It's gross." He makes a face. "I think it's a raccoon or something, but it's hard to tell. There are maggots everywhere," he adds. With flourish.

"Ew, gross," I hear her say as she moves back down the ladder. Michael turns back to me and just stares. He can see I've been crying, and I think he's just going to leave, but before he does he mouths, "Wait here," then he is back down the ladder.

"I've got to clean this up," I hear him say, back on the ground. "And it's going to take a while. Why don't I come over to your place when I'm done?"

"I can wait," she says, her voice low and teasing, and there is silence for a while, and if I wasn't scared of her seeing me, I'd move over to the wall in front where there are cracks between the planks, and I'd peer through, knowing I'd see them kissing.

"You go," he says. "I'll take a shower after."

"I could wash your back," she teases, low and sultry.

"Yeah, and my mom would chase you out of here with a giant skillet." He laughs.

"Okay," she grumbles. "Don't be long."

When she leaves, I do scooch over and peer out the crack, but Michael's gone, too. I don't know what to do, but I figure I'll wait a bit, at least to make sure the coast is clear. And then I see Michael come back out of the house, and he's got a bottle of Gatorade under one arm, and he's holding a big Ziploc bag in the other hand.

He climbs up, dumps the Gatorade and the bag on the pillow, and I'm not nervous at all anymore, because it is just Michael, after all, and this is the tree house I know like the back of my hand, and I don't feel seventeen and pregnant right now, I feel thirteen and filled with possibility; the feeling that anything is possible with my best friend by my side.

"You picked a good day," Michael says. "My mom just baked a fresh batch of thin mints." He opens the bag and hands me a bundle. "You still like them, right?"

I nod. They are still my favorites. I hadn't expected him to remember. When we were . . . friends, his mom set a mission to re-create the perfect Thin Mint cookie because she was completely addicted to them and she could never find enough Girl Scout stands to buy them. She'd buy them in bulk whenever anyone was selling them, but she'd eat pretty much a box at a time, so she decided she had to figure out how to make them herself.

Michael and I were her guinea pigs. She'd bring trays and trays out to the tree house, where even her rejects would be hungrily devoured.

Finally, using a chocolate fudge cake mix instead of attempting to make them completely from scratch, she got it. I've never been able to

eat a Thin Mint cookie without being transported straight back to the tree house, and even though we ate hundreds and hundreds, enough to put me off for life, they remain my favorites.

He remembers.

We don't say anything for a while. It's weird in that it isn't weird. Michael shoves a handful of cookies in his mouth, then grins, looking so like the young boy he used to be I almost want to cry.

He swigs Gatorade, then passes it over to me.

"Great," I sneer, although I accept it and swig. "Let's follow a shit-load of sugar with a shitload of sugar."

"You want water? Go get it yourself," he says, but his voice has no malice in it; it is teasing. Like it used to be. In the old days, I would have gotten it myself. I would have climbed down the ladder and gone through the back door, and Mrs. Flanagan would have insisted I take something else out there, or a blanket in case we got cold.

For years, this house felt more like home than my own. It was the one place I felt safe. No Mom being drunk and shouting. No women who weren't my mother pretending to be my mother and stealing my dad.

Just a place where I was accepted for me.

I do want water, but I don't want to get it myself. I don't want to walk through the door and see Mrs. Flanagan, or have her see me. It has been too long, and I am pregnant, and even though this black cardigan kind of covers it up, she will either think I have put on tons of weight and gotten huge, or she will know that I am pregnant.

Honestly? I don't know which would be worse.

Usually I love the way I dress. I take pride in the fact that I have a nose stud and several piercings in my ears, that my hair is blue-black and my makeup dramatic. I like getting stares. I ride up the escalator in the mall, staring people down. Sometimes, when girls whisper about me and giggle, I go over and raise my hands like a bat and whoop at them, just to freak them out.

Which it does.

This is not how Mrs. Flanagan knows me. She knows me as a slightly chubby and shy girl, with mousy brown hair, in jeans and sneakers. I don't want to show her how I've grown and grown up. I don't want to show her my deliberately provocative piercings and dye. I feel, suddenly, ashamed of the way I look.

I do not want Mrs. Flanagan to see my armor. If she has to see me, I want her to see me as the girl she used to know, and because that girl no longer exists, it is better she does not see me at all.

Michael's eyes flicker to my stomach, and I wonder if he knows.

"I'll get you water," he says, and before I can stop him, he jumps up and climbs down the ladder. I wonder if he did it because he wanted to get away because he is uncomfortable with me, but I do not hold on to that thought because I am not uncomfortable in the slightest, and I cannot imagine he feels anything but normal.

When he comes back, I wait for him to ask why I am there, but he doesn't, and I am grateful.

All those expressions: *What's up? What's going on? How you doing?* seem so trite. And yet I want to tell him, and I'm not sure how to start if he doesn't ask me how I am.

"I heard you weren't going to college," he says eventually, grabbing some pillows and propping them up against the wall, leaning back. His T-shirt rides slightly above the waistband of his jeans. I am shocked to see a tanned, firm stomach, the slightest line of hair running down from his navel. I forget that he is waiting for an answer, and I just stare.

"You're staring." He grins.

"You grew up," I say, but that isn't what I'm thinking. I'm thinking about the boys I have been hooking up with, any one of who is potentially the father of Bean. They are as pale and stringy as strands of spaghetti. Their bodies skinny and ghostly, their pubic hair stark, dark shocks against the near transparency of their skin.

They are as uncomfortable in their skins as I am in mine. Our couplings are brief, in darkened corners of bedrooms, or in the backs of cars—sometimes outside in a park or on a beach.

The only clothes removed are the clothes necessary to facilitate sex. Or blow jobs. Or whatever it is you are doing. It is one of the things that makes it okay for me: I do not have to reveal my body. I do not have to risk anyone's laughing at me, or noticing that one of my boobs is higher than the other, that my stomach is round, that my thighs rub together.

Sometimes, if I'm at the doctor's office, or in a place where there are a stack of magazines, I will pick up something like *Cosmopolitan*, and when I read about sex, and orgasms, and positions, I am bemused at what it is they are talking about.

None of it is about me, that much I can tell you. Not that it feels bad. It feels great when they're inside me, but better is when they hold me. Better is the feeling of being loved, even if only for a few minutes.

Even if they are these skinny, awkward, inexperienced boys, better is the feeling of being loved.

Michael doesn't look like those boys. I am staring because he looks . . . like a man. The line of hair tracing down looks like an invitation, and I am startled, stunned, to feel a jolt of lust.

I look away, quickly, as Michael just grins.

"Would you just cover yourself up?" I mumble belligerently, to hide my . . . discomfort? *Lust? NO!* Not lust. Not with Michael. That wouldn't be possible . . . Would it?

"What? It's a stomach, for God's sake." He is still grinning.

"It's just . . . inappropriate," I say.

"Fine, Miss Prude." He pulls the T-shirt down. "There. Happy?"

I shrug.

"So. College. You should go."

"I will," I say. "I'm just figuring out what I want to do. Also,

remember, I'm the youngest in the grade. Really, I should be going into my senior year now."

"Yeah. I forgot you're a secret genius."

"Not anymore." I shrug. Which is true.

"So what are you thinking? English?" he continues.

"Ha. No. I mean, sometimes, but I'm really interested in art school."

Michael nods, thinking. "Yeah," he says finally. "I could see that. You were always really creative."

There is another silence.

"So. That . . . Jenna. Is she your girlfriend?" There is a sneer in my voice that I hadn't intended. "Is she nice?" I add quickly, in more of a normal voice, just so he doesn't think I'm jealous or anything.

"We're just . . . friends."

"With benefits?"

He shrugs. "Is there any other kind of female friendship?"

"Uh, yeah." I roll my eyes. "Actually there is."

His face grows serious. "You're right. I'm sorry. You know what, Em?"

My heart does a tiny sentimental flip when he calls me Em. It is so thoughtless, so natural, that I forget we haven't spoken in years, and that we are supposed to ignore each other when we pass in the hallways.

"I fucking miss you."

My heart turns over.

"But you're just so fucking weird. I mean, you're not, okay? I know you're not *really* weird, but you don't do yourself any favors by wearing all this black and these piercings and stuff. This whole emo goth thing just makes everyone want to avoid you, so no one knows the cool person you are."

A million things run through my head, the first being to tell him to

go screw himself, but as I open my mouth to shoot something back, something mean, something that will take the hurt of what he just said and give it right back to him, a lump rises, and from nowhere a sob comes out, and suddenly I am sobbing, and I am so embarrassed I want to die.

And I can't stop.

Twenty-three
· · · · · · · · · ·

Oh, Jesus, Em." Michael sits up and comes to sit next to me. He doesn't put his arm around me or anything, but he takes hold of my little finger, and he sits, just holding my finger as I cry, and after a while he stretches out his T-shirt and holds it out, and I look down at it confused, hiccuping, and he tells me to blow my nose, which I do.

Which, by the way, is really gross, but he just lets it fall and we sit there as my hiccuping becomes slower and the jagged intakes of breath become less, then I am just slumped, exhausted.

"I'm really sorry," he says. "I did not mean to upset you like that. I never should have said you're weird. You're not weird, okay? I didn't mean it."

"It's fine. I mean, that's not why I was crying."

"Oh. Okay."

And I want him to ask me why I'm crying so I can tell him, even though I don't really know, other than I am overwhelmed, and scared, and as much as I want Bean, I know my life is never going to be the

same again, and honestly, I can't even think about school right now because my future has never looked so uncertain or terrifying.

I shake my head in disbelief. "Aren't you going to ask me why I was crying?"

"Do you want me to?" he says carefully, dipping his head and looking up at me nervously.

"Jeez, Michael. You're still weird, too. You may be this big handsome jock with muscles and golden skin, but I know better. You're still the weird geeky kid. I bet you still have all those *Star Trek* pins you bought on eBay."

"Totally!" He feigns shock. "They are my most prized possessions." And then he grins. "You said I was handsome!"

"Oh, shut up. I bet Jenna doesn't know about your secret Trekiness."

"She wouldn't understand. So why were you crying?"

I think about making this some big dramatic moment, but it doesn't feel dramatic as I pull my cardigan tightly over my stomach to show off my bump, Michael takes a sharp intake of breath, and when I look up, I see he knows.

"That stinks," he says. "And it's kind of awesome, too."

"I know!" I breathe. "That's exactly it, right? It stinks, and it terrifies me, and I can't believe I'm having a baby, and then I can't believe I have a life growing inside me, and I'm going to be a mom!"

Michael is staring at my stomach.

"You want to touch it?" I ask tentatively.

"Can I?"

I take his hand and lay it on my belly, keeping my hand on top of his, and wouldn't you know it, at that moment, the Bean takes a lazy tumble, like a slow somersault, and both of us not only feel it, but you can see my stomach move, a big wave of movement from left to right.

"She's rocking," I say.

"And rolling," he says, and he is as awed and overcome as I am, and the moment is swiftly broken as his phone starts buzzing. He picks it up, frowning, then turns it off, chucking it to the other side of the tree house.

"Jenna?"

"Yeah. Wondering where I am."

"Do you have to go?" I look away, so he doesn't see how very much I want him to stay, how very much I need him to stay.

"No. I don't," he says, and this time when he lies back and fires questions at me, I don't ask him to pull his T-shirt down, and I answer everything, and we move through all the questions about the pregnancy, and what I'm going to do, and how I'm going to tell my parents that no, actually, I'm not going to be putting my child up for adoption as they believe they can convince me to do but am going to raise her myself.

"Thank God." Michael exhales loudly. "You can't give your baby away. No fucking way. That kid will grow up knowing he wasn't wanted from the get-go, and you never get over rejection like that."

"It's a 'she,' " I say quietly, knowing Michael is talking about himself.

"She. He. Whatever. The point being you are totally doing the right thing, keeping this baby, and don't let anyone tell you different."

I nod once, to show that I understand, I get it, I know where this is coming from, then we move on to school, friends, life, and what the hell we are all going to grow up to be.

And the reason I don't ask Michael to pull his T-shirt down after it has ridden up yet again is not because I am ogling his stomach, but because it's no longer relevant. For while he may now be this big bronzed god at the high school, his handsome features morph during the time I am there, and when I look at him, all I see is my gawky, geeky, former best friend.

"We should do this more often," I say after dusk has fallen, and we both climb down from the tree house, a good four hours having passed. "This was just like the old days."

"I'm off to school in a couple of days," he says. "And I probably won't be back until Thanksgiving."

"Right." The disappointment floods my voice. Of course he's going away. I was so caught up in my pleasure at rediscovering our friendship, I had forgotten. Everyone's going away. Except me.

"I'll write, Em," he says. "Swear."

"Thumb swear?" which was this stupid thing we did as kids when we decided pinkie swears were just too girly.

"Thumb swear." He grins, holding out his thumb and pressing it hard against mine.

I don't know how to say good-bye. We stand there, and he wishes me luck, and then he pulls me in for a tight hug, except it isn't that tight because my stomach is in the way, and he says, "You better call it Michael if it's a boy."

"It's not a boy," I say.

"Michaela then," he says, and the next thing you know, he's let me go and run off to the house with just a final wave, and I walk back home feeling something I haven't felt in years.

Happy.

Twenty-four

· · · · · · · · · ·

A ndi is the one trying to be upbeat, trying to pretend that there is something fun about this process: meeting the couple she had picked out online, a couple who lives six hours away, who have flown in to try to persuade Emily that she should pick them; that they, above all others, would be the perfect people to give her baby a home she cannot give it.

It has been the hardest thing she has yet had to do, but Ethan has left her with little choice. Each time she looks at a prospective adoptive mother, she sees herself. Each time she reads about them, she is reading about herself.

Adeline and Greg Blackman have been married for seven years. He is a real estate developer, she is a professional musician—a violinist—which is, she writes, the perfect job for a mother because she can accept or decline engagements at will.

They have many pictures on the adoption agency's website. Adeline is Asian, pretty, and petite, and Greg tall, with kind eyes. They look like they would be good parents. They have spent too many years

and too much money doing IVF treatments before making the final decision to adopt.

Adeline has an older brother, and Greg is from a family of seven children. They had always dreamed of a large family but have now realized that they would be equally blessed to have even one child.

They like reading, and animals—a chocolate Lab called Mudston features in several of the pictures—and are both avid cooks. They are blessed to have a large house, with two acres, in a neighborhood where there are lots of children. The inference, Andi couldn't help but feel, is that they can give this poor, blue-collar, possibly child of an alcoholic a home and a life that it would not otherwise have had.

Well, Andi thought. They were perhaps right about only one thing, although Emily seems to have stayed away from the alcohol.

People like us, Andi kept thinking, do not give babies away. People like us, like Adeline, forty-one, and Greg, forty-six, and Andi, forty-two, and Ethan, forty-six, give gorgeous homes to babies that need them.

We feed them organic gourmet baby food that we steam and purée ourselves, scooping it into ice-cube trays for easy access later. We clothe them in the *cutest outfits ever* from Baby Gap, and enroll them in Gymboree classes before they can even walk.

We decorate their nurseries with the finest furnishings money can buy, the plushest toys, the heaviest curtains to ensure not a crack of light filters through the windows when our beloved darlings go down for a nap in the middle of a sunlit day.

We are the people who raise the babies that no one wants. We are the people who, if we are unlucky enough to have a seventeen-year-old daughter who becomes pregnant, step in as the grandparents du jour and raise the child as our own.

· · ·

Adeline and Greg; Andi and Ethan. They are almost interchangeable. And the pain of getting to know them, realizing how alike they are, is almost unbearable for Andi.

This should be Ethan and her, raising this child. In years past, it *could* have been Ethan and her, looking for a baby. If Ethan had agreed to adoption, this *would* have been Ethan and her.

She thought she was okay with his decision, had talked herself into believing she can see things from his point of view: they already have two healthy children; he doesn't want to be in his sixties with a child graduating from high school; think of how they treasure their "kid-less" weekends, how awful it would be to give them up; that was why he was so against the idea of more kids.

Andi thought she had bought it, despite her heart's sinking every time a period arrives, but since Emily's pregnancy, since Ethan refused to back down on giving away the baby, she has found herself simmering with a resentment so strong, it is the reason she pretends to be asleep in the mornings, the reason she has found herself struggling even to look at the man who was once the center of her world.

Twenty-five

· · · · · · · · · ·

o Andi picked a diner on the outskirts of Oakland, which is pretty funny. This couple probably thinks they're rescuing some crack baby from the rough badlands of Oakland rather than the suburban glory—and yes, I am being sarcastic here—of Mill Valley.

No one talks on the ride over. I'm used to not talking, but I am so not used to my dad and Andi sitting in silence. Usually they're yammering away about something, but these days they're barely speaking. It was pretty awkward.

My dad asked me if I felt okay, and I just shrugged. What am I supposed to say? I am so not interested although, for once, Andi didn't push it. A few days ago, when she decided we should meet this couple, she asked me once if I wanted to see their profile on the computer, and I said no, thinking she'd start trying to persuade me, but she just shrugged and turned away.

Which was fine. It's not like there's any point in me seeing who these people are. They have no idea I'm keeping Bean, and I'm not telling them until the last minute. I know that if I say anything before,

they'll do everything they can to take her away, so if I have to, if it comes down to it, I'll just refuse to sign the papers in the hospital.

Let them try to stop me bringing Bean home then.

Hey, I've watched Lifetime, I've seen those movies; I know how it's all going to go down. The only bit I haven't figured out yet is what we're going to do after Bean is born, but it's going to be fine. My dad will definitely take care of us until I find a job, even if Andi bitches and moans.

What's he going to do, throw his daughter and granddaughter out on the street? I don't think so.

Besides, Andi's not really bitching and moaning anymore. She's barely speaking to my dad, but she's pretty nice to me, and the one thing I'm sure of is that she'll back me in keeping the baby.

Oh, my God, do you think I don't see Andi's eyes every time she sees a baby? If someone pushes a stroller past us on the street, Andi has to stop them and coo over the baby and ask all kinds of questions. I used to think it was ridiculous, except the other day I was in town and I swear, I wanted to look in every stroller that passed me.

Andi loves babies, and I know she always wanted one. This may not be hers, but she can babysit her anytime I'm busy. Seriously. Anytime.

My dad puts on his big fake smile as we push open the door of the diner, and I spot them as soon as we walk in. They look really nice. They have nervous smiles, and they do a half wave, and Mary, this mousy woman from the adoption agency, is with them, and suddenly I feel really bad that they think they're about to get a baby when they're not, and I really wish I could turn around and walk away, quickly, before this goes any further.

It's too late. Adeline is already up and holding her hand out, telling me it's nice to meet me and asking how I'm feeling.

"Okay," I mumble, feeling really, really bad. You can just tell everything about this woman is nice, and neat, and pretty, and good. And I have this flash forward about both of them sitting anxiously outside my hospital room, with a freshly painted nursery at home, and a closet filled with designer baby clothes, and a nurse coming out and telling them that they're not getting this baby after all, and I can practically see them crumple in pain.

Oh, God. Now I feel so horrible, I can't even stand to look at them.

I stare at the table as everyone introduces themselves, and then we're all sitting down, and where do we go from here?

It's so nice to meet you," Adeline reaches across the table, extending a hand, which I have no choice but to take, and I shake it limply before allowing my hand to be dropped. "How are you feeling?"

"Okay," I mumble, not caring whether or not Adeline has to struggle to make conversation. I look at her quickly, and she's looking at me eagerly with a bright smile, willing us to have some kind of connection.

"So you're still in high school?" Adeline asks, and although she's making herself sound normal, I can hear that her voice is a bit shaky. I look her in the eye for the first time as I nod, and I can see she is desperate for me to like her, desperate for me to choose her. It's what my eyes used to look like before I decided to hell with everyone, that it was easier for me just to hate them first.

"You must be a senior," her husband says.

"No. I was a year ahead. I just graduated."

"A year ahead! Wow!" Adeline laughs, and she and her husband exchange a relieved look. "You must be clever."

I shrug. I don't want to be here. I don't want to like them. I don't want to feel anything, and right now I feel horrible.

"So . . ." Greg takes over. "Which school are you off to?"

"Emily's going to take a year off," my dad interjects. Which is fine because I really can't see the point of saying anything. "Because she's so young, we decided she ought to see a bit of the world first."

"Great idea!" Adeline practically jumps with excitement, and I can see, in that moment, she'd probably be a great mom. Not like my mom, angry and drunk, and never interested in either of us. She'll be the kind of mom who encourages her daughter with everything, tells her she's brilliant, and beautiful, and loved.

She's the kind of mom I always wish I'd had.

The kind of mom I know I'm going to be.

"I had a year off," she says, "before Juilliard. I went all over Europe on a Eurail pass. I can't even begin to tell you some of the adventures we had. I slept on more park benches than I could count."

"Really?" I look up. "You don't look like the sort of person who would sleep on a park bench."

"Oh you'd be surprised. I may play the violin, but I'm also incredible at woodwork."

"She's modest, too," Greg says dryly. And I can't help it, I smile. Just a bit.

"Oh shut up," she jokes, giving him an affectionate rub on the arm, and you can just tell they are totally in love. Like my dad and Andi used to be. "He's just jealous. I built all the bookshelves in our house."

"I am a little jealous," Greg admits. "She's incredibly precise. I try to do stuff, and everything winds up crooked."

"Yeah, because he doesn't believe in levels. He just eyeballs everything, then wonders why one side is six inches lower than the other. I'm all about the level. In fact"—she reaches down to her purse— "I'm totally embarrassed but look!" She draws out a key chain with a look of delight, and triumphantly holds it up for all to see—a tiny level on her key chain.

"That's funny," my dad says. "Andi has a high-heeled pump on her key chain. What do you suppose that says about her?"

"I was going to tell you how much I love those ballet flats!" Adeline bursts out excitedly. "I knew you were a shoe lover, too! A woman after my own heart! Emily?" She turns to me. "Your mom and I are clearly cut from the same cloth."

I can't do this anymore. I can't let these people think they are getting my baby. I feel so bad, but what's that expression? Being cruel to be kind? I have to end this now.

"She's not my mom," I say, buying time while I desperately think about how to do this without letting my dad know I'm keeping the baby.

"Oh." Adeline looks confused. "I'm sorry." She looks from Andi to my dad, then to the adoption counselor, who looks down at her papers, shuffling them in way that registers her own unease. "I . . . thought we were meeting Emily and her parents."

"Yes, I did think . . ." Mary says quickly, still shuffling, as if she will find the answer in the act of shuffling.

"I'm her stepmom," Andi says, sounding pretty tired, and then I have it, I know what I'm going to say, and even though it's going to be awful, I have to do it. Now.

"Yeah. I know we look like the perfect middle-class family." My voice comes out loud, and fast. It's breathy, like I'm about to lose my temper, except this time it's not; it's because I'm nervous and because I feel so bad.

"But if you're interested in adopting this baby, you should know the truth." I see them exchange an alarmed look, and I just steam-roll on. "So my mom's an alcoholic who doesn't want anything to do with me, and I'm pretty sure drinking runs in the family. As you can see, I'm not exactly the popular girl at school. In fact, I'm hated by pretty much everyone. I have no idea who the father of the baby is, but it's pretty likely that he also is a druggie, or at least drinks big-time. And by the way, I've also been drinking throughout this preg-nancy, and taking . . ." Oops. I stop then. I don't want to get arrested

here. "Whatever. The doctor already said the baby probably has fetal alcohol syndrome, so honestly, you seem like really nice people, but this is a kid who is going to come with a whole lot of problems." I trail off. "So, you might want to rethink," I say lamely, standing up and stepping away from the table.

Adeline looks like she's about to cry, and her husband just looks angry. I want to apologize. I want to grab them and explain, whisper to her why I just said it, but I can't.

I look at my dad, who looks as if he's shell-shocked.

"Can we just go?" I say, and, without waiting for an answer, I turn and march out the door.

Twenty-six

. . . .

The adoption counselor follows them out. Emily marches ahead of them, straight to the car, but Mary stops Andi and Ethan before they have a chance to get there.

"I know this is hard for her," she says, shooting a sympathetic look at Emily, now hunched in the backseat. "She's so young, and it must be overwhelming."

"Thank you for understanding," Ethan says.

"But . . . well . . . the things she said about drinking. And the fetal alcohol syndrome. Is that true?"

"There were no signs," Ethan explains wearily. "They looked for all the signs, and usually there are markers, and there weren't any. It isn't a given."

"I just wish you'd told us." Mary sighs. "We're very used to dealing with this in adoption cases, but we like to prepare the couples beforehand. You need to be honest with us. About everything. I'm also not happy that I didn't know Emily's mother wouldn't be present."

"Right now I'd say no one could be less happy than us," Andi says. "I'm sorry you didn't have the whole story, but it wasn't intentional, I can assure you. We didn't tell you because there was nothing to tell—everything about this baby is normal. I'm sorry for those people. I feel terrible. I need to go and say good-bye to them. Apologize. They were so nice."

"It's better if you don't," Mary says. "They're upset. It's best to just leave it. Let me talk to them, and we'll all check in later today. How does that sound?"

"Fine," Ethan says, ushering Andi away. "It sounds . . . fine."

Emily sits in the back of the car, staring out the window, her mouth tightly drawn. Andi fixes her gaze straight ahead, wishing she were somewhere else. She is so tired right now, tired of the unpredictability. How much longer can this go on?

"Can we talk about this?" Ethan starts, looking at Emily in the rearview mirror.

"No," Emily bursts out. "I don't want to talk about it. I don't want to think about it. They weren't right. That's all."

"But did you have to be so rude?" Andi can't help herself. "Did you have to say the things you said? Now you've jeopardized our entire relationship with the agency. Who knows if they'll even continue working with us."

"Jesus. I wasn't rude," Emily says. "I was just telling the truth."

"You were rude," Ethan says.

"Will you just leave me alone?" Emily starts to shout from the backseat. "You have no idea what I'm going through and"—she looks at Andi—"all you can think about is that I've been rude? What? I've embarrassed you? You're ashamed of me? Is that really all you care about?"

. . .

E nough!" Ethan's voice is loud, louder than Emily's, shocking her into silence and Andi into a glimmer of respect.

"Are you kidding me?" Emily is outraged. "You never stick up for me, you only ever stick up for Andi. You don't care about me. You haven't cared about me since she came into our lives."

Andi, the pain and hurt of the past few weeks finally welling up and bursting out of her, turns around to look at Emily face-to-face, shaking her head in disbelief.

"You ungrateful, rude, spoiled little . . ." She wants to say *bitch*, but catches herself.

"Oh, my God!" Emily says again, her voice dripping with sarcasm. "You were about to call me a bitch? Hear that, Dad? Niiice. Really nice. My own stepmother calling me a bitch. Wow. Just what I need right now, thanks for all your suppor—"

"No!" Andi says loudly, silencing everyone. She has had enough. "I'm done. I'm just done. Stop the car."

Ethan pulls over to the side of the road, scared. When Emily starts again, he roars at her to "shut the hell up," which he has never, ever done before.

She does.

Andi gets out the car, feeling the tears come, and she starts walking down the street, needing to get away. Just get away. A hand on her arm stops her, and she turns to see Ethan, as white as a sheet, holding her arm.

"What do you mean?"

"I'm done," she whispers. "I can't do this anymore. I can't take it. I love you, Ethan, but I can't stay in this. I can't do this anymore. I'm too hurt, and I don't think I can get over it."

Ethan blanches, stepping back in shock. "What? You're . . . What do you mean? You're . . . leaving me?"

"I . . ." she doesn't want to say yes. She hadn't planned this, had only thought about it as an abstract idea, but today's tantrum has just pushed her over the edge. It's too much. For too long. And today, she cracked.

"I don't know what else to do."

"Andi, get back in the car. Let's go home. We need to talk about this."

"I can't, Ethan. I can't get back in the car. I can't be around . . . this. I'm sorry, but . . . no."

"Please don't do this, Andi," Ethan begs. "Please. At least let's talk about this. Let me take Emily home and I'll come back and we can talk."

"I . . . don't know," Andi says. "I'm just so tired of this. Of talking about it. And arguing about it. And you saying things like, 'The two of you have to work it out between you,' as if I am somehow culpable, I am somehow to blame. I couldn't be a better stepmother." Andi looks up at him searchingly. "Honestly, I don't know how I could be any better. I don't react to her tantrums, I just walk away. I try and love her, and just when I think I'm getting through, when I think things are different, she goes and ruins it. I'm tired of you taking her side, of thinking that I, too, must be doing something wrong. I'm just tired." She takes a deep breath. "I need some space."

"It's *not* you," Ethan says quietly. "I haven't wanted to see that, but now I do. I see how you've been with Emily since the pregnancy. I see how you've looked after her, and how you've stepped up when her own mother abandoned her. And I see how Emily twists things, and manipulates, and . . . lies."

Andi blinks. She has been telling Ethan for years that Emily twists things, and manipulates, and lies, and he has always dismissed Andi, telling her it couldn't possibly be true, refusing to believe it about his darling daughter.

Now, finally, here he is, saying the impossible.

"It's not you," he says sadly, swallowing the lump that has risen in his throat. "It's her. I never wanted to believe it. I never wanted to think of my daughter as . . . I don't know . . . broken somehow, or in need of fixing. I know that her behavior stems from insecurity, from her wanting to be loved, but I also know it's about her, and nothing to do with you, and I know that it's not acceptable. Not anymore."

Andi blinks again, unsure of what to say. These are all the things she has been longing to hear: acknowledgment, admission, a desire to seek outside intervention. But is it too late?

Because on top of everything, on top of having to deal with Emily, is having to deal with her resentment at Ethan for not letting her have the only thing in the world she has ever wanted.

Is it too late?

Twenty-seven
. . . .

Something has changed with my dad and Andi, and I don't like it.

Since last week, since we met the couple who wanted to adopt the Bean, and no, after meeting me they no longer wanted to adopt the Bean, so mission accomplished, ha! But since then, and me losing it a bit in the car, they've both been weird with me.

And I did feel bad about losing it. I think I was just under so much pressure, and so scared about this adoption thing—I thought maybe somehow they'd find a way to go through with it—and it made me just freak out in the car. I didn't mean to say anything bad about Andi, I didn't mean to go after her in the way that I did, I really didn't, but once I got started I just lost control.

I said I was sorry to Andi, later. I went and apologized, and usually if that happens she gives me a hug and says everything's okay, but this time she didn't. She just stared at me without saying anything until I kind of awkwardly backed out the room.

Oh, God. I felt so bad. But I didn't know what else to do. And then

I was thinking, she said she was *done*. What does that mean? Is she done? Is she leaving us? And I thought I'd be really excited that we would finally have our dad back, but I just felt sad.

And scared.

Sophia was in her room doing homework, and I went in and lay on her bed. She totally ignored me, so then I told her what Andi had said about being done, and asked her what she thought.

She stopped her homework then. She swiveled her chair and started biting on the end of her pencil, which is what she does when she's thinking. Or nervous.

"Done?" she repeated, frowning. "How did she say it? What was her tone of voice?"

I said it as Andi had said it, although I think maybe I sounded more harsh than Andi. She sounded tired, and when I tried to say it the same way, it came out as sounding mad.

I tried again.

"I don't know." Sophia looked worried. "I'm going to talk to Dad."

"No!" I swore her to secrecy then. I told her that I'd find out and tell her when I knew, but not to bother Dad. I didn't tell her it was because he was upset enough already.

I stayed in Sophia's bedroom for a while. She went back to her homework, and I just closed my eyes. I thought about telling her then, about the pregnancy, but there's something I quite like about its being a secret. Maybe I'll tell her soon, though. I think she'd be okay with it.

At least she wouldn't disown me like my mom has done. My dad swears that isn't the case, but I'm not sure I believe him. And now that she has checked out, I don't know that I can do this if Andi's "done"; I don't know what I'll do if she leaves.

It's almost as if my hatred for her has changed into something else. I wouldn't say love, but . . . oh I don't know. Dependence maybe? Need. Whatever. I like her being around.

She has been amazing through this pregnancy, and I kind of feel that if I were to tell her my big secret—that I'm keeping the baby—and swear her to secrecy, she'd be okay with it. She'd support me.

Unless she's "done" with us.

I've wanted her to leave for so long, I can't believe that now it's actually here, now it may become a reality; it terrifies me, and the last thing in the world I want is for Andi to leave.

I don't know that I could ever tell her that, though. I don't know that she'd even believe me. I saw her face after I lost it in the car. I saw how she looked at me. I have spent years wanting to hurt her, but now that I actually have, *for real,* I want to make it better.

I know sorry isn't enough. I know I was causing pain, but . . . Oh, God. I don't even know how to explain it. It's like, when those feelings well up, when I'm overwhelmed, there is nothing, literally nothing, to stop them from coming out.

Even while I'm losing it, I know I shouldn't, and I want to calm down, but I don't know how to. It's like this white-hot rage that builds inside of me, this huge wave of anger and pain, and I can't keep it in, I don't know how not to let it out because if I didn't I might just . . . implode.

And I'm honestly scared that I might die.

When I was younger, I have to admit—and yes, I am a bit ashamed to admit this—but sometimes I would do it on purpose: lose my shit because I got what I wanted.

And when I was younger, when I did, genuinely, hate Andi, throwing a tantrum was a guaranteed way to split them up. She'd walk away and go off by herself, and my dad would sit with me for hours sometimes to try to calm me down.

Of course, I know that it was wrong—I told you I was ashamed. The thing is, it becomes self-fulfilling, and once I get started, I can't stop. Whether it's screaming at my parents, or sleeping with some boy

I just met, or trying to numb the pain, once I get started with any kind of self-destructive behavior, I don't seem to be able to stop.

I think that's how my mom is with drink. And it terrifies me. Because I worry that I'm just like her.

"Cutting" is the latest buzzword that everyone's terrified of. That one time I got caught smoking and my mom and dad came in to see the school counselor, she told them not to be surprised if I started cutting, and that was the next logical step for a girl with troubles like mine.

As if I didn't know that. Most of my friends have done it, and I quite liked this threat hanging over my parents, but I'm terrified of blood. There's no way in hell I would cut myself. Everyone talks about the release they feel, but even the thought of taking a knife and slicing my skin open makes me feel like throwing up. No way. Although it doesn't hurt that they don't know that.

I played on their fear, too. I was in the kitchen with Sophia, and she had just been on my phone, reading my texts, and I picked up the knife and told her I was going to cut myself with it.

Sophia turned white, and went running outside to call Dad and tell him. Of course I wasn't, but my dad was walking on tiptoes around me for days afterward, which was pretty damned cool.

So even though I have thrown tantrums deliberately, a fact of which I am not proud, last week wasn't deliberate. Honestly. I was just so scared, and it made it all so real, and I couldn't tell anyone that there's no way I'm giving the Bean up for adoption, and all those feelings just came out in a really bad way.

When Andi actually shouted—and let me tell you, Andi never shouts—and got out of the car, I was shocked. Then I was terrified that my dad was going to blame me, that this would ruin our relationship forever.

She didn't come back to the car, and I had to bite my lip all the way home to stop myself from crying. My dad refused to talk to me. He

did that thing where he clenches his jaw, and I know he's beyond furious, and I decided not to say anything.

But when we got home and he still hadn't said a word to me, I
couldn't help myself.

"It's not my fault," I said as I started to walk upstairs. "Now you're
blaming me and it's not my fault your wife's walking out."

"SHUT UP!" he screamed, and that really upset me because my
dad has never screamed at me before, and he's never, ever, told me to
shut up. It's one of the reasons why I prefer being at my dad's, even
with Andi there, because my dad is always calm. You can always talk
to him about anything, and he never gets mad.

My mom can be crazy. I love her so much, and when she's nice,
she's the most amazing person in the world, but she can turn on a
dime, and she screams at both of us all the time. You can be doing
nothing, and you'll hear her in the kitchen, snorting and working
herself up about who the fuck knows what, and she'll start screaming at you.

Actually, at me. She screams at Sophia but not nearly as much. I
start screaming back, then it just becomes this big mess usually until I
storm out, slamming a couple of doors as I leave. And then I just go
to Dad's, and he understands what a nightmare she is and why I can't
stay there.

Andi resents my being there on "kidless" weekends. I can tell.
She's fine, but cold, and I know that even though my dad welcomes
me there all the time, she doesn't. She's fine with us being there when
we're supposed to be there, but she hates when we show up unexpectedly.

Dad says that's not true, that she loves us and loves having us, and
that this is home and always open to us, but that's my dad: he'll never
say a bad word about Andi, he just defends her all the time and says
all this bullshit about her loving us, which I don't believe.

Although recently I could almost . . . almost believe it. Since the

Bean came along, I can kind of believe she might, if not *love* me, then maybe like me a little. When I'm sick, she makes me hot chocolate and sits on my bed and we read magazines together. When I'm sick, I don't have the energy to fight her, and she's actually quite nice.

That's why I felt bad about what happened last week. Since the pregnancy, she's been the only one who's okay with it. I see the disappointment in my dad's eyes every time he looks at me, which he barely does now.

So the other night I could hear them talking in their bedroom, and I crept along the hallway and listened. I do this a lot. Whenever they lower their voices, I can be pretty certain they're talking about me, and I stand just outside the room, as quiet as a mouse, and listen. Sophia always tells me I'm spying, but she wouldn't dare tell on me, and I've learned tons of shit by standing outside doorways.

"I don't know." I heard Andi say quietly. "I'm here, aren't I? I don't know what's going to happen. I really don't know anymore."

"This is temporary," my dad said. "It's the most stress any of us have ever been under, and it will be over soon."

"You've been saying that for five years," Andi said. "That girl has done everything in her power to get rid of me, and every time she treats me appallingly, you excuse it. She's stressed because of exams, or she's unhappy at her mom's, or she's under social pressure, and it will pass. And now she's pregnant, and quite apart from this being the biggest drama yet, the one thing that would solve everyone's problems, the one thing that would allow her to move on with her life and give us what we used to always talk about, is suddenly impossible. When we first met you knew I wanted a baby. Now, when it's actually within our reach, you won't even think about it."

What the . . . ? Is she talking about *Bean*?

"You can't let this break us up," my dad pleaded. "You and I have something that is so good. We'll never find it again."

"I will stay until this situation resolves itself," Andi said slowly. "Until Emily has the baby. And then we'll see where we are."

"What do you mean?" My dad sounded scared.

"I mean . . . I'm not going anywhere today, okay? But, I don't know. I honestly don't know if I can live with it. It's the best I can do. Every time I get hurt, it's like another piece of my heart shuts down, and I just feel . . . completely shut down right now."

There was a long silence, and when my dad spoke, he sounded like a scared little boy.

"You still love me, right?" he said.

"I love you," Andi said, but from where I was standing, it didn't sound like she was sure at all. "But I don't know if I can live like this."

"Are you serious?" my dad whispered, and then, I swear, he started to cry. I wanted to go in and smack her, but I couldn't because I wasn't supposed to be there; then I heard footsteps and I quickly went back to my own room so I wouldn't be caught.

The spare room is made up. My dad created some bullshit story about Andi having some highly contagious rash, so he's sleeping in the spare room. I had to walk out, I was so disgusted by his lying to me, but I couldn't tell him I knew the truth because then he'd know I'd been eavesdropping. And boy, does he hate it when I eavesdrop.

So they're sleeping apart, and when they are in the same room, it's totally fake, and the atmosphere is so icy cold you could practically freeze even though they think they're getting away with pretending everything's normal.

I feel awful for my dad. And I feel bad for Andi. I heard her crying in the bathroom the other day. I stood outside the door and listened, and I wasn't sure what to do, so I did nothing. But I felt kind of worried for her for the whole rest of the day.

Later that afternoon she brought me herbal tea, and when I fell asleep on the sofa, I woke up briefly to find her tucking a big fluffy blanket around me. I felt safe, and protected, and . . . okay. Yes. I'll say it.

I almost felt as if I loved her.

If it was possible for me to get bigger, which I didn't think *was* possible, I have gotten bigger. I am now thirty-five weeks, and I think there's very little doubt that I'm pregnant.

I'm not going out too much anymore. Even on my birthday, two weeks ago, we just got a cake and had it at home. Way to go to celebrate turning eighteen!

I'm spending most of my time sitting around the house, bored. I'm on the computer a lot—I've read every website there is about giving birth, and babies, and the various developmental points during the first year, but I have to be careful Andi doesn't see because she's still looking for another adoption couple.

Sophia's upstairs, doing some craft project in her room; Andi is outside doing yard work. I close down the computer and push open the door to Sophia's room.

"Can you knock?" she says nastily.

"Why? You're not doing drugs for God's sake, you're doing, what? Shrinky Dinks? I love Shrinky Dinks!"

"Yeah." She doesn't invite me to join in. "Still. This is my room, and I need privacy."

"Okay, okay, whatever." I collapse on her bed as she pretends to be busy doing homework, but I know she's waiting for me to speak. "Sophia? Can you keep a secret?"

"What kind of a secret?" She puts down her pen, and I know I have her full attention because Sophia is the best kind of secret-keeper. She will never tell anyone anything.

And frankly, although I kind of like having this secret, I don't like Sophia's not knowing, and I know I can trust her. It's time.

"You have to swear on your life you will not say anything to anyone."

"Cross my heart and hope to die."

"So you know I got really fat?"

"Yeah. You're pregnant," she says dully. "Is that it? The secret? Duh. What do you think I am, completely stupid?"

I'm impressed. "How did you know?"

"First of all, you look pregnant. I mean, you just looked fat up until about three weeks ago, and now you are definitely pregnant, and secondly, it's all everyone talks about in this house. Everyone shuts up the minute I walk in the room, as if that means I'll have no idea what I've overheard walking down the hallway. I know everything."

"Not everything."

"What don't I know?"

"Do you know that Dad and Andi think I'm giving the baby up for adoption?"

"Yeah. I looked up the history on the computer and looked at the couples. Some of them look really nice. I think it's so sad that they can't have their own children."

I grin in delight. Who knew that my perfect little sister had such a subversive streak. "You're pretty cool, you know that?"

Sophia just shrugs.

"Here's the secret. I'm not giving her up. I'm keeping her."

Her eyes grow wide. This, it seems, is a worthy secret. "Nooooo!" she breathes. "For real?"

I nod.

"Do you know it's a girl?" she says, awed.

"No, but I'm pretty sure. It feels like a girl. I call her the Bean."

"That's so cute!" She giggles, then frowns. "But you're not actu-

ally going to name her the Bean, right? Because that would just be awful."

"No!" I laugh. "I was thinking maybe . . . Michaela?"

"Michaela?" She makes a face. "No way. You can*not* call her Michaela. I had a Michaela in fifth grade, and she was so mean!"

"So what names do you like?" I say, thinking that even though Michael asked, Sophia is right. Michaela isn't my favorite name.

"How about Skylar!" she says excitedly. "I love that name. Or Madison!"

"God no!" I make a face. "I hate those names. I was thinking maybe Audrey. Or Evie. I kind of like old-fashioned names."

"I love those names!" Sophia's face lights up. "Evie!" She scoots over on the bed so she is sitting right up next to me. "Can I feel her?"

"Sure." I smile, and she takes her hand and lays it on my stomach.

Sophia frowns. "I can't feel anything."

"She's probably sleeping. She wakes up at night."

"Wow. This must be so awesome. So how do you think Dad will be when you tell him you're keeping Evie?"

"It's his first grandchild. He's going to fall in love. No one's going anywhere."

"That is so cool," Sophia says happily. "I'm going to have a niece! I'm going to be Aunt Sophia! At thirteen!"

"I know. But you can't tell anyone, okay?"

"Got it," she says. "Not a soul."

And as we lie there, during a rare moment of sisterly bonding, I wet myself.

It isn't like normal wetting myself. I didn't even know I had to pee, but suddenly I feel this warm whoosh of water, and I know I'm soaking and the sheets are soaking, and I'm completely mortified.

"Oh, God," I moan, as Sophia looks at me. "Get up! Get up!"

"What is it?" she says, scared.

"I just had an accident," I say, jumping off the bed. "Oh, my God! Soph, I'm so sorry."

"It's okay," she says, although she's screwing up her nose and I can tell she's as grossed out as I would have been if she had peed all over my bed.

I grab a bunch of towels from the bathroom and go back into Sophia's bedroom, and I have no idea what makes me do this, but I lean forward and sniff the wet sheets where I've peed, but they don't smell like pee at all. They smell like nothing. And I stumble backward and burst into tears.

"What is it?" Sophia says. "What's the matter?"

"Go get Andi," I cry. "Go get Andi."

Twenty-eight

· · · · · · · · · · ·

Andi rushes in to find a terrified Emily amid a pile of sodden towels.

"Oh, baby." She gathers Emily in her arms, all anger and resentment forgotten, seeing before her a terrified child. "Your water broke. It's fine. It's okay. I'm right here. We're going to ring the OB/GYN, then I'm going to drive you to the hospital. I'll just call your father—"

"No!" Emily shouts. "I just want you. Not my dad. Just you. Please?" And she looks up at Andi with large, frightened eyes, and Andi feels, as she has at every moment Emily shows her vulnerability, a rush of intense love, just as strong as she would feel if Emily were her own.

"Okay." Andi melts. "Don't worry. It's all going to be fine."

They have not prepared anything for the hospital, assuming it was at least five weeks away, and that first babies are usually late,

although Andi had found herself wondering if in fact that was an old wives' tale.

She had read somewhere that teenagers often give birth early, had expressed that fear to the OB/GYN the last time she took Emily in, but had been reassured that everything was looking great.

The phone call is brief. Andi flies around Emily's bedroom, putting together clean clothes, toiletries, her favorite blanket. She has nothing for the baby, she thinks with dismay, having expected to hand the baby straight to the adopting couple. There is no adopting couple yet, Emily thus far vetoing everyone Andi has picked since the disastrous meeting with Adeline and Greg.

Emily sits on the sofa, quietly crying, white with fear, as Sophia sits next to her, holding her hand and whispering how Emily should be so excited, the Bean is coming! Emily, when not shaking with fear, manages to acknowledge her.

"It's going to be fine," Andi reassures her each time she flies past, arms filled with things. "You're a brave girl, and we're going to be fine."

When Emily is strapped into the car, Andi runs next door to Drew, explains what's happening, urges him not to say anything to Ethan, and hands over Sophia.

"Are you sure I shouldn't come?" Sophia asks, her eyes searching out Emily in the car. "I'd like to."

"I know, sweetie," she tells Sophia. "We don't know whether it's happening now. We're just going to the hospital to check her out."

There is no way Ethan would want Sophia at the hospital. He doesn't even know she knows.

"The baby's not coming now?" There is disappointment in her voice.

"Hopefully not," Andi lies encouragingly. "We'll call you later."

. . .

D o you feel any contractions?" Andi asks, driving carefully.

"No." Emily shakes her head. "That must mean it's okay, right? If I was in labor, I'd be having contractions, wouldn't I?"

"I don't know, sweetie," Andi says. "We'll ask the doctor," and she turns just in time to see Emily's face crease up in pain. "What was that?"

"A stomach cramp. It's nothing. It's gone now."

"How many have you had?"

"I don't know. Just a couple."

"Are they five minutes apart, or ten? Roughly?" Andi's voice is now urgent.

"I don't know. Why? Are they contractions?" Emily's voice is filled with fear.

"I think so, Emily. I don't know for sure, but I think so."

"Oh, shit." Emily leans her head back on the seat. "I am so not ready for this."

"I don't know that anyone is ever ready for this," Andi says.

Emily closes her eyes and rests her hands on her stomach. Turning her head, she blinks, gazing at Andi, who looks over and smiles, reaching out and squeezing her hand reassuringly. When Andi thinks about withdrawing her hand, Emily holds it tighter. She won't let go.

Andi looks at her. "We have to phone the adoption agency. We have to figure out what to do when the baby is born. They may have a . . . foster home or something." She swallows hard, pushing aside her pain, knowing she has to be strong for Emily.

"Andi?" Emily looks straight ahead, her voice quiet. "I'm going to keep the baby."

"What?" Andi feigns shock, but in truth she is not surprised. Emily

had mentioned this before, but after Ethan's furious reaction, hadn't said it again. Ethan thought she had changed her mind, but Andi suspected differently.

Once upon a time, it might have made her happy. It might not be her baby, but it would still be a baby around the house, for where else will Emily go if not home? How will she support herself? How will they live? If she keeps the baby, she will have no choice but to stay at home. With them.

Instead of filling her with joy, it fills her with dismay.

If Emily keeps the baby, they get the baby, but they also get Emily. The pattern will continue. The screaming tantrums, which leave Andi discombobulated and terrified, interspersed with moments of loving calm, during which Andi feels a wave of love for her stepdaughter, a hope this signifies the beginning of a permanent change.

Andi feels a sinking in her stomach. Adopting Emily's baby was her last chance, the perfect solution. Andi would be a mother, and Emily would have her life back. She could go to college, go traveling, live the life she was meant to live instead of being tied down by a baby she doesn't want in a town she doesn't like.

It would have set Emily free and given them what Andi has always wanted, but keeping the baby now means the cord will never be cut.

Plus ça change, Plus c'est la même, she thinks, aching with sadness as she navigates the sunny streets to the hospital.

The more that changes, the more that stays the same.

'm scared." Emily sobs, breaking Andi's heart as Emily clutches her hand to stop her from leaving the room while the nurse snaps on gloves to perform an internal exam.

"Ssssh. Don't worry. It won't hurt, I promise. I'll be right outside the door, then I'll come straight back." Andi brushes Emily's hair off

her face, wondering again how it is possible that this child is having a child.

"Don't go," Emily cries.

The nurse looks up and smiles. "It's fine, Mom," she says. "You can stay right in here with your daughter."

This time, Emily doesn't correct her, doesn't scream that it's her stepmother, and she hates her. She just clutches Andi's hand tighter as Andi crouches, looking deep into Emily's eyes and whispering that it's all going to be fine, continuing to stroke Emily's hair back with her other hand, ssshing her and soothing her, and doing everything she can to let her know that Emily will be okay.

"You're just about ten centimeters dilated!" the nurse says cheerfully. "That means baby's about ready to come. Have you discussed what drugs you'd like to take, or whether this is natural childbirth?"

"Drugs!" Emily shouts, now in the midst of a stronger contraction. "Get me drugs."

"Let me get everything started for an epidural. We have to be quick and get it done before you start pushing. Don't worry. We're going to be fine," she reassures them as Emily's eyes widen with fear.

Andi continues stroking Emily's hair as Emily begs her not to leave, not for a second.

"Of course," she says. "But . . . I have to phone your dad."

"I don't want my dad here." Emily bursts into tears, but not the histrionics Andi is so used to. Quiet, genuine tears. "I know how ashamed he is of me."

Andi's heart breaks. "He's not ashamed of you, sweetie," she says. "He loves you more than anything. He doesn't know how to deal with any of this, that's all. He'll . . . get used to it. We have to let him know you're going to give birth."

"Okay." Emily nods reluctantly, knowing that Andi is right. "Call him."

. . .

E than is walking around a small garden in Sausalito when the call comes in. He has spent more time outside the past few days, hoping to find some solace in nature, for that was where he always found it before.

This time, it hasn't worked. He feels empty, and doesn't know how he will ever change that if Andi leaves him. He cannot believe he has let it go this far. He has a horrible feeling there is absolutely nothing he can do to stop his life from spinning out of control, and powerlessness is not a familiar or a comfortable feeling.

He and Andi circle each other like actors. They pretend to be husband and wife in front of the children, have conversations that might sound like the ordinary conversations of a married couple if you were to listen as an outsider, but there is no connection there, no warmth.

The intimacy that has always characterized their relationship has flown out the window, leaving two empty shells who are adept at going through the motions, who can fake the feelings when other people are around but who don't feel anything at all.

Except Ethan *does* feel. He feels lost. Confused. Terrified. Bewildered. He kisses his wife good night every evening, but not on the lips, not the long, warm smooches of evenings gone by, kisses delivered in bed as one of them rolls over and turns off their bedside light, but instead light pecks on her proffered cheek, for she turns her head now; a cheek is all he can hope for.

He pads down the corridor to the spare room, which is cold and unwelcoming. It is beautifully decorated in blues and whites, but it is not home: as much as he is a stranger in his own bedroom, he is starting to feel like a stranger in his home.

Every evening, when he walks through the front door, Andi is in

the kitchen making dinner. They sit at the dinner table, forcing small talk, with none of the easy conversation that has always flowed between them.

"How was work today?" Andi will ask. He will tell stories about his jobs, fill the silences with desperate stories because anything is better than silence.

"How about you?" he will offer when he has run out of anything else to talk about. "How was yours?"

Their time together is finite. Andi has been clear: they will reassess when the baby is dealt with, when life is back to normal. But what does that mean? That he has a few weeks to convince her to stay? A few weeks to fix something that right now feels as if it doesn't have a chance of being anything other than broken?

His phone buzzes in his pocket. He pulls it out, expecting it to be yet another client wanting something from him. Usually, he loves his job. He loves people. He takes enormous pride in being of service to his clients; there is nothing he loves more than walking around someone's garden and chatting about plantings and design ideas.

Not anymore. Now he is tired, too tired to chat lightly with anyone, but he looks cursorily at the phone, seeing it is Andi. He takes the call.

"Emily's gone into labor," she says quietly. "We're at the hospital."

Ethan starts to shake. "But . . . she's not due for another five weeks."

"I know. Her water broke. She's fine, but you should come now."

"But . . . the adoption," he sputters. "We haven't found anyone. What do we do?"

Andi is quiet. Should she tell him what Emily just told her? Should she share the news that is now weighing her down and bringing her to the brink of tears as she hears her husband's voice?

"Let's worry about it later," she says. "Let's just make sure this baby comes safely into the world."

Emily is pushing with all her might as the doctor and midwives urge her on. Andi sits at her head, encouraging her, and Ethan is pacing nervously up and down the hallway outside.

"I can't push anymore," Emily whimpers, her eyes crossed with exhaustion. "I'm too tired. I can't do it."

"One more!" the cheerful nurse says. "You're doing a great job! One more push."

"We see the head!" the nurse yelps. "You're almost there! Good girl! One more push!"

And then, slickly, suddenly, a purplish red tiny being, glossy with mucus and blood, is in the room, squawling angrily as Emily sinks her head back on the pillow.

"It's a boy!" the doctor exclaims, bringing the baby over to show Emily.

"It can't be," Emily mumbles, exhausted. "It's a girl."

"No." The doctor laughs. "That's very definitely a boy. Do you want to hold him?"

"Later," Emily says as Andi finally remembers to breathe.

"May I?" Andi's voice is an awed whisper. Emily nods as Andi's arms reach out for the baby. The tightly wrapped bundle is placed in her arms as Ethan walks in, seeing Andi, her face filled with joy and wonder, gazing at the tiny features, unwrapping the blanket slightly to see the tiny fingers and toes.

Ethan kneels next to her, putting his arms around her, and neither of them notices that Emily's head is turned to the wall and her eyes are tightly closed.

. . .

don't know what to say," Ethan says. "How *can* she keep the baby? She just turned eighteen. She has her whole life ahead of her."

"I agree. I agree with all of it. She's irresponsible; she's still a child. How can she keep the baby?" Andi stands next to Ethan outside the glass wall of the nursery, both of them unable to tear their eyes away from the perfect baby boy who is inside the room.

"But . . ." she turns to him slowly. "How can she not?"

Ethan shakes his head. "That's not Emily speaking. That's you. This isn't our baby, Andi." He looks at her, seeing the expression on her face when she held the baby moments after he was born; the pain she had truly gone through in finding out the perimenopause had made it so unlikely for her to have a child, and just what he had withheld from her by refusing to adopt, refusing to keep the baby.

He understands it all, and as he stands there, looking at his wife, he wishes, with all his heart, that this *were* their baby, that there wouldn't be a choice to make. But there is, and they can't, and it's too late.

"It's your grandson," Andi pleads.

"I know. But Emily is the mother, and she's simply not equipped to take care of a baby." He's saying what he said before, except this time he doesn't mean it in quite the same way. This time he is wondering whether they might be able to make it work.

"We would help. We could do it."

Ethan turns to her bitterly. "You haven't even decided whether you're staying or leaving. How can you commit to help raising a child when you don't even know if you're going to be around?"

"You're right," she says, not knowing what else to say, for her confusion has never been greater. She was definitely leaving. She wanted to forgive Ethan, but the resentment was too great. She'd made the decision, ever more clear when Emily told her she was keeping the

baby. Keeping the baby means keeping Emily. An untenable marriage of four.

But the baby! Holding that baby in her arms, Andi felt a rush of love she had never expected. She had heard of grandparents feeling that same rush of love, but Andi was not biologically a grand-anything, so where did this all-encompassing love come from?

Even now, she can't walk away from the nursery. Neither she nor Ethan has talked about leaving—standing outside the picture windows for two hours, gazing at the baby, waiting for him to be fed, hoping they can go in and hold him again.

He is dressed now, in a white cotton onesie with a tiny knitted cap on his head. Even when he sleeps, he jerks and twitches, moving his limbs. Andi wants to run in and scoop him up, hold him close to her breast, and never let him go.

"He's amazing, isn't he," she whispers, gazing in the nursery, feeling something shift between her and Ethan, feeling suddenly a warm ray of hope. "You're right about my not knowing what the future holds, but this might be the only thing I have clarity about right now. You can't give him up. Emily can't give him up. Whatever is supposed to be will be, but we have to bring him home." She isn't pleading anymore. She is calm. It isn't a question; it's a statement: this is the only way.

Ethan is quiet. "I just . . . I can't see how this is going to work."

"We don't have a choice." Andi says. "If Emily refuses to sign the adoption papers, there is nothing we can do."

"She's a minor. We can override."

"Ethan, she just turned eighteen. She isn't a minor anymore."

"Oh, God." He sighs dejectedly.

"You can talk to her as much as you like, but she is adamant. She wants to keep this baby."

Ethan leans his forehead against the cool glass and closes his eyes.

"I just don't believe this," he says. "I don't believe what is happening in my life."

"I don't, either," Andi says. "None of this is what we wanted. But . . . we have it now. We have to deal with it."

Ethan turns to her. "Together?"

She looks at him and nods, reaching down for his hand and squeezing it lightly before dropping it almost as quickly as she picked it up, unaware of how, in that second, Ethan's heart had lifted.

Turning to walk back down to Emily's room, Ethan isn't at all sure whether that just really happened, or whether it was merely a figment of his imagination.

Twenty-nine

. . . .

He's beautiful." Andi pulls a chair closer to my bed as I reach behind me to push the pillows up a bit so I can sit.

"I want to see him." I'm curious as to what he looks like. I want to hold him, to know what it's like. I want to feel the overwhelming love that I felt for the B . . . well, the baby girl I thought was inside my stomach.

The thing is—I know this sounds awful—I was so *sure* it was a girl. I was so sure it was Bean, and I connected with *Bean,* not with this boy baby that I don't know, and I don't feel any of that overwhelming love I felt when I was pregnant.

I just feel . . . kind of numb.

But I haven't even held my baby, and I'm sure that's what it is; I *know* those feelings will come. When I'm holding him in my arms and he's gazing up into my eyes, we'll feel it, and I will love him just as much as Bean. More, probably.

"I'll tell the nurse," Andi says as a frown crosses her face.

"Are you still feeling you want to keep him?" she asks carefully. "The adoption agency has been leaving messages. They would be

willing to take him and foster him until they find a permanent family."

She looks at me expectantly, and I shake my head vigorously. There is no way in hell I would let my baby go off with strangers. To a foster home? Are they nuts?

"No way," I shake my head again. "He's mine."

And I swear, Andi looks even more relieved than I feel.

The nurse comes in holding this tiny bundle, and she places it in my arms, showing me how to cradle him, and to make sure I always have one hand holding the back of his head to protect his neck muscles.

I sit there with this tiny baby in my arms, just staring at him. I can't believe this . . . human! . . . this baby came out of my stomach. I cannot believe that this is mine! I grew him inside me! I lift my other hand and stroke his cheek. It feels soft and furry. He stirs, then opens his mouth in a giant yawn, and it makes me laugh.

It isn't what I expected; he isn't what I expected, but look how sweet he is! Like a tiny little doll that moves!

"He's so cute!" I look up at Andi delightedly. "Did you see him yawn? I have a name for him."

Andi leans forward, and I hope she likes it. I hope she approves. I didn't have any boy names, obviously, but when I was lying here before, this name came to me, and it feels right.

"Callum," I say proudly. "Cal for short."

"It's a beautiful name." Andi smiles, stroking the baby's head, and her eyes instantly go all soft and tender. I wonder if my eyes do that when I look at him. I don't think they do, and I wonder if that's just because Andi's older. Maybe that will happen to me in time.

"Does he have a middle name?" she says, tearing her eyes away from him and looking up at me.

Of course he does. I made a promise, and I haven't forgotten it, even though I never expected him to be a boy.

"Callum Michael," I announce. "Do you like it?"

"Oh, Emily! I love it. It's a perfect name for him!"

And I have to tell you, I feel so proud right then.

The Irish nurse, Maureen, bustles over, cooing over Callum Michael. She's been in a few times already today, and I cannot believe how nice she is, clucking around me like the perfect mother hen. Just being around her warmth and big smile makes me feel taken care of.

"Would you look at the gorgeous boy! And the beautiful mother." She smiles and, for a moment, I could almost believe her. "Right, young lady. Time to introduce you to some nursing. Did you attend the classes?"

"Nursing?" I look up at her in panic. "I'm not going to nurse."

"Oh, yes you will," she says cheerfully, as if she didn't hear a word I just said. "A lot of mothers feel the same way when their babies are born, but it's wonderful once you get used to it, and far better for the babies. In the beginning, you're producing colostrum, which is filled with antibodies the baby needs, and it gets him off to the very best possible start. Let's just give it a go, I can help the baby latch on." She reaches out toward me, as if she's going to unbutton my pajamas or something, and I recoil away from her.

"No!" I yelp. "He's having formula."

"But Emily." Andi seems upset. "Maureen is right, it's so much better . . ."

"No!" I say again. God. They're not the ones having to get their boobs out in public. And the thought of a baby sucking on my nipple? Ewww. To say it grosses me out doesn't even begin to describe how horrific I think it is.

There is no way I am getting my boobs out. Ever. And no way I am having those huge, distended nipples. You think I didn't YouTube it already? Gross. I swear, I am grimacing just thinking about it.

"I was raised on a formula, and I'm completely fine," I say, which is true. My mom once told me that pretty much everyone back then was given a bottle, and it didn't seem to do me any harm.

"Just bring me a bottle," I say wearily, "and I'll feed him." I look down at him and, as if on cue, as if he heard me talk about food then got hungry, his tiny face scrunches up into an angry red bunch, and he starts to wail in this reedy, thin, baby voice.

"You know what?" I feel slight panic because I'm rocking him to try to make him stop, but the screaming just gets louder. "Can you just take him?"

I see Andi and Maureen exchange a look, but I don't care. I hold Cal out, and Andi steps up and takes him. Instantly, he's quiet again. She stands there, rocking him slightly, looking mesmerized, her eyes melting again as she gazes at his face.

"You've got the magic touch." Maureen looks on admiringly, and I don't care. Whatever. I just want them to go so I can go back to sleep.

Thirty

. . . .

Are you fucking kidding me? Again? I burrow my head under my pillow, pulling it tightly over my ears, hoping to drown out the ever-present bawling, and praying that he will stop, that somehow a miracle will occur and the baby will fall back to sleep by himself.

The wailing gets louder—he is in a bassinet at the foot of my bed, even though he has a perfectly good nursery, but apparently I have to keep him in my room until he's three months old. The law, according to my dad. Which sucks, because if he were in the nursery, I'm pretty sure Andi would get up and deal with these awful nights, because she's the one who seems completely entranced by my baby, and the nursery is next to their bedroom, but my dad says no.

I push back the covers and sit on the edge of the bed, unable to move for a while. My body feels like lead, but I have to stop the crying.

"Sssh." I stumble to the bassinet and lean over. His face is screwed up tightly, bright red, his fists clenched with rage. I retrieve the paci from where it rests, on the sheet next to his left ear, and put it back in his mouth.

"Ssssh." He sucks noisily on the pacifier, looking up at me with big eyes, and I lean down and give him my finger, which he squeezes tightly. Cute. If he were quiet like this all the time, maybe things would be a whole lot easier.

*C*olic, the doctor says. *Unfortunately, you have a colicky baby.* So? I said. Give him something. Give him medicine. Drugs. I don't care. Whatever it takes to stop his screaming.

"It's not that simple," she said, explaining that they weren't sure what caused colic, but that it would probably stop at around three months, and that there were measures we could take that might improve things, but ultimately it was time.

And yes, I know, three months is not a lot in the grand scheme of things, but when you are awake night after night with a screaming child, three months feels like thirty years, and that's pretty horrific.

I left the doctor's office with a list of suggestions. We changed his formula to soy, but that didn't work, and we give him these baby gas drops, but that doesn't work.

There are two things that work. At night, a pacifier, and during the day, his being walked. I spend hours every day walking around the neighborhood, up and down the canyons, pushing him in his off-road stroller, knowing that if I dare to stop, even a brief rest on a bench, he will start screaming again.

The only good thing about this is I'm getting in shape, but I don't care. I'd gladly give up a waistline and flattish stomach for a decent night's sleep and my life back.

You would think that my family would step up and help out a little more. Sophia takes him for walks, which helps, although she says she's nervous because he's so small. She keeps saying she's going to be an amazing babysitter, but he needs to get a bit bigger first, so she isn't so scared.

Tell me about it.

Andi's pretty good during the day when my dad's at work, but my dad has said, repeatedly, that if I'm going to be a mother, I have to be a mother, and it's not Andi's job to take over.

I heard them argue about it just the other night. Andi was saying it wasn't fair, it was too much for a young girl, and she's happy to help, happy to take the baby whenever, but my dad said absolutely not, that I had made my bed and now I had to learn to lie in it.

I never thought I'd say this, but right now? I totally hate my dad.

When he's at work, though, Andi always takes the baby. She works in the mornings now, which is when I have to walk him and walk him, but early afternoon, Andi gets him up from his nap, and if my dad's not around, she'll keep him for the afternoon just so that I can sleep.

Even then, even with afternoon naps, I am exhausted in a way I never dreamed possible. I don't always sleep, which is part of the problem. I get on the computer, which is about my only access to the outside world right now, and before I know it, my dad's pulling in the driveway and I have to take over so my dad doesn't think that Andi has been—heaven forbid!—helping me out by looking after Cal.

This is not what I expected. None of it was what I expected. For starters, as you know, I was expecting a girl, but male or female, I thought my baby was going to be perfect. It was supposed to be quiet, and cute, dressed in cool clothes, my tiny little partner.

Meanwhile, he's in onesies from Carter's, which Andi has bought, and everything's blue, and green, and yellow stripes, and I don't care. I just don't care that there isn't a single cool item of clothing in his closet. I don't have the energy to care.

He's cute when he's quiet, that's for sure. Especially since last week. Andi started yelling up the stairs for me, and I practically fell down them because she never yells, and I thought something terrible had happened.

"Look!" She dragged me into the kitchen, where Cal was strapped into this vibrating bouncy chair that was on the kitchen table.

The kid has more stuff than you've ever seen. Andi's gone nuts. Every day she brings back some other fantastic thing: toys that squeak and sing; chairs that bounce; mats you're supposed to lay him on, on his stomach, so he can strengthen his neck muscles by looking around although Cal just tends to lie there like a grub.

Sophia was sitting at the kitchen table with a delighted grin on her face. "You have to see this!" she said. "Andi? Show her!"

Andi leaned over and started making kissing noises at him. "Hey, baby baby," she crooned, and his face suddenly broke into a huge smile. He looked from her, to me, to Sophia, then back to her, and it was pretty awesome.

"Awesome," I said. "Hey, little dude." And I leaned down and kissed him on the cheek. I stood there awkwardly for a minute.

"Want to give him his bottle?" Sophia said. It seems she has become the babysitter earlier than planned.

"Nah, it's okay. I'm doing some stuff on the computer," I went back upstairs.

You see, that's the other thing that I don't get. Everything I read said being a mother was incredible, that the love you feel is the most intense thing you have ever felt in your life, that you would lay down your life for your child in a heartbeat.

I wish I felt that. I expected to feel that, and honestly, when he was in my stomach and I thought he was a she and she was the Bean, and when I was certain that I would be keeping the baby, and it was my secret, and my baby, and no one could take it away from me, I *did* feel that.

And I don't know why I don't feel it anymore.

Everyone loves this baby, and I just feel pissed off that I don't. I mean, I do, but . . . not in the way I know I'm supposed to. I see how Andi coos over him, how she cannot take her eyes off him. I see

how she cradles him and rocks him and sings to him, and I have tried to do that, I really have, but I feel self-conscious and weird. It doesn't feel natural, and maybe, maybe, I'm not the natural mother I thought I would be.

"You are overwhelmed," the leader of the teen-mom support group said, the one time I showed up. "Which is entirely natural. You are each incredibly brave, choosing to keep your precious children, and you need a tremendous amount of love and support, which is why it's crucial that you come to our group every week." She looked around at each of us four girls in there, smiling a beatific smile, this freaky fucking earth mother in her flowing diaphanous skirt, and I wanted to scream at her.

She could sit there and talk about being overwhelmed all she wanted, this old woman, but she had no idea what it was like to be me. She had no idea what it feels like to have your life taken away so abruptly, and by a baby who never stops screaming.

I looked cautiously at the other teen moms to see if any of them could become a friend, but Jesus, no way in hell I would have anything to do with any of them. Jennie was this big ugly moose—and seriously, how in the hell did *she* ever get laid; Sarah was one of the popular girls, so you could see how she got laid, but she looked shell-shocked at having got into this mess, and River, who looked like the hippie's granddaughter, beamed a beatific smile right back at her.

The other girls *shared*. River was the only one who seemed to love every second. Sarah said her parents were basically raising the baby, and Jennie, you could tell, was just thrilled that someone had actually had sex with her.

When it was my turn, I didn't say much. I knew I wasn't going to go back. I had nothing in common with any of them, and I might be dying of loneliness, but I'm still not desperate enough to go to that support group every week and reveal my innermost secrets.

We all brought our babies with us, and River's baby was first to start squawking. She had him in a sling around her body, and while we sat there, cross-legged on the floor, she unbuttoned her shirt and just started nursing.

That was when I almost started giggling, which was totally embarrassing because I know it's meant to be natural, except it isn't. It's just weird to see another girl get her boobs out. And I tried not to look, but I kind of couldn't help it, and when she switched breasts, she had these huge boobs with enormous nipples, and I seriously thought I might just have a fit of hysterics.

Then Jennie's baby started bawling, and like a line of dominoes, it set the others off. Thank God, the others reached into their diaper bags and pulled out bottles, so at least I didn't feel guilty about being the only one not getting her tits out in public.

Frankly, I couldn't wait to get out of there. And I'm beginning to think I might have made a terrible mistake in not doing the adoption thing. Adeline and Greg would have loved this baby. I see Andi with this baby, and I see how an older woman would have loved this baby. If not Adeline, someone else. Babies get adopted all the time, at any age, right?

But how can I turn around and say that I was wrong and they were right? How can I admit I made such a huge mistake, after the fights we had to give me the right to keep my baby.

I will find a way. I have to. My dad gave me such hell about keeping the baby; fights that were like nothing on earth. He said I was irresponsible; I didn't have a clue what it meant to be a mother, and I would get bored. He asked if I knew what it was like to be woken up night after night, all night, for years.

"I will do it," I spat back at him. "This is my baby, and I will take care of it." I cannot say he was right. I will not do that. I will find a way to make this work.

. . .

am in a deep sleep when I hear it again. At first just a squeak, and then a full-fledged bawl. I open one eye blearily and look at the clock—3:34 A.M. Twenty-two minutes since the last time he woke up.

I can't stand it. I can't stand it. I can't stand it.

I get up and walk to the bassinet and I do not mean to do this, I swear, I never meant to do this, but I stand over the bassinet and I scream back at him.

"Shut up!" I shout. "Shut up! Just SHUT THE FUCK UP!"

Thirty-one

. . . .

Andi wakes up late. She often does, these days. She wakes up every time she hears Cal scream, which happens every night, starting at around two in the morning, going on every twenty minutes until it is time to get up.

Andi now sleeps with earplugs. And a white-noise machine. But she still wakes up. She has gently suggested Emily remove the pacifier—the pacifier that helps him sleep is the same pacifier that falls out of his slack jaw once he is deeply sleeping, causing him to wake up screaming, roughly every twenty minutes or so, wanting the pacifier back.

Emily won't hear it. "I'm his mom," she snapped. "And I think the pacifier's great."

So Andi lies in bed, night after night, worrying about Cal. She worries that Emily hasn't bonded with him, that Emily has no patience, that Emily is so exhausted she may snap, and what will that mean for the baby if Emily snaps?

She hears him scream and wants to go to him, but she cannot, because she knows that Ethan is right.

"You cannot shield her from the responsibility of being a mother," he said gently. "I know you want to. I know you love him, and you could take care of him far better than her, but the only way she's going to learn how to do it is to do it."

"I just want to help her," she had pleaded.

"You are. And you can. But you cannot take over for her."

This past week she has heard Emily screaming at the baby. Numerous times. Then she has intervened. She met Ethan outside Emily's door, and both of them exchanged worried looks.

"I have to," she whispered. "I'm worried about what she may do." Visions of Emily raging as she has raged so often before fill her mind. The picture of Emily holding Cal up and shaking him hard to shut him up makes Andi sick with fear.

This week, Ethan hasn't stopped her.

They have both gone in to find Emily sobbing.

"Go to bed," Ethan has said gently to Emily. "We'll take the baby."

He has guided Emily back to bed and tucked the covers around her as Andi cradles Cal, carrying him out of the room, Ethan following her with the bassinet.

He has gone downstairs to warm a bottle and come back to sit with Andi as she feeds the baby.

"I'm worried about her," Andi said two nights ago. "I'm terrified she's going to snap and take it out on the baby."

"I hear you," Ethan said miserably. "I don't know what to do."

"We should take the baby at night. Or get a night nurse. A doula. Someone. We can't let her go on like this. She's exhausted, and she can't be a good mother when she's this tired. It's not fair."

"I agree," Ethan said finally. "You're right. A night nurse is a great idea."

"It's expensive," Andi said. "But worth it. We can do two nights, and maybe a night nurse for two nights. I'm sure she can handle two or

three nights a week, but not every night. You hear how she's screaming at him. I'm terrified she's going to . . ." kill him, she wanted to say.
But she couldn't say it out loud, as if putting it out there might tempt
fate.

"I know," Ethan said. "I know." He sat on the bed, next to where
Andi was cradling Cal as he sucked greedily on his bottle. "Isn't he
beautiful?" Ethan's whole face softened. "I could sit and watch him
for hours."

"I know." Andi sighed, with a smile. "Do you want to feed him?"

Ethan reached out his arms as Andi carefully tucked Cal in, reminding Ethan to tap the end of the bottle with his fingernail to keep
the baby sucking when his interest waned.

They lay side by side, both back against the pillows, Andi stroking
Cal's head, exchanging soft smiles, and Andi forgot she was thinking
about leaving. She forgot about the drama, and the crises, and the
hell of Emily when Emily explodes. She leaned her head on Ethan's
shoulder.

Anyone seeing them right now would think they were the picture
of a perfect, loving, happy family: mother, father, and beautiful baby
boy.

The late starts are becoming more normal for Andi, given how
much of the night is spent awake.

She sleeps in more and more, her body trying to catch up, waking
up at eight, and sometimes later. Today is a late one. Andi goes downstairs, expecting to find Emily in the kitchen, or the family room, giving Cal his bottle. Last night, Emily insisted on keeping him, said she
had slept all afternoon, felt so much better, there was no question that
she was going to keep him.

Last night, Andi didn't wake up. At all. She is stunned, but aware
that she is so exhausted, she must have needed to sleep. It is true that

this morning, after just one decent night's sleep, she feels like a new woman.

The house is eerily quiet. Ethan had gotten up earlier, as he does every morning of late, to get Sophia off to school, and the only sound is that of the passing cars.

Andi feels a flush of fear as she looks around for everyone. *I am being silly,* she tells herself. Emily has probably gone out with Cal on one of their epic walks. She goes back upstairs, her heart fluttering with fear, and pushes open Emily's door.

She gasps.

The closet doors are open. Instead of the mass of black clothing, squashed together, there are empty hangers dangling pathetically from the rail. The makeup that usually clutters the top of her desk is gone, as is Catso, the threadbare cat she has slept with every night since she was three months old.

Emily goes nowhere without Catso. Even at eighteen.

And the bassinet is gone.

Thirty-two

. . . .

As she pounds down the stairs, Andi's chest heaves painfully, panic spreading through her body in waves. She takes the stairs two at a time, breathless with terror as she grabs the phone to call Ethan.

The baby! Where's the baby! Where have they gone?

As she reaches the phone, she stops. She hears a squeak. Heart pounding, she pauses, phone in hand, to hear the squeak become a bawl.

Thank God! Thank God! She races upstairs, sobbing with relief, running toward the nursery, flinging open the closed door to find Cal lying in the bassinet, placed carefully in the crib, with a folded piece of paper tucked into the sheet at the top of the crib.

Andi scoops him up, covering him with kisses as she clutches him to her chest, still sobbing with the relief of his being okay. The note reads:

I'm sorry, I can't do this. You love Cal, and I can't. Not in the way I should, and I need my life back. Mom gave me

money, and I'm going away. I will be fine. Look after Cal for me.
Emily.

Andi stands, frozen, as Cal hiccups into her shoulder, and it is a good many minutes before she realizes her hand is shaking like a leaf.

Part Three

. . . .

PARENTS

Thirty-three

. . . .

Deanna opens the door and kisses Andi on the cheek before looking down at the large covered dish she is holding proudly in front of her. "What did you bring?" She smiles.

"Our favorite," Ethan says as he walks up the pathway proffering two bottles of red wine.

Deanna gasps. "Not the chocolate croissant pudding?"

"Yup," Andi says. "I know it's sinful, but how could I not? I may even do an Ashtanga class with you tomorrow to make up for the excesses of tonight."

Deanna throws her head back and laughs. "Since when have you even set foot in an Ashtanga class? You haven't been to my Hatha yoga class for three years. I doubt you could even do downward dog anymore."

Andi grimaces. "I know, I know. You're right, but what can I tell you? I'm busy being Mom."

"I know." Deanna pulls her in and takes the dish as they both head to the kitchen. "How is that little monkey?"

"Adorable and wonderful and perfect and gorgeous," Andi says.

"You look amazing. You just look so . . . happy."

"We are." Ethan slides a hand around his wife's waist and plants a kiss on her cheek. "Aren't we?"

Andi sinks into him with a smile as she nods. It is true. She is happy, but more than happy, she is *content*. Cal is now three, and the light of all their lives. Andi thinks of him as her little magician, for there is no question that he has filled all their lives with magic.

She thinks back, sometimes, to when Emily was pregnant, to those times when she was ready to leave, when all she could think about was starting again, without Emily, without responsibilities.

She is embarrassed to think that Pete—Pete!—was, albeit briefly, the subject of her most ardent fantasies. Pete, who now loves, and lives with, her best friend. Pete, who has become like a brother to her. How could she ever have even given Pete a second thought?

Andi glances over at Ethan, feeling herself smile. *What a wonderful man Ethan is,* she thinks. *How incredibly lucky am I?*

The peace that exists in their household started almost as soon as Emily left. Andi stopped tiptoeing around her own house, let go of any residual resentments she was holding against Ethan, found herself relaxing into the role of mother, a role she had always wanted, had never dared think she would play.

The threat of Emily's coming back didn't go away for a long time.

At first, Andi held back, terrified Emily was going to change her mind and come for him, reclaim Cal, take him away, but weeks went by, then months. They received the odd letter or phone call, all of which indicated Emily was not changing her mind.

In letters, she talked about herself, with, sometimes, a sentence asking if Cal was doing well. On the phone, she'd ask how he was, never seeming to be very interested.

Emily was in touch with her mother far more than with them, which would have been ironic, except Brooke was the one who had given Emily enough money to enable her to leave. Brooke had put

Emily in touch with a friend in Seattle, who gave Emily a room in her house while she was figuring out what to do.

She had worked in a coffeehouse for a while. Then, it seems, she came back to California for Burning Man, after which she lived on some kind of an artists' commune in Grants Pass, Oregon, with a bunch of people she met at Burning Man.

Andi doesn't miss her. On the rare occasions Emily calls, Andi's heart flutters with fear, but three years on, she is less scared. Three years on, she is more confident about her position in Cal's life. She might not have given birth to him, but she is his mother. No question.

There was an issue about what he should call them when he started to speak. They settled on Grandi for Andi, and Papa for Ethan. Sophia was Fifi—the closest approximation Cal could get to her name.

At two and a half, when Cal was in preschool for three mornings a week, he started calling Andi "Mommy."

"I'm not Mommy," she'd say, even though she was, and the fact that he was calling her Mommy filled her with a joy she hadn't expected. "I'm Grandi."

"No." He shook his little head. "You're Mommy."

"Baby, that's Mommy." She led him over and showed him a picture of Emily, for she and Ethan had been careful to tell him the truth.

"Emily's my Tummy Mommy," he announced seriously. "Grandi's my mommy."

Later that night, Andi had told Ethan.

"Where does he get that from?" Ethan was stunned. "Tummy Mommy?"

It turned out that Rory, another child in the twos' program, was adopted. He was proudly telling his friends that he had two mommies, and Cal announced that he did, too.

"He's right though," Andi had said. "He does have two mommies. And Emily is, I guess, his Tummy Mommy."

I am his real mother, she thought, but she didn't say it out loud. *I am*

the one who has raised him, and loved him, and gotten up with him in the middle of the night when he can't sleep.

I am the one who gives him a bath, who cradles him on my lap as we rock together. I read him stories and answer his continual questions. I am the one who tucks him in and kisses him good night, who goes in five minutes later because I cannot bear to be away from him, and I am the one who pulls a chair up to the side of his "big boy bed," just to watch him sleep, unable to believe the capacity for love we each hold within us.

"I guess this is the same as adoption," Ethan mused aloud. "Emily isn't here, and we are, we have become, his parents. I would never have suggested he call you Mommy, but if he does, is it really wrong?"

"Let's just see what happens," Andi said, her heart lifting. "It's not something we have to decide categorically."

She was Mommy from that day forward. It cemented her place in his life, and eased her fears about Emily coming home. She couldn't replace *this*. Andi was Mommy now, and that wasn't something that could ever be taken away.

Sophia, at sixteen, is no longer an aunt but a sister, not to mention a willing babysitter; but she is also a teenager, and they are careful not to ask too much from her, to allow her to have a social life.

The four of them are happy in a way Andi never thought possible. Finally, finally, she has the life she has always wanted. Finally, finally, her dreams have all come true.

Thirty-four

. . . .

W here's Pete?" Ethan asks, peering around the kitchen.

"Bringing more wood in for the fire. We figure it's almost Thanksgiving, so a fire's entirely justified. Pete even turned the air on this afternoon so we could get the full fall effect."

"It's the one thing I continue to miss about New York." Andi smiles wryly. "Nothing like the proper seasons, although winter was evil. I do not miss months of filthy grey slush and bone-chilling cold."

Ethan gives her a kiss. "I'm going to go help Pete." He heads out the back door just as the front doorbell rings.

"I thought it was just us?" Andi asks quizzically.

"Nope. I asked the boys, too. Drew called today and I said if they weren't doing anything, they should come."

"Yay! I'll get the door." Andi turns, but the boys have already let themselves in and are standing in the hallway. "I'm still angry with you." She attempts a frown as she approaches.

"We'll still come and visit." Drew puts his arms around Andi and pulls her close. "And you can come stay with us in the city anytime."

"But I don't like the city." Andi pouts, leaning her head against Drew's chest.

"Liar," he croons as Topher comes over and steals her for a hug of his own.

"You better not let anyone awful buy your house," she warns. "You have to let me approve all potential buyers."

"Forget it." Topher shakes his head. "You won't approve anyone because you're waiting for another us, and there's only one of us."

"That's true." Pete finally comes in, kissing Andi and hugging Drew and Topher. "And we have kind of forgiven you, plus you're going to have to find a new trainer, and you're never going to find one as good as me."

"We're not going to have to find a trainer," Topher says. "We're talking about a half-hour commute in the middle of the day. Drew's still going to come out to the gym."

"Great! Can we have lunch afterward?" Andi's face lights up.

"Of course!" Drew says. "You wait. Once we move away you'll probably see me more than you've seen me for years although you're the one who's never around. Every time I look up, you're whisking Cal here there and everywhere. Has he started piano lessons yet?"

"Next week," Andi says.

"Are you serious?" Pete turns to her in horror.

"No, I'm not serious," Andi says. "We're waiting at least another month." And everyone laughs.

In the living room, Pete appears holding a tray with filled champagne flutes.

"What are we celebrating?" Drew asks as Deanna hands out the glasses.

"Well," Deanna stalls until everyone is holding a glass, then walks over to Pete and takes his hand.

"Well," Pete says. "We wanted you to be the first to know that Deanna has agreed to marry me."

"Oh, my God!" Drew jumps up so quickly he knocks the champagne glass over, but he is too busy flinging his arms around Deanna and Pete to care. "I'm so happy! That's such great news!" he says, swiftly joined by everyone in the room.

"It's wonderful!" Andi squeezes Deanna hard. "You absolutely deserve it."

"I'm so happy," Deanna says. "I really didn't think I would ever be this happy again. I didn't think I deserved it, but now." She gives a sweet shrug. "I know I do."

A ndi's in the kitchen, rooting around the fridge for some cans of cranberry-lime seltzer that are, apparently, nestling in the back, when Drew comes in.

"Hey," he says quietly, bending down so his head is next to Andi's. "You okay?"

"Me?" She is confused. "I'm great. Why?" She pulls her head out of the fridge. "Why wouldn't I be?"

Drew drops his voice. "I know you always had a bit of a thing about Pete. I mean, I know it was a while ago, I just wanted to check you were okay with everything."

"Oh you are so sweet." Andi smiles. "But nuts. I never had a thing about Pete. I just thought he was cute for about two seconds when I first met him. I couldn't be happier. Shoo. Go back in the living room. I'll be in in just a second."

She finds the seltzer, and pauses as she cracks the can open. Of *course* she is okay with everything. If anything, she is embarrassed at how she read so much into one night of flirting all those years ago,

and relieved she didn't make a move, or reciprocate other than by privately fantasizing that he was the man for her.

When Deanna started teaching yoga classes at the same gym and announced one day that he had asked her out on a date, Andi was taken aback.

"I know this is stupid"—Deanna had smiled bashfully—"but I feel like I'm betraying you somehow. I mean, I know you're married, and I know you probably aren't interested in Pete, and let's face it, even if you were, you're married!" She attempted to make a joke. "But I still feel weird saying yes."

"Don't be so ridiculous!" Andi commanded, feeling utterly betrayed. This had happened just after Cal was born, when Emily was still at home, when Andi was entertaining fantasies of leaving, of Pete possibly being the man for her. "He's adorable, and you must go."

"But that night," Deanna had pressed. "When we went salsa dancing . . ."

"Oh stop!" Andi said. "It was fun to flirt, that's all. I'm married, Deanna, and you absolutely do not have to ask my permission. Go have fun. He's cute as a button!"

The morning after their date, Andi had to sit on her hands to stop herself from calling. It was all she could think about. At lunchtime, she couldn't resist, then felt sick as Deanna gushed about what a wonderful time they had had, that they were seeing each other again the next night.

She hated herself for hoping it would end. Was furious with herself that she harbored a wish for it to go wrong, and when, after four weeks, Pete told Deanna he thought he might have fallen in love with her, Andi's smile and exclamation of delight felt false and wrong.

Then Emily left, and Andi was far too busy looking after Cal to think about Pete. When Deanna suggested the four of them have dinner, Andi spent far longer than usual doing her makeup, chose a

colorful dress that made her feel beautiful and sexy, wore higher heels than she had worn for years.

"Wow!" Ethan wolf-whistled when he saw her. By that time, they were back in the master bedroom. They were sleeping together without sleeping together. No sex for weeks, but they were back in the same bed, and slowly, slowly, the affection between them was growing.

Andi wanted Deanna to be happy. But she also wanted Pete to look at her and think she was gorgeous. She wanted to show him what he was missing. Even though, yes, she knew she was married if not entirely happily.

They met at Frantoio for dinner. Deanna was in jeans and boots, and Andi felt ridiculous; more so when she saw that Pete clearly had eyes only for Deanna.

Andi had mistakenly thought there was all this chemistry between them, chemistry that was indicating she might have made a terrible mistake in marrying Ethan, but clearly it was all in her imagination. There wasn't a spark of anything. He was nice to her, but no nicer than anyone in the same position would have been.

In many ways, the death of the fantasy enabled Andi to open up to the possibility of Ethan again. Here was a wonderful man who loved her, who was good to her, and who, she increasingly realized, she loved in return.

When Emily left, when Andi saw just how good a man Ethan was, how much he loved Cal, how tenderly he held him, how solicitous and caring he was with Andi, she started to fall in love with him all over again.

Their relationship became far more solid than it had been prior to Cal's arrival. Emily was the knife that had always threatened to splinter their relationship, to drive it apart. Once she had gone, Cal became the glue that bonded them together, a bond that was more secure than Andi would ever have thought possible.

So secure she never gave her brief attraction to Pete another thought, assuming she must have imagined a chemistry between them the night of the salsa dancing, and thanking God she hadn't done anything stupid, hadn't embarrassed herself in any way.

How easy it would have been, back then, when she was so unhappy, to let herself be pulled into an affair, if not with Pete, then with someone else, someone who offered her a glimpse of the greener grass elsewhere.

Thank God for Ethan.

Standing in Deanna's kitchen, Andi pours herself a seltzer, putting the can in the recycling bin, and smiling when she thinks of Drew coming in to check she is okay with Pete and Deanna getting engaged.

She is better than okay. She is thrilled. And it is genuine.

Walking back in, she perches on the arm of the chair next to Ethan, runs a hand through the dark curls at the nape of his neck.

"What?" He turns to her with a grin, interrupting his conversation with Topher. "You look all loving and mushy. What's going on?"

"Just wedding talk. It makes me very glad I married you." She smiles, leaning forward and kissing him softly on the lips. "I love you, mister." She leans back, looking deep into his eyes.

"I love you, missus," he says as Topher sighs and shakes his head.

"You two." There is mock disdain in his voice. "Could you just get a room?"

Thirty-five

. . . .

inally!

Two people at the bar stand up, getting ready to leave; I grab Sally's hand and shove through the crowds, dragging her behind me to get those barstools before one of the other million students here gets them first.

"Got it!" I plant my butt firmly down on the seat, a triumphant grin on my face as I pull the other stool closer for Sally. "Quick," I warn, seeing another girl approach. I shake my head at her, and she scowls and walks away.

"Nice work." The barman grins approvingly, having watched my handy little maneuver. "You ladies deserve a free drink, I think."

Sally grins. "Thanks, Chad, but we would have been even happier if you'd reserved seats for us an hour ago."

"Sally!" He recognizes her and reaches over the bar to give her a warm hug. "No one told me you were coming in, although your wayward brother's here every night. Where the hell is he, anyway?"

Sally looks at her watch. "Twenty minutes late. Less about the wayward, please. I'm fixing him up."

Chad gives me a sympathetic grin as I roll my eyes. "I hate blind dates. Not to mention jocks. I pretty much hate jocks, too, although wayward might be interesting."

"So what do you like?" Chad says with a hint of flirtatious smile.

I'm about to say "barmen," just to fuck with Sally a bit and, okay, to lead Chad on a bit because even though he is totally not my type, it seems I might be his, but Sally intervenes.

"She only thinks she doesn't like jocks because she hasn't met Craig. I mean, really, isn't he the unjockiest jock you've ever met?"

I shake my head. "Even if he's totally unjocky, you know I like artists. And sometimes musicians."

"How about bartenders?" Chad chimes in.

"It has been known." I give him a sly grin.

"Hello? Chad? She's out of bounds." Sally turns back to me. "And by the way, you're twenty-one now," she says, like I'm an old lady. "It's time to grow up. You don't have to date hopeless men anymore." She shoots a look at Chad. "Including bartenders."

I tap her on the arm to get her attention. "They aren't hopeless."

Sally plants a hand on her hip and stares hard at me.

"Okay, okay," I mutter. "Maybe a bit. But it's not like I'm looking for a relationship. Anyway, I'm not moving here for another month."

"Love can conquer any distance," Sally says in a stupid voice, flinging her arms out dramatically, and I burst out laughing.

"You look beautiful, you know," she says seriously when the laughter subsides.

"I do?" I am blown away at this unexpected compliment. I look past Sally, to the mirror behind the bar, and I barely recognize the girl staring back at me. I don't think it's a push to say I look better than I have in years.

My hair is now a natural brown, just past my shoulders. The last vestiges of the blue-black dye was cut off a few months ago, so finally, thank God, I don't like a raccoon anymore.

My skin is lightly tanned thanks to the farmwork I do every year on a small fruit farm just outside Portland. It's freaky how much I love doing the physical work, and more, how much my body has changed as a result. It helps that I'm vegetarian now, too, but every now and then I stroke my arms because I can't believe how lean and sinewy they are.

My whole body is completely different. I'm thin, without ever trying, or even thinking about it. I think back to how I was, what I looked like as a teenager, how I never stopped eating, trying to eat away the pain, and I cannot believe that that girl has grown into this.

That overweight goth girl, filled with shame and anger, desperate to hide her body in layers of drapey black clothes, was someone else. Many lifetimes ago.

Sometimes I think that I cannot believe this is who I have grown up to be, that a miracle must have happened, not just for me to feel beautiful, but, at times like this, to catch glimpses of myself in the mirror and know that I *look* beautiful, too.

When I think back to who I used to be, I want to go back and tell her, the overweight girl who never felt good enough, the child who was always screamed at by her mother, that it's all going to be okay. I want to put my arms around her and whisper that she will find her place in the world, she will be beautiful, and she will be happy.

But you know what? She wouldn't believe me. A lot of the time I still can't believe it myself.

Working on the farm has changed me most of all. I cannot believe how much I love the hard, physical work. I love that at the end of the day I crawl into bed totally exhausted, every muscle aching, but I have achieved something tangible. That huge pile of vegetables now sorted into boxes? I did that! Me!

My body is doing exactly what it was designed to do. I love that my muscles ache, and love that I have become naturally thin. I eat huge amounts, but not of the sugary shit I used to sneak when I was living

at home. Vegetables. Fruit. Salads. Nuts and grains. I am healthy and strong, and never in a million years would I have thought that I, the teenage loser, would turn out like this.

So?" Chad the barman is still waiting while I lose myself temporarily in my head. "A drink?"

In the old days, I would have ordered a double vodka with lots of lime and a splash of soda without even thinking about it, but the farmwork has changed my drinking habits, and waking up with a hangover at five in the morning is really not so fun. Even though I'm not working tomorrow, I've gotten used to waking up feeling good, and I've slowly weaned myself out of the habit of drinking on a regular basis.

And I do not want to end up like my mom. Even though we have grown so much closer since she got sober, even though I'm now seeing the best parts of her, and only the best parts of her when she comes up to see me, I never want to go through what she went through; I never want to treat people the way she did when she was drunk, and let's just say I'm aware that I'm not exactly my best self, as Oprah would say, when I've had a few drinks.

"Can I just have a seltzer with lime?" I say. I await the inevitable comment about why aren't I drinking, and go on, you can't possibly have just seltzer, but Chad just nods.

"Nice drink," he says, as Sally orders a Budweiser.

"Cheers." We toast each other, settling in to wait for Sally's brother and his friends to arrive.

We hear them before we see them. A whoop goes up around the bar, and we turn to see a group of young men stopping every few feet to give those dumbass "man hugs" to pretty much everyone

in there. The guy in front is clearly the ringleader, and my heart sinks as Sally jumps up from her stool and flings her arms around him.

He is so not my type it's not even funny.

"You must be Emily." He turns to me with a pleased-with-himself smile, and I can tell from the slight slur in his voice that they have probably spent the last few hours drinking.

My heart sinks.

I know this is Sally's brother, and I know I have to be nice, but there is no way in hell anything is ever going to happen between us.

"You must be Craig." I plaster a smile on my face and extend a hand to formally shake hands when I pause, convinced I hear someone call my name. I frown, and turn to Sally. "What?"

"What?"

"Did you call me?"

She looks at me as if I'm nuts. "No."

I hear it again.

And I look past the big bulk that is Craig standing in front of me, and behind him, totally freaking me out, with a disbelieving expression on his face, is none other than Michael Flanagan.

Thirty-six

. . . .

My mouth has dropped open in shock.

"Michael?"

Craig looks from Michael back to me, bemused and disappointed. "You two know each other?"

"Michael!" The shock disappears as a feeling of pure euphoria fills my body. I jump down from the stool, feeling like I'm going to just burst with excitement, and without planning this, I swear, without even consciously thinking about what I'm doing, I jump into Michael's arms, wrapping my arms and legs tightly around him as I laugh maniacally, which threatens to turn into tears of joy and relief.

And Michael, God love him, does not freak out but holds me, squeezing me tight, and when he finally, finally, puts me down, the grin on his face is so huge, it looks as if his face might crack, and the two of us just stare at each other with delight before we start totally cracking up.

"I guess the answer's yes." Craig looks at Sally, sounding not exactly pissed but disappointed, I guess.

"Who is he anyway?" I hear Sally ask Craig with a frown. Her voice drops to an almost whisper but I still hear. "He's cute."

"A friend of Jed's," Craig says. "He's just in town for the weekend. Good guy, though. Even if he does seem to have stolen my date."

So here's the thing. For the last three years I have fantasized about seeing Michael in a situation almost exactly like this. I have wanted so badly for Michael to see who I have become, but I wanted it to be a surprise. I wanted to run into him somewhere, and have him not recognize me, and . . .

Okay. I'll admit it. So I wanted Michael to see me without knowing that it's me, and he would fall madly in love with me, or at least think I was the hottest girl he'd ever seen, and I had pictured his face as it slowly dawned on him that this amazing girl is me, and honestly? I never actually thought it would happen in real life!

My fantasies do not come true.

Really. Never ever.

Michael and I keep in touch on Facebook and stuff, but I deliberately had an anonymous profile picture and never put photos up. If other people put up pictures of me, I untagged myself, and that was all because I wanted this moment to happen; I wanted Michael to be shocked. And thrilled at what I now look like.

Okay, so it didn't go quite like it did in my head. Michael was the one who spotted me first, and I can't have changed that much because he recognized me instantly, but that hug! The way he's looking at me now! The way neither of us can stop laughing!

It is almost . . . almost . . . better than I could have imagined it. Michael's here!

I know what you're thinking: *Is that it? Your fantasy is just about Michael seeing you looking amazing and falling in love?*

Well . . . no. I do take it further, of course. I still have a picture

in my head, as clear as day, of his taut, tanned stomach, the line of hair stretching down from his navel, and I still shiver when I think about it. I picture him kissing me, and stroking my hair, and holding me. I tend not to take it much further, though. It's not about the sex, but the feeling of being loved. That's what I think about. I never get as far as sex.

Sometimes they freak me out. I start thinking I must be in love with Michael . . . but no. I can't go there. I *won't* go there. My fantasies are just my fantasies, and admitting to myself that I feel more for him only opens myself up to a whole world of hurt I am just not ready for. No way.

It is enough that we are friends, for now. It is enough that we stay in touch via computer and e-mail even though we haven't seen each other for three years. Three years! I can't believe I haven't been home for three years. Michael often asks if I'm going back to Mill Valley for Christmas, or Thanksgiving, or in the summer, but I haven't been ready.

I needed to stay away because I have this huge fear that the Emily I've become isn't the real Emily, that the old Emily, the unhappy, angry Emily, will take over again if I go back home. I'm terrified that going home means I'll be unhappy again, and I don't want to be that person ever again, so I've had to let the past go and keep looking forward, keep moving ahead.

Michael has turned into this awesome letter-writer. Which I tease him about, frequently, given his one-liners from sleepaway camp all those years ago. His e-mails are long, descriptive, and funny. The laptop my mom gave me when I left died a few months after I left—that's what happens when you're drunk and trying to send e-mails in the bath, and the damn thing falls in—but I've never been able to afford a new one.

I go to the public library to use the computers there. I tend to

write short ones home, saving the long ones, the ones filled with all my thoughts, and plans, and all the stuff I'm going through, for Michael.

My parents e-mail me regularly. My dad sends pictures of Cal from time to time, or pictures of the family, and Cal is in them. It's weird to look at him because I still don't feel anything. I mean, he's cute and all that, but I don't feel like he's mine, don't feel any urge to rush back and be his mother.

Part of me thinks that it might happen, that I'll just wake up one day and be ready. Old enough, mature enough, responsible enough to want to step in and do the right thing.

And I do believe it is the right thing.

Every now and then I think about Michael and what he used to say when we were kids about being adopted: his mom didn't want him enough to keep him, and he spent his whole life knowing he wasn't good enough.

I feel sick that Michael might think that about me, that I was cold enough to give away my own baby even though I know this is different. It's not like I gave Cal away to strangers. He's with family. It is different.

Isn't it?

It's the one thing Michael and I don't talk about in our letters and e-mails. He doesn't bring it up, and neither do I, and I am terrified even to go there in case I am judged by him.

But I have this nagging feeling, always, that I should be looking after Cal. Even though I don't want to, even though I'm not nearly ready even to think about it.

That's why I try to stay in the present, not worry about the future and what might happen. My life is settled. I am happy. I have no desire to upset the apple cart, not when, for the first time in my life, everything seems to be going right.

• • •

S o what the hell are you doing here?" Michael asks, his eyes still
filled with delight and warmth.

"I live here, dumb-ass!" I tease. "Well, just outside the city, remember? More to the point, what the hell are *you* doing here, and
why didn't you let me know you were coming?"

"I forgot you were near here," he says. "I'm visiting my roommate
from college, and I totally forgot you were so close. I thought you
were living on some artists' commune somewhere."

"That was two years ago! Now I have my own apartment on a
farm. For the summer, anyway. They've converted one of the barns
into apartments, and they let the workers stay there for free. God. Do
you remember anything I tell you? Ever?"

"Sorry, Em." He grins. "But you look *amazing*! I know you said
you didn't have dyed hair anymore and you were healthy, but Jesus!
You look awesome!"

"Thank you. And you don't look so bad yourself. You're even more
buff than when I last saw you!" I reach out a hand and place it on his
arm, and he flexes his bicep in response and grins. I'm impressed.

"It's rowing. Keeps me in great shape. So have you been home at
all? How is your family?"

Do you realize that neither of us can stop smiling?

"Everyone's good." I try to wipe the smile off only because I feel so
stupid, but I can't. It's stuck. "I haven't seen them in a long time,
though. I'm kind of thinking I might be ready to pay a visit home. I
feel like it's time, you know?"

Michael nods. "That would be amazing. Wasn't your mom here
recently?"

"Yeah. She comes to stay quite a bit, and she brought Sophia last
spring break, which was awesome. Weirdly I've become really close
with my mom. She's a totally different person since she got sober.

My dad hasn't been, though. I still can't believe I haven't seen my dad in three years." I shrug, attempting to hide the sadness.

"If you wanted your dad to come, why don't you ask him?"

"Because I want it to be just my dad. Not my dad and Andi, and he'd never come by himself."

Michael nods. "Yeah. I see your point." And that, I remember, is exactly what I love about him. He always makes me feel heard. "So maybe you're right. It is time to go home."

"Maybe," I say. "I'll think about it."

"Christ." Michael shakes his head suddenly. "Do you have any idea how great it is to see you?"

And I smile into his eyes, hoping he isn't noticing the hot blush that is staining my cheeks a bright, glaring red.

Michael and I don't stop yammering all evening. It's like the rest of the people in Sundown—friend, stranger, *everyone*—disappear completely, and it's just the two of us, catching up.

At some point, Craig yells that he's got a text that there's a party going on, and we should all head over there. We leave and head to the liquor store, then carry on walking down the street, making our way to the party.

Michael and I finally split up during the walk over, but I know it's only temporary. There is just so damn much to talk about. I feel like I could spend the rest of my life here with Michael, just the two of us, and I would never have to worry about anything else, ever again.

Sally grabs me from behind, linking her arm through mine, squeezing up as I try to help her walk in a straight line—she has definitely had too much to drink, as have most of this group, other than, well . . . me. And Michael. We've been too busy talking, getting high off the fact that we are together, no alcohol necessary.

"He's so cute!" Sally whispers furtively. "What the hell is going on? There I was, about to fix you up with Craig, and suddenly a handsome stranger appears, and you're like, totally engrossed in him for the whole evening. Are you interested?"

"Michael? Oh my GOD no!" I have no idea why I lie, but I want to keep this private. If, in fact, there is anything to keep private. And God, how I hope there is. Please, God, let it all come true.

"You so are interested!" Sally insists. "I can tell."

"No," I bluster. "He's just my oldest friend."

"Riiiight." She squints at me, and, damn it, I burst out laughing. I can't help it.

"So there is so much chemistry between the two of you it's like, freaky."

"Bullshit," I say, but the smile on my face gives it away.

The party is crazy crowded. My heart sinks slightly when we walk in because I can't see Michael. I can't see anything, other than a mass of people crushed together, drinking beers and trying to dance in a small, sweaty apartment, the only dim light coming from a few colored lightbulbs someone has screwed in.

And then Michael is in front of me, and he grabs my hand and pulls me through the crowd, and I swear, I am so instantly calmed it is like I just had an IV hit of Xanax or something, and I have no idea where he is leading me but I really don't care. At this point he could jump out the window, and I'd be right there, jumping with him.

"Trying to find some space!" Michael turns around and yells in my ear, and I just nod as I mutely follow him. Eventually we are on the other side of the room, and it's really not much better. It's like we're trapped in some giant game of sardines.

Michael turns to face me and shakes his head in disbelief.

"This is crazy!" I shout, then Michael's face is right there, and

suddenly he's not smiling anymore, and my heart jumps because—
thank you, God! Thank you, God! Thank you, thank you, thank you!—
there's this huge charge of electricity between us, and his face gets
closer, and I move toward him without even thinking about it, then
his lips are on mine.

It is the sweetest, softest kiss I have ever had. Tentative, nervous,
searching. We pull away for a second, open our eyes, and look at each
other, and I have no idea why but I am so scared; then he smiles, and
I know it's all going to be okay. He kisses me again, and his arms are
around me, and our tongues are intertwined and I am so happy, I
think I may be about to cry.

I have never been kissed like this before. And as crazy as this
sounds, this feels like so much more than a kiss. I can literally taste
the tenderness and love, and when he sighs, "Emily," and pushes my
hair gently off my face, I think I may have started to dissolve.

Thirty-seven

. . . .

My head is pounding before I even open my eyes. When I do, it's slow, and I am completely disoriented. The sheets don't smell like mine, nothing smells like mine, and as my eyes gradually come into focus, I remember where I am.

I turn my head very slowly, just to check, and no, it wasn't a dream.

Michael.

In bed.

With me.

I snuggle under the covers, not nearly ready to get up. I have no idea what will happen: Will Michael be cold? Distant? Will he say it was a terrible mistake, or that he loves me but only as a friend and it will never happen again?

A familiar dread fills my head, but I force it out and instead go over every detail of last night. I press mental rewind, and in slow motion go through the moment I first saw him, wrapping my legs around him, trying to remember everything we talked about, everything he said, through to him kissing me, and then, eventually, to coming back here.

. . .

We left the party, all of us, in the early hours of the morning, and walked back to Jed's apartment. Everyone sat in the living room for a while, watching TV and talking as Michael and I curled up on a sofa at the back of the room, not really joining in, just cuddling up. He kept one arm wrapped tightly around me, and with the other he kept taking strands of my hair and stroking them across his lips, just like he used to do when we were kids in the tree house.

"I can't believe you still do that!" I watched him do it in amazement.

"I can't believe your hair still feels the same. Don't ever dye it again, okay? Promise?"

"Promise." I smiled as he kissed me again, and I wondered if that meant he was thinking of a future, for why else would he care?

"I think we have to call it a night," Michael said to the room in general, after everyone had slumped into a silent fixation on some rerun of the game.

"I'll crash here," Jed slurred, half-turning and raising an arm from his prone position on the other sofa. "You guys take my room."

We mumbled thanks as Michael led me out of the living room and down the hallway to the bedroom.

"Don't be scared," he whispered as he kicked the bedroom door shut with his foot and took my face in his hands, kissing my eyelids, cheeks, nose, then lips. "It's only me." And I don't know how he knew I was scared, and I have no idea, in fact, why I was, but the minute he said that I started to relax, and as he continued kissing me, unbuttoning my shirt, cupping my breasts in his hands, I found myself sighing with pleasure.

I slid my hands under his shirt, feeling the muscles in his back, how strong and solid he felt; then I slid my hands around to the front, tracing my fingers ever so lightly down the line of hair from his navel downward, and it was his turn to gasp.

I had to keep opening my eyes because I wanted to see him. This was *Michael*!

Michael!

This is what I haven't even been able to openly admit to myself I had been wanting to do for years. And I was! And it was so, so, soooo much better than any fantasy I had ever occasionally allowed myself, it wasn't even funny.

He's a man. I sighed to myself as he lowered me to the bed, and when he asked me what I was smiling about, I just shook my head and kissed him, but it was true.

Michael is a man. And maybe . . . maybe . . . he might be my man. Even if only for one night.

I didn't think about very much at all after that. Michael moved down my body, and I panicked slightly—I'm not ready for this; I'm not ready to expose myself so fully—and I tried to pull his head up, but Michael pushed my hands away and whispered that I should just relax and enjoy, and suddenly I was lost in all these new sensations.

I had never felt anything like this before, and then this . . . this . . . wave, this huge wave of pleasure started to build and build, and it was flooding my whole body with pleasure, and I could hear someone moaning over and over and I was wondering who the hell was making all that noise, and I came back to earth, and Jesus H. Christ.

It was me.

Michael's face was then above me, and he was smiling down at me, and he said he was glad I liked that.

And I burst into tears.

Really? *Never* before?" he said, again, later that night, long after we made love, and it was, for the first time in my life, truly making love. "You really never had an orgasm before?"

I shook my head. Embarrassed.

"But . . . you've had a baby!" he said. "You're experienced."

"I know." I had no idea how to explain it myself. "All these years I'd heard people talk about orgasms, and I just hadn't had one. After a while I thought I was just someone who couldn't. And you don't miss what you've never had."

"So was it . . . good?"

"Are you kidding?" I looked at him in disbelief. "Did you hear that crazy lady shouting? It was *amazing*!"

"Amazing awesome? Or amazing good?"

I burst out laughing. "Would you like more compliments? Shall I tell you how wonderful you are all night long?"

"Woudja?" he'd shot back, as eager as a puppy. We both laughed, and when we went to sleep, I was wrapped tightly in his arms.

turn my head.

Michael.

His face pressed into the pillow, mouth slightly open, his golden bare back rising and falling, the comforter pushed down to his waist.

I fight the urge to reach out and touch him. I want to stroke his back, bury my nose in his neck just to smell him, savor every inch of him just in case.

Just in case this is the last opportunity I ever get.

I don't dare.

As long as he's sleeping, I can hope that last night means something. As long as he's sleeping, I can continue with the fantasy that this is just the beginning, because honestly? If this turns out to be a one-night stand, I think my heart might actually break.

I can't stand the not knowing. It would be easier to . . . leave. That way, at least, I won't get hurt, and if Michael wants me, he knows where to find me. It's 8:42 A.M. I can easily tiptoe out, gather my clothes off the floor, get a ride back to the farm without waking him.

In an ideal world you don't want to leave without saying good-bye, but I'd rather do that than have to put up with that awful, uncomfortable dread that comes when the man you have woken up in bed with knows he made a terrible mistake.

I push the covers back slowly, then jump. Michael's hand is clamped around my wrist. Too late. Damn.

"Where are you going?" he mumbles, one eye open.

"I was . . . going to get dressed," I stammer as he pulls me back over to where he is lying.

"Liar," he says. "I know exactly what you were doing. You were trying to sneak out because you thought it was going to be all weird and that we'd feel awkward, so you were leaving before I woke up."

"I wasn' . . ." I start, then, because he pulls me close to him and nuzzles my hair, I turn to face him. "Okay. I was. Sorry."

"S' okay. Pull the covers up. Bet you never knew I was psychic."

"Well, if you're so psychic," I tease, relief flooding my body, "how about telling me what's going to happen between us."

Oh, shit.

Shit!

I cannot believe I just said that. I cannot believe I just said something as pathetically insecure and needy as that. What the fuck am I thinking? As soon as the words are out, I want to inhale them back in because this is not who I want to be with Michael. This is sure to drive him away.

"Oho." He raises an eyebrow, which is pretty impressive given that one eye is still closed. "Let's see. First"—he nips at my upper lip and a shiver goes through me—"I'm going to make sure you have an even better time than last night, then"—he sweeps his tongue over my left ear—"we're going to go out for breakfast. After that I hadn't decided. Maybe a hike?"

"Do I get any say in the matter?" I am so reassured, so filled with a warm bubble of delight, I pretend to be exasperated just to try

to play it a bit cool, although granted, even I know it's a bit late for that.

"No." He pulls me closer to kiss me, then leans his head back. "You just get to gaze at my gorgeous body. Don't pretend you hadn't noticed. Ow!" He grins as I hit him.

"I can only get away with saying that to you," he murmurs after we have kissed long and hard, and before we have taken it further, although his hand is already sliding over my thigh, "because you know I'm really a geek underneath."

"And I can get away with smacking you every time you get too arrogant because you know I'm really an angry goth girl underneath, and if you don't stay in line, there'll be hell to pay."

"Em?" Michael breaks off from kissing me, stroking my hair with a tenderness that makes me want to weep. "You are so beautiful."

I feel like I have fallen into some sappy romantic Kate Hudson movie by mistake. Our day is so perfect, I can't quite believe this is happening to me. We do all the things that Michael has planned: we talk, laugh, cuddle, kiss, and I'm not scared at all anymore because this doesn't feel like something I could lose.

This feels like home.

In the late afternoon, we find a small coffee shop that is filled with the warm smells of fresh-baked cupcakes and cookies. We grab cappuccinos and a lemon bar to split, then settle in at the table by the window.

As Michael puts his head down to sip his coffee, he looks at me thoughtfully over the top of the cup.

"What? Do I have crumbs?" I wipe my mouth instinctively.

"No. It's not that. I was just thinking. You should go home."

I put down the napkin and frown. "Home?" I am confused.

"To California. I told you, I'm taking a year off before graduating,

maybe even two. I've got a job in the city, and I'm going back. You could be with me. It's time you were with your family again. And . . ." He pauses and reaches over to take my hand. "I know this is uncomfortable for you to talk about, because you always avoid the subject, and you never say anything about him in your letters and e-mail, but I have to ask. What about Cal?"

I look at him blankly. I feel a combination of guilt, defensiveness, doubt. No one here knows about Cal. I haven't heard Cal's name spoken by anyone other than my parents, and I know Michael must be sensitive about Cal given how he feels about his own birth mother. I bristle instantly.

"What about Cal?" My voice is defensive. "What are you saying?"

"I'm not saying anything. Relax." He puts his hands up. "I'm asking. Do you see yourself as having a place in his life? I mean, whoever's raising him, you still gave birth to him. You *are* his mother."

"I don't know that I am," I argue. "You wouldn't say *your* mom *wasn't* your mom, would you? She's still your mom even though she didn't give birth to you."

"It's true, she is, but there is also my birth mother."

"Whom you've never met."

"Whom I've never met, but not for want of trying, and you know how hard my life has been, knowing she gave me away."

I shake my head. "You know what, Michael? This is totally different. I didn't give Cal away, he's being raised by family, and I could still be around if I chose."

"That's all I'm asking," he says. "If you could be around, wouldn't you choose to be?"

No, I think. That's precisely the reason why I've stayed away for three years. I haven't wanted to be around. But now . . . things may have changed. I'm starting to think that maybe I should be with my family. Maybe I should get to know Cal. Maybe Michael has a point.

Maybe, even, the three of us could start again? I think about find-

ing a little house, or a garage apartment, making a home. I think about Michael coming home from work, and me working on a farm, and Cal being with my parents during the day but then me picking him up on the way home from work, making dinner for everyone. Being a family.

And it feels weird. And wrong. Maybe it's a thought I have to play with for a while. I don't have to make any decisions. Maybe I just need to think about it and see if I can get used to it.

"I don't know," I say. "It's confusing. I don't, or, I *didn't* . . ." I change the emphasis because I want to please Michael; I want to do the right thing; I want to tell him what he wants to hear, but I'm not sure. Not yet. ". . . want to be a mother, I mean, a full-time mother. I don't think I could handle it. I don't feel old enough. Or ready."

"I'm not saying be a full-time mother." Michael sounds patient in an exasperated kind of way. "Just be in his life. I'm only saying this because I know what it's like, and you can't do that to Cal. It would be better for everyone if he knew you, if you were, at least, around. And, Em? Selfishly?"

I meet his eyes, only for Michael to take a deep breath, suddenly awkward.

"I think . . . you and I . . . I don't know. It feels . . . right. I mean, I know that's nuts, I only just turned twenty-one for God's sake, but . . . I don't want to just walk away from this. I want us to give this a shot. And I'm going to be back in California, and I'd love you to be there, too. And, I don't know, maybe we can build a relationship with Cal together." He swallows, then looks at me.

"Oh, my God," I whisper, shaking my head, then I put down my coffee and throw myself, once again, into his arms.

Thirty-eight
· · · · · · · · · ·

A ndi sits Cal down in a corner of her showroom, empty-
ing out a basket filled with toys to keep him busy. Later
today, a new interior-design client will be in to sign off
on boards Andi has put together for her master bedroom.

The past couple of weeks have been frantic, getting hold of the
right fabric samples, the paint swatches, having the freelance artist
sketch the new bedroom, pinning it all together to look delectable.

If all goes according to plan, the client is likely to give Andi the
whole house. Right now, she doesn't think she needs to do much to
the rest of the house, perhaps re-cover some furniture, she said, buy
some matching pillows. Andi bit her tongue when she first went over,
merely nodding and agreeing that the tables she bought from the
consignment store were, indeed, fabulous, and no, no one would know
they were made from MDF.

The client is wealthy enough to spend significant amounts of
money on the best decorators in the area, but, as she laughingly said
to Andi, "It's just not my thing." Her husband demanded the master
be renovated to give them his and her closets and a bigger bathroom,

and Deanna, who teaches the client yoga, suggested she might want to meet Andi to fully take advantage of the newly renovated room.

She and Andi had hit it off, had met again to leaf through magazines to enable the client to show her what look she liked. Andi is confident she will love what she has put together.

It has been hard only because she picks Cal up from school at one P.M., and he is no longer napping. And she doesn't have a babysitter even though there are times when she desperately needs one, because she is his mother, and endlessly grateful that that is the case, and why would she hand him over to someone else in the afternoons unless she absolutely had to?

Even those times, like now, when she absolutely has to and Sophia is busy, she won't, preferring to try to manage it all, for isn't that what the modern woman does?

She puts the cardboard cup of coffee from Peet's on her desk— thank God for strong coffee, it's the only thing that enables her to make it through the days—and sits behind the computer, scrolling through to check the e-mails.

The e-mails take her off on tangents—she looks at sales going on at various manufacturers to see if there is anything her clients might like, spends some time browsing Visual Comfort for sconces for a house she is doing in Tiburon, and responds to the numerous e-mails from suppliers, Realtors, and clients, both potential and real.

She looks up, finally, to where Cal was sitting, but he is no longer there.

"Cal?" Her voice has an edge of panic. "Cal?"

"Here, Mommy," his little voice says. She turns the corner and finds Cal standing on the bench, both hands flat on the table. He grins in delight as he sees her and lifts his hands to show her.

"Look, Mommy! I painting!"

"Oh, shit!" Andi runs over. It is not paint. It is glue. He has spent the last twenty minutes smearing glue all over the board for her client.

Her beautiful presentation board, the one she has spent hours putting together, is covered in white, viscous glue.

"Cal! Get down! Oh no!" Andi is shouting, fury and despair filling her body. Cal, scared, knowing he's done something wrong, climbs down from the bench.

"No! Don't touch anything. Oh, GOD!" Andi grabs him by the hand and whisks him into the bathroom, where she scrubs his hands. "Why did you do that, Cal? You know you're not allowed to touch Mommy's work."

"I wanted to paint." He shrugs, not understanding why his mother is so mad, nor what, exactly, he did wrong.

Andi dries his hands, then goes back to look at the board. It is ruined.

"I don't believe it," she whispers, fingering the fabric that is now sodden, the wallpaper that is transparent. And she bursts into tears.

This is the mothering that no one had told her about, no one had warned her about. She thought it would all be hearts and flowers, she and a darling child, laughing and loving, and sharing moments of bliss.

No one warned her of the exhaustion. Of the nights when a three-year-old would come into your bedroom, over and over again, complaining of bad dreams, so every sleep pattern would be broken, and you would never feel that you had a decent night's sleep, that you would hit a midafternoon slump when you truly didn't know how you would get through the rest of the day.

No one warned her that she would be ratty and short-tempered because of the tiredness. That as much as she loves her son, there would be times when she would just run out of patience, which was less to do with him and anything he had done—he was, after all, just being a normal three-year-old—and everything to do with her.

No one told her how to deal with balancing motherhood and work—that she would constantly feel guilty, stretched, unable to complete anything with the ease and detail she had brought to her work pre-child.

And yet, she would not change anything. Even now, with her board ruined, with Cal's little face looking strained and sad, she would not change a thing. Ethan has suggested, numerous times, they hire a nanny, but how can she?

Even when she is entirely overwhelmed, she refuses to leave the child-rearing to someone else. She waited too long for this baby, has him only because fate intervened, finally, when she had given up hope entirely, choosing to smile on her.

"Come here, baby." She holds out her arms guiltily as Cal climbs onto her lap and rests his head on her chest.

"I'm sorry I shouted," she says. "I didn't mean to shout at you, I was just angry that something I'd worked on very hard was ruined."

"I sorry, Mommy," he says. "I won't paint again."

"Of course you'll paint again, but you have to ask Mommy first, okay?"

"Okay, Mommy," he says.

"All right, darling, let me just make a phone call. You sit here, and I'll be back in a minute." Andi walks to the phone to call the client and rearrange.

W as she okay?" Ethan is calling between jobs to see if Andi wants him to pick up dinner on the way home tonight.

"She was great. She said it worked better for her anyway, and hopefully by this time next week I can get the samples redelivered."

"How's our darling boy now?"

"Sleeping. He crashed out on the sofa. He still really needs these afternoon naps, but he just refuses to go down."

"What does the pediatrician say?"

"Not to worry about it. That they stop them when they're ready and he's obviously ready." She sighs. "He's not, though. The poor little monkey's exhausted."

"Well. It's good that he's sleeping now. You know"—Ethan hesitates—"you could always call Brooke. She'd take Cal in a heartbeat."

"She's working today, isn't she?" Andi says quickly.

"Right, but maybe she would find someone to cover?"

"Maybe," Andi says, although even as she says it, she knows she would never ask Brooke for help. Her experience of Brooke, at least in those early days when Brooke was drinking, was so unpleasant she still wants as little to do with her as possible.

"She's great with Cal, you know," Ethan reminds her.

"I know," Andi says, but there were too many years of discord for Andi just to forgive and forget.

"Speaking of Brooke, she phoned me earlier. She wants to talk to me about something. I'm going to pop in there in a bit."

"She needs to see you? Why can't you just talk on the phone?" Andi hates herself for sounding whiny.

"I don't know, but she asked me to come over. It's fine. I should be home by seven. Should I pick up something?"

"No, don't worry. I have some of Drew's tomato sauce left. I'll make pasta. That okay?"

"Sounds great. I love you, baby."

"Love you, too." She puts down the phone with a frown. What could Brooke possibly want?

Thirty-nine

. . . .

No one is more surprised at Brooke's life today than Brooke herself. She is three years sober, and grateful every single day. She no longer wakes up feeling foggy and hungover; no longer explodes with rage at her children; no longer finds herself filled with resentment at the world, knowing that everyone is against her.

She no longer itches to get home so she can pour herself a tumblerful of wine to take the edge off her day, loving the numbing feeling that spreads through her body, removing herself from the trials and tribulations of life. And Lord, were there trials and tribulations.

Not so today. Today she wakes up early, bright and alert. The shadows under her eyes have long since disappeared; the whites of her eyes, astonishingly, are white.

She is productive, and happy, and busy. Two and a half years ago she got a job, part-time at a florist's, and today she manages the store.

Newly sober, she had a series of disastrous relationships with men she met in recovery, all against the advice of her sponsor, who

advised her to wait for a year before embarking on any romantic relationships, particularly those with people who were managing their
own sobriety.

Eventually, she listened, and eighteen months later John came into
the store to order flowers for a colleague. He was funny, and charming, and a confirmed bachelor, which suited her fine—she had no
wish to be married again.

They have been together just over a year, and Brooke is happy.
John is her friend and partner, and well versed in recovery, having
been the child of alcoholic parents.

"There are no coincidences." He smiled at her when she was ready
to confess her past, taking it all in his stride, and understanding entirely that three or four times a week she would disappear for up to
two hours to attend meetings.

She now sponsors a number of people, and meets them for breakfast at Toast Cafe before work, helping them do the step work she did
when she first came in, the step work that she continues, knowing
how crucial it is to her recovery.

The best thing of all about being sober is the relationship she has
rediscovered with her daughters. Sophia, always so easy, is a joy to be
with. They have taken up knitting together, joining a mother-
daughter knitting circle on a Wednesday night, where both of them
have unexpectedly formed new and solid friendships.

Emily was not so easy, but then, Emily has never been so easy. For a
while, Brooke heard nothing from Emily, just bits and pieces of news
that Ethan would relay when he showed up to drop off Sophia. He
forwarded Emily's e-mail to Brooke, and Brooke would write to her
regularly, telling Emily all about her new life, her job, funny or interesting things that had happened to her that week.

She was careful to keep it light, not to give Emily a guilt trip, for it
was, after all, Brooke who had given Emily the money to go away. She
never knew if it was the right thing, but, newly sober, was aware that

she was doing the best she could; she was trying, for once, to get it right.

Poor Emily had been so unhappy back then. So filled with anger, how could it possibly be worse for Emily to start a new life free of the baggage that she would only ever associate with being unhappy.

She had a child she didn't want and wasn't prepared to take care of, a stepmother she hated, a father she loved but resented, and a social life that was filled with budding alcoholics, drug addicts, and misfits.

Brooke hoped by sending Emily away, it would force her to grow up, show her what independence meant, help Emily become a whole person.

It took time. Often Emily wouldn't respond at all to Brooke's e-mails, but slowly brief e-mails started coming back. One night, the phone rang; Emily was on the other end.

Brooke had braced herself, expecting Emily's life to have fallen apart, waiting for Emily's request for help, or money, or something. But Emily had not asked for help. Nor money. She had talked about her job, and sharing an apartment, and although she hadn't said much, she had sounded different. Lighter.

Brooke had been different, too. No guilt trips. No criticism. She had listened to Emily, really listened, for perhaps the first time ever, and in doing so had given Emily the space to phone again.

Emily started phoning regularly. When Brooke tentatively said she'd love to see Emily's new apartment, Emily immediately offered an invitation.

Brooke drove up to see her, pulling her battered old Volvo up outside a small redbrick apartment building. The door flung open, and a slim, pretty girl had squealed in delight as she ran over to the car. Each of them had wrapped the other in her arms, and clung on tight.

Brooke never said anything, but she felt she had gotten her daughter back. The real daughter. The one she had until Emily turned thirteen years old.

Emily, who has never discussed this with her mother, knew she had her mother back. The real mother. The one she had never known but had always hoped was there.

They are now close in a way neither of them had ever thought possible. When Brooke goes to stay with Emily, they go shopping and laugh, and Emily tells Brooke about boys she is dating.

Brooke tells Emily a little about Cal, but she is careful. It is the one area Emily is reserved about. Brooke tells her she sees Cal, but does not say she takes him one day a week, every week, or that being a grandmother has become her greatest joy.

Brooke missed out on her daughters' early childhood. Both of them. She was far more consumed with her next drink, counting down the hours until she could have her first, grumpy and irritable until the buzz of the alcohol calmed her down.

Brooke never had the patience to sit and read stories for hours and hours, as she does to Cal, with him curled up on her lap, happy to be read to.

She never had the patience to take the girls to the playground, push them on the swings, or chase them through the trees as they giggled and tried to get away from her, gathering them in her arms and covering them with kisses, as she does to Cal, every week.

Brooke would love to see Cal more than once a week. Occasionally, of late, she has had Cal for sleepovers, but not as often as she would like. She suspects Andi is not keen. She was not, she knows, a good ex-wife to Andi. For years she was bitter and angry, helping fuel the hatred Emily had for Andi.

When Emily complained about Andi, all those years ago, Brooke would agree, pretending that she was validating and supporting Emily, knowing, and enjoying that she was undermining any possibility of Emily's having a good relationship with her stepmother.

If Emily said Andi was controlling, that her dad did whatever Andi wanted, Brooke would say she had noticed the same thing, would

make a point of accusing Ethan of changing in front of Emily in a bid to create an alliance between Emily and herself, an alliance against Andi.

Months into her recovery, months after she joined A.A., became sober, she found herself doing Step 9.

Made direct amends to such people wherever possible, except when to do so would injure them or others.

Brooke went to see a somewhat bemused Andi, explained how jealous she had been, how difficult a time she had had with Ethan finding happiness when she was drowning in a well of pity and despair. She explained and talked for what felt like hours, and then, at the end, she had stood and opened her arms up to Andi for a hug.

Andi felt awkward and embarrassed, and while it was very nice of Brooke to apologize, it was really very unnecessary, and a hug? Really?

As soon as Brooke was safely out the door, Andi picked up the phone to call Ethan and tell him all.

"I know," he'd commiserated. "It's hell. I sat there for four hours last week."

"But . . . it's so weird," Andi had sputtered. "I didn't know what to say, and half of what she was saying I didn't know. I hadn't realized how awful she had been until she sat in my showroom and confessed all."

"So you haven't forgiven her?"

"She didn't ask for my forgiveness. She said she just needed to make amends although God knows what *that* means. She came out with all this stuff, then hugged me, then left. And now I'm stuck with it all."

"I'll take you out to dinner and you can download it all on to me. We'll talk about how nuts she is together. How does that sound?"

"The whole thing is bizarre. Are you *sure* you prefer her sober?" she asks doubtfully.

"Trust me. This is infinitely better than when she was drinking."

. . .

Two and a half years later, Brooke's relationships with everyone are better. Even with Andi. They are not friends, will not perhaps ever be friends, but they are on friendly terms, with a shared grandchild.

That, for starters, is more than either of them could have hoped for.

Ethan rings Brooke's doorbell, and hears her footsteps come to the door. The door opens, and there, in front of him, is a young girl with a huge grin on her face.

He stares as she flings herself at him and wraps her arms around him.

"Daddy!" she yells, as his arms go tightly around her back.

"Emily?" he whispers, lifting her into the air, his voice filled with disbelief.

And joy.

Forty

. . . .

A ndi?" I hover in the doorway as my dad yells excitedly up the stairs. "Andi? Are you home?"

"Just getting Cal out of the bath," I hear her shout down. "You okay?"

"Yes." He turns to me and grins before telling her to come down, and I shuffle awkwardly because I don't think this is going to be the amazing family reunion he thinks it will be. Let's face it, Andi and I have never seen eye to eye.

"You changed the hallway." I look around. "I like it."

"Lots of changes," my dad says, and I follow him through the dining room and into the kitchen, and this bubble of excitement rises in my throat as I see the back of someone's head, sitting on the sofa watching TV.

My dad looks at me and grins, an arm still around my shoulders because he cannot believe I'm here, and it feels so good to be back with my dad, so good to be home, that I get all emotional and have to look away for a second.

"Sophia?" he says, trying to sound normal but he is smiling so hard it makes his voice sound kind of weird.

"Hey, Dad." She lifts a lazy arm, but doesn't turn, and I am shocked at how old she has gotten since the last time she came to stay with me. This is my baby sister, but even from here, even seeing the faintest hint of her profile, I can see how grown-up she is.

"There's someone here to see you."

She turns around—it kind of feels like it's in slow motion—and stares at me, blinking. She frowns slightly, and I know she isn't sure, and I am smiling, and eventually I just can't help it.

"Jesus, Soph." I laugh. "It's me! Your sister? Remember?"

"OhmyGod!!" Sophia leaps over the sofa and grabs me, screaming in delight, and we are both lifting each other up and burbling with happiness. "Emily!!! You look amazing! OHMYGOD! You're home!"

We scoot around the kitchen, hugging and hugging, and my dad is laughing with us. Then he comes over and the three of us have this huge group hug, and the only reason we pull apart is because Andi walks in.

And with her, holding her hand, is a very little person who looks a bit like me.

Forty-one

. . . .

W hat's all the noise?" Andi stands there, an awkward smile on her face because she clearly has no idea who I am. She looks different. Older. And tired. And although I had been kind of dreading seeing her, I have to admit it is nice to see her. She looks familiar, and however much I might not have wanted her, she is, I guess, part of my family, and I feel an unfamiliar burst of warmth and something very close to love toward her.

"Hi." she walks over, extending a hand to introduce herself. "I'm . . ." and she falters, looking at my dad, then at Sophia, then at me, and we are all grinning. And the thing is, I watch the expression on her face go from detached politeness to delight, but before she rearranged her features into delight, I see something else.

Dismay.

Disappointment.

Dread.

And fear.

I see them all. It doesn't last long—she covers up quickly—but I see them, and instantly I feel all those things myself. I feel, just as I felt back when I lived here, unwanted. Suddenly, I don't want to be here anymore, and I have to remind myself that I am a grown-up, and that I no longer live in this house, and none of it matters.

"Emily!" Andi covers it with a laugh and reaches out to give me a hug. I hug her back, then break away, stepping back so I can see Cal. It's pretty amazing. I crouch to see him better, and he definitely looks like me.

"Wow." I shake my head as I look up at my dad with a smile. "He totally has my eyes."

"I know," my dad says. "And your temperament. He's just as stubborn as you were when you were his age."

Cal is half hiding behind Andi's legs, but he's looking at me curiously, and there are the beginnings of a shy smile. I have to admit, he's kind of cute. I feel, while not maternal, proud of myself for producing a kid like this. I did a good job.

"Hi, Cal," I say softly, reaching out toward him, but he scoots back. "I can see you hiding. Do you know who I am?"

Cal says nothing.

And without really thinking about it, I just say, "I'm your mommy." I hadn't thought that I would say that, and I swear, I wasn't trying to upset anyone, I just thought he knew, and I was trying to be honest. It's not like I'm trying to take him away, I just wanted him to know who I am.

It was clearly the wrong thing to say. Cal breaks into an instant wail, and the noise is outrageous and I catch Andi giving my dad one of her classic warning looks.

"No," Cal wails. "You're Emmy. You're my Tummy Mommy. Not real mommy."

I want to appease him, but I don't want to lie, so very gently I say, "No, sweetie, I am your real mommy." And I smile as I say it and

look at my dad for confirmation, but my dad looks really uncomfortable, and I know, suddenly, that I said the wrong thing.

Cal is wailing even more loudly, and I stand up and drop my hands to my side. "I'm really sorry," I mumble. "I wasn't trying to upset him. I didn't know . . ."

"Let's just talk about this later," my dad says, as Andi quickly scoops Cal up and starts to head out of the kitchen.

"I'll just take him up and read him a story," she says, and I feel like I've totally screwed up, as usual, and I really do want to try to make it better.

And I think about Michael, and what he said about feeling abandoned, and how much he wishes his birth mother had had a place in his life, and I decide I'm going to be really mature about this, and I'm going to do the right thing.

For the first time in my life, I'm going to do the right thing.

I lay a hand on Andi's arm and stop her. "I'm really sorry, Andi," I say, and she can tell I mean it. She falters. "I'm not trying to upset him. I should never have said that. I honestly didn't think about it, and I'm not. You're his mother. I just . . . want to get to know him. I just want him to know me as a member of his family. I'd love to read him a story. Can I? Please?"

Forty-two
· · · · · · · · · ·

A ndi hesitates, fighting the urge to grab Cal and run far away, protect him from whatever onslaught must surely be coming, but how can she say no? How can she say no when Emily *is* his birth mother, when she has every right to be with her child.

Or does she?

Andi doesn't know. This is the moment she has dreaded for three years. The prospect of Emily's coming back was so frightening, she never dared think about what she would actually do.

Now Emily stands, looking at her pleadingly, and it is, after all, merely a story. How can she say no? But Cal's arms are wrapped around her neck, and she knows if she tries to turn him over, he will cry more. He is not happy about Emily's being back, this she can tell.

"Come up with us," Andi says eventually. "He needs to get to know you slowly." Emily nods and follows them up the stairs.

· · ·

A ndi is quiet, has been quiet all evening.

"He's amazing," Emily says as they gather around the kitchen table, scraping the chairs back to sit down to dinner. "He's so cute, and he looks like Sophia when she was a baby, don't you think?"

"That's exactly what I've always thought," Ethan says delightedly, his eyes shining with joy at his daughter's being home. "Just like Sophia. Same smile."

"But he's better-looking." Emily grins as Sophia smacks her arm.

Andi looks away. This family togetherness feels fake, as if they are all pretending to be relaxed and happy, all avoiding the elephant in the room. She wants to wrestle the truth out of Emily, find out her intentions, make her swear, on her life and the lives of everyone she cares about, that she will not steal Cal away.

This is, unquestionably, a different Emily from the one that went away. Not just prettier; she is calm, not weighed down by unhappiness. If anything, Emily seems light, happy. She makes jokes easily, is, in short, delightful.

If Andi were not so terrified about losing Cal, she would be thrilled to see the transformation that has taken place in Emily, thrilled she now has a stepdaughter who doesn't seem to burn up with hatred and resentment every time she looks at her stepmother.

"So Andi, tell me about the preschool Cal's in. Does he like it?"

"He loves it," Andi says warily. "It's child-directed, very Montessori-like, and he's become incredibly social. He loves his teachers and his friends, but it's only a morning program. He's with me every afternoon."

"I'd love to spend some time with him tomorrow," Emily says. "Could I pick him up from school?"

Andi looks at Ethan, then down at her plate. What is she supposed to say?

"Why don't you come with me to get him, and let's see how he is," she offers. "He's given up his nap recently, so he can be really tired

and cranky in the afternoons, and I'm not sure he won't freak out if I don't show up to get him, too."

"He'll be fine." Emily dismisses her. "Didn't you see how cute he was upstairs? By the time we were halfway through the second book, he was loving me! Remember? He said, 'Emmy, stay!'" And she laughs in delight at the memory as Andi feels a knife slice through her heart.

"Let's just play it by ear," Andi says.

"No. Let me pick him up and if it all goes wrong, I'll call you," Emily insists.

"I'd rather come with you." Andi's tone is equally determined.

There is a long silence, Andi and Emily staring at each other.

"I *am* his mother," Emily says eventually. Quietly. "He wouldn't be here if it weren't for me." The words Andi was dreading, the words she hoped she would never hear.

"No." Andi takes a deep breath. "You gave birth to him. And then you abandoned him. That doesn't make you his mother. You haven't shown any interest in him for three years. That doesn't make you his mother. He only knows who you are from photographs. You are not the one to get him up in the mornings, to comfort him, to bathe him and put him to bed. You are not the one he wants when he is sick, or sad, or scared. I am his mother, whether I gave birth to him or not. And that's the way he wants it," she finishes, her face flushed, her heart pounding with the effort of keeping her voice calm.

Emily sits up straight, taking a deep breath. "He's three years old. He doesn't know what he wants. I have the right to get to know him. I'm not trying to take him away, I'm not trying to replace you, but I have the right to spend time with him and to have him know me."

There is a long silence as the two women stare at each other, and Ethan closes his eyes. He can't bear it. He can't bear the roller coaster of emotions he has gone through in just a few short hours since Emily came home. The sheer unadulterated joy of having his

elder daughter home switching to the familiar tensions and discord of old.

With so much more, this time, at stake.

He doesn't want to lose Cal any more than Andi does. He will always be the grandfather, but he feels like the father; Cal is the son he never had, the son he always wanted. He recognizes, relates to Andi's fear, because he feels it, too.

Like Andi, he also realizes that Emily has a point. She isn't asking to take Cal away; she's asking to get to know him. Whether that's as a mother figure, or as a sister, he isn't yet sure, but how can he say no without seeming ridiculously unreasonable?

But how can he say yes? He is being asked to choose, to take sides, just like the old days, before Emily ran away: Emily always accusing him of taking Andi's side; Andi accusing him of taking Emily's. He sits, torn. Upset and uncomfortable in a way he hasn't felt for three years.

Ultimately it is Sophia who speaks. Slowly and gently, looking at Emily.

"Em, it's amazing to have you home." She lays a hand on her sister's arm. "I've missed you so much. We've all missed you so much. I know Cal's going to want to spend a ton of time with you, but he's a sensitive kid. He doesn't do well with change, and you have to take it slowly. He's adorable, and wonderful, and funny, and all the things you saw when you read him a story tonight. He's also three years old and not used to change. Why don't you go to school with Andi tomorrow, and let him get used to you in his own time. Trust me, you don't want to be on your own with him when he throws one of his tantrums. He's completely unstoppable, and the only one who can calm him down is Andi. You have your whole life to get to know him, you don't have to rush anything. Are you back for good? Are you going to stay in Mill Valley?"

Everyone starts breathing. Sophia has saved the day. Emily nods,

able to hear the sense in what Sophia is saying, and the mood instantly lifts.

"I really am sorry." Emily turns to Andi. "I guess I was a little overenthusiastic."

"It's okay." Andi offers a tight smile. "I understand."

Emily turns back to Sophia. "I'm not sure what I'm doing. I'm going to be staying with Mom for a bit, but Michael's looking at apartments in the city, and I may end up staying with him some of the time."

"Michael?" Ethan frowns as Emily blushes.

"Yeah. Michael Flanagan."

"Oh, I love Michael Flanagan!" Andi enthuses. "How is he? I didn't know the two of you were still friends."

"We're . . ." and Emily blushes some more.

"No way!" Sophia shrieks. "You're totally dating Michael Flanagan!"

Emily shrugs bashfully. "Kind of."

"Wow." Ethan grins. "He's a good kid, and the two of you were always inseparable."

"Yeah. It's nice. We have a good thing going."

"So Michael's back in Mill Valley, too?"

"For now. He's taking some time out from studying so he's back with his parents but has a job in San Francisco, working in private equity, and he's traveling a lot, but as soon as he spends a bit more time here, he wants a place of his own, and we're talking about being roommates."

"How about you?" Andi says brightly, trying to disguise her dismay at Emily's staying in the area. "Are you going to look for a job, or go to school maybe? What are you thinking?"

Emily shrugs. "I still love the idea of art school, but I haven't gotten a portfolio together, so there's no point in my even applying this year. I'm going to help Mom at the florist's for a while until I know

where Michael and I are going to be, then I'll probably get a job for a few months. I love farmwork, and there are some interesting cooperatives around her. Eventually, though, I'd love to put some money aside and get my photography going again."

"There's a great bachelor of fine arts program at the San Francisco Art Institute," Andi offers.

"I know. It may be one of the places I end up applying to next year."

"You seem like you really have your life together." Ethan smiles at his daughter. "I'm so proud of you. Who would have thought it?"

"Gee, thanks, Dad. Why not just tell me you spent your whole life thinking I was a loser?" Emily's tone is sarcastic.

"I never thought that. But you were . . . troubled . . . for a while. Your teenage years were hard. You just seemed so unhappy."

"I was," she concedes. "But life is good now. And Michael is great."

"Your first love!" sings Sophia as Emily blushes again, unable to hide the joy that lights up her face.

Cal was having a great time with Emily. Andi and Emily picked him up from school and took him to the playground. Emily pushed him on the swings, chased him through the trees, and although he was tired and growing fractious, Emily said she'd love to keep him for the rest of the afternoon. It would give Andi some time off, let her get back to work.

Andi was cautious, but said yes. In truth, she had the whole board to redo; it was always so hard to get anything done properly in the afternoons when Cal was in the office with her, and she could do with the time alone.

This is a blessing, she kept telling herself, driving to the showroom, marveling at how quiet it was without a little person pulling on her sleeve, asking her questions every other minute.

It was the most productive afternoon she had had in years. She worked for three hours solidly, barely looking up from her worktable, disturbed finally by her cell phone ringing.

"Hi, darling," she says to Ethan.

"Hey, love. Can you go get Cal?"

Her heart starts pounding. "What do you mean? Is he okay? What's happened?"

"Nothing bad. I think he's just exhausted, and he's been screaming in the parking lot of CVS for the last forty-five minutes. Emily doesn't know what to do."

"On my way," says Andi, who has already grabbed her coat and is running out the door.

Ethan doesn't want to tell Andi what actually happened, but how can he not. Cal grabbed a handful of candy at the checkout, and when Emily had told him to put it back, he had refused. Emily had said, "Give them to Mommy," prompting Cal to melt down in the mother of all meltdowns.

Emily tried to pick him up to calm him down, but he kicked and screamed, then lay on the floor of CVS, screaming, as Emily stood helplessly, having no idea what to do.

She phoned her mother, who could not leave work, then phoned her father, whose cell phone had no service. Twenty minutes went by, at the end of which Ethan had to listen to a series of ever-more-frantic messages from his daughter, pleading with him just to come and pick up Cal.

Emily had managed to maneuver Cal out to the car, but he refused to stay still, refused to get in the car seat, and she just didn't know what to do. Cal screamed until he was bright red, until Emily was terrified he was going to hurt himself, or throw up.

"Please!" she cried, when her father finally called her back. "Just come and get him, okay? Please!"

. . .

A ndi hears Cal before she sees him. She hears him as soon as she pulls into the parking lot. She finds him lying on the ground, bellowing, his voice hoarse. She ignores Emily, now crying herself, apologizing, to scoop Cal up, hold him close, and soothe him.

"Mommy," he cries, wrapping his arms and legs around her like a limpet as she rubs his hiccuping back. "Mommy."

"I'm here," she whispers. "It's okay. Mommy's here."

"She's not my mommy." He points to Emily as the tears start up again. "You're my mommy. Tell her!"

"Shhhh. She's knows. It's okay. I'm your mommy," Andi croons, rubbing his little back and turning her own back to Emily because she does not want to meet her eye, does not want Emily to see the blame in her own eyes.

She is so busy tending to Cal, she doesn't see Emily backing out of the parking lot, breaking into a run as she reaches the street. She doesn't know that Emily runs blindly, not stopping until she reaches her mother's front door. She doesn't see Emily's tears when she finally reaches the safety of her bedroom.

She doesn't care. She only cares that Cal is fine.

W e have to talk to her," Andi says later that evening, when she and Ethan are clearing up after dinner. "You have to talk to her. Do you understand what happened? It wasn't about the candy although that might have been part of it, but Cal started saying he wanted Mommy, and your daughter told him she was his mommy.

"Do you understand? Do you get why he freaked out? The poor baby is terrified. This stranger appears, and he thinks she's trying to take him away, and he is paralyzed with fear. All evening he kept

asking if I was his mommy and making me promise I was never going to leave him.

"This is not acceptable, Ethan. We can't have this. He's three years old, and he can't have his life disrupted like this. It isn't fair to him. Jesus. It isn't fair to any of us. She can't just come back and expect to step in like this. You have to talk to her."

"She knows, okay?" Ethan sighs. "You think she doesn't know how she screwed up? She knows she shouldn't have said it."

"How do you know she said it?"

"She told me. And she was embarrassed. She had no idea he would freak out like that, and she swore blind she wasn't trying to stir things up, she was just, as she said, telling him the truth."

"But that's the point." Andi's voice rises to a shout. "It isn't the truth. It isn't *his* truth. We are the only parents he has ever known. He doesn't want another mother. He has one. He doesn't want Emily. She doesn't have the right to come back and step into his life as his mother. I am his mother, for God's sake. Don't you get it? I am his mother. Not Emily."

Ethan closes his eyes, and when he speaks, there is fear in his voice. "But he is hers. What if she does want to be his mother. What if she wants him? What then?"

"She can't have him," Andi snaps. "He doesn't want her, it's as simple as that. I think," Andi continues, taking a deep breath, "I think we ought to go and see a lawyer."

Forty-three

. . . .

The next morning, the topic is still weighing heavily on both of them. They are careful with each other, knowing that they are not able to reach an agreement. Andi is terrified, but Ethan refuses to believe the worst-case scenario will happen. If it does, if Emily should want Cal, then, he says, and *only* then, he will see a lawyer.

"She isn't ready to be a mother," Ethan says. "Whether she realizes it or not, she doesn't have a clue. She may be romanticizing it, but it just isn't going to happen. Emily is still Emily, just three years older. Look at what happened yesterday—he threw a tantrum and Emily bailed.

"I promise you"—he reaches out and puts his arms around Andi, attempting to soothe her—"Emily is not going to want Cal. Not full-time. I almost think we should go away for a week and leave her with him. Let her have a taste of what it's really like, being a parent, having no sleep and no life."

Andi had spent hours last night explaining why she wanted to a see a lawyer. Not to set anything in motion, she lied, but to see where

they stood. To see what the law would be likely to do, whether Emily had a right, after abandoning her child, to remove him from the only home, the only parents, he has ever known.

Not to mention, she had pointed out, Emily's prior history with alcohol and drugs.

"It is a miracle," she had shouted at the height of their emotional discussion last night, "that Cal is so normal. Do you get that? Emily drank her way through her pregnancy, and I still spend every day worried that some hidden sign of fetal alcohol syndrome will show itself. What do you think a judge would think about that, huh? What would he have to say about that?"

Ethan had shaken his head. "That's precisely why we don't need to see a lawyer. I don't want to drag up all the past. I don't want to do that to us, or to Emily. Look at how amped out you're getting, and it hasn't even happened. All Emily has done is ask to spend time with Cal, get to know him. You're freaking out unnecessarily. Please. Just stop. We will cross whatever bridge we have to when we get there, but not yet, okay? Please stop worrying about a future that may never happen."

"What about her telling him she's his mother?" Andi pushed. "That's what freaked him out so much. She can't do that. It's not right."

"I agree," Ethan said. "I'm going to talk to her about that today. It's not right." Those words, more than any other, consoled Andi. Temporarily. Those words showed her he supported her.

For a minute, she was able to breathe.

Andi is still worrying. She lay in bed all night worrying about it, and this morning, even as Ethan puts his arms around her, she is still worrying about it.

"You know she wants to get him from school again," Andi says.

"But that's great!" Ethan says. "Look, Sophia gets him all the time, and you're grateful for the break. Look at this as a welcome break. You know it's not going to last. This is the thrill of the new. If Emily does stick around, and I'm not even sure about that, she'll get bored pretty damn quickly. Let her take him. You were telling me just the other day about how busy you are. Use it as an opportunity to get things done."

"You're right," Andi reluctantly agrees. "You're right. I'll try and relax. I'm sorry."

"It's okay. And it's all going to be fine. You know that, right?"

"I do." She smiles, this time wrapping her own arms around him. "Thank you for always calming me down and making me see that life isn't ever as scary as I think it's going to be."

Forty-four

. . . .

Now that I'm back, I cannot believe I stayed away for so long. It's like Mill Valley was the huge, terrifying root of all my unhappiness, but either it has changed dramatically in the last three years, or I have.

And something tells me it's me.

I used to think it was this suburban hellhole filled with Stepford mothers and perfect little Californian blond cheerleader types, and that I was hated by everyone because I was different. And maybe, back then, I was different, but I don't feel different anymore, and now I fit in, and I see that it is filled with all different types of people, and the thing is, everyone's so nice!

I have run into a ton of old teachers, and neighbors, and people I went to school with. Every time I go out, it seems I run into someone, and instead of avoiding me like they used to, or *me* avoiding *them*, everyone seems genuinely happy to see me. Even the dreaded popular girls, who are still as cliquey as ever, even after all these years.

We were at Woody's the other day, and they walked in, all these girls I hadn't seen in years, and instantly swarmed Michael. I was at the

counter waiting for our ice cream, so they didn't see me, and when they asked what Michael was up to, he told them he was dating me. I turned then to see confusion on their faces, and that's when I stepped forward, and they all looked at me like, well if you're dating that freak, Emily, who's the hot chick you're with now, and then I said hi, and the expressions on their faces when they realized that I was Emily were priceless!

They kept saying they couldn't get over how beautiful I've become, and how thin I am. It made me feel good, but it also made me feel sad because they are still as superficial as they ever were. They invited me to some girls' night out, and I said sure, to text me, but I was just being polite. I really have no interest.

I'm loving being around my family, though. My dad, and Sophia. Cal is very cute, and Michael is thrilled every time I tell him I spent time with Cal, so everyone seems to be happy, except for Andi.

But I get it. I get that she's terrified. I want to tell her not to worry. I have tried telling her not to worry, but I honestly don't know whether she should be worried or not.

Right now, I like being around Cal, but I am still so far from ever thinking I would want more than this.

Michael confuses things for me. I see how happy it makes him to know that Cal and I are together, and I wonder what I would say if Michael said, oh I don't know, something like he wanted to marry me, and he and I would raise Cal together.

I honestly don't know what I'd say because I so badly want to make him happy, and I so badly want to want the things that he wants. I'm just not sure that I do. Not in this case, anyway.

And so most of the time I don't think Andi has anything to worry about, but some of the time I think she might. I just don't know yet. This all takes time to figure out. In the meantime, I have this incredible thing with Michael.

He's supposed to be living at home with his parents while looking

for an apartment in the city; meanwhile, he's spending every night with me at my mom's. She doesn't mind—are you kidding? She *loves* him. She practically melts every time he walks in the door, and she's away this week, so it's just the two of us, pretending to be an old married couple in a house of our own.

Speaking of love, I haven't said "I love you" to him yet, but I know I do, and sometimes I have to practically squeeze my mouth shut so the words don't slip out, because I will not be the one to say it first.

I know he does love me, though, even though he hasn't said it yet. I see it in the way he looks at me, the way he treats me, the way he calls me up, for no reason, when he's at work, just to hear my voice.

And still I can't believe that he is mine; that life has turned out this good for me.

"You could have anyone!" I tease him sometimes.

"I don't want anyone," he says. "I want you."

"That, you have," I snuggle into him and cover him with kisses until he growls in fake annoyance and throws me off.

I'm in that half-awake, half-asleep phase, kind of listening to Michael pad around the bedroom getting ready for work, and waking up properly only when he leans down to kiss me good-bye.

"Hey, love"—he smiles down at me—"I'll see you later, okay?"

"You should have woken me." I stretch. "I would have made you breakfast."

"Oh, man!" He groans, patting his stomach. "You already made me dinner last night. What are you trying to do, fatten me up?"

"No. I just like cooking for you."

"When we find an apartment we like, you'll be able to cook for me every night."

"Are you kidding?" I give him a look. "You'll be taking me out for

dinner every night. I expect nothing but the best from my private equity magnate boyfriend, you know."

"Yeah, I wish. I'm just a grunt right now, but they're telling me they think I have the potential for big things. Hey . . . I like the sound of us living together," Michael says.

"I thought we were just going to be roommates?" I say slowly, because let me tell you, there is a very big difference between roommates and living together, and Michael has been very careful to describe it as roommates. Until now.

"Well. Whatever. I like that I would wake up with you every day. It's a total pain in the ass being back at home. Thank God your mom's cool with me sleeping over."

"And thank God she's away for a couple of nights. Kitchen table? Wild!" I purr at him to make him laugh. "Tonight we should try the living-room floor in front of the fire."

"It's a deal." Michael bends down to kiss me again before standing up. "What are you doing today? Working?"

"Yeah. Florist's until lunchtime, then I'm going to get Cal from school."

"Wow." Michael's face lights up. "That's every day this week. That's so cool! You're really getting to know each other. He's a great kid. I really enjoyed taking him to the playground on the weekend. He's funny."

"He is a great kid," I say slowly before sighing. "I kind of feel a little taken advantage of, though. I mean, in the beginning, Andi didn't even want me to read him a story, and now she expects me to pick him up every day and watch him until she gets home. I feel like an unpaid babysitter."

"Emily!" Michael looks horrified. "How can you say that? You're saying you resent him? You've only just come back in his life. Do you realize how selfish that is?"

I flush a deep red. That I have just been honest about my true

feelings, and that Michael's reaction is to call me selfish, feels awful. I am instantly ashamed and wish I hadn't said anything. Seeing Michael look at me like that, the disappointment in his eyes, terrifies me. I backtrack, quickly.

"I don't resent him. I didn't mean that at all," I bluster. "I totally love being with Cal. It's just, I guess, that I feel it's expected of me now, and that's what I don't like."

"But that's great," Michael says gently. "They *should* expect it. You *should* be with him more. Maybe one day, we'll even have him live with us."

I sit up in bed, shocked. It's not like I haven't thought about it myself, but every time I think about it, I push it aside because it feels so weird. But I guess I knew Michael would be the one to bring it up. I just didn't know how I'd react.

"You want that?" I ask doubtfully, because I'm really not sure I do.

Michael shrugs. "Honestly? I haven't thought about it much. I just feel so strongly that you should have a place in his life, and if it ends up with us being, you know, the real deal, marriage and everything, then maybe it is something we should be thinking about."

I look at him openmouthed. The real deal! The M word! And because I don't know what to say, I pull him down for a proper kiss good-bye.

"You," I say, when I finally let him go, "are truly the greatest guy I have ever known."

"That's how I feel about you," he says.

I fake-frown. "That I'm the greatest guy you've ever known? Great. Thanks a lot."

"No. You know what I mean. You are the greatest girl. Truly. You're amazing. I can't believe I've known you my entire life, and you're my best friend, and now you're the woman I love."

And I think my heart stops.

Did he say it? Does that mean . . . is it the same as saying "I love you"? I can't breathe, but I don't want to spoil the moment, and my ears are buzzing and I wish there were a rewind button so I could check he absolutely, positively did say it.

"I love you." He smiles gently down at me as my heart starts beating again, and I am able to breathe.

"I love you, too."

I try to go back to sleep after that, but I am too damned awake. Can you blame me? I lie under the covers for about half an hour, going over the words again, reliving that exact moment when he told me he loves me, and eventually it's clear I am not going back to sleep, so I fling the covers back and climb out of bed.

Padding down to the kitchen in bare feet, I fill the kettle and put it on the stove for tea, turning to take a croissant out of the bread bin. I get butter and homemade jelly and arrange them on the table, going outside to grab the paper at the end of the drive and sitting down at the table with a hot cup of tea and breakfast.

I feel like a grown-up. I said good-bye to the man I love, and now I am savoring breakfast while reading the paper although I'm not actually reading because my mind is still whirring, and I cannot concentrate on anything, so I'm just flicking the pages and feeling like . . . a woman who is loved. A wife. Setting a place for herself on the kitchen table, going outside in her robe to grab the paper from the ground underneath the mailbox.

When my mom's here, I still feel, at times, like a little girl. Not that she ever treats me like that, but this is the house I've lived in for years, this is where I was a little girl, so of course I'm going to feel like that.

With my mom away, and Michael here, it feels like mine, and I can

allow myself to pretend that this is our first home, this is our life: me kissing Michael good-bye in the morning before getting ready for work myself, creating a beautiful home for the two of us.

I chew thoughtfully on the croissant as I try to imagine what it would be like if Cal lived here, too. If I can find a way for it to work in my head, then I could see how it would work in real life.

What kind of a person must I be if I really don't have any maternal instincts? Surely they have to be in there somewhere. Don't they? I mean, surely if I spend a ton more time with him, really get to know him, my maternal instincts will kick in, no? Look how everyone adores him. Even my mom melts into a puddle of love at the very mention of his name.

I want this all to work. I want to know what it's like to be a mother, and I want things to work with Michael. I guess it's just going to take time, and let's face it, no one's going anywhere.

Especially now that we're in love! And it's official!

I grab my phone and quickly text Sally in Boston, telling her the good news, before skipping upstairs to jump in the shower and start my day.

Forty-five

. . . .

I t is a slow day at the florist's. Manuel and Pablo are busy in the back room, taking deliveries of wholesale flowers, making arrangements that are due to go out today, and I'm totally daydreaming at the register about this being the real deal, and how we're going to spend the rest of our lives, and okay, okay, I even think a little bit about what kind of wedding we're going to have, when my cell phone rings.

Michael.

"Em? What are you doing right now?" He sounds excited.

"I'm at work, thinking about you." I smile. "Why?"

"I'm standing in the most incredible apartment. You know Patrick? The guy I work with who's been guiding me with the takeover of the jewelry company in the UK? They're transferring him to London to run it properly, and he has to find someone to take over the lease of his apartment. He's got the whole first floor in an old Victorian house in Bernal Heights, and he just gave me the keys and told me to run over and take a look because he has to find someone quick.

"Em! It's incredible. It's really bright, with high ceilings, and a yard! We could get a dog!"

"It sounds amazing!" Michael's enthusiasm is contagious.

"So here's the thing. He has another three people coming to see it this afternoon, and he says whoever wants it first, gets it. Emily, it's perfect. You have to come and see it."

"What? Now?"

"Yes! You have to get in here now. How soon can you get here? If you leave now there shouldn't be any traffic. You could be here in half an hour. I'm telling you, Em, it's a great price, and we are not going to find anything like this again. He's giving us a break on the price, but you have to come now."

If Michael's voice weren't so urgent, I'd probably just say I couldn't because I did promise my mom I'd work every day, but . . . this is important. This is our first apartment, and it sounds incredible, and I think she'd understand. And frankly, my mom runs out all the time, leaving Manuel and Pablo here by themselves.

I don't see it as being a big problem. Manuel and Pablo are great, and I know they won't mind.

"Okay!" I say. "Manuel and Pablo can run things until Julia gets here to take over my shift. I'll leave now."

It's only as I'm crossing the Golden Gate Bridge that I remember Cal.

"Oh, shit!" I scream, feeling the color drain from my face as I realize I am supposed to pick him up in fifteen minutes. There's no way. Even if I turn around now, I'll never make it back in time. I'm completely stuck, and I realize I have to get someone else to pick him up.

I pick up my cell and scroll through, looking for Andi's number, trying to keep one eye on the road. Andi will probably go apeshit, but I truly forgot, and it's not like I don't feel bad. I feel horrible. If I could turn around right now and get to Cal in time, I would, but it's too late.

Of course Andi doesn't pick up. I leave a message, but now I've

got, like, twelve minutes, and I have to do something. I try my dad, but his cell is switched off, as usual, and I'm starting to feel sick and I'm wondering what the hell I should do.

And then a flash of inspiration hits. Yes!

Sophia.

can't," Sophia says. "I have classes all afternoon."

"Sophia, you have to," I plead. "I feel really bad, and I totally screwed up, okay? You have to skip your classes today and get there. Please, Sophia. Please."

"But, Emily, I have a huge test this afternoon. I can't. If there were any way for me to miss today I would, but I can't miss this. I'm sorry. You'll have to find someone else."

"There isn't anyone else." I finally lose it because I'm so damned frustrated, and I don't mean to shout, but I do.

"I'll phone Andi," Sophia says.

"I already did. Thanks for all the help," I know I'm being sarcastic, but I'm genuinely shocked that Sophia isn't stepping up to help. "I'll figure it out by myself."

Forty-six

. . . .

Cal is the last one in the class. He has been the last one in the class for the past couple of weeks, since Emily has been picking him up, but he doesn't mind. He quite likes it. His teacher makes a big fuss of him, giving him a special snack from her secret stash in the cupboard above the sink. Today it was Rice Krispies treats, which are his absolute favorites.

Today it's a really long time. His teacher keeps looking at the clock and picking up the phone, trying to reach his parents, but no one is answering. He is beginning to get a little scared.

There is a soft knock on the door frame. Mrs. Gundell, Cal's teacher, looks up with relief, only to see a man she doesn't recognize shuffling awkwardly in the doorway.

"I here to get Cal," he says as the teacher and Cal both frown at him, Cal trying to think how he knows him.

"Hello, Cal." A lovely, if toothless, smile spreads over his face. "I am Manuel. Emily's friend? From the flower store? Emily, she send me to pick up Cal," he says.

"Oh." Mrs. Gundell frowns. "I don't have a note. We have a policy

of not releasing children to anyone other than regular parents unless there is a note."

Manuel looks worried. The teacher looks worried. Cal starts to cry.

"Look." Manuel scooches over and drops to one knee. "I brought you flower, man." He extends a pot with a plastic flower, pressing a button on the base, which starts music playing, as the flower bobs and weaves.

Cal instantly stops crying and smiles, bewitched, stretching out a hand to touch the dancing flower.

Manuel looks up at the teacher. "I give you Emily's cell? You talk to her?"

She sighs loudly. "This isn't what I'd normally do, but . . ." She shakes her head. She was supposed to be home five minutes ago. "Okay," she finally mutters reluctantly. "Let me call her."

She flicks through her notebook, looking for contact numbers before picking up the phone and dialing.

"Emily? This is Lisa Gundell. Cal's teacher? I have someone here saying he is picking up Cal, but I have no note."

"Oh, my God, I'm so sorry," Emily gushes. "I totally forgot I was supposed to pick him up and I only realized when I was already on the Golden Gate Bridge. I tried to get hold of Andi and my dad, but I couldn't get anyone, then my sister has a test, so she couldn't miss school, and Manuel is the only person I could think of. I am so sorry, but Manuel's great. He works with my mom at the florist's. Cal will be fine, and I'm coming straight back out."

"So it's fine to release him to the care of . . . Manuel?"

"Totally fine."

"Okay." She sighs. "But this cannot happen again. Next time we need a note in the morning."

"It won't happen again." Emily almost collapses with relief. "I'm really sorry."

• • •

Two minutes later, Cal is climbing into a beat-up old red Chevrolet Silverado pickup truck. There are no car seats, and the seat belts are broken. Manuel drives very slowly and carefully back to the flower shop, where Cal happily immerses himself in making sculptures out of florist's foam, eating chocolate, and endlessly pressing the button that makes the dancing flower dance.

Forty-seven

. . . .

Michael was right. This is totally worth it. The apartment is like something out of a magazine, and I cannot believe that after living in farm outbuildings for the past three years, I might actually be living someplace like this.

Michael and I walk slowly from room to room, and I cannot wipe the smile off my face.

We start with the master bedroom at the front of the house. High ceilings, a large bay window onto the street, surrounded by the original wood-paneled shutters. A queen-sized bed with a twin sofa at the foot of the bed, and an antique desk in the bay, with a sleek crystal lamp.

There are large walk-in closets on either side of the fireplace, and off to one side, a small en suite bathroom with a shower stall, sink, and toilet. A large hallway, with floorboards covered with old Dhurrie rugs, leads down to the rest of the house. A tiny spare room with a large window overlooking the garden. I walk over to the bookshelves and stand dreamily for a minute, running my fingers over the spines of the books, as Michael comes up behind me.

"You know this room could be perfect for Cal," he whispers, and I freeze.

"Michael, we haven't even talked about that properly. I don't know where I am with that."

"I know, I know," he says. "I don't necessarily mean permanently. I mean when he comes for sleepovers."

If he comes for sleepovers, I think. But I don't say anything. It is slowly beginning to dawn on me that Michael, bless his heart, is something of a romantic. I know he feels strongly about me having a place in Cal's life, but I'm also starting to realize that he has this romantic notion of having an instant family, and it isn't the slightest bit grounded in reality.

I'm kind of stunned that I can see this so clearly, that I'm mature enough to realize this, and I know we're going to have to talk about it at some point. It's the same fantasy of how he would be a happier person, or more secure, if he hadn't been adopted. I wasn't adopted, I always used to point out, and I'm even more fucked up than him.

Part of me loves that he has a romantic fantasy about how our life is. But I worry that his fantasy inevitably involves Cal.

We walk out and on through the rest of the apartment.

The kitchen, next to the living room, is a bright square room with gleaming stainless counters and subway-tile backsplash.

"Patrick put a new kitchen in last year." Michael, doing the sales pitch, tells me as I sigh with pleasure over the glass-fronted Liebherr fridge.

"We'll have to keep a tidy fridge." I gesture at the huge bowl of perfect white eggs at the front of the fridge.

"I already checked it out." Michael comes up behind me and reaches over, moving the bowl aside, revealing a mess of jars, cartons, and ancient Tupperware.

"Phew! Because that fridge was going to be a dealbreaker. I was worried it was all too much for me to keep up with."

"It's not too much, is it?" Michael asks. "It's perfect, right?"

"Sssh." I hold a finger to my lips. "Don't say anything until I've seen the whole thing."

We walk, finally, into the light-filled living room with French doors onto a small, pretty, enclosed yard.

"Did you see the floors?" Michael can't help himself, he has to start pointing out the features. "They're the original wide-planked oak. Patrick said he sanded them down himself. And that fireplace? It works. And isn't the shower awesome?"

"It's all awesome." And finally I turn to him. "It's perfect. I love it." I spin around, hugging myself as I dance around the room like a schoolgirl. I cannot believe that the first apartment we stumbled upon is as perfect, and as perfect for us, as this.

Thank you, God. Thank you, Fate. Thank you, whatever angels are smiling down upon us.

"Here's the best thing." Michael sinks down on the huge white sofa. "See this furniture? He's leaving it all. He wants to rent it furnished, so we don't have to buy a single thing."

"It's amazing." I shake my head, then frown suddenly. "Are you sure we can afford it? I mean, you? I'm going to try to earn money, but I don't even have a proper job, and I have no idea how much I'm going to . . ."

"Stop," he says gently. "Relax. With the bonus I've been promised thanks to this UK deal, yes. We can definitely afford it. I can afford it on my own. We're fine."

"Yes. Yes! Yes!" I collapse on the sofa next to Michael, lean my head back, and shout up at the ceiling, "I love it! This is it! Our first home!"

Michael checks his watch, then looks at me with a sly grin. "I think perhaps our new home needs christening, don't you? It will bring us luck."

"C'mere, big boy," I growl, taking hold of his waistband and pulling him close. "We can christen it as much as you like."

Forty-eight

. . . .

At four o'clock, Andi's alarm on her cell phone goes off.

"Oh, gosh. I'm so sorry," she says to Diana, one of her clients, whose house goes on the market next month. Andi has just been rearranging the furniture in the living room to show off the rug she picked out that was delivered this morning. "I have to go and get my son."

"Don't worry." Diana cannot tear her eyes away from her new, improved living room. "And thank you. Seriously. I cannot believe how perfect the rug is and how you've transformed the living room. Our Realtor will be amazed."

"I'm so glad you like it," Andi says, giving her a quick hug. "Let's talk next week about the new house, okay?"

"Perfect." Diana walks her to the front door.

On the drive home Andi rings the house to let Emily know she's on the way. She has been clear to Emily: Cal needs to be home by four, and Andi will be back at four-fifteen to take over.

There's no response at the house, which is odd. Andi rings Emily's cell, listening to it ring. And ring. She tries repeatedly, punching out the number with more aggression each time, a sliver of fear wedging itself into her being and growing every time the phone is not answered.

Where are they? Why isn't Emily picking up the phone? Images of car accidents fill her head. Cal falling off a high piece of equipment at the playground. A vicious pit bull escaping its chain link fence and savaging . . .

Stop! She tells herself. But the fear is growing, and with it, her ghoulish fantasies.

Where are they?

She calls Ethan, praying he's somewhere with service, practically crying with relief when he picks up.

"Don't worry." He is calm. "Emily's probably upstairs with him and can't hear the phone."

"I've called the house phone and her cell. A million times. She'd hear one of them."

"Maybe she left the phone in her purse, and they're in the yard. Relax, Andi. There's going to be a perfectly reasonable explanation. Stop thinking it's the worst thing possible; you'll just get yourself into a mess. Please, Andi. Everything's going to be fine. Call me when you're home, okay? And take some deep breaths."

"Okay," Andi says, but when she turns the corner and sees their house, there are no cars in the driveway. Emily and Cal are not home.

Where the hell are they?

She runs into the house, her heart pounding, feeling sick with fear. Grabbing the phone, she punches in Sophia's number.

"Hey, Andi. What's up?"

Andi forces her voice to sound normal. "Hi, Soph. I don't know where Emily and Cal are. Do you know?"

There is a pause. "Emily said she couldn't get him today," Sophia says slowly. "She called to see if I could, but I had that huge test."

"What?" roars Andi. "What do you mean she couldn't get him?"

"She said she had to go meet Michael in the city to see an apartment."

"Oh, my God," Andi shrieks. "Where is he? Where is he? Where the hell is my baby?"

"Call the school," Sophia has a calmness and maturity that, under different circumstances, would surprise them both. "Then call me back. I'm on my way home."

A s Sophia drives home, she is unaware that she is grinding her teeth and shaking her head. All she can think about is Emily, how she hasn't changed, and how furious Sophia is with her right now.

Sophia loves her sister. Emily is, has always been, the one Sophia looks up to. Sophia may act like the older sister, the mature one, the one who knows what to do; but she has, nevertheless, always looked up to Emily, has spent her life longing for Emily to be the big sister she always hoped she would be.

Emily's return was a dream come true. This time, Sophia thought she might stay. This time, Sophia thought they might truly be able to be a happy family, all together, after all. Instead of the constant screaming and backbiting, the flouncing around and slamming of doors that Sophia remembers from when Emily was last at home, there has been calm.

It helps that Emily is not living in the house, but Emily has been so different, so . . . happy.

But today, as Sophia grinds her teeth, thinking incessantly about her sister, she realizes that despite the outward appearances, despite the natural hair, and the hippie clothes, and the calm demeanor, Emily hasn't changed a bit.

She is still the self-obsessed, irresponsible, immature girl she always was. And Sophia cannot believe she allowed herself to think that Emily had truly changed, cannot believe that she, Sophia, had been that dumb.

Mrs. Gundell? I'm sorry, but she's left for the day. Can I take a message?"

"No!" Andi shouts. "My son is missing! I have no idea who picked him up from school. I need to find him! I have to speak to her!" Her voice is rising to a scream.

"Don't worry," the school receptionist says calmly. "Let me check the dismissal notes for today." There is a silence, Andi hearing only the rustling of papers.

"That's odd. I don't have anything," the receptionist says. "Let me check again."

"Please." Andi is now crying. "Just give me her number."

"Let me get Mrs. Gundell on the other line," the receptionist says. "We'll get to the bottom of this."

Ten minutes later, Andi screeches to a stop outside the florist's shop. Banging the door open, she runs in to find an empty store. There is tinny music coming from the back room. Panicking, she runs frantically through to where the music is coming from, to find, sitting on a high stool against a counter, his mouth smeared with chocolate, his fingers covered with green foam, Cal.

"Mommy!" He smiles when he sees her. "Look what I made! Train!"

"Oh, Cal." Andi tries to smile as she scoops him up and squeezes him tight, but she bursts into tears.

"Why you crying, Mommy?" Cal examines her face as he pats her on the back to comfort her, in much the same way she does to him.

"Because I'm so happy I found you," she says. "I was so scared. I didn't know where you were."

"I was not lost." Cal frowns. "I was here."

"I know." She closes her eyes briefly. "I know. Let's get you home." She turns to see a dark-skinned man shuffling awkwardly.

"I sorry, Missus."

Andi takes a deep breath. She is filled with a fury she has never known, but it is not against this man. It is not his fault.

"You're Manuel?"

"Yes. I sorry, Missus. Emily phoned. I did not know what to do."

"It's okay. I just had no idea. Thank you for looking after him."

"He is a good boy." Manuel smiles and crouches to say good-bye to Cal.

"Up high." Cal gives him a high five. "Down low. In the middle. Too slow!" Cal giggles as he pulls his hand away and looks delightedly up at his mother.

"Who taught you that?" she says.

"Manuel. Can we come again?"

"We'll see," she says, picking him up and walking out the door.

The fury does not abate. The longer she thinks about it, the stronger her rage. She does not let it out in front of Cal. At home, she sits him in front of his play cube and goes up to the master bedroom to phone Ethan.

"That's it!" she screams down the phone. "That's it! I'm done. Your goddamned daughter let a stranger pick Cal up from school today. Do you realize what could have happened? He could have been anyone. For three hours, our son was with someone none of us know. I feel sick when I think about it. I'm done, Ethan. Do you understand me? That's it. That girl is not going to be taking Cal anymore. I can't do this. I can't do this." Her voice breaks, filling with sobs. "She comes

back, and with her comes all the goddamned drama. Our lives have been so peaceful for three years. I've never been so happy, and the minute she's back"—Andi can't even bring herself to say Emily's name—"there's drama.

"I've had enough, Ethan. She is not going to have anything to do with Cal. Not anymore. We gave her a shot, and today, she blew it. I am going to see a lawyer, and I'm going to tell them what happened today, and about the drugs and alcohol, and we are going to get custody of Cal. Officially." Andi runs out of steam. She clutches the phone, waiting for Ethan to say something, but there is just silence.

"Well?" she says finally. "Don't you have anything to say?"

"I . . ." And she realizes he's crying, too. "You're right. This can't happen again. Ever. Make that appointment."

"Can you get home now? I have no idea where your daughter is, but right now I'm ready to murder her, and I'm not joking. You need to be with me, and together, we're going to tell her."

"I'm on my way." Ethan puts down the phone and drops his head into his hands.

Forty-nine
. . . .

Michael pulls his suit pants back on and reaches down to help me up from the living-room floor. I can't believe we christened our apartment already! So cool! I stand up and wrap my arms around his neck.

"Maybe we should have some champagne to celebrate?" He cranes his head back to look at me. "There's a wine bar right around the corner—VinoRosso. Shall we quickly run in?"

"Definitely." I grin, taking a last look around the apartment. "Wow. I can't believe we're going to live here." And as we walk up the road we can't stop talking about what our life is going to be like, and how great it's going to be when we start our new life here.

My phone is on vibrate, and it's at the bottom of my purse, and I swear, I never heard it ring once. By the time I get it out to check it, when we're in VinoRosso and Michael's in the bathroom, I realize that I have majorly, majorly, fucked up.

There are endless missed calls from everyone. I look at my watch,

and I gasp, because I swear, I swear on my life, I never ever realized what time it was, and that it had gotten so late.

I didn't think. I didn't think about anything other than the apartment. I know Manuel picked Cal up, but I was supposed to be back to take him home. And I'm not. And I feel sick.

I don't even know who to call. My dad or Andi would be out of the question right now—I start to listen to the voice mails, but Andi is screaming, and I can't listen. Sophia. She's safest. I call her cell, and she picks up immediately.

"Wow, Emily." Sophia's voice is heavy with sarcasm. "You really outdid yourself today."

"Jesus, Sophia. It was an accident, okay? I didn't realize what time it was. I feel horrible. I just wanted to check that Cal was home and was okay."

"Yes, he's home, but no thanks to you. You let Mom's flower guy who barely speaks English, and who she barely knows, pick up Cal? Nice move."

"What else was I supposed to do?" I end up saying because she's right, and I know it, and I don't know what to do about it or how to make it better. "You refused to pick him up yourself."

"How about not being so selfish and thinking about someone other than yourself all the time? That would be a good thing to do."

I can't tell her she's right. I won't. "Oh, my God, Sophia. Since when did you get so high-and-fucking-mighty," I spit, wanting to hurt her—feeling, in that moment, like I am fourteen again and having another childish fight with my sister, and I want to cause her as much pain as she's causing me.

"Oh right. I forgot. You've always been Miss Goody Two-shoes." My voice drips with sarcasm.

"You still don't get it, do you?" Sophia is incredulous. "Anything could have happened today. Manuel's worked for Mom for about ten weeks. We know nothing about him. Not to mention that

Cal went with Manuel in his truck, did you know that? And I've seen that truck. No seat belts and there's no *way* he had a car seat."

"You're overreacting. Mom leaves Manuel and Pablo in charge all the time. She obviously trusts him. I wouldn't leave Cal with a stranger."

"She leaves them in charge for ten minutes at a time if she has to do an errand. That's it. That doesn't tell you anything about whether she trusts him or not."

"He's fine, isn't he?" I end up asking wearily. "Nothing happened."

"Thank the Lord. He's home and yes, he's fine. If I were you, I wouldn't show my face around here for a while. Andi and Dad are ready to kill you."

"Why are you making such a big deal out of it?" I feel my voice catch, and I know I am on the edge of tears. "You said yourself, Cal's fine."

"It is a big deal. And what's more, you're not going to be allowed to spend any more time with Cal."

That's like a red rag to a bull. At least, right now. I'm angry, and defensive, and I cannot admit that I'm wrong. Sophia's saying this just pushes all my buttons.

"I am his mother, remember?" I say coldly. "Let them try and stop me."

"Okay. I will. I have to go now. Honestly? I'm ashamed of you right now. I don't even want to talk to you myself, and I wish you had never come back." The phone goes dead.

Fifty

· · · · · · · · · ·

y the time Michael gets back from the restroom, I'm a total mess. My eyes are red and puffy, and I'm crying so hard I can barely get the words out. I try to tell him what happened, between sobs, as he feeds me tissues, and when I've finished, I realize he's looking sad. And disappointed.

"God, Emily. I didn't know you hadn't found anyone to get Cal," he says quietly. "I would never have dragged you in to see the apartment if I'd known."

"What do you mean?" I snap. "You think they're right?"

"Em." His eyes are sad. "Of course they're right. You let someone nobody really knows get a three-year-old from school. It's totally irresponsible, not to mention, as they pointed out, potentially dangerous."

"Christ." I feel more judged than ever, and, as that old, unhappy Emily used to do, I start to shut down. When it hurts, shut it out or walk away. And this hurts. A lot. "Take their side, why don't you." I stand up in a fury, ready to walk out because I cannot take this pain, but Michael grabs my arm and pulls me back down.

"Listen to me. This isn't about taking sides. I love you, Emily. And I know you. And sometimes you can be a little . . . thoughtless. You screwed up today. Big-time. It's not the end of the world, but yes, you were wrong, and yes, you were selfish."

I can't believe he's saying this to me. I glare at him, trying to find the words, and as I glare, the fight suddenly goes out of me. I can't put up this fight. I was wrong. And the apartment isn't an excuse. Nothing is an excuse.

"I know." I close my eyes for a second. "I know I was wrong. I swear to you, I just totally forgot. I got so swept up in the excitement of the apartment, I forgot everything. To get him from school, and then to get him from Manuel and take him home. I'm sorry, okay? I'm sorry."

I don't know what else to say.

"I know you are." He is gentle. "But it's not me you have to apologize to. You have to talk to your dad and Andi. You have to make it right. They can stop you from seeing Cal, even though you're his mother, and my guess is if this went to court, it could be a large and messy battle. And expensive. You want to be with Cal, don't you?"

I look away. God. I wish he'd stop talking about it. I ask myself this question every day. I know I *should* want to be with him; it's what I'm supposed to want, how everyone expects me to feel.

It's not like I don't want to be with him, nothing as concrete as that, but . . . full-time motherhood? The thought gives me a fluttery feeling in my stomach, not in a good way, which is why I always push the thought aside.

But Michael seems to want something else. I look up at Michael, knowing what he wants to hear.

And I nod.

It's what Michael wants me to do. And I want to make him happy.

"So you have to be a mother to him," he says gently. "You have to prove to them you can do it."

"Okay." I lean into his chest so I don't have to look him in the eye. "Thank you. I love you."

"I love you, too. And so do your parents."

"Andi doesn't," I mutter, knowing how immature I sound but not caring.

"You know, I think she does, even though you don't make it easy for her. Start by saying sorry."

I sigh and sit back. "Okay. But I can't deal with it tonight. The shit is totally hitting the fan. If I let them cool down overnight, I can go over tomorrow and apologize."

"Sounds fine." Michael pulls his BlackBerry out and starts frowning at the screen.

"Oh, man." He shakes his head.

"What?"

"I sent Patrick a text saying we'd take the apartment, and he's just texted me back."

"What does he say?"

"He says we can't have the apartment. He needs to talk to me immediately, can I come and talk to him and Tim at five."

"Tim?"

"The big boss. Oh, shit. This does not feel good at all."

Fifty-one
. . . .

A ndi is first out of the car, up the path, and to the front
door, desperate to be with Cal, but so tired she can
barely put one foot in front of the other.

"Hey, guys." Deanna looks up from where she is sitting on the floor, playing with Legos with Cal. "How did it go?"

"It was . . . interesting," Andi says. "Thank you for the recommendation. You were right. She seems like an incredible woman."

"I swear, she's the best custody lawyer for miles. People come from all over the state to see her. I'm just grateful she lives here and can help you."

"Yeah." Andi sinks into a chair and reaches down to put Cal on her lap. "I'm just grateful she does yoga. If you hadn't known her, I don't know how we would have gotten in."

"See? It's amazing who I meet through teaching. So? What did she say?"

"You know what, Deanna?" Andi sighs. "I want to tell you, but I just can't talk about it right now. I'm sorry. It's all good, but I just haven't got the energy. Can we talk tomorrow?"

"Got it," Deanna jumps up and kisses the top of Andi's head. "Do you need anything before I go?"

"I'm good. Thank you, sweetie."

"You're welcome. I loved looking after Cal, by the way. He is so delicious."

"I know, and truly, I meant thank you for understanding, for being such a good friend."

Deanna pauses. "You know what? Why don't you and Ethan have some time alone tonight? Why don't I take Cal for another couple of hours? You look like you just need a break."

Andi looks from Cal to Deanna. Normally, she would say no. Normally, she cannot wait to get back home and be with Cal, but tonight she can do with the break.

Tonight, she's finally going to admit she's not Superwoman and accept help when it's offered.

Once Deanna and Cal have left, Andi thinks very hard about moving, but the thought won't translate. She slumps, almost paralyzed, too tired to do anything other than stare off into the middle distance.

"I made you green tea." Ethan appears, holding a large steaming mug.

"Thank you, sweetie." Andi smiles gratefully as he places the tea on the table next to her, lowering himself into another chair, leaning forward, his elbows on his knees, his chin resting on his hands.

"What did you think of the lawyer?" he says quietly.

"I thought she was amazing."

"She seems to think we have a very strong case."

"Of course we have a strong case. Emily's a disaster, and we have tons of evidence to prove it. Plus, as she pointed out, we're the only parents he's ever known. The court must do whatever's in the child's

best interest, and she seems to think no judge in the country, let alone state, would think it was in Cal's best interest to be with Emily."

"So you want to go ahead and file a petition to be appointed Cal's legal guardians?"

Andi puts her mug down and looks at Ethan. "Do you?"

"Yes."

"Thank God." She closes her eyes, opening them to reveal tears. "I know how hard this is for you. I know how much you love Emily, and how painful this is, to have to make a choice. Thank you."

Ethan frowns. "Why are you thanking me?"

"Because you're doing the right thing for Cal."

"I know," Ethan says softly. "But it's also about us. I spent so many years trying to make Emily happy. I thought that if Emily were happy, then everyone would be happy. Her moods seemed to control everyone in the house, so I bent over backward trying to keep her mood good, convinced that if I managed it, then life would all be fine."

Andi nods. He rarely speaks about Emily. The subject is so emotional for both of them, Andi has learned to avoid the conversation, and the subsequent fights that always arise.

"And then, when she ran away, I saw how different things were when she wasn't here. The house was peaceful. Everyone was peaceful. Emily always blamed you, saying if you hadn't come along, life would be great, and"—he inhales sharply—"as painful as this is to admit, I wondered if that were true. I didn't blame you, but I thought this was something you had a part in, too."

"I know." Andi reaches out a hand and squeezes his knee gently.

"When she was gone, I realized it wasn't you. And we had Cal. When Emily was pregnant, I just wanted the problem to go away, and I was so furious when she refused to give him up for adoption. I thought having this baby was going to ruin all of our lives.

"I guess some part of me knew, or suspected, that the baby would

be dumped on us, and I didn't want it. I didn't want to have to resent my daughter for constantly treating us like babysitters, and I didn't want to have a baby around. I'm forty-nine, for God's sake. I've done the baby thing, and I know how tiring it is.

"But the minute he was born, I knew I'd drop everything for this child. And the minute Emily left, I knew that I would raise him, that although officially I'm the grandparent, I'm his father, and there is nothing I want more in the world.

"I loved, still love, seeing you as a mother. I know how much you wanted children, and how hard it was for you to accept you couldn't have them, but I didn't realize how much of a loss it must have been. I didn't really know until I saw you with Cal.

"Andi, I have fallen in love with you all over again through watching you be Cal's mother. I am stunned, every day, by your patience, and love, and the way you guide him through this world, and I am so proud of you. I am so proud of us. Of my family."

His eyes fill with tears. "I love Emily, but I can't fix her. I tried fixing her for years, and it didn't work. I can't let her break up this family. She isn't Cal's mother. I don't care that she gave birth to him, she isn't his mother. You are.

"I love my daughter, but she is not equipped, in any way, to be a mother, which she has proved to us, numerous times, since she's been back. I'm still"—he shakes his head—"appalled that she allowed someone who is practically a stranger to pick Cal up. I know she's apologized, but I can't forgive her. I will. Of course I will, but I can't just yet.

"If this is about what's best for Cal, and if that lawyer is right, the courts will recognize that and will revoke her parental rights and give us custody. I hate that it has to go that far, but I can't hope that Emily sorts herself out anymore. I can't wait for things to get better.

"I want to file the petition as soon as possible."

Andi just sits, looking at him. This is the most he has spoken

about Emily ever, and the most honest he has ever been. She knows
how hard it is for him, can see the pain etched on his face, is filled
with a wave of all-consuming love for this man who—right now she
cannot believe this was ever the case—she almost walked away from
three years ago.

"I love you so much." Andi stands, walks to the chair, and sinks
onto Ethan's lap, wrapping her arms around his neck. "I love you for
your bravery, and your quiet courage, and your integrity."

They hold each other tight.

Andi turns her head slightly to ask gently, "Do you think this will
turn out okay? Do you think we'll get him?"

"I think we will," Ethan whispers. "I somehow think this is all
going to work out exactly the way it is supposed to."

"I hope you're right," she says.

"I am," he whispers, kissing her on the neck, then on the cheek,
then moving to her mouth.

"Ethan!" She laughs, craning her head back. "You cannot be serious! How can you be in the mood for sex? We're going through the
most emotional time of our lives, and you want sex? What's the matter
with you?"

"I can't help it." He shrugs. "I love my wife, and we have an empty
house for the next two hours. Come upstairs with me, lovely wife.
Let's make the most of it." Andi allows herself to be led upstairs before opening her arms and pulling him in.

Fifty-two

· · · · · · · · · · ·

stare at myself in the mirror and slide a Juicy lip gloss over my lips, smacking them together to spread the gooey gloss evenly. I'm trying to look mature. Responsible. I'm trying to prove that I'm not a little girl anymore, but a woman. A girlfriend. A mother.

I'm trying to be the kind of woman who strides confidently down a street, secure in her skin. The kind of woman you would trust.

God, I wish Michael were here with me. I said I could wait until he came back, but he says I have to do this now. He's on a Virgin Atlantic flight on his way to Heathrow Airport, and I know I just have to get this over with.

Still, if he were here, he would be with me, and I know it would be so much easier. One of the things I love most about him is how he calms me down and helps me to see things differently. I know I'm not the easiest person in the world, and Michael might be the only person who truly knows how to handle me.

He helps me to see things differently and is the only person I trust to tell me the truth. Plus, I can hear it from him because I know,

finally, it doesn't change his feelings about me, and I know that when he tells me stuff I don't want to hear, it's not because he's trying to hurt me but because he wants life to be easier.

I was thinking about Andi this morning. How Michael has helped me to see that I don't hate her, that it became a story I told myself, a role I played, and that it's okay to let it go and let us be friends. Although right now, Andi wants nothing to do with me.

And I was thinking about what Andi says about marriage. She always says she doesn't believe women should get married before the age of thirty-five, which isn't exactly surprising given she was ancient when she and my dad married. But she says women change so much in their twenties, they can't possibly know who they are, and the choices they make before the age of thirty are rarely good ones.

So I was thinking about that, and how that couldn't be right. Look at childhood sweethearts—they meet and fall in love as children, and many stay happily married forever.

I have no doubt that Michael is my childhood sweetheart, the boy I was always destined to be with. Even though it's much too early, I also know that if he asked me to marry him tomorrow, I would say yes. I mean, I would want a really long engagement and everything, but I know. Already. This is it.

Not that we've talked about marriage, not properly. But we are talking long-term, and I'm not worried. It's not like marriage is the big be-all and end-all anyway, but I have to confess—and please, don't ever let anyone know this—I did pause in front of the magazines in the bookstore last week, and somehow a copy of *Martha Stewart Weddings* made its way to the cash register.

I am so not the kind of girl who has spent her life dreaming of, and planning, her wedding. For the longest time, I thought I would never get married, and then, if ever I allowed myself to think about the

possibility, I knew that I would never wear white, or be some pouffy meringue-wearing bride.

I am not into hearts, and flowers, and lace, and big white dresses. I do not care about wedding cakes, and bridal showers, and what brides-maids should wear. But when I got that wedding magazine home, I memorized every single page and, I swear, I have never seen anything more beautiful in my life.

And now I lie in bed, on those nights when I can't sleep, and I allow myself the odd fantasy about my wedding. Sort of like a treat. I don't do it often, but every now and then I will think about what kind of dress I will wear, and what kind of flowers, and where I will get mar-ried, and how proud my dad will be, and I can see, I can truly see, the look of pride and love on Michael's face when I take those first tenta-tive steps down the aisle.

I limit myself to those fantasies twice a week. Weekends only. A forbidden, but delicious, treat.

It's so much nicer losing yourself in fantasy than in reality. Every time I think about what I have to say to my family today, I get a clutch of nerves, and I wish someone were here to help me. My mom isn't back until tonight, but I can't wait anymore. I need to get this over with, need to tell everyone what's going on, so we all have time to adjust be-fore getting on with our lives.

It's not like waiting is going to make it any easier, and there is no way in hell I can go through another night like last night. I barely got any sleep. Michael and I talked for hours about what to say, how to say it; then he went straight to sleep and slept like a baby all night as I lay there, for hours, going over and over what I was going to say.

Then I tried *not* thinking about it. I tried to force myself to think of other things, even indulging in the wedding fantasy for a good fifteen minutes, which was much longer than the allotted time, but even that couldn't take my mind off it.

Talking to my dad and Andi, the speech, the words I have to say would drift back in, and the next thing you know, an hour's gone by, and all I've done is stress.

And now it's here. I smooth my hair back, check it in the mirror before I take a deep breath, and walk down the stairs.

This is like acting, I tell myself. If I act like a grown-up, it will all be fine.

Fifty-three

· · · · · · · · · ·

Andi and Ethan sit stiffly at the kitchen table, watching Emily, who looks equally uncomfortable.

They have seen her since the incident with Cal and Manuel only once, when Emily came to apologize. Michael came with her, and Emily had the good grace to own up to her behavior, or at least to appear contrite. She said she knew it was wrong and that it would never happen again.

"Damn right it will never happen again," Andi said, noticing that Emily was stopped from barking something back by Michael's squeezing her hand so hard that Emily noticeably winced.

Last night Emily phoned. She wanted to talk to them, had some news, would rather tell them in person.

Neither Ethan nor Andi had a clue. Was she going back to Oregon? Did she have a job? Was she pregnant again? Could she have gotten engaged? They went through every possible scenario until Ethan commanded them to stop, saying the process was exhausting, and irrelevant. They would find out this afternoon.

Now she is sitting across from them, looking, oddly, like a businesswoman, or at least, how someone thinks she ought to dress when she is trying to come across as a businesswoman.

Andi is so fascinated by this strange transformation, she cannot take her eyes off Emily. She is wearing what appears to be one of Brooke's suits, which seems to belong to the early eighties. It is black, with a knee-length skirt, a fitted jacket with big square shoulder pads over a white shirt, buttoned up to the collar.

Andi doesn't know that Emily tried to get the shoulder pads out this morning but realized she couldn't do it without cutting the lining, and her mom would freak out if she'd cut the lining. The shoulder pads had to stay.

Her hair is back in a chignon, she is wearing red lip gloss and high heels. She looks as nervous as they do, and is speaking in a slightly stilted fashion, as if she has rehearsed.

Andi's fascination suddenly gives way to a giant bout of fear.

This is horrible. I have never felt so uncomfortable in my life, and I'm in my own home. Well. It used to be my home. But I know I am about to change everything, and I don't even know whether it's the right thing to do.

But what else can I do? Michael wants it, he says it's the right thing, and I want to want it, too. I want to feel the same way he does even though right now I feel a bit like I'm on a runaway train and don't know how to get off.

So I clear my throat and clasp my hands on the table in a way that I think makes me look grown-up, and I look them both in the eye, one at a time, as Michael told me to do to get them to trust me.

"I wanted to talk to you both together," I say, just as we rehearsed. "Actually, Michael and I were going to talk to you both to-

gether, but then he had to jump on an early flight this morning, and we didn't want to wait any longer.

"So Michael's been working on this big deal for his company, where they're taking over a jewelry business in the UK. One of his colleagues has been sent over there to run the company. In fact, we were going to take over his apartment, that was the reason why . . ." I trail off. No reason to go over that again. "Anyway . . ." I shake my head to dislodge the memory, wishing I'd never brought it up and hoping they're not thinking about it, too, but I can see from the hard expression in Andi's eyes that she is. Damn.

"So Patrick's gone to London," I continue, "and they called Michael in and told him they're sending him with Patrick to form part of the UK team."

"That's great," my dad says. Warily.

"Right. We're so excited. I've never been to London, and I've always wanted to go, and Central Saint Martins is there, which is, like, the best art school in the world, so I really want to go and get an art degree, and it's the most incredible opportunity." As I'm saying it, which, by the way, wasn't part of the planned speech, I realize how excited I am about all of this, and that this really is going to change my life forever.

"Wait," Andi says slowly, putting up a hand to stop me, as if she didn't understand what I just said, and needs a minute to digest it. "You mean, you're going, too?"

I nod. "Can you believe it?"

And I see Andi exchange a look of relief with my dad, and I want to stand up and run out right now. Before the hard bit. While they're still happy.

"Emily! That's great!" Andi enthuses. "Oh, my gosh, what wonderful news. No wonder you wanted to come and talk to us. It's just great!"

And I can see that she is ready to dance with delight; I can see exactly what she's thinking: *She's leaving! We're safe!*

"Congratulations!" My dad takes my hand across the table and squeezes it hard, and when he smiles at me it is warm, and filled with love. "I'm thrilled for you, Em. A fresh start, hey? And with a great guy. I couldn't be happier."

And I want to accept their joy. I want to bask in their love and acceptance, which feels entirely genuine, but I can't because I am about to throw a bomb at them.

"There is one more thing," I say nervously, and they both look at me, completely unprepared, still smiling.

I take a deep breath. I can do this. This is what Michael wants. This is what I'm going to want, even if I don't want it right now. It's the right thing to do, and this, above all else, proves that I am finally a grown-up; I am ready to take on the responsibility; I am ready to do the right thing.

"We're going to take Cal with us."

There. I said it. It wasn't so bad. There is silence. I look from one to the other, but they just stare at me as if they haven't understood.

"Excuse me?" my dad says. He shakes his head. "What did you just say?"

And this we prepared for although I hadn't anticipated how much my heart would be pounding.

"I'm sorry. I know you love him, and you've been amazing to him while I've been away, and I could never thank you enough for stepping in and playing the role of his parents. Now it's time for Michael and me to take over. I know we're young, but Michael's being paid really well, and we have the financial stability to look after him.

"Really. Thank you. For everything you've done for Cal." I am acting now, and doing quite a good job. I sound mature and calm, and I am pleased that this seems to be going surprisingly well.

My dad and Andi are just staring at me. They haven't screamed. They haven't exploded. They're just listening to what I have to say. For the first time in my life, I think that I am being heard by them. I

am being treated as an adult, and they are actually responding. Or not responding, which is the point. I think they're going to be okay. I do. I think they're weighing it up in their minds, and they realize that everything I'm saying is sensible, and it's all going to be fine.

"I'm leaving to join Michael in two weeks." I am confident now, matter-of-fact. "Obviously, Cal can stay with you for the next two weeks, but I'd really appreciate it if I could spend time with him, too, to get him used to the idea."

I look from one to the other, waiting for a reaction, but there is none. I wait. And wait.

"Well?" I ask eventually. "Aren't you going to say anything?"

Andi is the first to speak. She is gritting her teeth, holding the edge of the table so tightly her knuckles have turned white.

"I have something to say." Her voice is dangerously quiet, and, I suddenly realize, trembling with rage.

"Over my dead body."

Fifty-four

Andi's fists are clenched as she speaks, and she looks like she is about to explode. I guess, as stupid as it sounds, there was a part of me that hoped they would accept it. Sure, I knew they'd be upset, but they'll get over it.

I didn't expect anger, though. Tears, yes, but Andi looks like she is about to explode, and I have to remember that whatever she says, however they react, I will stay calm. If I am the adult I am telling them I am, responsible enough to take Cal, to raise him in the way they would want, I have to behave like an adult.

Even when the adults around me aren't.

Andi stands up, looming over me, her voice low and sinister.

"You come back here after three years of showing no interest, and you think you can just take Cal after spending a few hours with him? You think you can offer him stability and the type of security a child needs? Are you out of your mind? He doesn't even know you, and the few times you were supposed to look after him, you either forgot about him, sending a *stranger* to get him from school, or rang your father to come and help because you had no idea what

to do when he was upset. Are you kidding me, Emily? Is this some kind of sick joke?"

"That was a mistake." God. Why does she have to keep bringing that up? I said I was sorry. Over and over. "I felt terrible, and it will never happen again. And yes, I am new to this, but I will learn, and I will learn from doing it. I will learn from mothering. Because, Andi, however much you would like things to be otherwise, I am his mother." I astonish myself at how strong I sound. My heart is pounding, but my voice is calm, and purposeful. Seriously. I wouldn't want to mess with me right now. I am going to win this. No doubt in my mind.

"No. You're not. As I have said many times before, you merely gave birth to him." Andi's voice is shaking with emotion. "There's a big difference. You are *not* a mother. You don't *know* what being a mother means. Being a mother, Emily, means you are there through thick and thin. It means never forgetting your child, or letting, heaven forbid, someone you don't know go and get him from school.

"Being a mother, Emily, means that when your children scream or cry, or keep you up all night, every night, because they are sick, or sad, or scared, you comfort them, and you *stay*. You *stay*. You *stay*." She repeats these words, over and over, staring at me accusingly like a crazy woman. "Do you understand? You do not run away when you are overwhelmed. You *stay*. And let me tell you something else. I would give my own life, happily, before I let anything happen to Cal. You know why? Because he's my child. Regardless of who carried him in her stomach until he was born, *he. Is. My. Child.* Do you understand? You can't understand because you are not a mother, and you're not equipped to be a mother."

She is glaring at me, breathing hard, waiting for my response. I take a deep breath.

"No," I say. "I can't understand in the same way because this is new to me. I'm learning, and I will continue to learn, every day. I have

made mistakes, but I've owned up to them, and each time I have done something wrong, I have learned how not to do it next time.

"Despite what you seem to think, Michael and I will be good parents. I am not the same girl you knew, and I am willing to do whatever it takes to make this work.

"And as for not being equipped to be a mother? You're wrong. Michael's job is secure and well paying, and we're going to be able to provide Cal with a good home. We may not have the financial assets you have, but that doesn't matter. The most important thing is for a child to be loved, and Michael and I will love him. Do love him," I correct myself quickly.

Andi snorts contemptuously. "The very fact that you just said all a child needs is love is an indication of just how ill equipped you are to be a mother. Not to mention that providing a child with a home is not what I was talking about by being *equipped*. I'm talking about being mature, responsible, selfless. Oh, and by the way, Michael is not your husband, he's your *boyfriend*. And has been for, what? Five minutes? How stable do you think *that* is?"

I blink at her, momentarily stunned at the sarcasm dripping from her voice, at her obvious contempt for me. You see, I always suspected she felt this way about me; no matter how sweet she would pretend to be, she never actually *liked* me, was just putting on an act to try to please my father.

But I never actually *knew* it for sure. Until this minute. She doesn't like me. She never has. Finally, she's stopped putting on the act, and a part of me thinks, *Ha! I knew it!* Like I should feel gratified or something that I was right, but to actually *see* her hatred? To *hear* it? To know how she really feels about me? It's unbelievably painful. More painful than I ever would have thought, and I look up at her, standing above me, and I just keep blinking like an idiot, willing myself not to cry, not to show her I'm upset.

I am here because I have a right to be here. I am here because I am

Cal's mother. I am here because Michael and I are going to raise Cal, and there is nothing they can do about it. I repeat those words to myself until I know I can speak.

"You know, Andi," I say quietly, when I am sure the lump in my throat has gone, "you have made it very clear that whatever I do will never be good enough for you. Despite what you may think, I am not the same girl I was when I lived here. I've been away for three years, and I have grown up. I have worked for three years, I have supported myself, and I have changed.

"You can think whatever you like about my lack of responsibility, or lack of stability, or fickle nature, or whatever else you might want to throw at me, but it doesn't change anything.

"None of it is relevant. What's relevant is that I have a right to have my son live with me, and I'm going to exercise that right. I know you love Cal, and I know how you feel about me, and I am sorry that life isn't going the way you planned. But I am a grown-up now. I need to take responsibility for my life, and that includes my son. I have a legal right to raise my child, and I am going to bring him with—"

"That's enough," my dad says softly. I look up at him, his voice sounds so different, and he doesn't say anything else so I keep talking.

"I haven't finished—" I say, and then I jump as he slams his hand down on the table.

"Enough!" he says. This time he shouts, and I am so shocked, I shut up.

"I can't do this anymore." He sounds tired, and sad. "I can't take this, Emily. You've been back a few weeks, and in those weeks, I have been on a roller coaster of emotions. When I opened Brooke's front door and saw you there? I thought I was going to explode with joy."

I watch my dad, even though he's not looking at me. He's talking, but he's looking down at the table, as if he can't bring himself to look at me, and even though he just said he thought that he was going to

explode with joy because I came home, I'm suddenly scared about what he's going to say next.

Why can't he look at me?

"I hoped and prayed that you had grown up. That you had found happiness and peace. You seemed like such a different girl from the one who left, and I was so thrilled. But then you started acting in ways that made me think you hadn't changed that much, that it was all superficial." Then he looks up at me, and that's when it hits me. I'm looking in my father's eyes, and I see nothing there.

"You let someone you didn't know pick up Cal because as soon as something came up that interested you more, you abandoned him. Just like you did when he was three months old.

"Andi is right. You aren't Cal's mother, and you are not equipped to be. If you were, you wouldn't have forgotten about him. If you were, you would never have entrusted him to the care of a man you didn't know. I feel sick to my stomach every time I think about what could have happened.

"Andi's greatest fear has always been that someday this day would come, but I never actually believed it because I trusted that you knew your limits, that you knew, just as we do, how incapable you are of being a parent.

"I have made many, many mistakes with you, Emily. I indulged you and spoiled you, and tried to give you everything you ever wanted in the hope that it would make you happy, even when nothing ever did. I wish, *God, how I wish*, I had been firmer with you, but those days are over. This is not something I'm going to give you.

"I will not let you take our son. It's just not going to happen. Frankly, I don't care what explanation you give, how grown-up you think you are, or what you and your boyfriend's plans are when it comes to Cal. You do not get a say. And you do not get to come back and ruin our lives.

"We are Cal's parents, and I have had enough of . . ." And he

sighs deeply and shakes his head, as if he can't believe what he's about to say, and when he says it, his voice is almost a whisper. "I've had enough of you."

I can't believe what he just said. I sit, stunned, like a deer caught in the headlights, my eyes wide with fear.

My dad's voice is cracking now, and he sounds like he's about to cry, and this has become the worst, the most painful, the shittiest day of my whole entire life.

"I've had enough of you, Emily," he says again, and now I am swallowing the lump, and I feel like I'm in some kind of awful nightmare and have to wake up soon. Please let me wake up.

"I love you, but I cannot live with you. I love you, but I do not want to be around you. Not anymore. I will not let you disrupt our lives in this way; you are not taking Cal."

"You can't stop me," I say weakly, but I'm not even thinking about Cal. Not anymore. I'm thinking about what he just said.

My own father.

He's had enough of me.

"I can. And I will. We have already sought counsel, we have a lawyer in place, and are filing a petition in family law court to be appointed Cal's legal guardians, for full custody. The court must do whatever is in the child's best interest."

My dad is now looking straight at me, but this time I can't meet his eyes. I'm concentrating on a spot on the floor, willing myself not to cry.

My dad has had enough of me.

"The judge considers the character of the parties involved. Home environment and stability, financial stability, ability to care properly for the child. All past transgressions with alcohol and drugs will be taken into account. Our lawyer has already stated that there isn't a judge in the country who would choose you over us. And just in case I have not made myself clear, let me say this. We will spend every

penny we have to fight you on this. We will take you to court, and we will win."

I can't move. I am using every ounce of strength I have not to break down in tears, and never, ever, in a million years, did I expect my father to disown me.

My own father.

"I can't believe you would say that to your own daughter," I whisper finally.

"I can't believe you would try and take our son away," my dad says, and the sadness and disappointment in his eyes are like a knife twisting in my heart.

"You're the worst parent in the world," I manage to whisper as I stand up, my legs wobbly, knowing I have to get out of there before I break. I have to leave. Quickly. My voice is shaky, but I want to wound him as much as he has just wounded me. I want him to hurt, too.

"No, Emily," he says sadly. "*You're* the worst parent in the world. And we will prove it in a court of law. We have spent three happy years peacefully raising our son, without you. Your coming home has only brought drama and pain, and now you want to bring more. I won't let you do this, and if you insist on trying, I will fight you every step of the way, and believe me, we will win."

I can't take it anymore; I have to get out; I don't know what I've done.

The chair goes crashing to the floor as I run out, but I keep going, blindly heading for the car, and I don't even know how I make it home because I'm crying so hard I can barely see anything, and I'm driving away from the pain except I'm not, and I'm praying that I have a crash, that someone drives into me, that something happens to stop this pain, and what have I done?

What have I done?

Fifty-five

· · · · · · · · · · ·

A ndi sits at the kitchen table, unable to move. She has been sitting here trying to make sense of her thoughts, but there is no way to make sense of them, as there is no way to make sense of what just happened.

Today she saw the very worst thing happen, and the very best. She saw Emily say the words she had been dreading, the words that would destroy her life, and saw Ethan, finally, saying no.

She cannot believe how Ethan has stood up to Emily. She cannot believe how firm he was.

And she cannot believe the worst-case scenario has come to pass.

Andi looks up at Ethan, his face still with bewilderment and pain. As they listen to the car screech away from the house, Ethan, suddenly, bursts into tears.

Andi gets up to stand behind him, wrapping her arms around his back, resting her head on his shoulder.

"Sssh," she croons. "It's okay. It's okay. It's all going to be okay."

But she doesn't know that's true. She would cry, too, if she wasn't

shaking so hard, if she knew that Ethan was going to be the strong one.

He has been the strong one for their entire marriage.

Now it's her turn.

She will not cry. She will be strong enough for both of them.

Fifty-six

· · · · · · · · · ·

The Prius pulls up outside the pretty cottage, and Brooke, after kissing John good-bye, turns and smiles at her house before walking up the garden path.

How I love this house, she thinks, leaning down to snap off the dead geranium stalks as she walks past the pots. It has been a wonderful few days in Mexico with John. Idyllic to drift around the hotel's infinity pool like a couple of honeymooners, lying on the beach with a stack of good books; the hardest decision of the day being whether to have a virgin strawberry daiquiri or a piña colada.

Brooke hadn't had a real vacation in years. She had mentioned this to John, in passing, and three days later he had presented her with a brochure and plane tickets. She forgot to mention she really didn't like going on vacation, hence the reason she had not done so for so long, but it would have been churlish to confess when he was watching her reaction with such devoted expectancy.

The truth was, she didn't like the *idea* of vacations. Once there, she loved it, but she was perfectly happy at home and always homesick after four days.

Home, she thinks with pleasure, opening the front door, then pausing as she hears what sounds like crying.

"Emily?" She drops her bag and dashes upstairs, finding Emily in her old bedroom, lying on the bed, heaving with sobs as she realizes her mother is home.

"Emily!" Brooke sinks on the bed and gathers Emily in her arms. "What is it? What's happened? What's the matter?"

Boyfriend trouble, she thinks, recognizing the soul-wrenching sobs from her own teenage years. This is what happens when you have been dumped.

Emily is so like her. So emotional. Brooke could go from zero to a thousand between dates one and two. She never merely liked someone, she was madly in love, just like Emily. When Brooke was dumped, it wasn't something she could just put behind her; it was heartbreaking. World-ending. Produced exactly the same sort of crying that she is hearing now from Emily.

That Michael Flanagan, she thinks, pursing her lips as she strokes her daughter's heaving back. She liked him, but he was too good-looking. The problem with heartbreakers, she thinks, is that they break hearts. She isn't surprised Emily has been dumped. If anything, she is slightly astonished it lasted as long as it did.

He certainly pulled the wool over her eyes, though, she thinks. At first she was convinced he was just using Emily, but when she saw them together, she actually thought they might have something there. He seemed to adore her, but that must have been false charm.

Poor Emily.

"Poor baby," she croons. "He isn't worth it. I promise you you'll find someone much better. I always knew he was too handsome for his own good. I know it feels like it's the end of the world, but it's going to get better. You're so beautiful, and you have your whole life ahead of you. It's going to be fine."

Emily has stopped sobbing, and is now hiccuping madly, looking at her mother in disbelief through red-rimmed puffy eyes.

"It's not Michael." She heaves.

"It's not?" Brooke sits back. Oh, God. What is it? Sophia? Cal?

"What is it?" Brooke's voice is a whisper, her heart clamped in a vise of fear.

"It's Dad. He said he wants nothing to do with me." Her eyes well up again. "He hates me!" And she dissolves, once again, into tears.

B rooke stirs the water in the bathtub, easing herself up to get Emily, leading her gently in, almost like a child, wrapped tightly in Brooke's own favorite robe.

"There," she says soothingly. "I've filled a lovely hot bubble bath for you, with some lavender bath oil. You sink in for a while, and I'll go and make some tea. When you're ready, come downstairs, and we'll talk."

Emily nods like a little girl as Brooke gently closes the bathroom door, her feet as heavy as lead.

She managed to get the whole story out of Emily: How her father hates her, has threatened her, is going to take Emily to court—Emily wailing for hours that her own father has abandoned her.

Brooke left the room only once. She told Emily she had to go sort out an issue at the store, but that she'd come straight back as soon as she resolved it. Instead, she drove around the block and called Ethan to get the other side of the story. Brooke loves her daughter, and knows her tendency for histrionics, for making herself the victim.

She knows because, prerecovery, Brooke did it herself. For years.

Ethan tells her what happened, and Brooke nods sadly, for it is exactly what she had thought. There were no threats, just Ethan telling Emily what he would do if she tried to take Cal away.

Brooke loves her daughter. She wants to support her daughter.

But Cal is her grandchild, and she, *all of them,* must do what is best for him. This is why she is sitting numbly at the kitchen table, waiting for her daughter to finish her bath and come downstairs to join her.

This is why she gets up, after a while, and phones her sponsor. She needs some help on how to handle this, how to handle Emily. She needs some help with the right words, the words that will enable Emily to hear.

Brooke is certain that Emily doesn't want Cal. Emily might have spent a little time with Cal since being home. She might have talked about how cute he is, but she hasn't demonstrated an overwhelming *need* to be with him.

In fact, Brooke would go as far as to say she hasn't seen any maternal instinct at all.

She has watched Emily with him, and Emily, true to form, gets bored very quickly. It is fun to play at being mother for a while; but the minute Emily wants to do something else, she will hand Cal over to whoever is closest at hand.

Even, Brooke shudders, to Manuel. Not that there's anything wrong with Manuel, who has a family of his own and seems sweet enough, but the fact that Emily allowed someone to pick up Cal whom Cal didn't even know, whom any of them barely know, fills Brooke with horror.

Thank God he could be trusted.

Unlike Emily, who is as mercurial today as the day she was born. Emily as Cal's full-time caregiver? It's unthinkable. A child raising a child. A child who has neither the patience, commitment, nor stability to raise Cal.

A child who doesn't even *want* a child of her own.

Please, God. She shuts her eyes for a few seconds and prays. *Show me what you want me to say.*

Fifty-seven

. . . .

ow are you feeling?" My mom slides a mug of chamomile tea over the table, and I take it gratefully, exhausted from all the emotion, and sadder than I have ever been. I warm my hands around the tea as I lean my head down to take a sip.

"Are you ready to talk about it?" says my mom gently.

"About how my father hates me?"

She shakes her head. "He doesn't hate you."

I look up sharply. "You weren't there. You didn't hear him!"

"Emily. I know you heard that he hates you, and I understand that's how it feels. I think he was shocked and scared, and he probably said some terrible things that he didn't mean."

"He meant it," I whisper, wincing at the pain of the memory. "You didn't see the look in his eyes. I saw hatred. He doesn't want anything to do with me. My own father!" Tears start to well up again as I think about it.

"He loves Cal," Mom says. "He was simply panicking at losing Cal."

"He said he would fight me for as long as it took." I look at my mom, waiting to see her reaction, and I want her to feel angry on my behalf. I want her to stand up for me. I want her to protect me.

"Which bit hurts more?" she asks softly.

"What?" Of all the things she could have said, I was not expecting that.

"Which is harder for you? That you think your father hates you, or that he'll fight for Cal in court?"

"Both. He'll fight me. That's the same as hate."

"It isn't, Emily. It isn't about fighting you. Okay, let me ask it differently. Does it hurt more that you think your father hates you or that you might lose Cal?"

Wow. Talk about getting to the crux of the matter. I know what I should say. I know what I should feel. I just don't know if I can say it out loud.

"It's important, Em," my mom coaxes. And I wonder suddenly if she knows what I really feel.

"Both," I say finally, because I don't know how to say it, but my mom pushes me.

"And if you absolutely had to pick one, if your life depended on it, which one would you pick?"

I look up at my mom. "Cal?" I say, and I can't help asking it in a question. I can't say it as a statement because I know it's not true, and I am sure that somehow she's psychic, and she knows it's not true.

"So it hurts more that you could lose Cal than that your father hates you?"

"Oh my *God*!" Diversionary tactics are called for. "You just said it yourself! You said it yourself. *He hates me.*"

"No. I'm trying to understand what's really going on here. Em, you adore your father. You've always adored him. When you were a tiny baby, he was the one you always wanted to go to." Her face softens at the memory of me as a baby, and I sit rapt, because the one thing I

love more than anything else is hearing about when I was a baby. "I'd walk into the room, holding you in my arms, and as soon as you saw your father, your face would light up, and you'd stretch your arms out to go to him."

More. I want more. I need more. Especially now.

"Your first word wasn't, like all the other babies, Mama, but Dada. And you've always been inseparable. I imagine that thinking he hates you must be incredibly painful."

I nod. I can't speak because there's suddenly a huge lump in my throat, and my eyes start to drip big wet tears silently, and I lay my head on my arms, on the table, and squeeze them shut.

"And I imagine"—my mom lays a hand on my arm—"that's even more painful than the thought of losing Cal, isn't it?"

For a while I don't move. And then I nod. Almost imperceptibly. But I do. Because she knows.

"I think you feel an extraordinary amount of pressure, now that you're home, to be Cal's mother. I understand why you've stayed away, and I understand that in coming back, you have to revisit your past even when you might not want to."

"I do want to be with Cal." I lift my head then and look her in the eyes.

"I know you do," my mom murmurs. "And you should. But being with him as a beloved aunt, or a sister, is very different from being a mother. Let me tell you something, Emily." She sighs. "Not wanting to raise a child doesn't mean you don't love him." She closes her eyes for a second, almost as if she's praying, before continuing.

"Michael loves you, and I know you love him. It's very easy, when you're first in love, to get swept away in romantic fantasies of what your life will be like."

I smile slightly. That's exactly what we've both been doing. I've been fantasizing about a wedding, and Michael? He's been fantasizing about Cal.

"Some of those fantasies, I'm sure, involve Cal," my mom says, and I honestly don't know how in the hell she knows. "The three of you forming an instant happy family. Going off to London now! So exciting, and you must be thinking of all the things the three of you can do!"

I nod, because that's exactly what Michael's been talking about.

"Fantasies aren't reality, Emily. I could sit here and tell you how hard it is to raise a child, particularly when you're living far away from home and haven't got your mom around to hand the baby over to when it all gets too much. I could fill your head with horror stories, but I won't, because I think you've got swept up in pressure, and fantasy."

"I haven't," I say. Weakly.

"I think you feel obligated to take Cal even though you don't really want to. I think you are caught up in a fantasy, but that deep down you know it's not going to work out."

I know she's staring at me, but I can't look her in the eye.

"Listen to me, Emily. Leaving him here doesn't mean you don't love him. It also doesn't mean you're abandoning him. We all love him, we're all playing a part in raising him, and you can, too. Sometimes . . ."

I look at my mom, only to see her wince.

"Sometimes, leaving the ones we love is the only way we can take care of ourselves, and it's the hardest thing in the world to do. But sometimes it's the right thing to do." She reaches out for my hand, and I let her take it, remembering when I was tiny, before she started drinking, when all I wanted was to hold my mommy's hand.

"I know. I did it. Remember when I first got sober? I couldn't see you. I had to leave you for a while to take care of myself. It didn't mean I didn't love you." Tears are streaming down her face as she says this. "It meant I loved you *more*. I loved you *enough* to leave you. Do you understand?"

"No." I shake my head as I stare at our hands, fingers intertwined, and now I am crying, too.

"I loved you enough to take care of myself because it was only by taking care of myself that I could be a better mother, that I was able to take care of you. You have your whole life ahead of you. You can start again in London, go to school, get a job, have fun being with Michael instead of trying to juggle school and caring for a three-year-old. You can live the life you're supposed to instead of struggling, because it will be a struggle.

"And you can be in Cal's life. Not because you feel you have to be but because you want to be. It takes a village, and we're all here doing it together. Don't take him away. It's not the right thing to do.

"Oh, Emily," she says finally. "I love you so much. I see you as this talented, bright, beautiful girl who is itching to spread her wings. A child will hold you back, and I know you know that. I know you know that leaving him here is the right thing, but you feel guilty about admitting it."

And she squeezes my hand and keeps squeezing it for a long time.

"I'm right," she whispers, after many minutes. "Aren't I?"

The weight lifts from my shoulders as I look up at her, finally, finally, able to meet her eyes. I nod.

"But how do I tell Michael?" I whisper. "He's the one who wants this. He's the one constantly talking about the three of us. What if he doesn't want me without Cal? What if he dumps me. And . . ." I stop, thinking again about my father.

"How do I tell Dad? He never wants to speak to me again." And I let my mother take me in her arms and hold me as I weep.

Mostly with relief.

Fifty-eight
· · · · · · · · · ·

My head is pounding. It feels like the hangover to end all hangovers, but as I gradually force my poor, swollen eyes open, I remember that I didn't drink. Not alcohol, not this time, but too many tears and too much emotion.

I get up and go to the bathroom, gasping when I look at myself in the mirror, then crawl back into bed, burrowing under to where it's warm, glad that my mom is downstairs and that for the first time in what feels like ages, I feel safe.

My mom knocks on the door, then pushes it open.

"Em? I've brought you some coffee. You awake?"

"I am now." I sit up in bed, and my mom puts the coffee on the bedside table and sits down on the bed. She squeezes my leg under the comforter, and smiles at me as if I were a little girl, and I realize that this is what my childhood with her would have been like if she had been sober; this is how I would have felt: safe, secure, loved.

"Michael phoned. He said he's been trying your cell but it's going straight to voice mail." I pick up my cell and sure enough, it's out of

juice. It's not like the service is great anyway—the likelihood of my getting a call in this house is practically nil.

"He says to call him back on the office number in London. I've got the number downstairs." She smiles, then leaves the room, pulling the door closed softly behind her as I gaze at my old posters on the wall—Siouxsie Sioux glaring down at me, Robert Smith's kohl-ringed eyes from classic posters of The Cure—and wonder what the hell I'm going to say.

I have to tell Michael. Today. Now. Last night was huge. It was truly as if my mom could see inside my head, and she voiced all the things I'd been too terrified to admit, even to myself.

I realized that so much of my thinking I should be a mother to Cal, even though I didn't really want it, was because of guilt. What kind of a person must I be to have a kid and not feel anything toward it other than relief that someone else has stepped in to take care of him?

I knew, coming back home, that I'd have a place in his life, but I never thought, seriously, about taking him away. That was never part of my plan until Michael showed up.

And that's when I started to feel guilty. Michael never said I was selfish, but I felt judged by him, and I felt like that was what he thought: how could I not want to raise my child?

Last night, my mom showed me that Cal is in the best place; there was no reason to feel guilt at not having maternal instincts, not wanting to mother. She showed me that Cal was in the best place for him, and I knew that. On some level, of course, I always knew that, but I was trying so hard to do the right thing.

And because she didn't judge me, but understood, she has made it okay to be me, living exactly the life I'm living now. She's made me realize that going to London, pursuing photography, or whatever else I may end up doing in my future, *is* the right thing. For me.

If anything, she said with a smile, it's being self*less*. It's not just

better for me. It's the right thing for Cal. And my parents. It is, to get slightly cheesy for a second, for the greater good of all concerned.

Except perhaps for Michael. I have no idea if he'll understand. There's a part of me that's terrified he'll change his mind about me, that he will think I am selfish, and cold. But then . . . I have never been able to shake the feeling that he is buying into the fantasy, and that perhaps, deep down, he might be as unsure as I have been.

I know on the surface he was the one who wanted this so much, and he was the one who said I couldn't abandon Cal, but I'm not.

That's the thing. I mean, I know I did, right? I know that for three years I showed no interest, but now I've met him, now I've come to know him. I'm happy to be his big sister.

And it's not like I'm going to be seeing him a ton anyway, unless Michael decides to dump me and I end up living back at home in Mill Valley. Oh, God. That just cannot happen.

I love my family. I do. But when I'm home, I feel like I can't breathe properly, I regress to a teenager, and I hate who that person was, I hate hearing myself talk in her voice. I know it's not my parents' fault. I know they were doing the best they could, but I think it's better for all of us if I get on with my own life, away, if I'm free to be myself without the past coloring the present.

I love Michael. And I want to go to England with him. But not with Cal. I know he'll be shocked. The more he talked about taking Cal with us, the more it seemed a fait accompli, and even though I think he wasn't as sure as he seemed, what if I'm wrong?

What if he loves me *because* I have a child? What if he loves the idea of the whole package? He was the one who wanted us to be a ready-made family, who said I couldn't walk away from Cal. So how's he supposed to feel when I walk away not just once, but twice?

Because I'm not staying. If Michael ends it, I'm going back to Portland. The only thing I am totally certain of is that I'm not staying here.

The coffee is cold. I throw back the covers and step out of bed, feeling as if I have a weight the size of California on my shoulders, and I push my arms into the sleeves of a well-worn robe that I have had since I was about ten that doesn't really fit me but it is the coziest, most comfortable thing I own.

The worn sisal on the stairs feels reassuringly familiar as I walk down, curling up on the sofa to make the call from the house line.

Please, God, please, please, God, let Michael understand. Let him still love me.

So your mom said all these things and you realized she was right?" Michael's voice sounds . . . weird. My own voice sounds weird; high and breathy, and I can't tell what he thinks. I've told him everything, and as I wait for him to say more, I lift my right hand—the one not holding the phone—and I'm not that surprised to see it's trembling.

"Yes." My voice comes out in a whisper. *Jesus, Emily!* I think. Where is strong Emily? Who the hell is this scared, whispery girl freaking out? I take a mental deep breath, and the next time my voice comes out, it is back to normal.

"I don't know what else to say. I know you've talked about this ready-made family, and I know you love . . . the idea of it, but that's what it is. An idea. A fantasy. It's like fantasizing about the grass always being greener, until you get there." I look down at my legs, and run my hands over them, feeling the stubble, wondering, from this moment forward, if I'm going to be shaving them every day as I have since Michael and I got together, or whether I'm going to let the stubble grow in, not caring because no one's going to be seeing my naked legs.

I pull the robe over them tightly so I won't think about it anymore.

"I love the idea of having Cal, too." I stop. "I don't want to lie to you. I don't love the idea of it. I've been *trying* to love the idea of it, because I can't stand the guilt. But every time I indulge myself in this fantasy you have of this ready-made family, it feels . . . wrong.

"It doesn't feel like it's supposed to be *my* reality. Because it's not. I'm not ready to be a mother, and I don't want to disrupt everything in that kid's life. Everything in all their lives." I trail off sadly.

"My mom was only pointing out the truth. My dad and Andi *are* his parents, and he's better off with them. They love him, and he loves them. They're the only parents he's ever known, and look how much he freaked out whenever I said anything about being his mommy. We can't do this to them.

"And I don't want to. I gave birth to him, it's true, but I was a . . ." I struggle for the words, knowing I'd just read them somewhere in some magazine article about surrogacy. ". . . a gestational carrier! I'm not his mom. And I don't want to be. I was trying to do the right thing, but this isn't the right thing. The right thing is to leave him to grow up where he is."

There is silence on the other end of the phone.

I think I might throw up. My heart is beating so loudly it's making me think I'm deaf. That maybe Michael is speaking, and I'm not hearing him because all I can hear is this thumping in my ears. And then I hear him.

"You're sure this is what you want? You're not just saying this because your dad terrified you by talking about the legal fight?"

"What my dad said is a whole other issue. But yes. I'm sure. I'm so sorry. I totally understand if you want to . . . I don't know . . . break up with me. I mean, I get it. I know you wanted the whole package, and I get it if you . . ." Now I really do feel sick.

"Emily!" Michael jumps in. "Will you stop? I only wanted what's best for you. I thought you *wanted* Cal. I've been supporting you be-

cause I thought, I . . . assumed . . . that's what you wanted, that's why you were so willing to come back to Mill Valley."

"I came back for *you!*" I'm kind of stunned at what he just said. "You knew that! That was the only reason." I don't want to have a fight with him, but what kind of bullshit is that?

"I have always been reluctant about taking Cal." I know I sound a bit pissed now, and I lower my voice. "Whenever you talk about it, and it's always *you* who brings it up, I either said nothing, or told you that I wasn't ready, but you never wanted to hear it. You had this fantasy about Cal and where he should be in our lives, and I was too . . . scared to tell you I didn't feel the same way in case I . . . in case I lost you.

"Seriously, Michael? It's bullshit that you would even think I wanted this. I never gave you any indication of that. You could see I was uncomfortable. I never actually said that I wanted this, too, I just didn't give you a definitive no."

"I'm not a mind reader," he says angrily. "If you didn't give me a definitive no, how was I supposed to know?"

"Oh, come on," I say. "I may not have spelled it out, but surely my lack of enthusiasm counted for something?"

I am amazed at what I am saying. Amazed that I am wading into what does appear to be a fight, but in saying all this stuff, I realize how much I have changed.

I think about all the times I've done stuff to make other people happy—my God, those awful boys I fucked, not because I wanted to but because I wanted to be accepted—and I realize I'm finally being honest. I'm saying what I really feel, and stating what I really want, and I'm not lying down like a doormat and letting myself get walked over.

I may have been a holy handful with my family, but I wasn't like that with everyone else. When I was a teenager, I hated everyone,

mostly because I presumed they would feel the same way, and I figured I'd get there first.

Unless I wanted you to like me. Then I would twist myself into a pretzel to become whomever you wanted me to be.

I'm thinking about this as Michael and I have our first phone fight, and I start to smile, which is totally weird, and I can't figure it out until I realize why I'm smiling. For the first time in my life, I'm secure enough to be honest, and I'm secure enough to have a fight! And not just that, I started it!

Do you have any idea how huge this is? Huge! Monumental! I don't have to be who I think Michael wants me to be in order for him to love me.

And that's why I'm smiling. Because it's all going to be okay. If Michael loves me, he'll accept me, even if my life plans are different from his. And if he doesn't? I'm still going to be okay. If my life is supposed to be in London with him, then great, but if I'm supposed to go back to Portland by myself, that's . . . okay. Yeah, I'll have a bit of a broken heart for a while, but I'm looking after myself, and I'm going to be fine.

If this relationship stands a chance, if this really is "the real deal," we have to be honest with each other, even when we're worried about what the other might think.

Oh my God! Does this mean I'm finally growing up?

knew you came back for me, but it's not fair to say . . ." And then Michael pauses. For a long time.

I sit quietly and wait, amazed that instead of freaking out, I am surprisingly, almost eerily, calm.

"You're right." When Michael finally speaks, his voice is quiet. "I *have* had this fantasy. I wanted you to be involved in Cal's life because I have spent my life feeling like my own mother abandoned me, and I

guess I . . . I saw things in black or white. I thought it was either take him, or ignore him. And ignoring him felt like you'd be abandoning him, doing what my birth mother did to me."

"But why would you think that?" I am stunned. "I haven't ignored Cal since I've been back. We had some great times, and I've loved being with him. When I was allowed."

"I know that. I think that's why I started to think it could be . . . permanent. I thought that we, together, were able to offer Cal a stability you would never have been able to give him as a single mother, and I thought you would like that. Or, I thought it would change things for you, that maybe that was the reason why you hadn't wanted him."

"I never said that." My voice is quiet.

"I know," Michael says. "I guess I thought I knew you so well, I knew what you were secretly thinking."

"Well. You were wrong."

"I was. I'm so sorry, Emily. I'm sorry for trying to force you to want something you didn't want. And I'm sorry for not hearing you."

"I'm sorry, too." The relief that washes over me is indescribable. "I'm sorry that I wasn't honest about my feelings." I stretch out my legs, grinning at my stubble, knowing that it won't be there for very much longer. "So . . . you're okay with it? You're okay with not bringing Cal? With me being a big sister to him, but that's all?"

"Yes," he says, and I can tell he means it. "I'm very okay. You're in his life, that's the most important thing. I'm never going to make assumptions about what you're thinking or feeling again."

"Michael?" I am now serious. "Can we make a pact? That we talk about everything in the future, that we never have this kind of breakdown again? I want us always to be honest with each other, and not to keep quiet because we're frightened of what the other might think."

"I agree. Were you frightened of what I would think?"

"Terrified." I laugh then. It comes out as a high-pitched giggle,

which doesn't sound like me at all, and I know it's nerves. "I thought you'd end it."

"End it?" Michael is shocked. "Emily! I love you, and you're my best friend. I wouldn't have ended it. I'm just grateful your mom intervened so we were able to talk about it in time instead of making a huge mistake. And I do see how your dad and Andi love him, and how he's happy."

"Thank you." I am filled with a wave of love for this good, good man.

"So . . . when are you going to tell your dad?"

"Today. My mom's going with me." I don't know if this is the right thing, but I do know that the thought of even walking up that garden path by myself, like I did yesterday, makes me feel sick.

"Oh, God," I groan. "I just want to turn the clock back to six months ago, when everything in life was good."

"Great. Thanks a lot," sniffs Michael.

"Not you! I just mean this shit with my dad and Andi. You cannot even begin to imagine how awful yesterday was. And the worst part was I turned back into a teenager. I came back here after three years, feeling like I was going to show them how mature I am, and how grown-up, and instead I sat there feeling angry, and resentful, and hating them."

"Hating them, or hating Andi?" Michael asks gently.

Of course it was hating Andi. I have always hated Andi, but as I think that, I realize it's not true. I felt it for years, but there were moments, so many moments, when I came so close to loving her, when I thought that perhaps we could find a way to be friends, find a way through.

I came back thinking it's time to put the past behind us, and instead I could tell, from the moment Andi walked in and saw me, that nothing had changed. I might have changed, but she hasn't.

But do I really hate her? I think about how she looked after me

when I was pregnant. I think about her being there, holding my hand, making sure I was okay during the birth.

I think about the way she stepped in to look after Cal, and look after me at the same time. And I realize I don't hate her. Not anymore. Perhaps I never did, but I hated that she didn't love me; that, unlike Sophia, I never felt like her child.

Hate is a strong emotion, and as I sit talking on the phone with Michael, thinking about my life, I realize that I haven't got the energy for it anymore. I haven't got the energy to hate Andi. I just want us all to be okay.

"Em?" Michael prompts. "You still there?"

"Sorry. Just thinking. I can't hate Andi anymore. There's no point, and I'm tired of fighting with her. I'm tired of fighting with them, but I don't even know if they'll ever forgive me. Even when I tell them I'm not taking Cal, I don't see them forgiving me. I think I just fucked up my relationship with my dad, and my family, forever." Tears spring unexpectedly into my eyes as I say this, and I blink them away, hard.

"Nothing is forever. You're his little girl. Trust me, I know these things. Daddies love their little girls forever. They may not immediately forgive you, but you can make a start by apologizing. Then it just takes time, but now's your chance to show them you're doing the right thing."

"I wish you were here," I say. "It would be so much easier to do this with you here."

"You're going to be fine," he says.

And I know it's true.

Fifty-nine

. . . .

As they turn the corner home, Ethan takes a moment to register before slowing the car. They are returning from filling out the paperwork to file an instant petition in court to prevent Emily from taking Cal, when they see Brooke's car in the driveway, Brooke and Emily standing on the doorstep.

"Oh, Jesus," whispers Andi, lifting a hand to her forehead as a familiar wave of panic washes over her. "I can't do this today. I don't want to see her. I don't even want to look at her. Why is she here? Why are they here?" These last words come out in a hiss as Ethan lays a hand on her arm.

"I don't know," he says. "Stay in the car, and I'll find out. If it helps"—he exhales loudly, with a shake of his head—"I don't want to see her, either."

He opens the car door and stands there, looking at both his ex-wife and daughter, waiting for an explanation. Emily cannot meet his eyes. Brooke seems to be nudging her, urging her to say something. She doesn't.

"I'm sorry we're descending on you like this," Brooke says eventually, uncomfortably, still looking to Emily to interject. "Emily has something to say to you."

"What is it?" Ethan's voice is short.

"Well, it's to both you and Andi. Could we maybe go inside?"

"No," Ethan says. "Andi and I are exhausted and upset. We just can't do this. We're really not that interested in hearing what you have to say. Not anymore. Please." His voice softens as he starts to choke up. "Please. Just leave." He drops his hands to his side, his shoulders slumping in defeat.

"I'm sorry, Daddy." Emily's words come out in a rush. Ethan thinks of all the times he has heard those words, over all the years.

I'm sorry, Daddy.

Those words have always torn at his heartstrings. Whatever transgression she has made, whomever she has screamed at, however powerful the tantrum, he has always, *always*, instantly forgiven all upon hearing those words.

Not anymore.

"Please. Just leave," he says again quietly, wearily, turning to go back to the car.

"Ethan," Brooke commands sternly, grabbing his arm, forcing him to turn back around and face them. "She's still your daughter. I know terrible things were said yesterday. She's not here to apologize. She's here to explain."

"I'm not interested," Ethan says, noting that Andi has put the car window down slightly and is listening. "We're not interested. We'll see you in court."

"I don't want him!" Emily grabs Ethan's arm to physically stop him. "I came here to apologize, and to tell you that you can keep him. I'm not going to take him, okay? I was trying to do what I thought I *should* do, feel what I thought I *should* feel, even though I . . . didn't. You were right. About everything. I don't want to be his mom, and I

don't want to raise a child. I know he's happy here, and I know you're his parents, okay? I'm going to London with Michael, and I'm not taking Cal. You can keep him. He's yours." She looks frantically from her father to Andi, waiting for a reaction, but neither of them speaks.

Ethan stands, frozen, unsure of what to believe, what to think. He turns only when he hears the car door, and sees Andi, walking up to them, reaching out and taking his hand.

Andi knows she shouldn't be feeling the relief she is feeling. Emily is so mercurial, how does she know Emily won't; turn around next week and demand him again?

But somehow she knows that won't happen; the nightmare is finally over. They will go through the process of legal guardianship, and all will be well.

All will be well.

"You'd better come inside." Andi, her voice low and calm, pushes past them to open the front door. "I guess we do have things to talk about after all."

Epilogue—Emily

know everyone complains about the Northern Line all the time, how it's the worst line on the Tube, but honestly? Even when it's totally crowded at rush hour, and I'm standing squeezed in between hundreds of hot, sweaty strangers, I still think it's completely cool.

Michael thinks I'm hilarious. After three years in London, he says I'm supposed to be taking it in my stride, but how can I take it in my stride when it's so different from anything I ever knew before, and I still pinch myself every day, knowing how lucky I am to live here.

So every day, when I'm getting the Tube home, I don't care that I'm shoved into a corner, and I still think it's funny that if I nudge someone by mistake, or fall against them when the Tube jolts, they're the ones who will look up and say *sorry*.

I guess it's an English thing.

Tonight, I'm lucky. A woman gets off at Warren Street, so I get a seat pretty much the whole way home, and it's lucky because I'm carting back a ton of food to get ready for the family's coming for Thanksgiving.

I had to go grocery shopping during lunch. A bunch of the other

students were going to the pub around the corner, and they invited me to go with them, but there's no other time to get this stuff done, so I had to say no. I try to say yes when I'm invited, because now, at the grand old age of twenty-four, I'm so much older than them, I want them to know how grateful I am to be included at all. I just couldn't do it today.

It's strange being back at school at this age. I love that I'm at this incredible art school, but it's weird being the oldest and, I guess, weirder still that I actually want to learn.

Most of the others are a few years younger and living a different life entirely. Booze, clubs, partying. *Been there, done that.* I pretend to be interested, but boy, am I happy that's not my life anymore.

I never expected to feel so grown-up, but working for the past four years, saving money to put myself through school, going home every day to my boyfriend in a country that isn't my own, has definitely made me mature way faster.

I had so many lifetimes before I even touched the soil in the United Kingdom. My childhood in Mill Valley, then life postdivorce with all the terrible teenage trauma that came with it—oh, my *God*!—how grateful am I *those* days are over—then the pregnancy; being a mother for all of five minutes, working on the farm and discovering who I am over in Oregon, and, finally, Michael.

We are now talking marriage. Not actually doing it, not yet, but definitely recognizing that this is it for both of us. Someone said to me recently that they didn't think relationships as good as ours existed. I laughed, but it got me thinking. I absolutely did think that relationships like this existed; I just never thought it was going to happen for me.

I was always scared I'd end up a lonely, middle-aged woman, with skanky boyfriends and no hope. And here I am, with a boyfriend who's not only clever and handsome and cute and brilliant and funny, he's also been my best friend for more than ten years.

And let me tell you, that counts for one hell of a lot.

I get off at Chalk Farm and walk quickly down the road, not stopping to window-shop like I usually do. It's freezing here, the kind of freezing I don't ever remember experiencing on the West Coast of the United States, and I'm wishing I thought to bring a hat and gloves when I left the house this morning.

Actually, I'm wishing that I even owned a hat and gloves.

I rest the bags on the doorstep as I fumble for the key, then I'm in, and it's toasty warm, and I go down the hallway to the kitchen and dump everything on the counter.

A quarter to four. My family won't be here until seven. There was some mix-up with the flight, and they had to have a layover, and the whole thing's messed up, but I'm relieved that I can get ready for them.

I love having them here; having them see me as a grown-up; hosting them in my home. We started having Thanksgiving here two years ago. It was Andi's idea, and I was happy because the Thanksgiving before that we went to some friends' here in London, people Michael works with, and although it was great to have all the usual food—their pumpkin pie was insane!—it felt kind of sad for me, not being with my family.

I never minded before, which is weird. When I left Mill Valley for Portland, nothing dragged me back for three years, but everything changed after they adopted Cal.

I flew back to sign the papers. I stayed with my mom, but I spent a little bit of time with my dad and Andi. It was pretty hostile between Andi and me at first. We never talked about the time I said I was taking Cal, and the awfulness of that day, and how I thought she had always hated me.

Now I know that isn't true. She never hated me.

I think I hated myself.

But on that trip Andi and I were both superpolite with each other.

My mom said Andi didn't believe I was really going to go through with signing the adoption papers, and no one could blame her for not jumping back in to be my best friend.

I did sign the papers. We all went to the lawyer's office together, and when it was done, Andi came up to me in the waiting room, and said thank you. She started crying when she said it, but tears of happiness, I think, and I said that's okay; and then it was really freaky: we just kind of fell into each other's arms.

I never would have expected it, but we stood there for a really long time, both of us crying. I think I was crying more from relief than anything else, and she . . . well. She was just over the moon.

I saw my dad a few times after that, before I flew back to London, but I didn't see Andi again. We all agreed it was best if I left her, and Cal, alone.

One night my dad called and said they were thinking about coming to London for Thanksgiving. Everyone. Sophia and Cal, too. I got so excited, I was practically dancing around the living room.

Michael and I went all out. I got up at five A.M. to roast my first-ever turkey, and Andi came over by herself in the morning to help me with the sides.

I did the sweet potato pie and green bean casserole, and a nut roast for me, and she made the cranberries, mashed potatoes, and creamed onions. That's what we now have every year. I had no idea what I was doing that first time, but Andi helped me, and we had fun. Together. Who would have thought it?

She wasn't fake, or judgmental, or a bitch. I didn't feel that she resented me, or hated me, or thought I was hopeless. She was relaxed and happy, and I wanted her to be there. I wanted to tell her about my life. She felt, for the first time, like a really good girlfriend.

She completely messed up the onions the first time around, and then she messed it up again—we were talking so much she forgot to check them, and not just once, but twice. The second time it hap-

pened we were upstairs—I was showing her some photographs I'd taken recently—and we smelled burning.

"Shit!" she yelled, and we flew downstairs to the kitchen. She took the lid off, and sure enough, there they were again: black onions. Burnt to a crisp. And she looked up at me in despair, and suddenly we both started cracking up. But not regular cracking up: this was clutching our stomachs, sinking to the floor, tears falling down our cheeks cracking up.

Honestly, to this day I have no idea what was so funny, only that it took us about half an hour to recover, and for the rest of that day all we had to do was catch each other's eye, and we'd start giggling again.

"What's the matter with the two of you?" my dad kept asking with this big smile, and I could see that what he was happiest about was that Andi and I were getting along. We tried to explain, but nobody else got the joke.

It marked a turning point for Andi and me. That night, at the Thanksgiving table, I made a point of saying grace, and I changed it, on the spur of the moment, to say that I was so thankful for my family: my sister Sophia and my brother Cal.

I opened my eyes when I said that, as did Andi. We looked at each other across the table, and she nodded at me. If it is possible for a nod to contain acknowledgment, gratitude, and love, I would say that nod contained all three.

Things have gotten better and better since then. I used to sit on the phone with them, but now we Skype, and we do it all the time. I can start with Andi, then Sophia will come home and shove Andi out of the way, while Cal leaps up and down behind them, making me laugh.

I have come to know him, truly know him, thanks to technology, and I can honestly say that I love him. For real this time.

Giving him up was a way to let go of the guilt that kept me away

those three years with barely any contact. Giving him up gave me the space to get to know him, to really enjoy him, on neutral terms. Since the minute I signed those adoption papers, I have felt nothing but pleasure at getting to know, and love, this truly great kid, and my truly great stepmother.

I have a family that I love. Without exception.

Life may not have turned out the way any of us expected, and God knows there have been some harsh and painful twists and turns, but today it feels like it is all supposed to be, it all happened for a reason, even though we couldn't see it at the time.

And it's all good.

I go into the spare room and make sure there are clean towels in the bathroom, and flowers on the table. Sophia always stays here, my dad, Andi, and Cal in a hotel in Swiss Cottage.

Last year Sophia tried to persuade Cal to have a sleepover here, with her, but the lure of the indoor swimming pool was too much, and he refused. He's six now, and hilariously strong-willed. If Cal decides he isn't going to do something, hell will freeze over before he does it. I can't think where he gets it from.

I unwrap the cheeses and put them on a platter with fresh organic grapes and the gluten-free crackers that Sophia likes, and put the white wine in the fridge. Dad said he wanted to take us all out for dinner tonight, and it would be fine to bring Cal because he'd be on California time so it would be lunch for him, but we're going to meet here for drinks, like we do every year, before tomorrow's Thanksgiving feast.

Oh, my God! He's gotten so big!" My hands fly to my mouth as they walk in, and hugs are exchanged, and coats are handed to Michael, who throws them on the bed in the spare room, and every-

one's laughing and talking, and saying they can't believe how cold England is, and I can't take my eyes off Cal: six years old! I know I see him on Skype all the time, but I didn't realize how tall he'd gotten! So tall, and grown-up, with a big-boy haircut for the first time ever.

"How about our boy, eh?" Andi sidles up and nudges me with a smile, seeing me staring at Cal, saucer-eyed. "I told you he'd grown!"

"He's beautiful," I say, and I like that she called him "our boy," even though he's not. I only gave birth to him; he's their boy.

"He's just like you," she says with a laugh. "Two peas in a pod."

"Let's hope he doesn't turn out like me." I make a face, attempting a joke, but also thinking about my teenage years of drinking, and doing drugs, and hooking up with really, really awful boys.

Andi steps back and frowns at me. "Are you kidding? You're a beautiful, brilliant, talented woman. I hope he turns out to be *just* like you. Nothing would make me happier." There are tears in her eyes as she says it, and she means it. I can tell. There is nothing fake about her words, and I just stand and stare at her, mumbling something about the bathroom, and I go in the bathroom, shut the door, and lean back against it.

I am not used to compliments. When I get them, I usually just brush over them, or pretend I didn't hear; that they don't mean anything to me, but what Andi just said *means* something. They are the words I have been waiting to hear ever since she came into our lives. Not that she hasn't said stuff like that before, but this is different. This is real.

I take some steps over to the vanity and lean on the counter, looking at my reflection in the mirror, trying to ignore everyone shouting outside the door for me to hurry up, with my dad asking, as he always did when I was a kid, if I've fallen in.

"Be there in a sec," I yell, taking some deep breaths, Andi's words

reverberating in my head. I lean forward, my face inches from its reflection, looking myself in the eye, noticing the shimmer of peace, and joy, and love.

"You know what?" I whisper, a slow smile spreading on my face, a glow of contentment radiating out from my heart.

"I hope he turns out just like me, too."